"Damn you,"
Ivy whispered.

"Is this my cue to melt into your arms? Do I say, 'Oh, Alex, I love you, too,' and forget that this problem exists?"

"No, I guess not," he said sadly. "We seem to be at an impasse. I won't say I'm sorry for wanting to protect the rarest, most precious thing I've ever had in my life." He opened the door and glanced at her one last time. "Maybe it's a question of need, Ivy. You can't bring yourself to need someone in the same way you need air to breathe and food to eat. That's too much of a risk, isn't it?"

Through Ivy's anguish, she scrambled to find an answer to his question, but before one came, Alex was gone. The door closed softly behind him, and Ivy crumpled onto the bed, sobbing her heart out....

ABOUT THE AUTHOR

Connie Bennett's previous Superromances
have garnered uniformly excellent reviews
from both her peers and trade magazines. Not
content to rest on her laurels, Connie felt the
need to stretch as a writer by creating two
very complicated—but extremely likable—
protagonists, and a plot that's sure to keep
readers guessing. Fans are sure to enjoy
Playing by the Rules. Talented Connie makes
her home in Missouri.

Books by Connie Bennett
HARLEQUIN SUPERROMANCE

Playing by the Rules

CONNIE BENNETT

Harlequin Books

TORONTO • NEW YORK • LONDON
AMSTERDAM • PARIS • SYDNEY • HAMBURG
STOCKHOLM • ATHENS • TOKYO • MILAN

Published August 1990

ISBN 0-373-70416-X

For Barb,
who was beginning to wonder
if "we" would ever
get this one finished.

PROLOGUE

THE PRESS WAS HAVING a field day.

Except for the family of the victim, no one had taken much notice of the first murder back in January. The police had hit the case with their usual dogged efficiency, but after a month had passed and no significant suspect or motive had presented itself, they had put the case on the back burner and gone on to other things.

Until February, when another victim was found to have been killed by the same method. Strangulation.

All the deliberately left clues were bizarre, and the Brauxton police began to suspect that they had a serial killer on their hands. The press came to the same conclusion, and the media circus started.

By the time the killer struck again in March, the newspapers were, of course, calling the murderer the Brauxton Strangler, and the mayor was ready to start pulling out his already thinning hair. The city's 724,000 people were putting pressure on him, and he, in turn, was putting pressure on the police commissioner. The commissioner took his foul mood out on his precinct captains, who passed the pressure down the line, until every duty sergeant, detective, patrolman, clerical worker and janitor in the department knew that the case would have to break soon or heads would start rolling.

A special task force was formed with great fanfare and grandiose promises of immediate results, but winter gave way to spring, spring turned into summer, and by July, both tempers and temperatures were sizzling. Six unsolved murders held the city in appalling terror, and the only thing people talked about for any length of time was when the killer would strike next. Every attractive woman in her mid-twenties to early thirties lived in fear that she would be next, but the killer went on killing, methodically, inexplicably, leaving unfathomable clues behind.

He was playing a game, the newspapers said. A game whose stakes were too high. And like a master tactician who craved greater and greater challenges, each death was designed to challenge the police to find someone among their ranks who was worthy of playing the game with him.

CHAPTER ONE

"I WANT ALEX DEVANE back on the force," the mayor said in a tone that brooked no argument, but Police Commissioner Len Eversall was so shocked by the announcement that he forgot it was unwise to enter into a debate with his boss.

"You can't be serious, Whit. Alex Devane is a nut case."

Whit Jablonski leaned back in his chair, practicing the patient look he usually reserved for press conferences. "I prefer to think of him as eccentric."

"He had a nervous breakdown, for crying out loud."

"But he's functioning well enough now, I understand. Got his own business and everything," the mayor replied. "And anyway, from what I hear, the reports of his breakdown were greatly exaggerated. He'd just survived a terrible series of tragedies in both his personal and professional life, so he decided to resign from the force." He smiled coolly. "At least that's the line I'm going to feed the press when you convince him to come back."

"Forget it," Len said flatly, thinking of the unpleasant confrontations he'd had with Devane through the years. "Nothing I could say or do would lure Alex back to the department, and I'm not sure I want to try."

"*I* want you to try. That's all that should concern you. We've got six unsolved murders on our hands, and your people are no closer to catching this lunatic than they were in January. Your handpicked task force is costing this city a fortune and getting no results."

"That's not true," the commissioner snapped, but his voice lacked conviction. "We're making some progress. In fact, I think we're getting closer every day."

"Save it for the press," Whit advised him. "The only thing you know so far is who *didn't* kill those poor girls. You haven't the faintest idea who did."

Knowing he couldn't argue with the truth, Len tried a different tack. He had to talk the mayor out of this ridiculous idea. Alex Devane had no respect for authority, no desire to be a team player. He was the proverbial loose cannon, and Len didn't want him back on the force. "But why Devane?"

"Isn't it obvious? Not only was he a good cop, he was a brilliant detective. He's got an IQ that makes Sherlock Holmes look stupid."

Len eyed the mayor archly. "You're exaggerating, Whit."

Whit smiled. "Of course I am. I always exaggerate. How do you think I got elected mayor?"

"But—"

"No 'buts,' Len. Your job is on the line here. And mine, too," he replied, coming forward in his chair to indicate that he'd heard all the arguments he would listen to. "We're not dealing with an ordinary homicide here, and it should be plain by now that this so-called Brauxton Strangler isn't a run-of-the-mill lunatic. All your psychiatric profiles on him say that he's a twisted genius with an astronomical IQ who's just toying with the police, daring you to catch him. Well, it's about time you did."

Len nodded. The mayor was up for reelection in November, and if Whitney Jablonski lost the race, Len Eversall would be out of a job, too. If he opposed the mayor on this decision, he could be out of a job by tomorrow. Wearily, he said, "All right, Whit. I'm not sure I agree with you, but I'll give it my best shot."

"Excellent. We're going to use a genius to catch a genius," Whit said with a satisfied smile. "Nervous breakdown or no nervous breakdown, by tomorrow morning I want Alex Devane in charge of your task force. End of discussion."

THE RARE BOOK ROOM of the J. J. Philpot Memorial Library was so quiet that even the gentle tapping of keys on the portable computer sounded like hailstones pounding against a tin roof. Several bespectacled, scholarly types glanced irritably in the direction of the noise, amazed that the librarian would allow such riffraff to penetrate these sanctified halls.

For long moments at a time, the intruder would stop typing and return to the book from which he was apparently transcribing carefully selected passages. He would read awhile, key whatever he'd found worthwhile into the computer, then read awhile longer. Read and type, read and type. The process went on ad infinitum, irritating the other occupants to no end.

Of course, Alex Devane wasn't the only person to invade the Rare Book Room with a computer, but the scholars might have had more patience with him if he hadn't looked so...so...unkempt. Devane's black hair, liberally peppered with gray, hadn't seen a pair of barber's shears in months, and his cutoff blue jeans and paint-stained, short-sleeved sweatshirt would have been far more appropriate in a gymnasium or softball game than a prestigious reading room. Nearly everyone who saw him at the library thought someone ought to inform Mr. Devane that the hippie movement had ended almost two decades ago.

If Alex realized the disturbance his presence was creating, he gave no sign of it. He cared very little what others thought of him and even less whether or not they were impressed by how he looked. In fact, if the truth was told, Alex cared very little about anything these days. Caring was dangerous to his health—and the health of others.

Books, on the other hand, were simple, nonthreatening and interesting. Since the day he'd started doing research for people who wanted information but didn't have the time or the inclination to find it for themselves, not one single person of Alex's acquaintance had died. Except Mr. Potter, the old gent who lived next door to Alex. But he had been ninety-three when he'd passed on, and Alex didn't think anyone, including Potter, could hold the former homicide detective responsible for old age.

The scholars on the other side of the room breathed a sigh of relief when the interloper gingerly closed the hundred-year-old book he'd been working on, but Alex didn't oblige them by taking himself elsewhere. His hands returned to the computer keyboard, and hailstones rained a few minutes more.

When Len Eversall slipped into the room, Alex was the only one who didn't look up and acknowledge his arrival. Though he could see the commissioner out of the corner of his eye, Alex kept typing away, his concentration apparently unbroken by the intrusion. Len approached his table, stopped and leaned one hip against the sturdy oak desk.

"You're a hard man to find, Alex," he said quietly, but his voice still sounded like thunder in the silent room.

As though Len hadn't spoken, Alex continued with his computer input, then finally punched a button to save his research and exited the program. He switched the computer off, closed the lid and finally turned his dispassionate gray eyes on the real interloper in the room.

He stared at his former boss for just a moment, taking in his disheveled appearance and the hint of desperation that hovered just beneath his urbane veneer. Alex knew that nothing short of an act of Congress would force this man to come looking for him, which meant only one thing: the Strangler case. Alex wasn't going to bite.

"No."

Len blinked once. "What do you mean, no? I haven't asked you anything yet. Is that any way to greet an old friend?"

Alex smiled and met sarcasm with sarcasm. "Len, you and I were never friends. As I recall, the day I resigned from the force, you threw a party to celebrate."

The commissioner thought back three years to the night in question. "That was my wife's birthday party."

"And I wasn't invited. That hurt, Len. That really hurt," he said, affecting an appropriately injured expression.

"You were in the hospital, Devane."

"It's the principle of the thing, Len. After all we'd been through together, you could have at least sent me an invitation as a gesture of courtesy." He stood, picked up his portable computer and started out of the room.

Len fell in beside him. "Devane, you are an irreverent, irritating smart aleck. You always have been, and you always will be. And not only that, you're a real pain in the—"

"Tsk, tsk, Len." Alex cut him off with a Cheshire cat grin. "Didn't they teach you at police commissioner's school that you should never insult someone from whom you need a favor?"

They reached the end of a corridor that emptied into the cavernous main lobby, and Alex marched briskly toward the front entrance with Len hustling to keep up.

"How do you know I came here to ask you a favor?" he asked, bristling. Alex Devane could get to him in a way no other human being ever had because he took nothing seriously. The ex-cop had a smart answer for everything. Worst of all, underneath all the wisecracks, Devane had a brilliant, analytical mind that made all who knew him feel as though they were in the fourth grade, sitting in the corner of the classroom wearing a dunce cap, being laughed at. It wasn't a comfortable sensation.

Alex let Len's question hang in the air until they reached the security guard, who stopped them at the door to make certain Alex wasn't trying to hide a copy of *War and Peace* in his computer case. Alex placed the case in front of the guard, and for good measure, turned the pockets of his jeans inside out, palming his car keys to keep them from spilling onto the floor. He grinned at the guard. "Wanna frisk me?"

"Wiseacre." The guard grunted and snapped the computer case shut.

"So I've been told." He picked up the case and marched out onto the wide concrete veranda that fronted the building. "Now, let's see, what was that question you asked?" he said, not looking at Len as he started down the long flight of stairs. "Ah, yes. You wanted to know how I deduced that you had a favor to ask. Well, it's simple, Len. You haven't read anything deeper than a comic book in twenty years, so I know you didn't run into me in the library by accident. Also, your introductory remark in the reading room indicated that you had been looking for me."

Without a pause, he continued. "Since I have a very loyal, efficient secretary who guards my privacy like a pit bull guards her pups, you could only have learned where I was by bullying her or playing on her keen sense of civic duty. Ergo, you tracked me down because you need to ask a favor, and as I said before, the answer is no."

"How can you say no before you even hear what the favor is?"

"It's simple," Alex said, stopping near the bottom of the steps so abruptly that Eversall almost tripped over him. "All you have to do is place the forward edge of your tongue against the hard palate on the roof of your mouth and force air through the glottis.''

Len looked at him as though he were inspecting a creature from Mars. ''They should have kept you in the funny farm, Devane.''

Alex's eyes narrowed with the first hint of real emotion he'd allowed to surface since the commissioner had found him. ''I was never in the funny farm, Len, and you know it. That was just a vicious rumor you circulated to get the press off your back about the Tanya Ringwald shooting.''

''That's a lie,'' Len said hotly, even as he silently acknowledged the truth of the accusation. The shooting of a six-year-old child by one of his detectives had turned into a media circus, and to defuse the situation, Len had quietly spread the word that the cop in question would be seeking psychiatric help for a nervous breakdown.

Of course, he had no intention of admitting that to Alex. ''I'm not here to debate the past with you, Devane. I came because the mayor sent me.''

''No kidding?'' Alex feigned surprise. ''Are you two planning to go into business together after he loses the election?''

''If we catch the Strangler, Jablonski will be reelected by a landslide.''

Alex considered the irony of the situation. ''Now, that does pose an ethical dilemma for me. I never imagined myself rooting for a killer to escape justice, but that reason alone might tempt me.'' Actually, Alex had nothing against Mayor Jablonski, but the rules governing snappy repartee had dictated a sarcastic comeback, and that was the best Alex had been able to come up with on short notice.

''You mean you'd stand by and let more innocent women die between now and November just to get the mayor out of office?''

"I'm not standing by doing anything except wasting time talking to you. I didn't kill those women."

"I know," Len said smugly. "You were in Philadelphia doing research when Miss March was murdered."

Alex didn't think there was anything in the world that could shock him anymore, but this bombshell did. "Do you mean to say that I was a suspect?"

"We considered you for a while, quietly—strictly off-the-record. After all, you do fit the profile—a mentally unbalanced, emotionally immature genius with a sick sense of humor and a penchant for playing games. If that doesn't describe you, I don't know what does."

Alex raised one hand modestly. "Please, you'll turn my head with all that flattery."

Len decided he'd had enough. "Look, Devane, let's cut the crap. I'm here because the mayor wants you back on the force. Personally, I think he's got a screw loose, but that's what he wants, so that's what he's going to get. Effective tomorrow morning, you're in charge of the Strangler investigation."

For the second time in one day, Alex was surprised. He'd suspected that Len had been instructed to get him on the case, but he hadn't anticipated that the offer would be quite so extravagant. Just the thought of all that responsibility made Alex want to run for his life.

"Sorry," he said as he started a leisurely jog down the last of the stairs. "Please give the Academy my thanks, but tell them that I cannot, in all good conscience, accept the Oscar at this time. Personally, I think it should go to Clint Eastwood, instead. That would really make my day."

Len charged after him down the stairs, across the lawn, past the Keep Off the Grass signs and into the parking lot, haranguing the ex-cop all the way. "Look, you impudent, smart-mouthed, egotistical lunatic, I didn't want you brought in on this case, but the mayor wants you, and by God, he's going to get you!''

"Wanna bet?" Alex called over his shoulder as he fumbled for his car keys.

"Damn it, Alex! Listen to me!"

"I tried, but you didn't say anything I wanted to hear," Alex said calmly. He opened the car door, but Len caught up with him and shoved the door shut in a move that was so macho it was laughable. Only quick reflexes kept Alex from being pinned to the car like a butterfly on a board. He eyed the commissioner dispassionately. "You've been watching too many Burt Reynolds movies, Len."

"Just shut up and listen," Len said harshly between deep breaths. "I know you, Devane. I don't *like* you, but I know you. You're running scared because you're afraid of responsibility. That's why you quit the force. It's why you're hiding out in libraries. But I've got a news flash for you— you can't hide from this case. It's been eating at you all year long, hasn't it? It draws you like a moth to the flame, because you like puzzles and intricate little mind games. You've been following this case since the very beginning, devouring every crumb of information you could get your hands on. Can you deny that?"

Alex just stared at him, letting his silence be his answer.

"That's what I thought," Len said smugly. "You're such an egotist you'd like nothing better than to go one-on-one with the Strangler, just to prove that you're smarter, that you're better at the game than he is. Admit it, you've been dying to get in on this case for months."

There was a long pause before Alex replied, "Go away, Len."

"I can't, because these murders aren't going to go away. There's a serial killer on the loose, and as much as I hate to admit it—particularly to you—we're no closer to finding him than we were six months ago. The mayor thinks that the

only way we're going to catch the murderer is to put someone on his trail who thinks the way he does.''

"You mean, it takes a psycho to catch a psycho?''

Len almost smiled. ''The word the mayor used was genius, not psycho, but that's the gist of it.''

"And do you agree with him?''

The commissioner shook his head. ''No, I think psycho
is more accurate than genius.''

Alex laughed, surprised for the third time. That had to be
a record. ''That was good, Len. I didn't know you had a
sense of humor.''

"I wasn't joking.''

"No, but your timing was impeccable, and that counts for
something.''

His insolent attitude finally pushed the commissioner to
the limit. ''You know what your problem is, Alex?''

"I thought we already covered that.''

Len ignored the response. ''You'd do anything, say anything, to keep from making a commitment. Your wife knew
that. It's probably one of the reasons she killed herself.''

Alex went very still, immobilized by a wash of painful
memories. The commissioner was an incompetent fool,
more concerned with his own aggrandizement than with
running an efficient, safe police department, but he was
smart. Alex had to grant him that. He knew how to pin-
point an opponent's weakness and capitalize on it. ''I'm
leaving now, before I do something we'll both regret,'' Alex
said softly, his voice tinged with something dangerous that
made Len shiver.

He knew he'd gone too far but an apology wouldn't have
been accepted or believed, so he didn't offer one. ''You're
not going to accept the mayor's offer.'' It wasn't a question.

"No.''

"To spite me, you're going to let a madman run loose, let more women die?"

"It's not my problem. As you pointed out earlier, I don't want the responsibility." Somewhere inside, Alex cringed at his own words. It wasn't like him to turn his back, not if he could help. His callous statement struck at the very heart of the reasons he'd become a cop in the first place, a lifetime ago. But he'd stopped being a cop when he'd started hurting more people than he helped. He'd driven his wife, Brenda, to suicide, and then only weeks later, he'd murdered a little six-year-old girl. People had died because of him. There was no reason to believe that things would be any different if he went back to the force now.

Opening his car door again, he smiled humorlessly at the commissioner. "Keep in touch, Len. We'll have to do this more often."

"Wait!" Len stepped forward and Alex took an exaggerated leap backward as though he feared Len was going to do his macho act again.

But the commissioner merely stood there, keeping the open door between himself and the nutty ex-cop. He shifted his weight indecisively, then, as a last resort, reached into his breast pocket and removed a sheet of paper. "This is a note he left us last month pinned to Erin Selway's body," he said softly. "So far, we've managed to keep it under wraps. Read it, Alex. If you can look at that and still reject the mayor's offer, I'll go away and leave you alone."

Alex stared at the paper for a long moment. It was a piece of standard xerographic bond, folded in quarters lengthwise. Not the Strangler's original note, but a copy.

The desire to leave was intense, but so was the need to know what the clever murderer had to say to the police he obviously took great delight in baffling. Finally, with a gesture of irritation, Alex snatched the note from Len's hand and unfolded it.

Before he looked at the words, he swiftly took in all the salient details of its appearance: a salutation and two paragraphs composed on a word processor with a twenty-four-pin printer, the margins justified. Obviously the killer was a neat freak. He couldn't stand anything out of place, not even the right-hand margin of a page.

To Whom It May Concern,

Frankly, gentleman, I am disappointed. Though I had not anticipated being captured, I did, at least, think you'd be a little closer by now. Are my clues too obtuse? Or are you simply too literal-minded to interpret them? This is no fun at all. Perhaps two victims during the month of July might spur you into action. A game is only as good as its weakest player, you know.

And by the way, can you get the press to stop calling me the Brauxton Strangler? I deserve something a little more original, don't you agree?

It was the arrogance that got to Alex. He knew that Len had expected him to be piqued by the implicit challenge in the note, but that wasn't what did it. Six women were dead because some supercilious psychopath was bored. Real people were his pawns, to be used and discarded, toyed with and disposed of. And if he made good his threat, the death toll was going to start doubling very quickly.

For three years, Alex had avoided anything that resembled obligation or accountability. He'd left the police force and simplified his life. No one died because of him anymore.

Now, Len Eversall and Mayor Whitney Jablonski had changed that. If Alex refused their offer to head the task force, if he refused to at least try to find the killer, the next death would be on Alex's conscience for the rest of his life.

And it was too crowded in there already.

Without looking at Len, Alex stepped to the car and placed his computer on the floor behind the driver's seat. "One condition."

The commissioner was flooded with equal parts of relief and dread. "What's that?"

Alex looked him dead in the eye. "I won't carry a gun. Never again."

If he hadn't known the reason for Alex's ultimatum, Len might have laughed. But he did know, and he couldn't resist one last dangerous dig. "Then we'll all sleep better at night, won't we?"

CHAPTER TWO

IVY KINCAID STARED at the blurring amber dots on her computer monitor and decided she'd had enough of this to last a lifetime. It was only 10:00 a.m., and already her shoulders were aching, her derriere was numb, and her fingers were cramping from her staccato keyboard input technique. And what was worse, the stack of Strangler files on her desk showed no signs of diminishing. Every time she keyed in one set of reports or interview results, two more took its place. Like this entire case, Ivy's job was long, frustrating and seemingly never ending.

"Maybe I should take up a new line of work," she grumbled to no one in particular as she filed an interview that would be cross-indexed with hundreds of others. "Like strip-mining. Or maybe auto mechanics. I've always been good with my hands."

"Talking to yourself again, Ivy?" Mort Adamson asked smugly as he turned from his desk. "One of these days the men in the white jackets are going to cart you away."

She batted her long eyelashes at him rapidly. "But you'll be my hero and come to my rescue, won't you, Mort?"

"Not on your life. I've been dodging the funny farm for years."

"Haven't we all," Ivy said wryly. "This entire task force is going to be committed long before this case is solved."

"Oh, ye of little faith," Mort said with a grin. "Just because we're overworked, underpaid and outclassed by some lunatic with a weird sense of humor doesn't mean that we're not accomplishing anything."

"You mean like spending the taxpayers' money?"

"Exactly."

"Kincaid!"

Ivy jumped at the sound. "What?" she yelled back, swiveling her chair to look at one of her fellow detectives, who was glowering at her menacingly.

"What the hell is the computer password today?"

"It's not a password, Jordy, it's an access code, and I'm not about to scream it at you from across the room. There are two dozen reporters just outside the door who would love nothing better than to find out how to break into our computer network."

Jordan Brubaker gave her a smile that looked more like a ghoulish leer. "If I come over there, will you whisper it in my ear? Pretty please?"

"You'd better watch it, Jordy," Mort warned. "You keep that up and sweet little Ivy here is likely to slap you with a sexual harassment charge. She's done it before."

Ivy heaved a mental sigh, wishing that horrible episode of her early career with the Brauxton Police Department would go away. Unfortunately, it followed her everywhere, coloring her comrades' perceptions of her, and she'd found that the only way to deal with it and retain her sanity was to pretend it didn't bother her. "Very funny, Mort. You try grappling with a two-hundred-pound desk sergeant in the property room one of these days and see how you like it."

Mort frowned as Ivy picked up a pen and wrote the access code word on a slip of paper. "I thought it was a lieutenant in a holding cell."

"Actually, it was Colonel Mustard in the conservatory with the candlestick. Some detective you are." She stood and headed across the room. Any excuse to get away from her desk was welcome. "Here, Jordy. Don't let it out of this office."

The beefy Brubaker glanced at the code word that would allow him to patch into the task force's vast supply of information on the Strangler. He frowned at her. "Ace... aceta... acetaminophen?"

Ivy shrugged. "I had a headache last night. It was the best I could do."

"I can't even pronounce it. How am I supposed to type in?"

"Here." His central processing unit was on and the monitor was blinking its request for the proper access code. Ivy leaned over the arm of Jordy's chair, swiftly keyed in the word and walked away before the computer had time to respond. "It's all yours."

On the way back to her desk, she stopped long enough to pour some wretched coffee into a foam cup, then returned to work with a resigned sigh. This job was really getting her down. When she'd first been assigned to the task force only weeks after her long-overdue promotion to detective, second grade, she'd been convinced that her career was on the right track. Then she'd found out that the only reason she'd received the plum assignment was that someone had told the commissioner she typed one hundred words a minute and was a wizard with a computer.

So far, Ivy hadn't set one official foot out of the station house. She had not been allowed to view any of the crime scenes. She did not interview potential witnesses. She was not encouraged to hypothesize. What she did all day, every day, was draft other detectives' reports into the network, cross-reference them and complain. The way she looked at it, she had little to lose by making her dissatisfaction known. She had joined the force to be a police officer, not a key-punch operator. If that was all she was going to get to do from now on, she might as well do it in a place where she could earn a decent salary.

"Morty, what's all the ruckus about outside?" she asked as she sat, using her coffee cup to gesture toward the reporters outside the squad room door. "They don't camp out there in droves unless Ever-Stall Eversall is going to make an announcement. Did someone crack this case and forget to tell me?"

Mort swiveled his chair around and slid closer to Ivy's desk. "Haven't you heard? Rumor has it that Grumberg is being replaced."

"Why doesn't anyone ever tell me about these things! I like to gossip, too, you know." She leaned forward conspiratorially. "What's the dirt? Who's going to be the new head of the task force?"

"I'm not sure."

"Come on, Morty, don't fail me now. You know everything that goes on around here. Your brother-in-law's sister is married to the commissioner's nephew. What's up?"

Mort pursed his lips thoughtfully, a gesture that was anything but attractive on him. With his dark, close-set eyes and puckered mouth, he reminded Ivy of a goldfish she'd once had to flush down the toilet. "Frankly, Ivy, the rumor I heard is so bizarre that it can't possibly be true."

"Let me be the judge of that."

"Well—"

Before the unconfirmed rumor could be spoken, the reporters in the hall came to life, and the sudden clamor made everyone in the squad room sit up and take notice. A flood of incandescent light spilled through the door's small-paned windows, indicating that cameras were rolling, and a couple of the detectives strolled in that direction, hoping to catch a glimpse of the press conference just getting under way.

Ivy wasn't one of the gawkers and neither was Mort. They stayed in their chairs, figuring that someone in authority would probably come in sooner or later to tell them what was going on. If not, they'd catch the announcement on the six o'clock news. After all, they only worked here. Employees, like wives, were always the last to know.

The press conference was unusually short. Chased by questions he obviously didn't want to answer, Commissioner Eversall backed into the squad room, waving ineffectually at the shouting reporters. "Please, please. The mayor will be issuing a statement later today. You'll be notified when and where. In the meantime, that's all I have to say."

He held the squad room door open just long enough for Alex Devane to saunter through, then Len closed the door quickly and pointed toward the office at the back of the room.

"Well I'll be a monkey's uncle," Mort Adamson murmured under his breath.

"Who's that?" Ivy asked, her attention riveted on the gorgeous, casually dressed man with the commissioner. "He looks like a refugee from some TV detective show."

"That's Alex Devane," Mort answered, leaning over Ivy's desk. "I heard he was coming back, but I didn't believe it."

"Devane? Why does that sound so familiar?" she asked, unable to take her eyes off the newcomer.

"He was on the force until about three years ago."

"Of course! Wasn't he involved in a shooting?"

"Yeah. It was a real freak accident," Mort said sadly. "He was chasing down a junkie who'd just robbed a liquor store. The kid was hopped up on PCP and started shooting indiscriminately into the crowd, so Devane returned fire. He pumped four slugs into him, but the kid was so high he didn't even feel it—just kept on firing. One of those slugs connected with Alex's shoulder, and the impact spun him around. His gun discharged into the crowd and killed a little girl.''

''I remember now,'' Ivy whispered, feeling a sickening tightening in her stomach. The story was right out of a nightmare every cop had had at one time or another. ''He quit not long after that, didn't he?''

Mort nodded. ''Turned in his resignation while he was still in the hospital. I heard a rumor that he went off the deep end, but I don't believe everything I hear. Alex was always a little strange, but he was a damned good cop.''

Other pieces of the story were returning to Ivy, pieces Mort hadn't mentioned. Maybe he'd forgotten, or maybe he just thought they were better left in the past, but Ivy seemed to recall that only a few weeks before the shooting incident, Devane's wife had committed suicide. The two tragic events, one upon the other, would have been enough to make anyone go off the deep end. ''So you think he's decided to come back to work?'' she asked.

Devane and Eversall had entered the office currently being occupied by Gene Grumberg, head of the task force, but Ivy could still see the ex-detective through the slats of the open miniblinds that covered the windowed wall.

''I think he was asked to come back.''

That spun Ivy around toward her compatriot. ''You mean he's our new boss?''

''According to the grapevine,'' Mort confirmed. ''And I'd say the fact that he's here pretty much proves it.''

''But why?'' Ivy looked through the blinds across the room again. A red-faced Grumberg was waving his arms, and Ivy didn't have to be any closer to imagine the expletives that were spewing forth. Eversall had his back to her, but he appeared as calm and unflappable as always, even in the face of the abuse Grumberg was hurling, no doubt because he'd just been informed that he'd been replaced.

But it was Devane who ultimately captured her full attention. He was so impassive and unconcerned that he looked almost comical leaning against the wall. Dressed in faded jeans, a tie-dyed T-shirt and a lightweight, wrinkled jacket with the sleeves pushed up toward his elbows, he looked, from the neck down, like Don Johnson after a particularly long night.

From the neck up, he looked even better. His wavy, unkept black hair framed a face that was handsome in an offbeat sort of way. His nose was a little too long, his eyes a little too round, his lips a little too thin, yet the individual features came together to create a face that was arrestingly appealing, disarmingly attractive.

Or maybe it wasn't the face that attracted her, Ivy reflected. Maybe it was just the indifferent, amused-by-the-world aura he projected that caught her attention and made her heart beat a little faster. Whatever it was that Alex Devane had, Ivy liked it.

When she realized that Mort was answering the question she'd asked, Ivy drew herself away from her inspection and started paying attention. Attractive or not, a new boss meant that things were going to change around here, and Ivy had to find a way to capitalize on that. She was sick of being everybody's secretary. Somehow she would make Devane realize that she was capable of contributing more to the Strangler case than just her speedy fingers.

"My guess," Mort was saying, "is that they asked him to come back because he's a genius. He's got an IQ of about 170 or something ridiculous like that. I've seen him take the most intricate puzzle imaginable and unravel it in a matter of minutes, while the rest of us stood around scratching our behinds. He just sees things different from the rest of the world."

Mort shook his head in amazement, remembering. "Do you know, he used to keep a chessboard on his desk and he played against himself because no one else could give him a good game."

"Really?" Ivy asked, intrigued. She'd done the same thing herself, hundreds of times. A friend had once told her that it took a really warped personality to be able to do something like that. Maybe Alex Devane was a kindred spirit.

"Yeah, really. He liked every kind of game imaginable, and he couldn't refuse a challenge, no matter how small. That's probably why they wanted him. The game angle, I mean, though the challenge probably got to him, too."

Ivy nodded, understanding what Mort meant. The Strangler had a really perverse sense of humor. Alongside every victim the police found some piece of a game or puzzle, and with each killing, the clues were getting more intricate. The January clue had been so subtle that it had been overlooked for several weeks. Beverly Coit's body had been found in her dining room with a tiny metal thimble sitting just under the table, inches from her lifeless fingertips. It had been identified as a token from a Monopoly game, then discounted as insignificant, a piece lost from a game she had no doubt been playing with friends in the days or weeks before the murder.

But friends were questioned and no one could remember Beverly having played Monopoly since she was a child, though they did recall that she had spent a weekend at a hotel on the Boardwalk in Atlantic City a few weeks earlier. No one had connected the coincidence until Miss February was found with a yellow wedge from a Trivial Pursuit game lying just beyond her outstretched hand. Miss February, a lovely high school teacher by the name of Nancy Monroe, taught history during the week and helped out at her father's bakery on the weekends.

This was before the task force had been formed, but Ivy, recently assigned to the homicide division, had heard about the puzzling clue and pointed out that in the game of Trivial Pursuit, yellow denoted the history category, and the wedge was known as a piece of pie. Two clues for the price of one.

Unfortunately, the price was murder, and no one thought the Strangler's sense of humor was amusing.

To Ivy's right, across the room, the door to the lieutenant's office was suddenly thrown open, and all eyes were drawn there as if by magnets. Grumberg, who seemed to be hanging on to his control by a fraying thread, stalked into the squad room with Commissioner Eversall right behind him and Alex Devane following at a more leisurely pace. He stopped just outside the door and leaned negligently against the wall.

"Listen up, people!" Grumberg shouted, but the effort was unnecessary. It was already so quiet in the room you could have heard a paper clip drop. "Commissioner Eversall has an announcement."

"Here it comes," Mort murmured under his breath.

Eversall stepped forward. "Gentlemen—and ladies," he added in deference to Ivy and a few other women scattered throughout the room, "at the mayor's request, former homicide detective Alex Devane has returned to the force to join us in our efforts to apprehend the Strangler. Effective immediately, Detective Devane will be reinstated and promoted to the rank of lieutenant and will assume control of this task force."

Murmurs of surprise rippled through the squad room, indicating that a few of Ivy's fellow officers hadn't been privy to the grapevine, either. Eversall raised his voice above the mumbled comments, silencing them. "This is in no way a reflection on the devotion Lieutenant Grumberg has shown to this case, but the mayor believes that Lieutenant Devane has a few special qualifications that make him the best person for the job." He turned toward Alex.

"Lieutenant Devane, do you have anything you'd like to say to your staff? Any questions you'd like to ask?"

"Yeah." Alex stepped forward. "Where's the coffee-pot?"

Eversall gritted his teeth, and Grumberg actually groaned out loud, whirled and stormed from the room.

"It's over here," Jordan Brubaker said, rising from his chair. Devane headed toward the coffee urn, and Brubaker plotted an intercept course. "Welcome back, Alex." He extended his hand and Alex accepted it.

"Thanks, Jordy. It remains to be seen whether or not it's good to be back."

Everyone watched in silence while the new lieutenant poured his coffee, added two packets of sugar and one spoonful of nondairy coffee creamer. He stirred, sipped, grimaced, then took in the room with one encompassing glance. "I want all the physical evidence that was collected at each crime scene on my desk within the hour," he said without preamble. "And there's got to be one person in this room who knows more about the case than anyone else. I want to see that individual in an hour, too."

"That would be me," Jordy piped up. At that moment, Ivy thought she might actually throw up, but the damage was already done. "I've been acting as senior supervisor, collating the information before it gets passed on to Lieutenant Grumberg."

Alex headed toward the office. "Then you bring yourself and the evidence into my office. And from now on you collate nothing. All the information comes straight to me." He stopped at the door and surveyed the room again. "And the rest of you, pass the word—if anyone has any ideas, theories, hypotheses or hunches, I want to hear them. If your Aunt Gertie is psychic and sees the Strangler in her sleep, I want to know about it. My door is always open, unless it's closed, so don't hesitate to drop by. I'll be getting around to talking to all of you in the next few days, so keep doing what you're doing until you hear otherwise from me.''

He took another sip of coffee, grimaced again and gave one last order. ''And find somebody in the department who can make a decent cup of coffee. This stuff will kill us all.''

He disappeared into his office, and when Eversall moved to follow him, Alex shut the door, leaving the commissioner standing in front of eleven detectives, five uniformed officers and a half a dozen clerical workers.

Eversall turned. ''You heard him, people. Now get back to work.''

The commissioner left, but no one paid too much attention to his edict. They were all too busy speculating about Alex Devane's triumphant return and gossiping about his tragic past. Jordy motioned for Mort Adamson, and both men headed toward the property room to start collecting the evidence the new boss had requested.

That left Ivy no one to gossip with, but she had better things on her mind. Through the window blinds, she watched Devane settle into Grumberg's chair and turn toward the glowing screen of his computer console. She saw that he was already into the system and wasting no time.

Unconcerned by the adage ''curiosity killed the cat,'' she turned to her own keyboard and worked a little of the computer voodoo for which she was famous. In seconds she had covertly interfaced with Devane's CPU, and her monitor showed her everything the new lieutenant was seeing. His initial request had called up the complete list of Strangler files. Aside from the six principal murder reports, there were dozens of subdirectories on each incident and scores of reports and lists.

Ivy had expected Devane to glance through the individual crime scene reports first, but he surprised her. With considerable finesse, he initiated a tricky cross-reference command and pulled out all the relevant data on the games the Strangler had used. Ivy smiled appreciatively as she watched her monitor flicker. Devane scanned the information, then began flashing back and forth between fact files that captured his attention. He arranged and rearranged data with lightning speed, filed it for future reference under a simple code only he—and Ivy—would be able to access, then went on to other files.

The man knew what he was doing, that much was obvious, Ivy reflected. Like most of the detectives on the force, Grumberg had used his computer sparingly and under protest. He had mastered only the simplest commands, and consequently, he'd had no idea what an invaluable tool it could be in a complex case like this one. But Ivy knew. And apparently Alex Devane knew it, too. That was an edge she would find a way to use to her advantage. If Devane listened to her ideas and treated her as an equal, there was a good chance he'd let her go out into the field occasionally.

Reluctantly, she left the lieutenant to his job while she returned to hers. For the remainder of the morning, Jordy and Mort came and went from Devane's office, carrying in box after box of evidentiary material. Two other veteran detectives were called into Devane's office, as well, and the five of them spent most of the afternoon huddled in conference. When the four detectives finally emerged, Devane closed his door and pulled the blinds, cutting himself off from his task force. He remained that way for the rest of the afternoon.

As was her custom, Ivy signed out at five o'clock but stayed at her desk through the shift change. As the day force left en masse, the skeletal evening crew came on duty, and Ivy learned that most of them had heard about the unexpected change in command; they all wanted her impression of the new lieutenant. She couldn't tell them much, because she hadn't had the privilege of meeting Devane face-to-face, but she hoped to change that very soon.

Ivy liked this time of the day, when the large room was mostly empty and the phones weren't ringing nonstop. It was quiet, and this was when she did some of her best work—work that wasn't specifically assigned to her. She was on her own time, so she was free to play with her computer files, indexing and cross-referencing, looking for the one thread that would unravel the mystery. It had to be there somewhere—she was convinced of it. All someone had to do was find it, and Ivy wanted to be that certain someone.

Every person on the force, from Grumberg down to the janitor, knew that Ivy was putting in extra time on the case. Most of them teased her about it. They accused her of wanting the glory that would come to anyone who could single-handedly catch the Strangler. And Ivy, always ready with a snappy comeback, agreed with them wholeheartedly, making jokes about how the city would have to give her a ticker-tape parade and how the mayor would have to promote her to police commissioner.

But the real reason Ivy spent so much time on the case was much more prosaic. It was fear, pure and simple. Every one of the murderer's victims had been an attractive female between the ages of twenty-six and thirty-two. Ivy was two months away from thirty. All of the victims had been career women who lived alone. Ivy fit nicely into that category, too. The victims all had blond hair and were between five feet four inches and five feet eight inches. Ivy was a five-foot-seven-inch dishwater blonde.

Being a cop didn't make Ivy immune to fear. There wasn't an intelligent, rational woman fitting that description in the city who wasn't terrified that she would be the next victim. Ivy wanted the threat of the Strangler removed so that she could go home to her apartment every night without worrying that a madman was somewhere inside, waiting to make her the next pawn in a very unfunny game.

Of course, Ivy would have died before letting another living soul know about her secret fear. Her mother constantly begged her to dye her hair or move back home, and Ivy jokingly told her that she'd rather take her chances with the Strangler. But when she was alone she worried more than she knew she should. Ivy's grandmother had been as superstitious as they came and had been blessed with what she'd always called "the sight." Gram had always seemed to know things before they'd actually happened, and she'd claimed it was both a blessing and a curse. She'd also claimed that Ivy had "the sight," too.

Ivy didn't believe it, of course. She was much too pragmatic to believe in superstitions. That didn't stop her from experiencing occasional "bad vibes," though, in the form of dreams that seemed to come true or feelings that wouldn't go away. Most of her life she had laughed those bad feelings off, but now that was harder to do. She had a recurring dream about suffocating that was just too vivid. When the murderer was caught, the dream would go away. In Ivy's opinion, putting in a few extra hours at work every day was a small price to pay for peace of mind.

At six-thirty, Alex Devane's door opened, and Ivy stopped what she was doing to watch him. Apparently lost in thought, he ignored the inhabitants of the room and headed straight for the coffee urn. He added all the appropriate ingredients to his cup, tasted it, shook his head in disgust and carried the cup back into his office. But this time he left the door open.

Smiling to herself, Ivy pulled her purse and an empty thermos out of the bottom drawer of her desk, then started toward the door to the corridor.

"You leaving early tonight, Ivy?" Violet Dodgson asked.

"No such luck. I'm just going to run down to Ernie's and grab a decent cup of coffee," she answered, stopping at her friend's desk. Like Ivy, Violet was a junior grade detective who spent a lot of time processing files for senior detectives who hadn't mastered the computer. She also screened the dozens of hot line calls that came in every night.

"How boring. I thought maybe you had a hot date."

Ivy grinned and leaned one hip against the desk. "Are you kidding? I haven't had a date in months."

"Tell me about it. You ought to try organizing a social schedule while working the night shift. I haven't had a date in so long that I've forgotten what one looks like."

"It's a little wrinkly thing, about the size of a prune."

"I meant a man, silly."

"So did I."

Violet blushed to the roots of her hennaed hair, and Ivy laughed. "Hold down the fort, will you? I'll be back in a few minutes. You want me to bring you anything?"

"No thanks, I brought my dinner. See ya."

Ivy waved and headed quickly out the door. With a cursory wave at everyone who spoke to her, she hurried down the stairs and ignored the pandemonium that always reigned around the front desk. There were still several hours of daylight left, and the early July heat was oppressive. Normally, she would have deferred to the temperature and assumed a leisurely pace, but today she had a mission. She had to get to Ernie's and back before Lieutenant Devane decided he'd done enough work for one day. He'd said to drop in any time the door was open, and Ivy was about to take him up on that offer.

CHAPTER THREE

THERE WERE HALF A DOZEN PLACES along the four-block route to Ernie's Delicatessen where Ivy could have gotten coffee and sandwiches, but Ernie Lebowitz was the undisputed King of Coffee in downtown Brauxton. He used only freshly ground beans of the highest quality and then added a secret ingredient or two. If Lieutenant Devane craved a good cup of coffee, Ivy wanted to be the one who satisfied that craving. It was the perfect way to introduce herself to the new boss.

Twenty minutes later she was back, and Devane's door was still open. Hurrying, she stowed her purse away, grabbed a couple of foam cups from the break table, took a deep breath and launched her assault. She moved to the lieutenant's door and found him focused on the computer. His back was to her, so she rapped her thermos lightly against the door frame.

"Hungry?" she asked as he slowly swiveled toward her.

Alex surveyed his visitor casually, inspecting her from head to toe, and Ivy allowed it. In fact, she discovered that she rather enjoyed it. Up close, he was even more attractive than she'd thought. Watching him from across the squad room earlier, she hadn't experienced the full impact of his charismatic gray eyes, nor had she noticed the intriguing hint of sadness that dwelled just behind them. Whether he knew it or not, Alex Devane challenged a woman to succumb to his charisma, uncover his secrets and take away the sadness.

Knowing that Devane was performing a similar instant assessment of her didn't bother Ivy. She knew what he would see: an attractive but not beautiful woman of average height and weight, with average features that were well placed in her square face. If she was any more average, she would be invisible. The only thing that people ever seemed to remember after meeting her—if they remembered her at all—was her unique sense of humor. Those who liked her described her as fascinating and fun to be around. Those who didn't like her said she was impudent and irritating.

Because Devane was her new boss, Ivy hoped that he wouldn't fall into the latter category, but she had no intention of altering who and what she was just to please him.

Apparently, Devane found the results of his inspection to his liking because he returned his scrutinizing gaze to her face, capturing her eyes as he said, "I'm starved."

"Good." Ivy took that as an invitation and swept into his office. Conscious that he was watching her every move, she found the only clear spot on his cluttered desk and unloaded two sandwiches from the white deli sack. "Pastrami on kaiser or turkey and Swiss on whole wheat?"

"Turkey and Swiss."

"That's good. I wasn't going to let you have my pastrami, anyway." He chuckled and Ivy decided that was a positive sign. She uncapped her thermos, poured a cup of coffee, then dumped in two packets of sugar and a smidgen of real cream that she'd appropriated from the deli. She stirred it once briskly, handed it to him with a flourish and stepped back to watch him while he tasted it.

Alex approached the cup suspiciously and sipped cautiously. The moment the rich brew hit his taste buds, his shoulders relaxed, and Ivy saw the makings of a wonderful smile on the way. "Ernie's, right?" he asked.

"That's right."

"This is the only thing about working downtown that I've missed," he said, taking another sip.

Ivy poured a cup for herself and took a chair without being invited. "Detective Ivy Kincaid." She thrust her hand across his desk and he accepted it. It was strong and warm.

"Alex Devane."

"I know. I get paid to keep current on little details like that."

"Are you good at it?"

Ivy took her hand back, but her eyes were locked with Devane's gray ones. The humor she saw sparkling there made her feel right at home. "I'm a lot better at it than most people give me credit for."

"Well, you certainly have good taste in coffee. I'll give you credit for that. And your timing is impeccable." He peeled the plastic wrap off his sandwich. "Is this your way of buttering up the new boss?"

Ivy smiled at him. "Of course."

Alex captured her eyes, his own gaze steady. "Why? Are you planning on seducing me?"

He was only half-serious, and Ivy got the impression that half-serious was about as deep as he ever got with strangers. She could relate to that. "No," she answered, her impish smile never wavering.

Alex sighed. "That's too bad. It's been a long time since I've been seduced."

"Oh? Sorry to hear that. I can give you the name of a computer dating service that vice has been investigating."

"No thanks," he answered good-naturedly. "I prefer a little more subtlety in my conquests."

Ivy started to ask just how many conquests he had made through the years, but she wasn't quite that bold. If the effect he was having on her was any gauge, the number was probably astronomical.

The sparkle in his eyes told Ivy that Devane had sensed the train of her thoughts, but they both let the subject drop—for the moment. "So, how are you enjoying your first day, boss?"

"I'll let you know when it's over. Do you always put in extra hours?"

Ivy nodded. "Usually. I keep hoping someone important will notice and make me police commissioner."

"Is that your goal in life—to be commissioner?" he asked, taking a bite of his sandwich.

She sipped her coffee and settled back in the chair. "At the moment, my only goal is to get out from behind my computer occasionally."

"Ah! And you think bribing the new boss will accomplish that."

"Of course not!" Ivy said with feigned indignation. "It's obvious that a man of your caliber can't be bought with coffee and a sandwich. I was going to offer you part of my salary, too."

Alex chuckled. "Considering what you make, Detective Kincaid, you'd be better off sticking with the coffee." He leaned back in his chair and eyed her speculatively. "So, you're dissatisfied with your assignment within the task force."

Ivy shrugged. "Someone found out I can make the computer do just about anything I want it to, and I haven't seen the light of day since."

"Some might say that's efficient utilization of manpower."

"Some might. I wouldn't." She grinned. "I'm a good detective. I'd like the opportunity to prove it."

Alex spread his arms expansively. "Be my guest."

Ivy accepted his challenge eagerly. "All right. This morning you asked to speak to the one person who knows more about the details of this case than anyone else. Well, here I am. In one way or another, I've handled every piece of information that has come through this office. If I didn't key it into the computer personally, I assigned it to the person who did. And then I did the indexing and cross-referencing of that information with all the other files.''

Pausing for effect, Ivy came forward in her chair, planting her elbows on Devane's desk. "About the only thing I haven't done, Lieutenant, is view the crime scenes and personally interview potential witnesses. There are a lot of good people working on this case, but they only have bits and pieces. I have it all—'' she tapped her forehead "—right up here. I can help you solve this case if you give me the chance. Anything you want to know, just ask me.''

"All right," Alex said, leaning forward, mirroring her position. "Who is the serial killer?''

Ivy sighed impatiently and gave him a disgusted glance. "You had to start with the hard stuff, didn't you?''

Alex grinned. Ivy Kincaid was effervescent, irreverent and altogether too intelligent for her own good. All in all, that made her one of the most intriguing women he had met in a long time. She was also pretty in a nondescript way; her features were nothing extraordinary. Her eyes were lovely and shrewd, though, and they flashed with an inner fire that indicated there was a lot to be discovered inside this woman.

Unfortunately, Alex wasn't interested in exploring Detective Kincaid's feminine psyche. She was probably a very complicated person, and Alex liked things simple these days. He was interested in her perceptions of this case, however, and he had no intention of dismissing her offer of help. Brubaker, Adamson and the other detectives he'd talked to today had given him the bare facts but had offered no insights or creative possibilities. These men were good, solid, dependable police detectives, but they weren't creative thinkers Alex could bounce ideas off.

Instinctively, he knew that Ivy Kincaid was different. She had charged his office with energy and excitement just by walking through the door, and Alex liked that. Granted, part of that excitement was sexual—an intriguing man-woman awareness that was strong and undeniable—but he would make certain that their relationship stayed professional.

"Let me rephrase my question, Detective," he said. "In generic terms, who is our serial killer?"

"He's a psychopathic genius who likes to play games."

"Shucks. Why didn't I think of that?"

"Don't be so hard on yourself, Lieutenant," Ivy said with mock sympathy. "You'll get the hang of it after a while. Anything else I can clarify for you?"

"Why does everyone assume the Strangler is a male? The victims are strangled with a rope, not bare hands. None of them have been sexually molested. Couldn't the killer be a woman?"

"I'm happy to see that you're an equal opportunity sleuth, Lieutenant," she said with a grin. "Our consulting psychiatrists aren't so broad-minded. Historically speaking, there have been very few female serial killers, and those who have been caught were driven to kill men, not other women. The fact that none of the victims were raped merely suggests that the killer is either impotent or has a very low sex drive—someone who prefers the cerebral to the physical."

Alex cocked his head thoughtfully. "Why does *he* choose young, attractive blondes?"

A shutter clicked over Ivy's expression for just a moment as he touched her own irrational nerve regarding this case. To hide her discomfort, she quipped, "He has good taste?"

Alex recognized the defense mechanism and fell back in his chair thoughtfully. "You fit the profile of all the victims, don't you?"

Ivy's blood ran cold. Other than her mother and a few close friends, no one—particularly here at the office—had made that connection. "So do about a hundred thousand other women in Brauxton and its suburbs."

"But they don't have access to all the facts of this case, nor do they spend their days with absolutely nothing to focus on but who the Strangler will choose as his next victim. It must be disconcerting for you."

Devane was striking too close to the bone, and Ivy wanted to deflect his scrutiny with a diverting quip. Unfortunately, her rapier wit failed her. "It does cross my mind from time to time, but paranoia isn't my style. Next question."

She was lying, but Alex let it pass. "All right. This task force has been working on the case for four months, without results. What was Lieutenant Grumberg doing wrong?"

Ivy smiled again, the impish twinkle lighting her eyes. "You mean other than not allowing me to have a crack at the Strangler?"

"Yeah, other than that," Alex said, his own smile returning. Her humor was contagious.

Ivy shrugged. "I don't think he was doing anything wrong, technically speaking. We've been following sound, solid, proven detection methods. Unfortunately, the Stranger isn't playing by any of the rules. On the face of it, he isn't even following the accepted psychological pattern of the average serial killer. Not that there is an average serial killer," she added quickly.

"What do you mean, 'on the face of it'?" Alex asked.

"The two psychiatrists who worked up profiles on the Strangler both agreed that this killer—like every serial killer—wants to get caught. That's why he leaves bizarre little clues. But these killers usually follow predictable patterns, whereas our Strangler has thrown in some odd little variations that don't add up."

"But there is a clear pattern in the selection of victims," Alex reminded her, playing devil's advocate.

"True, but everything else in the case appears to be arbitrary. None of the murder dates coincide—he doesn't strike consistently during the first week of the month or the third, and he doesn't favor a particular day of the week. There is no apparent pattern to when he will kill."

"Maybe he does it when the mood strikes him." Alex offered the suggestion and earned a wicked little smile from Ivy, because they both knew that he didn't believe that particular theory.

"Possible, but not likely. Some aspect of each victim's life relates to the game clue he leaves, which means that he has to do meticulous, time-consuming research before choosing whom he will kill next."

"What about the games?"

Ivy grinned. "That's where it really gets complicated. The games must have a special, psychological meaning to him, but his use of a *different* game piece for every murder is inconsistent with the pattern killer profile."

"Why is that?" Alex felt a little like a teacher leading his favorite pupil through a complicated exercise in logic. So far, Ivy had passed every test. She hadn't told him anything he hadn't already learned today, but she certainly hadn't exaggerated the extent of her knowledge. Ivy Kincaid was sharp.

"A normal pattern might be for the killer to use different pieces of the *same* game because it has some deep psychological meaning to him."

"Such as?"

"Who knows?" She shrugged expressively. "If his mother was a blonde in her late twenties who deserted him when he was a child and ran off to Atlantic City with the mailman, then he might fixate on the Monopoly game and use only pieces from that game as clues. But that's not the case here. Obviously, the killer isn't fixated on one single game."

"Which means?"

"That the games themselves aren't important," Ivy answered, knowing that Devane was testing her. His mind had already traveled this route; he had already drawn his own conclusions. But she didn't mind taking his quiz, because he was listening to her answers and evaluating their worth—something no one else on the task force had ever done. Also, there was something exciting about the connection that had formed so rapidly with Alex. There was a tension in the room that was almost electric. It snapped, crackled and popped between them like the white-hot filament of a light bulb. Alex's eyes were locked on Ivy's, and they shared the knowledge that they were both feeling—and enjoying—the heat.

"If the games aren't important, then what is?" he asked, almost holding his breath as he waited for her answer. He'd covered this ground with Brubaker and the other detectives this afternoon, and none of them had given the logical answer.

"The key is in the sequence of the games he's used."

"Bingo!" Alex cried, jumping up. Finally, he'd found someone who looked at the case the same way he did. "Give the lady a prize—the sequence is the key. The Strangler isn't fixated on games, he's fixated on a *list* of games." With almost manic energy, he began pacing the space behind his desk. "These aren't crimes of passion. There's no sexual assault of the victims, no mutilation, even the method of strangling is almost...antiseptic. He uses a rope, not his hands, because he wants to make it as clean and impersonal as possible."

"As though the victim herself is irrelevant," Ivy interpreted, shuddering as she did so. How anyone, even a madman, could consider human life irrelevant was beyond her comprehension.

"That's right. The victim is only a pawn. It's the game that's important to him, and the key is in the sequence of games—Monopoly, Trivial Pursuit, chess, Risk, Othello and Pentathlon. Six games, six murders. If we can ascertain the seventh game in the sequence, we may be able to figure out who the next victim will be."

Ivy saw where he was leading, and her excitement mounted. This was an idea that had skirted around on the edges of her consciousness, but she had never addressed it head-on. Lieutenant Grumberg had operated the investigation on the assumption that the Strangler was choosing each victim first, then finding a board game that in some way related to the victim's life. It was that particular assumption that had created the discrepancy the psychiatrists had pointed out. Having no discernible pattern to the games wasn't consistent with the profile of a pattern killer. But according to Devane, there was a predictable pattern in the sequence.

Unfortunately, only the killer knew what it was.

"That's an interesting theory," she commented.

"But you don't buy it?"

"On the contrary. It makes about as much sense as anything we've come up with so far. In fact, it makes more sense in some ways. The problem is, if the list of games isn't random, how do we determine the origin of it?"

"We look for the common denominator. Everything down to the tiniest detail is important in this case. In fact, the solution to this puzzle might be so ridiculously simple that everyone has overlooked it," Alex said, taking his seat. "I doubt that that's the case, but we have to start at the beginning and find the one common thread that connects every murder."

"The games."

"Yes."

Ivy had given them a great deal of thought, so she had no trouble offering him an immediate answer. "All right. One, all the games are played on a board. Two, they all have at least one piece that is unique to that particular game—and that's the piece the Strangler is using." For clarity's sake, she listed the clues found at the crime scenes: a Monopoly thimble, a Trivial Pursuit wedge, a chess queen, a Risk army, a black-and-white Othello disk and a Pentathlon gold medal.

"Three," she said, "all the games are immensely popular."

"That's true," Alex said. This was an angle he hadn't considered before. Of course, he hadn't had a lot of time to do much considering, since his only previous contact with the case had been through newspaper accounts, and most of this information had been withheld from the newspapers. "There's not an obscure one in the bunch, is there? There are hundreds of board games on the market, yet he chooses only games that just about everyone in the world has heard of. We'll file that thought for future reference."

"All right," Ivy murmured, liking the way he was saying "we'll" not "I'll". She continued listing things the board games had in common. Alex would add to her list when she ran out of ideas, and then she would be off and running again. They fed off of each other as though they had been working together for years.

Somewhere in the back of her mind, Ivy realized that she and Devane were able to communicate almost without speaking. They both organized their thoughts sequentially and they were both extremely logical. And as they traded ideas, it became obvious that they shared a twisted sense of humor that could rear its perverse head without warning.

"All right, we've covered the similarities," Alex announced, filling in a small, thoughtful silence that had fallen between them. He downed the last bite of his turkey sandwich. "Let's go after the differences."

Ivy changed gears and started listing again. "Each game is designed for a different number of players, all the pieces are of different sizes and shapes—"

"They're made of different materials—"

"Not all of them," Ivy corrected. "Except for the Monopoly thimble and the jade chess queen, the pieces are all plastic. That queen, by the way, is probably our best clue. It's from an expensive, antique, hand-carved set that may very well be one of a kind."

"But no one's been able to determine where it came from," Alex said, thinking of the report he'd read just before Ivy arrived. A dozen antique dealers had been questioned about it, and none of them had been able to tell the police anything except that it was more than a hundred years old and of Chinese origin. "So what other differences have we got?"

"The initial letters of each game, in sequence, do not spell anything—"

"You thought of that, too?"

Ivy nodded. "Try as I might, I couldn't make a word out of *mtcrod*. I haven't been able to anagram it, either."

Alex shook his head. "That's invalid, anyway, since we don't have the entire list of letters. Unless he's planning on committing a finite number of murders, the initial letters can't be an anagram of something."

"Good. I hate anagrams—they're the only type of puzzle in the world that I am absolutely worthless at." She paused, trying to think of other differences in the games. "Some use dice, some don't. All the game pieces left at the crime scenes were different colors—silver, yellow, green, blue, black-and-white and gold."

She whipped off the list without hesitation, and Alex grinned. She really did know the facts of this case—even the smallest details—backward and forward. "True. There is no repetition of color."

"Coincidence?"

Alex shook his head. "I don't believe there are any coincidences in this case. Everything's neatly tied together."

Ivy took a deep breath and her eyes widened appreciably. "Do you realize that you're suggesting a puzzle of mind-boggling proportions? If there are no coincidences— no random elements at all—we'll never catch this guy!"

"On the contrary. The more complex this puzzle seems on the surface, the more likely it is to unravel neatly once we learn which threads to pull." He grinned. "Pardon the mixed metaphor."

"You're forgiven," Ivy told him generously. "Personally, I'm rather fond of mixed metaphors."

"How about mixed drinks?"

Ivy tilted her head to one side and eyed Devane speculatively. "I've been known to imbibe on occasion. In moderation."

"Then why don't we continue this over something cold?" he suggested. "I've been cooped up in here so long that I'm developing cabin fever."

"And it's only your first day," she reminded him. "Just imagine what it must be like for poor, pitiful me, stuck out there—" she made a pathetic gesture toward the squad room "—day after day, week after week, seeing nothing but those four big walls that seem to close in on me..."

Alex held up his hands in surrender. "I get the picture, I get the picture."

"Does that mean you're going to rescue me from my ivory tower?"

"I'll think about it" was all he would promise her.

Ivy frowned. "My hero."

Alex grinned. "Don't press your luck, blondie. You want that drink or not?"

Fighting back a laugh, Ivy leaned forward and lowered her voice confidentially. Alex wondered if she was aware of how sexy the husky tone sounded. He certainly was. "Do you realize, Lieutenant, that if we leave together, it's going to cause rumors? By tomorrow morning, it will be all over the precinct that we're having a torrid love affair."

Ivy's eyes had tiny flecks of dark blue that stood out in contrast to the paler azure of her irises. Alex had to struggle to ignore what those intriguing, sparkling eyes did to his insides. "Is the rumor mill really that bad around here?"

"Oh, yes," she assured him gravely.

Alex assumed an air that was half shock, half overwhelming gratitude. "Thank God you warned me," he said hoarsely.

"Why is that?"

"You may have saved my career! Earlier this afternoon I almost asked Jordan Brubaker to go out with me and discuss the case over dinner! I certainly won't make that mistake again," he vowed fervently.

"Well, I should hope not," Ivy said, barely managing to swallow another laugh. "Come on, boss, we'd better move you out of here before you think of something else that will really get you in trouble."

"You take such good care of me." Alex grinned and swiveled his chair toward his computer. He hit the appropriate buttons and put it to sleep for the evening.

Ivy stood as Alex began collecting some printouts he obviously planned to take home. "Where are we going, by the way?"

"Someplace quiet and discreet, I should think," Alex answered. "We wouldn't want Jordan to see us together and get jealous."

"Of course not," Ivy exclaimed. "He might challenge me to a duel, and I'd have to defend your honor."

"Would you really do that for me?"

"Sure, I would."

"Thank you. I suddenly feel so safe and protected," he said with a sigh. "Come on, let's blow this pop stand." He headed for the door and Ivy fell in beside him, smiling. This wasn't a date—it was purely business, she reminded herself—but already she'd had more fun with Alex Devane than she'd had with her last six dates combined.

"I have to make a quick stop at my desk," Ivy told him, starting in that direction. "I need to get my purse and change the computer access codes so no one can infiltrate our files."

"No problem." Alex followed her through the nearly deserted squad room. He leaned casually against Ivy's desk while she completed her computer housecleaning chores, but before they could effect their escape, Ivy's phone rang.

She glanced up at him with an apologetic smile. "Sorry. It's probably the Strangler calling to turn himself in because he's heard that you're going to let me have a crack at catching him."

"No doubt."

Ivy stabbed at the flashing button on her phone and lifted the receiver. "Kincaid."

"You're still at work, naturally," Mavis Kincaid, Ivy's mother, said with patient censure in her voice. "Don't you have anything better to do, darling?"

"No, Mother, I don't. But if it will make you feel any better, I was just getting ready to leave. What's up?"

"I just had a very interesting phone call, and I'm going to need your help."

"With what?"

"Shopping," Mavis said succinctly. "Gil Hatchet just called to ask me for a date, and I haven't a thing to wear."

"Mom, that's wonderful! Who's Gil Hatchet?"

"He's a retired businessman I met at the community center bingo game last Saturday night."

Ivy glanced at Alex, who was unabashedly eaves-
dropping on her end of the conversation. She shrugged and
mouthed the word "sorry" to him, then went back to her
mother. "This one doesn't have warts or cheat at bingo, I
presume."

"Of course not! I wouldn't be going out with him if he
did."

"Naturally." Ivy was grinning from ear to ear. Her
mother had been divorced from Ivy's father for nearly
twenty years, but until she had retired two years ago, she'd
never even considered dating. Her daughter and her work
as a legal secretary had taken precedence over men, but now,
with time on her hands, Mavis was discovering the joys of
socializing with the opposite sex. And Ivy was discovering
a fascinating, heretofore untapped side of her mother's
personality. "So when's the date?"

"Sunday afternoon. We're driving up the coast to a little
inn called the Breakers."

"You're letting him take you to an inn on the first date?"
Ivy asked, coming forward in her chair, alarmed.
"Mother!"

"It's only for lunch and a walk along the beach, Ivy,"
Mavis said with exaggerated patience. "I know what I'm
doing, I just don't know what I should wear. I was hoping
you might go with me to Broadricks this week and help me
choose something appropriate."

"Of course I'll help, Mom," Ivy promised. She glanced
at Alex and found that he was grinning broadly. She could
only guess what he had divined from the one side of the
conversation he could hear. "I'm not sure what my schedule looks like for the rest of the week, though. Why don't I
call you later and we'll firm something up. I want to hear
more about this Gil Hatchet, but I'm a little busy right
now."

"Oh, honey, I'm sorry. You said you were leaving. I didn't realize you were busy."

"I was just on my way out to have a drink with my new boss. We're going to discuss the case."

"Your new boss?" Mavis asked with interest. "Would that be Alex Devane? I saw him on the six o'clock news tonight."

"That's him."

Mavis lowered her voice confidentially. "He's very attractive, Ivy, though he could use a good haircut. Is he married?"

Ivy had to smother a grin. "I don't know, Mother. He's right here. Let me ask him—"

Mavis shouted, "Ivy Lane Kincaid! Don't you dare!"

But Ivy ignored her, drew the phone away from her ear an inch or two and grinned up at Alex. "My mother wants to know if you're married."

Alex chuckled despite himself. "No, I'm a widower," he answered. Only a small shadow darkened his eyes as he said it. "But tell your mother that I have a particular weakness for attractive middle-aged women, and I don't cheat at bingo."

Ivy went back to the phone. "Did you hear that, Mom?"

"I heard," Mavis said between gritted teeth. "How could you embarrass me like that? I thought I raised you better than that."

"Be nice, Mom, or I'll tell Lieutenant Devane you think he needs a haircut."

At that, Alex doubled over with laughter, and Mavis, hearing the deep, resonant sound, cringed with mortification—though heaven only knew she should have expected her daughter to pull something like this. Ivy had always been audacious and downright brazen. If the truth was told, Ivy's outrageous personality was one of the things Mavis loved and admired most about her daughter.

Ivy wrapped the call up quickly, and Alex was still chuckling when she hung up.

"You know, Detective Kincaid, they say *I'm* crazy, but I think you've got me beat by a mile," he told her with a deliciously wicked gleam in his eyes that would have jump started Ivy's heart even in subzero weather.

Ivy tilted her chair back and regarded him lazily. The atmosphere between them was sizzling again. "It's all just an act to keep people at a distance."

"Yeah? Me, too," he said, surprised at his own candor.

"You think we'll ever get past the wisecracks and really get to know each other?"

"Probably not."

"Meaning, you don't ever plan to let anyone get past your defenses and crawl around inside your head?" she asked, a knowing smile still teasing her lips.

"Nope."

Ivy tilted her face, unable to keep a coquettish lilt from her voice. "Not even casual visitors?"

Alex considered that for a moment. "I do have a short-term lease program."

"Oh, yeah? How short?" she asked, her tone provocative and challenging.

Sexual static crackled around them like Fourth of July sparklers. Gray eyes met blue and held on, prolonging the tension, dragging out the moment. Each dared the other to be the first to look away, the first to break the contact and extinguish the sparklers.

Surprisingly, it was Alex who finally caved under the pressure. Ivy Kincaid was one potent lady. "You are certainly something else, Detective," he complimented her. "Are you sure you're not trying to seduce me?"

"Positive," Ivy answered. "I can't help it if we have this—" she paused, searching for the right word "—chemistry."

"I guess that's true." He eased away from the desk as Ivy retrieved her purse and stood. "You know, Tracy and Hepburn had the same kind of chemistry between them."

Ivy gave him an innocent smile as she swept past him. "So did Starsky and Hutch."

Alex fell in beside her. "You think they ever slept together?"

"Nah," she said, breezing through the swinging doors that led to the corridor. "We'd have read about it in the *Enquirer*." She punched a button to call the elevator, then turned to find Alex Devane only inches away from her. His proximity almost took her breath away.

"Do you think *we'll* ever sleep together once this case is over?" The flirtatious quip didn't come out quite as lightly as he had intended.

Ivy met his eyes squarely. She wasn't promiscuous and she didn't believe in love at first sight, but at this very moment, she did believe that she had inherited her grandmother's ability to see the future. "It does feel inevitable, doesn't it?"

Alex sighed as the elevator doors whooshed open. "Yes. Heaven help us."

"Amen."

Grinning, they stepped into the elevator and the doors whooshed shut.

CHAPTER FOUR

ARMED WITH A SHOPPING BAG containing his own thermos of drinkable coffee from Ernie's Delicatessen, Alex Devane jogged up the stairs to the second floor of the station house and moved briskly past the elevator toward the squad room. It was only seven forty-five in the morning, but already the corridors and offices were bustling with activity. Phones were ringing and uniformed officers were hurrying in and out the door to the squad room, pointedly ignoring a couple of bulldog reporters who were camped in the hallway.

Alex recognized one of the reporters instantly. Phil Danker was a no-talent, unscrupulous hack who worked for a sleazy Brauxton tabloid that specialized in sensationalizing anything its editors got their hands on. The accidental shooting of a six-year-old, defenseless child had been right up their alley. After Tanya Ringwald's tragic death, it was Danker who had led the crusade that crucified Alex in the press. Needless to say, the reporter wasn't high on Alex's list of favorite people.

Both reporters spotted Alex at about the same time, and they sprang forward eagerly, barraging him with questions.

"How does it feel to be back, Lieutenant Devane?"

"Any breaks in the case, yet?"

"Any comments on Grumberg's handling of the case?"

"What do you plan to do first?"

"Sorry, guys, no comment," Alex said, trying to brush past them.

"Have you found a new perspective on the case?" the younger of the two reporters asked, blocking his way.

"No comment." He sidestepped that reporter, but Danker quickly barred Alex's escape.

"You mean you haven't collared the Strangler yet, Lieutenant?" he said with an unmistakable sneer in his voice. "I thought they brought you in to get fast results."

"If you want fast results, take an antacid."

"May I quote you on that?"

"You will, anyway." Disgusted, Alex feinted to the right, then dodged left, neatly circumventing Danker. He disappeared through the swinging doors of the squad room, ignoring a question shouted at him by the younger reporter.

Several detectives were already at their desks, and Alex returned the greetings of those who spoke to him as he made his way to his office. Ivy Kincaid's desk was conspicuously vacant, and Alex smiled at the memory of the way the vivacious detective had barged into his office the previous night determined to capture his attention. And she had succeeded—in spades. Ivy was smart, funny and vibrantly attractive.

She was also as knowledgeable about the Strangler case as she had claimed she was. She had proved that in his office last night, and later, over drinks at Coopersmith's, a trendy little bar down the street from the station house. They had stayed there until nearly midnight, but when they parted company and Alex went home, he'd felt that Ivy was still with him—firmly implanted in his imagination. He'd spent the rest of the night thinking of little else. Fortunately, since they'd spent most of their time together discussing the case, Alex could assuage his conscience by telling himself that thinking about Ivy Kincaid was tantamount to thinking about the Strangler.

It was a small bit of self-deception that worked reasonably well.

Alex stepped into his office and stopped abruptly. Someone had definitely been in the room, and Alex placed his money on the former task force commander, Gene Grumberg. The beach-bunny swimsuit calendar that had been hanging on the nail to the left of the desk was conspicuously absent, as was the horrible hunting poster that had been hanging to the right of it. The mostly dead spider plant that had sat withering on the windowsill was gone, thank goodness, and so were the framed photographs, pipe tobacco, ashtrays and other personal paraphernalia that had marked Grumberg's occupancy.

The room was considerably less cluttered now, but the institutional green block walls were dismally bare. As Alex moved to his desk he made a mental note to do something about that as soon as possible. Maybe a couple of nice watercolors would liven things up a bit. They certainly couldn't hurt; the room was so depressing that even a couple of strategically placed sticks of dynamite would make a vast improvement.

As he removed his thermos and his "I loathe mornings" mug from his shopping bag, Alex reached over to the computer and brought it on-line. He sat, poured a cup of Ernie's coffee and devoted his full attention to the monitor. He wanted to glance over the reports filed by the officers on duty last night to see if any unusual phone calls had come in on the hot line.

Unfortunately, the computer would not cooperate. Bright amber letters blinked "Access Denied" at him.

"Morning, *mon capitaine*. I see you brought your own coffee today."

Alex swiveled toward the sultry feminine voice and found Ivy standing at the door. Dressed in lemon-yellow trousers and a bold floral-print blouse, she looked brighter and perkier than anyone had a right to look at 7:55 in the morning. "Don't tell me you're one of those obnoxiously cheerful people who start every day with a smile," he said grumpily, trying to squelch his own smile, which had started somewhere inside and was inching its way toward his mouth.

Ivy shrugged. "What can I say? I'm a morning person."

"Under my new administration, that could get you fired." Despite Alex's best efforts, the smile finally broke free. It was obviously a direct result of the effect Ivy had on him, and Alex decided that he liked it.

"I'll take my chances."

"You must like living dangerously."

"I live for excitement."

"I'm pretty fond of cheap thrills, myself," he told her. "Maybe you could give me one right now."

Ivy's delicately sculpted eyebrows went up. "Such as?"

"Tell me how to break into this damned computer."

"Try rosebud," she suggested, wishing her heart rate would slow to normal. After she'd left Coopersmith's last night, she'd spent quite a bit of time thinking about her new boss, and those thoughts had made her pulse race as it was doing now. She had tossed and turned in bed remembering the sizzling chemistry they'd shared, and she'd managed to convince herself that Alex Devane wasn't nearly as handsome as her fevered imagination was making him. She was wrong, though. He was even better looking than she remembered, hence, these irritating palpitations.

"Rosebud, huh? Are you a *Citizen Kane* fan?" Alex asked as he typed the access code into the computer and was rewarded with a blank screen and a blinking cursor.

"Who isn't? Now it's my turn to ask a question."

"Ask away."

"Are you going to use that nail?" She pointed toward the spot where Grumberg's swimsuit calendar had once hung. The nail in question was deeply embedded in the concrete block.

"Actually, I did have a There's No Place Like Home poster I was thinking of putting up there, but if you need the nail, it's all yours. Be my guest."

"Thank you."

"Of course, you realize," he added as Ivy swept toward his desk, "that if you pull it out of the stone bare-handed, you'll have to change your name to Arthur and take your rightful place as king of England."

"Oh, but I have no intention of removing it, Merlin," she quipped, producing a flat, rectangular box that she'd been hiding behind her. Deftly, she flipped the latch on the side of the box and spilled two velvet pouches onto the blotter in front of Alex, then opened the hinged box and leaned over his desk to hang it on the nail.

Alex looked at the small black-and-white checked board, and his grin widened. Ivy opened one of the velvet pouches and out tumbled sixteen black chessmen, which she quickly began placing on the board. "Magnetic, I presume."

"Naturally. It's a travel set my mother gave to me when I joined the high school chess club."

"Are you any good?"

Ivy reached for the second velvet pouch, capturing Alex's eyes as she spilled the contents. "I'm better than good, Lieutenant."

Alex felt his breath hitch in his throat. Ivy's declaration was a husky, low-pitched murmur that challenged him to a chess match, nothing more, but he couldn't help wondering what else the lovely Detective Kincaid might be good at. Would she be good at kissing? he wondered as he took in the smile that teased her lips. Yes, he decided. Her mouth was prettily bowed, her lips were full, and she had an inner warmth and energy that infused everything she did. That latter trait was one she could no doubt use to devastating effect in a kiss.

Would she be good at touching, too? he asked himself as she turned her profile to him and her small, graceful hands began placing the white chessmen on the bottom row of the board. He watched her nimble fingers arrange the men and realized that, yes, she would probably be very good at touching, too.

Of course, there was no question as to whether or not Ivy would be good to touch. As she leaned against his desk with her arms raised to the board, the soft fabric of her shirt strained against the delectable swell of her breasts and outlined her impossibly small waist. Her trousers clung to the curve of her hips. Her blond hair, long in the back but clipped short on the sides, highlighted the slender line of her neck—a neck that had obviously been made to drive a man to distraction.

Alex felt a swift, piercing shaft of pure, unadulterated desire course through him and was ashamed. Not because he wanted Ivy Kincaid, though. He was ashamed of himself because he was so thoroughly delighted by his desire for her. He hadn't exactly been a monk these past few years, but his few sexual encounters since Brenda's suicide had been cold, passionless and unfulfilling. He'd just been going through the motions. The last years of his marriage to Brenda had been the same.

It had been a long time since a woman had aroused in him a desire that brought a warm, exhilarating glow of expectation. It was going to be exciting finding out if or when that expectation might turn into reality.

No, Alex thought, *not if. When. Definitely when.* Once the Strangler case was wrapped up, Alex intended to devote a considerable amount of time to finding out what made Ivy Kincaid so fascinating. In the meantime, that was just one more reason to catch the Strangler quickly.

"Et voilà," Ivy said, stepping back a few inches when she had finished preparing the board. "The game, as they say, is afoot!" She reached out and moved the white queen's pawn forward two squares.

"Whoa! Hold on there, Sherlock!" Alex exclaimed. "Who decided that you get to make the first move?"

Ivy looked at him as though he were from Mars. "White always moves first."

"Yes, but who said you could be white?"

"It's my board—even has my name scratched on the back to prove it," she said smugly. "That means I get to be white."

"According to who?"

"According to Hoyle," Ivy retorted with a grin. "It's in the rules. If you don't believe me, look it up."

"Oh, I will. There's nothing I like more than calling someone's bluff."

Ivy gestured toward the board. "In the meantime, it's your move."

"All right," he said, rising. From a standing position, he could reach the board easily, but the move Alex made had nothing to do with chess. He stepped out from behind his desk and sat on the front edge. "I'm planning on paying a visit to each of the murder sites this morning, and I seem to recall that you expressed an interest in getting out of the office once in a while. Would you care to join me?"

Ivy's eyes lighted up like bright sapphire Christmas ornaments. Her pulse slammed into overdrive, but she somehow managed to project an ultraprofessional demeanor. "Why, yes, Lieutenant Devane. I'd be only too happy to accompany you."

"Good." Alex grinned. His reasons for wanting Ivy along had nothing to do with the fact that he enjoyed her company, but he couldn't help being pleased at the way she lighted up. More than anything, Ivy wanted a greater involvement in the case, and Alex was convinced she deserved an opportunity to prove herself. Alex knew from the years he'd spent with Gene Grumberg on the homicide squad that the irascible lieutenant didn't care much about equal rights for women. Assigning Ivy to a computer was probably as close as Grumberg would ever have come to giving her a real opportunity to develop her potential.

Alex had no such prejudices, though, and he was going to make sure the female members of the task force were afforded the same opportunities as the men. "We'll leave about nine," he told her. "I'll buzz you when I'm ready."

"I'll be waiting." Ivy headed for the door, then turned back, her smile fading as she regarded him sincerely. "Thanks for giving me this chance, Lieutenant. I won't let you down."

"Oh, don't thank me. I have an ulterior motive— you're going to pay me handsomely for this opportunity."

Ivy froze, and all her lightheartedness began to fade. Ever since she'd walked into Alex's office last night, they'd been playing a game of innocent flirtation, and clearly they'd both been enjoying it. Now, though, Ivy cursed herself for giving in to that unprofessional temptation. She'd been down this you-scratch-my-back-I'll-scratch-yours road before, and she had no intention of traveling it again. Flirtation was one thing—sexual blackmail was quite another.

She'd thought Alex Devane was different, but if he expected sexual favors in return for giving her the job opportunity she deserved, clearly she'd been wrong about him. The disappointment she felt was keen—almost painfully so.

"Exactly what did you have in mind as...payment?" she asked, unable to keep an edge of frost out of her voice.

Alex felt the chill that suddenly pervaded the room and realized that he'd carried their playful banter one step too far. He sobered and gestured toward the chessboard. "My intention was to blackmail you into allowing me to be white, but my joke backfired, didn't it? Sorry."

Ivy leaned against the door frame, immensely relieved and horribly embarrassed. "No, I'm the one who should apologize. I'm sorry I jumped to a stupid conclusion. A few years ago I had an unfortunate encounter with a desk sergeant who wanted to exchange favors. It's made me a little wary of innuendo."

"As I recall, you weren't too wary last night," he said, remembering that they'd shared more than one double entendre during the evening.

Ivy shrugged. "Last night we were exchanging information, but you hadn't given me any indication that you were going to allow me to have a greater involvement in the case. Today, you did, and I overreacted. I should have known better than to think you were a low-down, sleazy skunk who would resort to blackmail to satisfy your disgusting, lustful appetites."

Alex laughed. "Thank you. I think."

"Don't mention it." Ivy grinned. "It's gratifying to know that you are just a low-down, *sneaky* skunk who would use blackmail to satisfy a childish need to go first in a game of chess."

"Does that mean I get to be white?" he asked hopefully, delighted that their relationship was back to normal.

"Not on your life, buster. Blackmail is an ugly business, and I won't be a part of it. If I give in this time, there's no telling what you'll ask for next."

"Well, I promise you this, Ivy," Alex said, growing serious once again—so serious that Ivy's heart did a thrilling little back flip, "whatever happens or doesn't happen between us will have nothing to do with your job. I invited you to come with me today because this case needs some fresh viewpoints, and I happen to like the way you think."

"Thanks."

"You're welcome. Now get back to your desk before I put you on report for dereliction of duty."

"Aye, aye, Captain Bligh." With a mock salute, Ivy hurried out of Alex's office. Though she maintained a sedate pace back to her desk, inside she was turning cartwheels. She was getting out of the office today! She was finally going to view the murder scenes! Someone was finally going to listen to her opinions! And best of all, Alex Devane liked her despite the way she'd made a fool of herself with that blackmail business!

Ivy considered that last item with a modicum of guilt and reminded herself that she had a job to do. She came to the precinct every day to serve and protect the city of Brauxton, not to augment her meager love life. It was thoroughly unprofessional of her to be thinking of the charming, incredibly sexy lieutenant in personal terms, she told herself.

But on the other hand, Ivy had yet to meet any human being on this side of the planet who was able to keep business and pleasure totally separate. There was certainly nothing wrong with enjoying Alex Devane's company while they worked together, and if, after the job was done, something personal developed . . . well, that would just be icing on the cake.

It was a few minutes after nine when Ivy's phone rang, with the lieutenant on the other end of the line asking her to step into his office. "I'm on my way," she told him, then grabbed her purse and feigned nonchalance as she strolled to his office.

She rapped perfunctorily on the door, and Alex motioned her in with one hand while the other ripped a page from the computer printer that sat behind his desk. "Before we go, I want you to take a look at this," he said, handing her the paper. "It's the transcript of a call that came in on the Strangler hot line last night."

Ivy took the single sheet, tossed her purse onto one of the two chairs that sat in front of Alex's desk and dropped herself onto the arm of the other. She quickly skimmed the report.

The call, which had come in at 11:04, was from a Mrs. Ada McGivens. Mrs. McGivens had apparently felt compelled to inform the police that her next-door neighbor, Rupert Girrard, fit the profile of the Strangler. The lady included in her accusation a number of incriminating statements about Girrard's nocturnal activities that did seem to make her neighbor a likely suspect.

"What do you think?" Alex asked. "Worth following up on?"

Ivy tried to squelch a smile. "On the surface it does look promising," she admitted. "Unfortunately, poor Mr. Girrard isn't the only man in Ada McGivens's neighborhood who fits the Strangler profile. She's been calling in with a different suspect once a week for the past two months."

Alex hadn't actually expected McGivens's tip to be valid—in a case like this, crank calls were a dime a dozen—but even a long shot was worth considering. "She's a crank?"

"The crankiest," Ivy confirmed, handing the computer sheet back to Alex. "Last week she was certain the Strangler was Father Leo Whipkey, her parish priest."

"So much for blind luck and easy solutions," Alex muttered, crumpling the paper into a ball that he sent hurtling toward the trash can. "I guess we'll have to do this the hard way. Are you ready to give it a try, Sherlock?"

"Ready and waiting."

"Good." Alex started to turn toward his computer, but a voice from the doorway stopped him.

"Well, Devane, I see you've settled in."

Ivy whipped her head toward the voice, but not before she got a glimpse of the scowl Alex made no attempt to hide.

Commissioner Eversall stood at the door, with a small box tucked casually under his left arm. "Do you have anything significant to report yet?" he asked.

"There's going to be a full moon tonight," Alex replied lightly, leaning negligently back in his chair. The tension level in the room had risen drastically in only seconds, and Ivy glanced at Alex once again; his glacial stare did not match his cavalier tone. She turned back toward Eversall, feeling very much like a spectator at a tennis match.

"What's that got to do with anything?" Len demanded. "Do you think there's some connection between the phases of the moon and the Strangler's strike pattern?"

"No," Alex replied. "That's just the most significant thing I have to report. If you'd do me a favor and pass it along to the mayor, I'd be grateful. It'll save me a call."

Eversall seemed about to reply, but his glance slid to Ivy and he seemed to reconsider. "Kincaid, isn't it?"

"Yes, sir," Ivy answered respectfully. "If you like me to step outside..." She started to rise, but the commissioner forestalled the movement with a wave of his hand.

"Not necessary. This won't take long." He stepped toward the desk, reached into the box he carried and tossed a black leather wallet down in front of Alex. "I brought you your shield. I thought it might come in handy."

"Thanks." Alex reached for the leather-encased badge and tucked it into the pocket of his lightweight jacket without inspecting it.

"And your beeper." He laid it on the desk. "With this job, you're on call twenty-four hours a day. And I also brought you this." Eversall reached into the box again, and Ivy thought she detected a hint of smugness in the commissioner. It didn't take a Holmesian intellect to see that these two men disliked each other, and she couldn't help but wonder why.

She watched as Eversall withdrew a Smith & Wesson .38 Chiefs Special from the box and placed it on the desk. That threw the ball back into Alex's court, and Ivy turned to see his reaction. It wasn't pleasant. The tension level shot off the Richter scale, and Ivy fought the temptation to duck for cover.

The springs of Alex's chair creaked as he leaned forward slowly. "Get that thing out of here," he said, his square jaw locked so tightly that his voice was nothing more than a gravelly whisper.

"It's standard issue, Alex. You have to take it—it comes with the job."

"I told you I wouldn't carry a gun, Len. That was my only condition for returning."

"The gun is yours, Alex," Len told him. "What you do with it is your decision."

"Get it out of here."

Eversall ignored the command and placed the box on the desk. "Shoulder holster and ammunition. All signed out to you," he explained. "Don't bother thanking me. I'll just see myself to the door."

The commissioner sauntered out, leaving Alex fuming in his wake. He looked at the gun with ill-concealed distaste, and Ivy wondered which he detested more—the deadly weapon or the man who'd delivered it.

"Obviously you didn't get this job by trading on an old friendship," Ivy observed dryly when the silence in the room became oppressive.

Alex cut his eyes sharply toward her, then looked down at the gun. "I told him I wouldn't carry one of these, so naturally he had to show me who was boss. He's still ticked off because the mayor forced him to bring me in on the case."

He wasn't telling Ivy anything she hadn't already guessed. "My native curiosity is begging me to ask why you and the commissioner hate each other's guts, but since it's none of my business, I won't."

"Good."

"What I will do, though—" she stood, picked up the .38 and placed it back in the box "—is take care of this little number for you." Moving around the desk until she was beside Alex's chair, Ivy opened the deep lower drawer of the desk. It was virtually empty except for a couple of file folders that lay on the bottom. Ivy picked them up, deposited the gun—box and all—into the drawer and tossed the folders on top of the box.

"Out of sight, out of mind?" Alex asked.

Ivy nodded as she closed the drawer. "That's the general idea. It's not in view, but it's there just in case the station house is seized by a gang of Lilliputian terrorists and you need to defend yourself."

She had expected her quip to draw a smile, but it did not. Instead, Alex turned toward his computer. "I will never use a gun again. Not even for defense."

Ivy thought that was a somewhat rigid point of view, yet she couldn't help but sympathize. "Because of the little girl who was shot?" she asked quietly, sitting on the corner of his desk.

"That's right." He shut off the computer and turned toward her, capturing her eyes squarely. "A child is dead because of me. Nothing like that will ever happen again."

"Alex, that wasn't your fault," she said gently, not even realizing she'd used his first name with such ease. "It was an accident."

"It was my gun. If that doesn't make it my fault, what does?"

"What happened to you is every police officer's worst nightmare," she said, avoiding the question that had no easy answer.

"Well, my nightmare came true," he told her. "And once was enough."

His eyes were as cold as flint, and Ivy was deeply moved by the pain she saw beneath his hard, determined exterior. The police officer in her empathized with that pain; the woman in her wanted to reach out and gently take it away.

Instead, she chose a more appropriate course and tried again to lighten their mood. "Would you like me to take the gun and shove it down the commissioner's throat for you?"

That finally did the trick, and Alex grinned. "A stunt like that could get you fired."

Ivy waved one hand airily. "Oh, don't worry about me. I'll just tell him you ordered me to do it."

Alex laughed. "Thanks a lot, pal." He jerked his head toward the door as he picked up a cardboard box containing six case files. "Come on, let's get to work. We've got a strangler to catch."

CHAPTER FIVE

WITH IVY RIGHT BEHIND HIM, Alex stepped into the squad room and called to Detective Brubaker.

"Yes, Alex?"

"Jordan, I want you to see that these hot line calls are followed up on today." Shifting the cumbersome box under one arm, Alex took a sheet of paper off the top and handed it to his subordinate. "I'll be out most of the day, visiting the murder sites."

Brubaker glanced at the hot line list without really seeing it. "You want me to go with you?"

"No, you hold down the fort. Kincaid's going with me."

"Ivy?" Brubaker glanced sharply at Ivy, and the look on his face was one of such shock that she had the childish urge to stick out her tongue and go "Na-na-nana-na." But she didn't. She was impulsive, yes, but she wasn't stupid.

Instead, she told him, "I think the lieutenant wants a woman's point of view on this." She started to add "For a change," but stopped herself just in time.

"But the Strangler's a man," Jordan argued, not pleased that his place as senior detective was being usurped. He had been Grumberg's right hand, and he'd expected to continue in that capacity with Alex. But this morning, the rumor mill had been buzzing with the news that Ivy Kincaid had left the precinct with the new lieutenant last night after a long powwow in his office, and apparently the rumor was true. Somehow, she'd managed to insinuate herself into Devane's good graces overnight. Jordan didn't have to speculate long to figure out how she'd accomplished that feat.

"He's a man who kills women," Alex pointed out. "And I want to know how he's choosing his victims. Come on, Kincaid. Get on those hot line calls, Jordy." He started out and Ivy wiggled her fingers at Brubaker and followed.

After dodging questions from a bevy of reporters in the hall, they made a brief stop at the property room to pick up the keys to the apartments of the victims, then took a rear stairway down to the parking garage in the basement. Alex had been assigned an unmarked police car, but that little bit of anonymity wasn't enough to prevent them from being spotted as they left the underground garage.

"I want to do a drive-by of Beverly Coit's house first," Alex said, heading north toward the Riverside Parkway. "But I'd rather do it without an audience."

Ivy glanced out the rear window and saw a flashy red sports coupe pull into the stream of traffic behind them. "You think we picked up a reporter?"

"Yep." Alex would have recognized Phil Danker a mile away.

"What do you suggest we do?"

Alex thought a moment, then pulled into a left-hand turn lane and stopped at the red light. Danker made the same maneuver and ended up right behind them. "Can you get a make on his license plate?" he asked.

Ivy turned on the seat. "Inch the car forward a little bit." When Alex complied, Ivy had an unrestricted view of the bumper. She read the number aloud, then faced forward. "Now what?"

In answer, Alex picked up the microphone of the police band radio, tuned it to a closed frequency that couldn't be picked up on civilian CBs, then called the dispatcher to report the sighting of a stolen vehicle. The light changed and

Alex maneuvered a left turn onto Third Street as he described the red sports coupe behind him.

When he finished, Ivy threw back her head and laughed. "You are truly a devious individual."

"I do my best, ma'am," he drawled, grinning with satisfaction when he heard the unmistakable wail of a police siren. He glanced in the rearview mirror and watched as a black-and-white pulled Phil Danker over to the curb.

"And now?"

"Now—" Alex accelerated, made a quick right turn off Third and headed for the nearest entrance to the Riverside Parkway "—we go take a look at Beverly Coit's house. That all right with you?"

"After the stunt you just pulled, I wouldn't dream of contradicting you," she said. Still chuckling, she settled back to enjoy the ride.

Beverly Renee Coit, the Strangler's first victim, had lived in a two-bedroom house in one of Brauxton's older neighborhoods. At the time of her murder, no one had had any idea that her death would be the first in a long string of serial killings, and consequently, the police had released the murder site several weeks later. The homes of all the other victims had been sealed off indefinitely, but Beverly's house had since been sold. Alex knew he wouldn't be able to get in to have a look around, but he wanted to see the neighborhood, anyway. Nothing about this case had been left to chance, which meant that maybe the victims' homes had something in common. Or maybe not. Alex would have to see them all first before he'd know the answer to that one.

Ivy understood his reasoning without having to be told. "Beverly's house is near the neighborhood where I grew up. My mother still lives there, in fact."

Alex took his eyes off the busy freeway long enough to shoot Ivy a questioning glance. "You said that as though you knew her personally."

"My mother? Of course I know my mother."

"I walked into that one, didn't I?" Alex said with a half laugh. "I was referring to Beverly Coit, Sherlock. Did you know her?"

"Not while she was alive, no," Ivy answered. "But I feel as though I've gotten to know her since. I've studied the files so much that I feel I know them all."

Alex didn't have to be told that "all" meant the Strangler's six victims. "You feel a kinship with them, don't you?"

Ivy nodded, wishing Alex couldn't read her quite so well. He'd made a similar, accurate observation last night. "Yeah. Maybe too much so. It's the only time in my life that being a perky blue-eyed blonde hasn't come in handy."

Alex gave her remark the serious consideration it deserved. "Ivy, you're much too smart to let yourself get caught the way the others did."

Ivy turned on the seat and looked at Alex's profile. "They weren't caught, Alex. They were stalked, trapped and murdered in cold blood."

"But the odds against you being a victim are astronomical."

"Really? Maybe I should have my horoscope done to make certain I'm in the clear," she quipped, though she didn't at all feel like making jokes about this.

"I said astronomical, not astrological," Alex corrected her, chuckling. "You know, Ivy, having a serious conversation with you is even more difficult than having a serious conversation with me."

Ivy's eyebrows went up suspiciously. "Oh? Do you have many serious conversations with yourself?"

"You know what I mean. Usually I'm the one who whips off the snappy one-liners while someone else plays straight man. Being around you has thrown my timing off."

"Sorry," she said without a hint of apology.

Since Ivy had effectively diverted the conversation from a discussion of her personal feelings about the Strangler, Alex decided to keep the atmosphere light for the time being. Once they began investigating the murder sites, lightheartedness would be a lot harder to come by. "Tell me about yourself, Ivy. All I know about you personally is that you're absolutely outrageous, and you have a mother who plays bingo and goes to intimate retreats with virtual strangers."

"Leave my mother's love life out of this," Ivy said with a grin. "She discovered that life doesn't end at age sixty-two, and now I can hardly keep up with her. It wouldn't surprise me if one of these days I got a postcard from Aruba telling me she's run off with her ballroom dance instructor, Ramone."

Alex took his eyes off the road long enough to glance at Ivy. "Does she really have a dance instructor named Ramone?"

"It wouldn't surprise me one bit."

"What about your father?"

"He deserted us when I was ten," Ivy explained matter-of-factly. "Ran off with another woman and moved to Chicago."

"That must mean you didn't see him much."

Ivy sighed. "Try not at all. I got birthday cards for a while, and then nothing. He called me at Christmastime about ten years ago. He sounded a little...nostalgic, but we really didn't have anything to say to each other. He never called back."

Ivy was angled sideways on the seat, almost facing him, and Alex wondered if she was really as nonchalant about her father as she sounded. "His desertion must have been hard on you."

She grinned. "I was a tough kid, and I had a great mother. I survived."

Alex took his eyes off the traffic once again and pinned them on Ivy. "Without scars?"

Ivy's grin faded. "We all have scars, Alex. Should I ask you about yours?"

Alex thought of Brenda. "No."

"Then don't ask about mine."

"Deal."

They completed the trip in a silence that wasn't the least bit strained. The box of case files sat on the seat between them, and by the time they pulled up to the curb opposite the house where Beverly Coit had died, Ivy had the first file open on her lap. Alex shut off the engine and sat, surveying the quiet residential neighborhood. There wasn't much to see. No one was selling tickets to tour the home of the Brauxton Strangler's first victim, and the killer didn't seem to be lurking in the bushes, waiting for the police to show up and arrest him.

Alex got out of the car and moved toward the sidewalk, keeping the street between him and the small, white frame house. Ivy joined him, file in hand. Without being asked, she reached into the folder, extracted a set of photographs of the house and handed them to Alex. He compared the pictures to the real thing and found no significant differences. The trees that had been bare in January were now green. The new owners had added country-blue shutters to the windows. A couple of missing stiles in the white picket fence had been replaced. A lawn sprinkler was waving a delicate fountain of water back and forth over a section of parched grass.

"No sign of forced entry?" Alex asked.

"None," Ivy answered with certainty, not bothering to check the file. She knew most of it by heart.

"What did he do? Walk up to the door, say, 'Excuse me, miss, but my car broke down. May I use your phone?' and she let him in?"

"Possibly. Or maybe he was someone she knew well enough not to consider a threat."

"Possible, but not probable," Alex replied, shaking his head. "If the Strangler was someone the victims knew, we'd have found him by now."

"We?" Ivy questioned, raising one eyebrow. "You and I have both been watching this game from the fifty yard line, Kemo Sabe."

Alex grinned. "Figure of speech. Come on, Tonto, let's go before we get arrested for loitering." They turned to the car, and Alex headed for the site of the second murder.

He hadn't yet asked for an address, and Ivy was impressed with his memory. She knew them because she'd been on the case for months, but Alex had had less than twenty-four hours. He'd stuffed a lot of information into that brilliant mind of his in a very short time.

Nancy Monroe had made her home in a high-rise apartment building across town from Beverly Coit's more suburban-looking neighborhood. Here, the streets were teeming with traffic—both pedestrian and vehicular. Alex left the car in a restaurant parking lot down the block from the high rise, and Ivy put Nancy's file into her handbag, then got out of the car and locked the door.

"Is that a purse or a trash compactor?" Alex asked, eyeing the bag that hadn't seemed large until it had expanded to accept the file she'd stuffed into it. They headed down the busy sidewalk toward Nancy's apartment.

"Actually, it's a little of both."

"Well, watch where you swing it. You could probably lose Rhode Island in there."

Ivy chuckled. "If Rhode Island does turn up missing, at least you'll know where to look."

They reached the high rise and paid a quick courtesy call on the superintendent, introducing themselves and telling him they were going to survey Nancy Monroe's apartment.

The super was less than courteous and voiced his displeasure at having a perfectly good apartment sit vacant for five, going on six, months.

Alex listened politely to the man's tirade, then said a few meaningless, placating words about how the police department appreciated his cooperation and how the case would be wrapped up soon. Five minutes later Alex broke the yellow crime scene tape that sealed the door, and he and Ivy stepped inside.

A blast of hot, stale air slapped their faces, and it took them a moment to adjust to the heat. The room was in exactly the same condition as it had been in February when Nancy Monroe's body had been found—except for the white tape in front of the sofa that took the place of a strangled corpse.

Alex began slowly pacing the room, not really looking for anything, just getting the feel of the place in the same way he'd gotten the feel of Beverly Coit's neighborhood. Ivy, though, remained riveted at the door, unable to take her eyes off the spot where Nancy Monroe had died.

What was she thinking in those last moments of her life? Ivy wondered. Her death had been quick, but not so quick that she wouldn't have known what was happening to her. There had been plenty of time for her to feel the rope sting and burn and slice into her flesh. She'd had plenty of time to panic. More than enough time to feel the worst kind of terror. . . .

Unconsciously, Ivy raised one hand to her own neck. Her throat was as dry as cotton, and the acid taste of fear nearly choked her. Logically she knew that she was tasting the musty atmosphere of a room that had been sealed up for months, but emotionally she was putting herself in Nancy Monroe's place—or rather, the place Ivy irrationally believed might soon be hers. She could almost see Alex Devane walking dispassionately around her own small apartment, avoiding the white tape where her body had lain, looking for clues to her grisly death.

The thought brought her up short. *Get a grip, Ivy, or Alex is going to send you home without your milk and cookies.* As though to punctuate that thought, she glanced around quickly, looking for Alex to see if he'd observed her inappropriate reaction. He was standing at the other end of the long living room, dining room area, watching her. There was no censure in his eyes, but it was clear he knew what she was feeling.

"You okay?" he asked.

"Fine," Ivy replied, then coughed to clear her throat because her voice was little more than a croak.

"If you want to wait outside—"

"No!" She cut him off quickly. "I was just trying to imagine what it must have been like for Nancy—those last few moments."

Alex came toward her then. "That's not a good idea, Ivy."

"You detect your way, I'll detect mine," she told him in a tone that said "Hands off, buster."

"All right," he said slowly. He turned toward the sofa and crossed to the tape marks. Again, Ivy anticipated him and removed pictures of the body from the file in her purse. Prying herself from the spot where she had taken root, she traversed the room and handed him the photographs.

"Thanks." Alex compared the shots to the tape marks, then squatted beside Nancy's outline. He pointed to a single piece of tape near the edge of the sofa. "That's where the Trivial Pursuit pie was found."

"Yes," Ivy confirmed, even though it wasn't phrased as a question. The spot was only inches from Nancy's left hand. Ivy shuddered involuntarily.

Alex studied the area for several minutes, stood, handed the photos back to Ivy, then crossed to a sliding glass door that led to a balcony. He opened it and examined the lock. "He gained entry by jimmying this door, right?"

"Yes." Ivy joined him as he stepped onto the balcony. Five stories below them, the street was still buzzing with activity. "Apparently, he came up the fire escape and crossed those two balconies—" she pointed to the right "—to get here. That was probably about nine-thirty. One of her neighbors remembers Nancy's dog barking right about that time."

Alex studied the space between Nancy Monroe's balcony and that of her next-door neighbor. The distance was only five or six feet, but it would take a lot of confidence to make the leap from railing to railing. "So we know our Strangler is strong, agile and probably relatively young. I can't see a senior citizen making that jump."

"Agreed."

"But why did he feel the need to take that risk? He didn't break into Beverly Coit's house—for some reason, she let him in. Why didn't he use that same ploy on Nancy Monroe?"

From where she was standing, Ivy could see through the living room to the front door. "Look at that door. There are three locks on it, plus a security chain. And she had a German shepherd that was probably for protection rather than companionship. Offhand, I'd say that Nancy wasn't the type to open her door to a total stranger."

Alex nodded, remembering that Nancy's wasn't the only body found in the apartment. "What did he use to silence the dog?"

"A New York strip steak, generously laced with strychnine."

"How many other victims had dogs?"

"Just number five, Susan Anderson."

"Whose apartment he also broke into, rather than ringing the doorbell."

Ivy realized where he was leading. Three of the victims had probably opened the door to their killer, while the other three had been taken by surprise. And two of those three had owned pets that would have raised a ruckus had they not been silenced by the Strangler before their mistresses returned home. "I see your point. You're thinking that maybe he only breaks in if there's a dog in the house that has to be taken care of first."

"It makes a lot of sense. If Nancy's German shepherd had been alive when the Strangler attacked her, the dog would have been all over him. Even a small dog could do some damage," he pointed out. "That could explain the inconsistency in his methods of gaining entry."

"But he came in through a window at Erin Selway's house, and she didn't have a dog," Ivy countered.

"Oh, well." He sighed heavily. "Another brilliant theory bites the dust."

Thoughtfully, Alex left the balcony and walked toward the kitchen, leaving Ivy to close the door. She did so reluctantly; the temperature outside was already in the mid-nineties, but that was practically frigid compared to the stifling heat of the apartment.

For a moment, Ivy considered following Alex into the kitchen, but she changed her mind. She hadn't come along to be his shadow or his encyclopedia; she was here to investigate and form her own opinions. Striking off in the opposite direction, she skirted the outline of Nancy's body and wandered toward the bedroom.

There, as with the living room, the decor was modest but attractive. The carpet was an institutional beige, but a peaches-and-cream comforter on the bed and matching Priscilla curtains at the window made the room bright and airy. Dust clouded the surfaces of a modern oak bureau and a chest of drawers. A vinyl jewelry case lay open on the bureau, but the necklaces, rings and earrings neatly arrayed on its red velvet lining had lost their luster beneath five months' worth of accumulated dust. A forlorn-looking strand of faux pearls was draped casually over the raised lid of the box. Ivy could almost see Nancy Monroe as she'd gotten dressed for work on the morning of her death, holding the pearls against the bodice of the blue dress she'd worn that day and finally deciding that a simple gold chain looked better.

Disturbed by her vision, Ivy turned away and inspected Nancy's closet, then the bathroom. Then she went back into the bedroom again for one last look. There were pictures everywhere—mostly family, Ivy guessed, remembering Nancy's file: parents, a sister and two brothers, nieces and nephews. All of them were in mourning now.

"Any impressions?" Alex asked quietly from the doorway as he watched Ivy float around the room.

"She didn't deserve to die," Ivy answered softly without turning.

"None of them did," he said in a voice that was as sad as Ivy's. He wandered into the bathroom while Ivy took a tour of the kitchen, and finally they met back in the living room.

By tacit agreement, they left the apartment quietly, pausing outside only long enough to lock the door and place a fresh seal across it.

The rest of the day was spent in much the same manner, going from home to home, making private observations that they occasionally shared when they returned to the car. Other times, they merely rode from place to place in silence, absorbed in their own thoughts. The third apartment, that of Darlena West, was a little easier for Ivy to view, and Elaine McNaughton's house was even easier.

Of course, *easy* was a comparative word. Viewing the apartment of victim five, Susan Anderson, was easier than flying to the moon without a spacecraft, but on the whole, a day on the beach in Bermuda would have been a lot more fun.

"How are you holding up?" Alex asked as they headed toward the home of victim number six.

"I'm hot, hungry, exhausted, filthy—"

"And disappointed?" Alex asked, lowering the visor on the inside of the windshield to block out some of the late afternoon sun.

Ivy turned on the seat and frowned at him. "Why should I be disappointed?" she asked, even though one of the confusing emotions she was experiencing was indeed disappointment.

"Because you haven't solved the case yet," he answered, grinning. "You've visited the sites of five murders, and the case is still unsolved. Not one big, fat, juicy clue has jumped up and bit you."

Ivy hadn't wanted to admit that bit of folly even to herself, but once Alex said it out loud, she realized it was true. "You're right," she said wearily. "Deep down inside I had this romantic notion that if I could just get a close look at the crime scenes I could solve the case single-handedly. Not very professional—or realistic—right?"

Alex laughed. "Don't beat yourself up over it, Sherlock. I think I had the same idea, and I'm old enough to know better."

Ivy drew her shoulders up huffily. "I may be new to the detective squad, Lieutenant, but I'm not exactly a babe in the woods on the force. I spent eight years in a black-and-white, learning the streets. Don't make it sound as though I'm a greenhorn." An awful thought struck her. "Unless...you feel that I've conducted myself like one," she said quietly, remembering those first awful minutes in Nancy Monroe's apartment.

"No, Ivy, that's not what I meant," Alex told her, his voice endearingly soft. "You've comported yourself like a real professional. And not only that, you've been a big help to me. I have no doubt that if I'd brought Jordan Brubaker along today, he'd have stuck to me like a second skin and spent most of his time trying to prove to me how important he is."

"I take it you've worked with Jordan before," Ivy said dryly.

"More than once," Alex replied. He started to add that he hadn't noticed an appreciable change in the blustery Brubaker since the last time he'd worked with him, but he caught himself just in time. Ivy was so comfortable to be with that Alex felt free to say virtually anything to her, but it wasn't appropriate for a superior to denigrate a subordinate in the presence of another subordinate. The problem was, Alex wasn't accustomed to a command position. And besides that, Ivy seemed more like an equal than a underling. He had the feeling she bowed to the superiority of no man—or woman.

They chatted on aimlessly until they reached the house of victim number six, Erin Selway.

"The last one," Alex said with a sigh of relief as he pulled into the driveway of the Garden Avenue house and shut off the engine. He stepped out of the car and locked the door behind him.

"How I wish that were true," Ivy muttered.

They were both silent as they moved across the lawn, which was beginning to show serious signs of neglect. As before, they broke the police seal and went in quietly, collecting impressions. Erin Selway was the only victim whose body had been found in the bedroom, and Alex led the way toward the murder scene, his footfalls silenced by the lushly padded carpet.

"You could lose a dachshund in this rug," he mumbled.

"Yes, but who would want to?"

Alex stepped into the bedroom and studied the luxury Erin Selway had surrounded herself with. The unmade bed revealed satin sheets; across the room, mirrored doors ran the length of one wall. Three of those doors stood open, exposing a wardrobe of mind-boggling proportions. Alex moved around the king-size bed, and there, in front of the closet, was the clumsily taped silhouette of Erin's body.

"Let's get to it," Alex said with a sigh, holding out his hand to receive the photographs Ivy had ready for him.

CHAPTER SIX

UNTIL HER UNTIMELY DEATH, Erin Selway had been a successful model. She had been highly sought after for fashion shows and print work and had even appeared in a number of television commercials. One of her regular employers, a local department store, sponsored Erin's participation in the annual Brauxton Ten-Kilometer Charity Marathon. That charitable act might have contributed to her death; the game piece found alongside her body was a gold medal from Pentathlon—a board game in which the participants compete in five Olympic events.

Erin's lucrative career had allowed her to live a life of unquestionable luxury, and everything around her had reflected her expensive appetites. Her clothes were designer originals. Her spacious home was elegant and impeccably decorated with just the right artwork, perfect arrangements of silk bouquets in expensive vases and, as Alex had noted, wall-to-wall carpeting so thick that you could lose a small animal in it.

Ivy spent nearly an hour exploring the house, and not once in all that time did she envy Erin Selway. Her own efficiency apartment wasn't much to look at, her life-style was far from glamorous, and her wardrobe was straight from bargain basements, but she was alive to enjoy what little she had. Erin Selway wasn't.

"Are you about ready to call it a day?"

Ivy was in the fit-for-a-gourmet-chef kitchen rummaging through cabinets and well-ordered drawers when Alex spoke to her. She straightened guiltily, as though she'd been caught in some indiscretion. "I suppose so," she said with a weary sigh. "I don't know what I think I'm going to find in these cabinets, anyway."

Alex grinned. "You're desperate to find that elusive, case-solving clue, and this is your last chance. Don't feel badly. I ransacked the medicine cabinet and linen closet."

"I won't tell anyone if you won't." In one last, futile effort, Ivy opened the cupboard doors beneath the sink and looked in.

"Anything?" Alex asked.

"Dishwashing detergent, window cleaner, furniture polish, scouring pads, paper towels, some dishes—" *Dishes?* Under the sink? In Ivy's haphazard kitchen, plastic bowls stored under the sink might have been right at home, but in Erin Selway's perfectly ordered world, they were a definite inconsistency. Ivy reached deep into the dark cabinet, past the detergent and Endust, and latched on to the bowls. "Well, well, well . . . if ever we needed proof that the Strangler is smarter than we are, this is it."

"What?" Alex's view was blocked by the open cabinet doors, and he hurried toward Ivy.

"Well, maybe not smarter," she amended, "just better informed." She stood and held out two plastic dog dishes to Alex. "It looks as though your theory holds water, after all, Alex. Erin did have a dog. That's why the Strangler broke into the house rather than ringing the doorbell."

Alex shook his head. "But what happened to the dog? Why wasn't it found in the house? Where is it now?"

Ivy shrugged. "My guess would be that at the time the Strangler chose Erin as a potential victim, she owned a dog, but something must have happened to it. It probably died. One thing is certain—if the dog had been in her possession at the time of her death, its food and water dishes wouldn't have been stored away."

"But why didn't forensics find any dog hairs in the carpeting?"

"That's a very good question."

"Let's take a closer look at her file," Alex suggested.

"Can we do it in the living room?" Ivy asked, pulling Erin's file from her purse. "These shoes are killing me. I hadn't planned on being on my feet all day."

"I'll give you a little warning next time," Alex promised, leading the way into the sumptuous living room and settling onto the L-shaped sectional sofa. Ivy dropped onto the cushion beside him and made no protest when he took Erin's file out of her hands. As he leafed through it, looking for the forensics report, Ivy slipped off her shoes and dug her toes into the heavenly soft carpet.

She must have made some little noise of contentment, because Alex looked at her with one dark eyebrow raised as he said, "If you've finished wallowing in luxury, you might want to help me with these."

"Yes, sir!" Ivy snapped to attention but refused to shove her feet back into her shoes. With her toes still wiggling on the carpet, she leaned forward and cleared the surface of the chrome and glass coffee table in front of them, giving Alex the space he needed to lay out the contents of Erin's file. She pushed a floral centerpiece to one end of the table and laid a stack of magazines at her feet.

Alex immediately took advantage of the makeshift work space, and in seconds, papers were scattered from one end of the long table to the other.

"Here's the forensics report," he announced when he finally found what they were looking for. Shoulder to shoulder, they perused the eleven-page document, searching for any indication that Erin Selway had owned a dog.

The waning afternoon sun streamed in through a bank of multipane windows, bathing the sofa in warm light. Without air conditioning, the house was unconscionably warm, but as Ivy sat nestled against Alex, she knew she couldn't attribute a sudden flush of heat to the closed-up house. Alex's frame was lean, but his lightweight sport jacket did nothing to disguise the taut musculature of his arm where it touched hers. She allowed herself a brief moment to speculate on what other enticing masculine endowments were hidden beneath his casual clothing, then tried to focus all her concentration on the forensics report. It was safer that way, because her unprofessional musings were doing dastardly things to her insides.

"Look at this," Alex said, pointing at a section of the report.

Ivy was grateful for the interruption of her impure thoughts. She glanced at the paper, saw a string of chemical compounds and frowned. Apparently, Erin's carpet fibers had contained something Alex found revealing; Ivy found them unpronounceable. "What are they?"

"Cleaning chemicals—industrial strength. The kind you'd expect professional carpet cleaners to use," he explained.

Ivy was impressed. "Good work, Sherlock. You think Erin had her carpets cleaned after she got rid of the dog?"

"That would explain why no dog hairs were found by forensics. Now all we have to do is find out who cleaned her carpets. If we can determine when Erin got rid of her dog, that should tell us how far in advance the Strangler chooses his victims. It's not much, but it's more than we had five minutes ago." Alex thought a moment. "Did she have an address book?"

"Yes. It's in the property room back at the station. I cross-referenced the entries from all the victim's personal address books. Offhand, I don't remember whether she had a carpet cleaner listed or not."

"How about a veterinarian?"

"I honestly don't remember, but—" Ivy's eyes lighted up as she spied the antique rolltop desk on the other side of the living room. She was off the sofa in a flash. "I think maybe we're in luck. When I went through this earlier I saw..." Her voice trailed off as she rummaged through the nooks and crannies of the desk. "Aha! Here it is."

"What?"

Ivy returned to the sofa with a slender, leather-bound book. "It's a business card directory." Quickly, she flipped the divided plastic pages that housed four cards a page until she found one that read Dwyers Carpet and Furniture Cleaners. As might have been expected, the company's address was in one of Brauxton's more fashionable business districts. Nothing but the best for Erin Selway.

Alex grinned broadly at her, and Ivy's heart began doing the rumba. It was a truly devastating smile. "Good work, Sherlock."

Ivy muttered a thank you but found that she was having a hard time taking her eyes off Alex's mouth. His lips were full, and when he smiled, too small, endearing dimples appeared in his cheeks. Funny, she'd never noticed that before. But then, she'd never been quite this close to him, either. Dangerously close. He was so appealing, so devastatingly handsome, that it was impossible for her not to wish that he would lean a little closer and kiss her.

Embarrassed, Ivy quickly averted her gaze from his face and focused once again on the business cards. Was it coincidence, she wondered, that at that same moment Alex cleared his throat uncomfortably and turned away to study the forensics report?

Ivy hoped it wasn't. It would be humiliating to think that her foolishness was one-sided.

Just to fill the void of silence that was distinctly tension filled, Ivy flipped through the cards and found one for a veterinarian. Somehow, she wasn't surprised. Erin Selway had been as efficiently organized as she had been classy. If she'd had a dog—as Ivy was certain she had—she'd have had a veterinarian to care for the dog. One plus one equaled two, for a change.

She showed the card to Alex, then began reassembling Erin's scattered file. Ivy stacked the papers neatly, and Alex reached for the magazines on the floor. He placed them in a clump on the coffee table as Ivy returned the centerpiece to its original position, but there was something offensive about the arrangement. Erin had kept the magazines neatly arrayed in a colorful, symmetrical fan, and Alex felt gauche for not returning them to their original configuration. It was like defiling a shrine or something.

Keeping the bottoms together, he splayed the tops an equidistant one and one-half inches, but all he came up with was a lopsided lump. He started the process from scratch and out of the corner of his eye saw Ivy's shoulders shaking with silent laughter.

"You think this is funny?"

"I think it's hysterical," she said, giggling. "You're more compulsive than Erin Selway was."

"Yes, but I am true of heart and stalwart of spirit."

"Not to mention humble."

"That, too. Unfortunately, manual dexterity was never my strong suit."

Ivy laughed again as she stuffed Erin's file and the business card directory into her purse. Alex tried to imitate the magazine fan one last time, then gave up and spread the periodicals out evenly, tops and bottoms parallel to the edges of the coffee table. A copy of *Vogue* rested on top, and beneath that was the June edition of *Working Woman*. Forgetting his attempt at neatness, Alex picked up the *Working Woman* and fanned the air with it thoughtfully.

"Didn't I see a copy of this in Susan Anderson's apartment?"

"Yes," Ivy confirmed. "They both subscribed. And Darlena West subscribed to *Vogue*, too. A couple of the victims subscribed to various other women's magazines, but we couldn't find any pattern. Elaine McNaughton didn't have any magazine subscriptions at all, so we ruled out the possibility that the Strangler is choosing his victims from some sort of mailing list."

Alex returned the magazine to its slot. As he did so, he uncovered a copy of *Perplexities*, a popular game periodical. In a case so closely tied in with games, the presence of a magazine devoted to games could be significant. Alex quickly checked the back cover and found the computer-generated sticker with Erin Selway's name and address. "Rats," he muttered. "It's a subscription."

Ivy's smile was gentle and indulgent—the kind of a smile a mother would give to a child who'd just discovered there was no Santa Claus. "You were hoping it was another clue? Something subtle planted by the Strangler?"

Alex sighed and tossed the magazine down. "Without hope, a man is nothing. I don't suppose any of the other victims subscribed to *Perplexities*?"

"Nope. Sorry. If it makes you feel any better, *I* subscribe to it."

"Somehow that doesn't surprise me." Wearily, Alex wiped his hands across his face and fell back onto a deep cushion of sofa pillows. "Well, partner, let's take stock. We've been at this—" he glanced at his watch "—nine and a half hours. What have we got to show for it?"

Ivy resisted the urge to lean back, too. Alex was half reclining on the sofa, and the position would have been a little more intimate than Ivy could handle. "Well...we know that Darlena West liked country and western music, Elaine McNaughton had a penchant for naughty underwear, Erin Selway probably had a dog at the time the Strangler targeted her for murder, I have blisters the size of water beds on my feet, and your face is smudged with dirt.''

Alex managed a weary laugh. ''Your feet and my face notwithstanding, we haven't accomplished much, have we?''

''I don't know about you, but I got a real kick out of Elaine's peekaboo undies.''

''You are truly a sick human being, Ivy.''

''That's probably why we work so well together.''

Alex raised his head from the comfortable pillow, looked at her and said musingly, ''We do, don't we?''

Ivy stared into his intelligent, sensual gray eyes and felt the onset of that God-I-want-him-to-kiss-me sensation again. ''Yes, we do.'' *Brilliant remark. Where's a snappy comeback when you really need one?* she wondered caustically. ''So what's next, boss?'' Another zinger. If she kept this up, before the week was out, Johnny Carson would be begging her to write his next monologue.

''It's too late to follow up on the carpet cleaner and the vet, so we probably ought to call it a day,'' he said, resting his head on the cushions again. ''The problem is, I don't feel like quitting. I want more answers than I've got.''

Ivy understood the feeling. The day had been emotionally depressing and physically draining, but intellectually it had been wonderfully invigorating. For the first time, she actually felt as though she were an integral part of the task force. ''We could catch a bite to eat and compare our impressions.''

''Of the meal?''

''Of the victims,'' she said with mock disdain.

''You're on. I want to go through the game angle again.'' He sat up and reached for the copy of *Perplexities*. ''Other than this magazine, we haven't run across anything that ties into the game pieces.''

"Or the list you think the Strangler's taking the games from," she added. Alex was flipping idly through the magazine, and Ivy saw that some of the crosswords had been filled in. A little shiver ran down her spine when she realized that she had worked some of the same puzzles as Erin Selway.

As Ivy watched, Alex closed the magazine and placed it with the others, halfheartedly attempting to maneuver the stack into the fan shape again. But Ivy didn't laugh this time. The cover of *Perplexities* was winking at her as Alex shuffled the magazines, and a memory that seemed suddenly very important was hovering on the edge of her consciousness. Her conversation with Alex yesterday began running through her mind—the part about the popularity of the games the Strangler was leaving pieces from as clues—and suddenly she realized what it was that seemed so significant. The list of games. She knew where the Strangler had come up with his list of games!

"I'm an idiot!" she shouted. "A certifiable, lamebrain, card-carrying idiot!"

Startled by her outburst, Alex watched as Ivy jumped off the sofa and dashed across the room to the long bookcase that was set into the wall. There, she dropped to her knees and threw open one of the doors that protected the lowest shelf. Plastic magazine files held back issues of all Erin's periodicals, and Ivy went through them quickly, going from door to door, until she found the back issues of *Perplexities*.

"What are you doing?" Alex asked, wondering if his lovely partner had misplaced a marble or two.

"I am solving this case!" she cried, returning with the magazine case.

"Oh, really? How do you figure that?" Alex kept his voice lackadaisical, but Ivy's excitement was contagious. He could feel his heartbeat revving up.

"You wanted the Strangler's list of games, I'll give it to you." She rifled madly through the back issues until she found the January issue she needed to verify her newly formed theory. Quickly, she consulted the index, flipped to the right page and shoved the magazine at Alex. "Look at this," she instructed him.

Alex glanced at the bold, black headline, "The Best of Last Year," and below that in smaller print, "*Perplexities* Readers' All-Time Favorite Games." His excitement growing, Alex scanned the list of twenty games, mentally comparing the sequence of the first six to the six games the Strangler had used. The lists were almost identical, but almost wasn't good enough. Alex felt his heartbeat slow as his excitement faded.

"Close, Ivy-love, but no cigar." He handed the magazine back to her and watched as her look of triumph disappeared.

"Damn!" The expletive was only a whisper, but it was heartfelt. "I was so sure this was the list."

"It almost is." He leaned close and pointed. "Most of the games are there, but they're in a slightly different sequence. And Pictionary—the second game on the readers' poll—isn't on the Strangler's list at all."

"Yet," Ivy said softly.

"Yet," Alex agreed.

"But wait a minute," Ivy said, unwilling to abandon her lead. "Games are trendy, and those trends vary from year to year. Three years ago Trivial Pursuit was so hot it was unreal. Last year, Pictionary was the in game, so if the Strangler is using popular games, why isn't it at the top of his list?"

"We won't know that until we find his list," Alex said reasonably. "Ivy, you're grasping at straws."

She shook her head adamantly. "No, I know I'm onto something. This is important. You're the one who said that the Strangler must be operating off a predetermined list of games. Well, where else in the world are you going to find a list?''

"I'm sure game manufacturers have some kind of marketing list—bestsellers, that sort of thing. Maybe he's using that.''

Ivy shook her head again. "If he's using a list of last year's bestselling games, Pictionary would have to be at the top.''

"Maybe he's using a list from the year before last.''

Ivy's face lighted up again. "Then we could still be in the right ballpark, Reggie.'' She waved the magazine at him. "This is an annual feature. They run it in every January issue.''

Alex grinned, catching some of Ivy's excitement again. "Then it seems that it would behoove us to locate a copy of last year's January issue of *Perplexities* forthwith.''

Ivy's triumphant grin turned downright smug. "Would you believe that I know exactly where I can lay my hands on that very issue?''

"Don't tell me you're a collector.''

"No, I'm a pack rat. I never throw anything away.''

Alex stood. "Well, come on then, Sherlock, let's go.''

"I'm right behind you.'' They hurried out of the house, replaced the door seal and headed for the car.

"Where do you live?'' Alex asked as he climbed behind the wheel.

"Baker Street, where else?''

Alex had the key halfway toward the ignition, but his hand stopped in midair as he looked at her. "You're joking, right?''

"No. I live at 1221 Baker Street, apartment 4-B.''

"Seriously?''

"Seriously.''

"You moved there on purpose, right?''

Ivy gave him a self-satisfied smile. "I must admit, a Baker Street address was part of the charm. The rest was purely coincidental."

"Well, Sherlock, if your *Perplexities* lead turns out to be valid, I'd say that you deserve that semi-illustrious address. In fact, I may even give you a medal."

I'd rather have a kiss, Ivy thought as Alex pulled out of the driveway and headed for her home. But she didn't express her sentiment out loud. She was becoming almost as preoccupied with kissing Alex Devane as she was with finding the Brauxton Strangler, she reflected. And what was worse, she wasn't feeling the least bit guilty about it. The sun was finally going down, she was on the verge of finding an important clue, and her new lieutenant did crazy things to her blood and her brain.

All in all, not a bad day's work.

CHAPTER SEVEN

IF EVER A HOME reflected the personality quirks of its occupant, it was Ivy Kincaid's Baker Street apartment. She unlocked the door, flipped on the lights and hurried across the room to turn on the air conditioner while Alex stood in the narrow, almost nonexistent entry hall trying to figure out if he was really seeing what his eyes told him he was. Except for a small dressing room that led to a bathroom on the right, Ivy's apartment was one huge living room, bedroom and kitchen. The floors were polished hardwood, the ceiling was uncommonly high, and the walls were painted pristine white.

It could have been an elegant, attractive living space, but instead, Alex felt as though he'd fallen down the rabbit hole into Alice's wonderland. Nothing in the room matched anything else. To his left, a sofa, two mismatched chairs and several equally mismatched tables were arranged in a conversational grouping on an enormous blue-and-gold Turkish carpet.

Beyond that, a long counter filled with computer equipment separated the "living room" from a small, narrow kitchen that seemed seminormal. The stove and refrigerator looked to be of standard issue, but a three-paneled Japanese screen hid the far end of the kitchen, and Alex was afraid to wonder what might be hidden behind the screen. Whatever it was, it couldn't possibly be any worse than the "bedroom"—or more accurately, the bed—which was directly in front of him.

Mouth agape, he moved toward it like a sleepwalker. In his worst nightmares, he'd never seen anything comparable. The mahogany four-poster was a Gothic monstrosity. The carved headboard, fully six feet tall, was a mass of scrolls, curlicues and mysterious shapes he didn't dare try to classify. And rising above the headboard, perched at the top of the opposing posts, were two menacing winged gargoyles poised and ready to pounce on any poor soul who was silly enough to think that he or she might find a decent night's rest on the mattress below.

"Gorgeous, isn't it?"

"That wasn't the first word that came into my mind," Alex said cautiously, turning to look at Ivy, who had suddenly appeared beside him, her face beaming with pride.

"You don't like it?" she asked, her face falling.

"'Like' isn't a word that comes to mind, either."

She shrugged. "I guess there's just no accounting for taste."

"I guess not." Almost afraid to speculate on what he might see next, Alex turned and found himself staring at the end of the kitchen that he hadn't been able to see before because of the Japanese screen. On the wall behind a surprisingly normal-looking dinette set was a seven-foot neon palm tree flanked by two large neon flamingos.

Ivy studied the expression on Alex's face, which suggested he was going into sensory overload. "Don't tell me you hate the palm, too."

"No, no," Alex reassured her quickly. "I kind of like it, actually. It's just that you don't find many people these days who use flamingos and gargoyles to make a decor statement."

Ivy chuckled. "What can I say? I have an eye for the ridiculous and the sublime."

Alex turned back toward the bed, half hoping it would be gone. "Where did you get this . . . thing?" he asked incredulously.

"I found it at an estate auction a couple of years ago and fell in love."

Alex looked at her suspiciously. "Whose estate? Edgar Allan Poe's?"

She let the crack pass and pointed toward the kitchen. "And the palm tree was a present from a neon sculpture artist I used to date."

Alex felt his ears perk up at this personal revelation. "What happened to him?"

Ivy shrugged and headed across the room toward a set of double doors beyond the "living room." "Nothing that I know of. I read last month that he had a very successful gallery showing at the Artiste."

Alex followed a little way, then stopped beside a brass art nouveau floor lamp in the image of water lilies rising from a small pond. "You don't date him anymore?"

"No, he was a little too eccentric for my taste."

An unrestrained shout of laughter burst out of Alex before he could stop himself, and it was several seconds before he brought it under control. Ivy had unlatched the doors of a closet that had originally been built to house a Murphy bed, and she held on to one of the handles, smiling as she watched Alex laugh.

"This—" with one hand he made a broad sweep of the room "—is a joke, right?"

"Of course it's a joke," she answered. "How could anyone look at this room—or live in it, for that matter—and feel sad or depressed? And besides, if you consider each piece of furniture or decorative item by itself, they're not that bad. If you'd seen that art nouveau lamp at Erin Selway's, you'd have thought it was very distinctive."

Alex glanced around the room and realized that Ivy was right. With the possible exception of the bed, nothing in the room was in poor taste. The living room "suite" was mismatched, but not unattractive. The whole apartment, in fact, was just an odd combination of antique and contemporary extremes. It jarred the senses, but on the whole it was quite pleasant because, as Ivy had said, it would be pretty impossible to feel bad here. More than that, it reflected the personality of the woman who lived here. Like her apartment, she was delightfully one of a kind.

And she was also—as she had warned him—a pack rat. That became obvious when she threw open the closet doors and exposed floor-to-ceiling shelves that contained, among other things, rows upon rows of books, games and puzzle magazines.

Alex joined her at the closet. "How far back do these issues go?"

Ivy shrugged. "About three years, at least." All the magazines were in plastic files that kept them upright and orderly. There were dozens of issues of *Games, Dell Crossword and Variety Puzzles* and *Perplexities*. "I keep them because my interests vary," she explained as she pulled down two files, handed them to Alex and reached for two more. "Some months I only work the logic problems, but the next month I may be in the mood for crosswords or acrostics. I keep the back issues so I'll always have a puzzle that interests me."

Alex took the magazines to the sofa and began sorting through them, looking for an eighteen-month-old January issue. Ivy joined him and was the first to hit pay dirt. "Got it! January of last year." She looked at the index to find the page number of the annual readers' poll feature, then quickly thumbed through until she found it.

"Well?" Alex realized that he was holding his breath.

For several seconds, Ivy's face betrayed nothing. She looked the list over once, then twice, and finally a glorious, exultant smile began working its way to the surface. "By George, I think we've got it!"

"Are you kidding? Let me see!" He grabbed the magazine and Ivy followed it, coming to her knees and scooting across the sofa until she was pressed against his side so that she could read over his left shoulder.

"What did I tell you? That is it. It has to be!"

One look told Alex that Ivy was right, but he glanced through the list a second time to be certain. And he was. The list of game clues left by the Strangler matched the *Perplexities* readers' poll exactly. That was too much of a coincidence to be coincidence. For some reason, this periodical or this list had some special meaning to the Strangler. It was a start—the first major clue anyone had yet to discover in this complex case.

Alex wanted to feel some of Ivy's excitement, but strangely, none appeared. She was pressed close to him, with her hands resting lightly on his shoulders. Her color was high, her smile was radiant and her breathing was slightly erratic. She was ready to celebrate a triumph. But as much as Alex wanted to celebrate with her, he couldn't bring himself to turn and pull her into his arms for a congratulatory hug because there was so much left to do. He had the Strangler's list, yes, but he still had to decipher the list's special meaning, determine how the Strangler was choosing his victims, anticipate the date he would strike next and catch him before he killed anyone else.

"Alex?" Ivy was so excited she was practically jumping up and down, but her boss seemed considerably less enthusiastic. "What's wrong? Don't you think the list is significant?"

"I think it's very significant. There's no question that this is the list the Strangler is using."

"Then why aren't you singing hosannas from the highest rooftop?" She pulled away from him slightly, disappointed by his apathy. "You're the one who said that finding this list was the first step toward finding the Strangler."

"That's right, Ivy, but there are a lot of steps remaining."

"Hmm...." Ivy sat back on her heels, regarding him curiously.

Alex watched her studying him. "What's wrong?"

"Nothing. I'm just trying to decide if you're a pessimist or a cynic." She said it as though both choices were as loathsome as the black plague, and Alex found himself bristling. He knew he wasn't perfect, but it was irksome that Ivy had figured that out so soon. Obviously, she found him lacking, and his male ego didn't like knowing that this lovely, clever, vivacious woman was disappointed in him.

"Just because I'm not jumping up and down like a silly schoolgirl doesn't mean I'm a pessimist," he snapped irritably, knowing he was being irrational but unable to stop himself.

Ivy drew back as though he had slapped her. Slowly, she unfolded her legs and slipped off the sofa. "Sorry, *sir*," she said coldly. "You're the one who said that finding this clue was vital to solving the case. I apologize for being happy to have contributed something significant." Hurt and angry, she stalked off toward the kitchen.

"Damn," Alex muttered under his breath. He hadn't meant to bark at her like that, particularly since she hadn't done anything wrong. He prized logic and rationality, and lashing out at Ivy made no sense whatsoever. "Where are you going?"

"To the kitchen. Where does it look like I'm going? I'm starving."

Trying to frame an apology, Alex followed her, watching with fascination as she began opening and closing cabinets, slamming pots and pans onto the stove and mightily abusing the door of the refrigerator. She was so adorably self-righteous that he had to work at suppressing a smile. "Do you always throw things around when you're mad?"

"Yes," she answered succinctly, throwing a package of ground chuck onto the counter by the stove.

"Do you usually stay mad long?"

She shot him a withering glance as she returned to the refrigerator and retrieved a bag of tomatoes, an onion and a bell pepper from the crisper. "Long enough."

Alex leaned against the counter that separated the kitchen from the rest of the apartment. The silence mounted as he followed Ivy's abrupt movements around the small enclosure. She worked with energy and economy, but he could tell that she was having a hard time maintaining her irritation with him. "Has anyone ever told you that you're beautiful when you're angry?" he asked finally.

"Not and lived to tell about it." Ivy had to work at keeping a grin off her face. Alex was trying to cajole her out of her anger, and she had no intention of making it easy for him.

"Oh." Silence stretched out again as she began chopping the pepper on a large cutting board. The cleaver she was using with consummate skill looked deadly. Alex was almost afraid to ask, "What are you making?"

"Spaghetti."

"Do you ever invite ignorant clods who have insulted you to stay for dinner?"

Ivy stopped what she was doing, faced him squarely and waved the cleaver with casual menace. "Only if they apologize."

Alex grinned. "I'm sorry, Ivy. Truly."

"You're just saying that because you're hungry."

"No, I'm not," he replied, his tone serious. Heart-stoppingly serious. "You did a wonderful job coming up with that clue. It's just that once you found it, I realized how much more remains to be discovered. We're a long way from catching the Strangler.''

Now she understood why he had lashed out at her, and she could sympathize. She laid down the cleaver and wiped her hands on a dishtowel. "I know we don't have him yet, Alex, but we're a little closer than we were this morning— maybe even a lot closer. This *Perplexities* clue could open some of the doors the task force has been banging its head against. I'm excited about the possibilities, and I was disappointed that you didn't share that excitement. I'm sorry I called you cynical and pessimistic.''

They looked at each other for a long moment, and the man-woman chemistry that always sizzled between them evolved into something a little deeper and a lot more meaningful. "I am both, you know,'' he told her quietly.

Ivy had to work to keep her heart from shifting into overdrive. There was a haunting look of sadness in his eyes, and she wondered if he was thinking about the child he'd accidentally killed or his wife, who'd committed suicide. Alex had a lot to be cynical about. Probably a good deal more than she was aware of, yet his innate pessimism didn't negate her immense respect for him—or her intense attraction to him. It should have, but it didn't. "Yes, I know.''

He looked at her strangely, as though seeing her in a new light. "But you're not, are you? You're not the least bit jaded. You still believe in things like truth, justice and the American way.''

Ivy considered his observation. "I believe that there's a lot of ugliness in our world but that every now and then the good guys do win one. We have to take those little victories and make them mean something.''

"You're an idealist,'' he said accusingly.

Ivy grinned wistfully. "No, I'm a romantic. There's a big difference.''

There was a short pause. "Do you believe in love?" he asked, wondering why he'd felt the need to ask the question.

Fascinated by the direction their conversation had suddenly taken, Ivy levered herself onto the kitchen counter and sat, swinging her legs lightly against the cabinet below. "Of course I believe in love. Don't you?"

"No." Taking his cue from her, Alex slid onto the counter directly opposite her. They sat facing each other—studying each other—like two kids who were waiting for their mother to bring them their after-school milk and cookies.

"Why not?" Ivy held her breath, wondering if Alex would answer something so personal.

"I think love is a fantasy. It's something created by man out of a need to justify."

"Justify what?"

Alex shrugged. "Different things for different people. Some women have to believe in love in order to justify a basic biological need for sex," he explained. "And some men have to believe in love in order to justify giving up their freedom when they give in to a woman's nesting instinct. Mostly, though, love is a misguided need for belonging and security. People aren't happy within themselves, so they look to other people to make themselves happy."

Ivy frowned and shook her head. "Whew. That's one depressing theory you got there, fella."

"You disagree?"

"I told you, I'm a romantic. Romantics believe that somewhere in this world there is one special person waiting just for them. Someone who touches them on a level so deep that they're changed forever. Someone who needs them, respects them, even cherishes them. Someone who makes the world stand still and makes their hearts pound faster."

"Do you realize that you sound like a poorly written romance novel?" Alex asked without any malice.

"Is that a crime?"

He shrugged. "Not yet, but maybe it should be."

Ivy shook her head sadly. "I can't prove that you're wrong, Alex, but I know I wouldn't like living in the world you described."

"I'm not too fond of it myself," he admitted frankly. "But I've seen the destruction that can come from your kind of romantic fantasies, and I want nothing to do with them, either."

"Wait a minute," Ivy said. It didn't take a genius to figure out that he was referring to his late wife, and Ivy didn't like being compared to a woman who had committed suicide. "I'm being lumped into a category and condemned for crimes I haven't committed. You're talking in generalities, but you're thinking about something very specific. Why don't you spell it out so that I can defend myself?"

"You haven't done anything wrong, Ivy. You don't need to mount a defense."

"Oh, no you don't. You're not getting off that easy," she said as she jumped off the counter and returned to her cutting board and half-chopped green pepper. "According to you, I'm going to destroy the world—or some small corner of it—with my ideas about love and romance."

Alex cursed himself for having gotten into this conversation in the first place. "That's not what I meant."

"Yes, it is," she insisted, then softened her voice. "You were thinking about your late wife, weren't you?"

"I see the precinct grapevine has been working overtime. What, exactly, have you heard about Brenda?" he asked brusquely. He'd always wondered how much of the sordid story was common knowledge among his former colleagues at the station. Now was his chance to find out.

Ivy put the chopped pepper into a bowl and began working on the tomatoes. "Not much, really. Someone told me that you and your wife separated, and shortly after that, she...died."

"You mean she killed herself."

Ivy nodded and turned toward him. "Why did she do that, Alex?"

He looked at her without flinching as he answered. "Because I was a lousy husband. I was too wrapped up in myself and my job to give her what she needed."

"Maybe she needed too much," Ivy said quietly.

Alex frowned and jumped off the counter, shaking his head. He didn't want to discuss this any longer. "How the hell did we get into this in the first place?" He grabbed a paring knife from a wooden rack and joined Ivy at the cutting board. She shoved an onion at him.

They were shoulder to shoulder again, and Ivy was completely aware of everything about the lonely, sexy, disillusioned man in her kitchen. "We got into this discussion when you asked if I believed in love. Which you probably did," she added, "because we seem to be very attracted to each other, and you wanted to make your feelings on the subject of love perfectly clear to me."

Alex gave a short bark of mirthless laughter. "Do you always say exactly what you're thinking?"

"When it's important, yes."

He stopped chopping and looked at her seriously. "'We' are not important, Ivy, because there is no 'we'. There's you, and there's me, and there's the case that brought us together. That's all. If something of an intimate nature does happen between us, it won't be permanent."

Ivy stopped chopping, too, and faced him squarely. Only inches separated them. "Because you don't believe in love."

"That's right."

She smiled wistfully. "You do realize, don't you, that telling a woman you don't believe in love is like waving a red flag at a bull? It makes her want to charge in and prove you're wrong."

"It can't be done, Ivy," he said flatly, despite the painfully delicious stirrings of his body. Ivy Kincaid was potent medicine, and she was too close for comfort right now—both physically and emotionally. "If you try, you'll only get hurt."

Her smile became broad, as though she were highly amused by his warning. "Oh, that's good, Alex. Putting a dare on top of a challenge is a nice touch. That will really scare me away," she said sarcastically. "Why don't you place a bet on it, too?"

"I get the feeling you're not taking me seriously, Ivy."

"Of course I'm taking you seriously, Alex. I just don't think that deep down you really mean exactly what you're saying. Personally, I think that, like me, you're a hopeless romantic, but you've been hurt so badly that you're afraid to believe in love anymore. You espouse cold, bloodless theories about the nonexistence of love, when what you really want is someone to come along and make you believe again."

"You're wrong." It was a flat, lifeless denial, but somewhere in Alex's head—or maybe his heart—a tiny, grateful voice was congratulating Ivy on her insight.

"No, I'm not," she argued. "No one wants to be alone and lonely, not even you. I'm not saying that I'm the woman who can heal whatever wounds you're carrying and make you believe in love again, but you do want to find someone who can. Now—" she smiled brightly and turned back to the cutting board "—are we going to make spaghetti, or are we going to continue this pointless discussion? You've done your civic duty and warned me not to fall in love with you, so there's really not much more to be said."

There's a lot more to be said, Alex thought irritably, but he couldn't put his frustration into words. Simply put, he wanted Ivy Kincaid in the worst possible way. He'd wanted her since the moment she'd walked into his office last night, and the feeling hadn't stopped. All day long, he'd been aware of her in a way he'd never been aware of any other woman in his life, and that was disturbing, because no matter what Ivy said, he didn't believe in love and happily ever after.

Stymied by her attitude, Alex picked up his paring knife and started chopping onion again. Silence stretched out in the quiet room—a tense, aware-of-each-other silence that spoke more truth than any words could. Alex knew that their attraction for each other was strong and undeniable, but it would never be love. He wouldn't let it be.

If Ivy refused to believe that... well, that was her problem.

CHAPTER EIGHT

WITH ALEX'S HELP, Ivy finished making dinner, and they both ate as though the nation's breadbasket would be empty by morning. Their lunch had consisted of Rudy's Hungarian Hot Dogs, which they'd eaten while standing on the corner of Cypress and Third streets. Not exactly haute cuisine. Ivy's spaghetti—based on a recipe she'd stolen from a friend—was considerably more appetizing.

They ate the spaghetti, an endive salad with a mild vinaigrette and a small loaf of Parmesan bread until they were stuffed to the gills, and not once during the preparation or the eating of the meal did the subject of love crop up again.

They discussed cooking, movies, books and general police work—lightweight stuff, trivial but interesting—and after they had finished off the last swirl of pasta and fought over the remaining slice of bread, the subject they returned to was the Brauxton Strangler.

"So what's our next move, Kemo Sabe?"

Alex chewed the last morsel of the Parmesan loaf he'd had to pull rank to procure. He was refreshed, amazingly relaxed considering the circumstances and ready to go back to work. "We know the *Perplexities* list is relevant, so we study it until we figure out why."

"What was the seventh game?" Ivy asked. She'd been so overjoyed at finding the clue that she'd forgotten to mentally record the next game in the sequence.

"Scrabble, I think. And Pictionary was the eighth," Alex answered. Taking his glass of California rosé with him, he rose and moved into the living room. Ivy followed, carrying her own glass and the remaining half bottle of wine. Rather than relaxing on the sofa, which would have placed them temptingly close to each other, they chose to sit on the floor at opposite ends of the coffee table, where copies of *Perplexities* were scattered like autumn leaves. As soon as they were settled, they seemed to realize how much space they were giving each other, and Ivy grinned knowingly. Alex made a conscious effort not to.

He picked up the clue-laden copy of *Perplexities* and leafed through it until he found the readers' poll. "Yep, I was right. Scrabble. If this is the list the killer is going by, the next victim will be found with a piece of a Scrabble game beside her."

"Then to prevent that, we have to find a potential victim whose life in some way relates to some aspect of that game."

"What's the most obvious component of a Scrabble game? Letters, right?"

"Right." Ivy picked up a more recent copy of *Perplexities* and began riffling the pages absently. "So we look for someone who works with letters."

"A secretary?" Alex suggested.

"Or a teacher—kindergarten or maybe business education."

"A printer—"

"A commercial artist, a calligrapher—"

"Writer, reporter—"

"Vanna White—"

Alex threw her a disgusted look. "'And a par-tri-idge in a pear tree,'" he sang. Frustrated, he ran one hand through his already disheveled hair. Some of the thin gray streaks rearranged themselves, but overall, the gesture made no discernible difference.

Ivy nodded and tried not to notice that he still looked windblown and sexy. His jacket had long since fallen by the wayside, leaving him dressed in a pale blue short-sleeved T-shirt that highlighted every contour of his leanly muscled chest and arms. He was difficult not to notice, but Ivy made the effort. "You're right, this is getting us nowhere. We can't put the domicile of every twenty-six to thirty-two-year-old secretary, teacher, artist and writer in the city under surveillance."

Alex tossed her the eighteen-month-old issue of *Perplexities* and picked up another one. "Damn it, even with the list, we're no better off than before."

Ivy examined the magazine cover. "Why is this periodical important to him? And why did he choose the list from last year rather than this year—or the year before last, for that matter?"

Alex considered the question. "It could suggest that he put a year's worth of planning into this series of crimes. Or maybe something about this list is different from the others."

"Something that made him go off the deep end?" Ivy asked as she began scrounging through the piles of magazines until she came up with four January issues. She quickly found the readers' poll in each one and laid them out in the middle of the table in consecutive order.

Forgetting his need for space, Alex scooted around the corner of the table—as did Ivy—until they met in the middle. Together they compared the lists.

"See anything significant?" Ivy asked.

Alex shook his head. Except for random differences in the sequence, the lists were essentially the same. Monopoly, a sentimental favorite, was always in the number one slot. Trivial Pursuit had started in the number three slot, risen to number two and stayed there for two years until it was displaced by Pictionary. Risk, chess and Othello jockeyed for various positions throughout all four lists of the top twenty games.

Pentathlon, like Pictionary, did not appear anywhere on the first two lists; both games were relatively new to the market. However, Ivy did seem to recall from her earlier research that Pentathlon was one or two years older than Pictionary. Apparently, it had taken a little longer to catch on in popularity, but there was nothing extraordinary about that.

"I don't see anything," Alex answered finally.

"Nor do I," Ivy said, falling back against the sofa. "Tomorrow morning I'll key these into the computer and play around with them for a while—maybe I can calculate a pattern that we're not seeing."

Alex nodded his approval, but he had his doubts, as did Ivy. He began leafing through the previous year's editions, thinking out loud as he did so. "That list is in a January issue, and the first murder was committed in January. What do you think the chances are that he's tied that issue of *Perplexities* into his crimes in other ways, too?"

Ivy straightened, intrigued by the possibility. "Or with subsequent issues."

Alex looked at her and immediately realized that was a mistake. His mind was totally focused on the Strangler puzzle, but his body was viscerally aware of Ivy at every moment. Looking at her, seeing as well as feeling her vibrant energy, threatened to wipe all thoughts of his job right out of his mind. He quickly glanced away and pretended to study the magazine in his hands. "What do you mean?"

"The crimes were committed monthly, starting in January, and *Perplexities* is published monthly, starting with the January readers' poll."

"You mean maybe February's murder is somehow tied in with last February's issue?"

Ivy shrugged. "Anything is possible. You're the one who said there are no coincidences in this case."

"Let's check it out." Alex began searching for all twelve of the previous year's issues. When he had them stacked, Ivy pushed all the others out of the way and they each took an issue, looking for anything that might tie in with the murders. Alex went through the January issue page by page. Ivy did the same with February.

It was a time-consuming process, during which they finished off the rosé. Ivy went to the kitchen, and when she returned with a second bottle, she found that Alex had moved from his spot in front of the sofa. He had pulled her favorite high-backed armchair to the end of the coffee table and was sitting with the magazine in front of him, his knees spread wide to accommodate the table. Ivy didn't know whether to be insulted that he no longer wanted to sit beside her or pleased that he found her nearness disturbing.

Alex noticed that she was looking at him speculatively, and he felt compelled to explain why he had moved. "My bones aren't as young as they used to be."

Ivy looked deliberately from Alex to her sofa—which was a lot closer to where he'd been sitting and a lot more convenient to reach than a heavy chair that had to be moved four feet. She grinned. "Makes perfect sense to me."

"Are you suggesting that I chose this chair because I was afraid to share the sofa with you?"

Ivy gave him a look that was all wide-eyed innocence. "Would I suggest something like that?"

"Yes."

"Alex, I told you yesterday that I'm not trying to seduce you."

He cocked his head and looked Ivy up and down significantly, taking in every delightful curve and contour, from her bare feet and long legs, narrow waist and perfectly proportioned breasts, to her more-beautiful-by-the-second face. There, he captured her blue eyes with his intense, amused gray ones. "Maybe I'm fighting a losing battle to keep my-self from seducing you."

His look was so potently sensual that Ivy grew speechless and flustered, which delighted Alex immensely. It was the first time he'd seen her when she wasn't completely in control of the mystifying fascination they had with each other. He liked knowing that she could be caught off guard.

For the life of her, Ivy couldn't think of anything to say. Her mouth was as dry as sandpaper and her heart was beating like a big bass drum. She wasn't embarrassed, she was just suddenly very hungry for something other than spaghetti, and she didn't know how to handle a feeling that overpowering. She turned to the task of opening the bottle in her hands.

"What? No witty rejoinder?" he asked.

"More wine?"

Alex grinned and held out his glass. "You can dish it out, but you can't take it, huh? If I tell you that you're beautiful and whisper a few off-color suggestions in your ear, will you blush for me again?"

"No, but I might kick you in the shins," she replied sweetly. "And besides, I don't blush."

"Wanna bet?"

Ivy looked at him archly. "Wanna get back to work?"

Alex laughed. "Fine." It was good to have finally gotten in the last word. He picked up the March issue of *Perplexities* and began his page by page search. The magazine was a fascinating mix of variety puzzles, commentary on industry trends and short feature articles on games, new and old. Unlike many puzzle magazines, *Perplexities* listed bylines for every contributor, even their free-lance puzzle creators. Alex suggested that they investigate the puzzle contributors to see if any of them lived in the Brauxton area, and Ivy promised to get on it first thing in the morning.

"Hmm.... This is interesting," Ivy said thoughtfully. She was sitting near the end of the sofa—as far away as she could get from Alex's chair. "Last year's April issue has a feature on Risk and several other world domination games. Coincidence?" The clue found beside April's victim had been a Risk army token. "It was written by someone named Michael N. Montaugne."

Alex looked up from the March issue. "Let me see."

Ivy slid the publication across the coffee table toward him, putting a little too much effort into it, and the magazine fluttered to the floor.

"Good shot, Sherlock." Alex retrieved the magazine. "What page?"

"Fourteen, I think." Ivy reached for the May issue on the sofa beside her, then stopped dead still. Alex, too, had frozen. They looked at each other, almost afraid to voice what they were both thinking—two coincidences were two too many. April victim Elaine McNaughton had been killed on the fourteenth of the month.

Wordlessly, Ivy scrambled toward Alex, taking a position on the floor by his chair while he hurriedly relocated page fourteen. They stared at the article that featured the fourth most popular game of the year—Risk.

"This can't be a fluke," Alex said firmly. "The Strangler is using page numbers from these magazines to choose his murder dates."

"But none of the other murder dates correspond with anything in the issues I looked at," Ivy protested. To prove her point, she grabbed the February issue and turned to page twenty-five—the date Nancy Monroe had been killed. "See. It's just a logic problem. There's no mention of Trivial Pursuit anywhere on the page—or in this entire issue, for that matter."

"This can't be a coincidence," he insisted. But when they matched up the murder dates with page numbers from the other issues, no further similarities were found. Neal Steward's March maze on page six had nothing in common with the chess piece found on the sixth of March beside Darlena West's body. The same held true for the other comparisons.

They had reached another dead end. "Damn it!" Alex cursed. "I feel like Tantalus, stuck in that damned pool in Hades, unable to reach food or drink. Every time we find a solid lead, it vanishes before we really get a good grip on it."

"I'll feed all this into the computer tomorrow and see what I can come up with," Ivy promised, refusing to be daunted by something as insignificant as a brick wall.

He grinned at her, making a concerted effort to shake his frustration. "I thought you wanted to get out from behind your computer."

"And I did, thanks to you," she told him with a grateful smile. "I know it's been a frustrating day, but we really have accomplished a lot, Alex. We know now that the key to finding the Strangler is somewhere in these magazines. That's a lot more than we had yesterday. We're close. I can feel it."

Alex looked down at her, admiring her optimism—and her beauty. "You are really something else, you know that?" he asked softly, unable to keep himself from reaching out to gently cup one of her soft, peaches-and-cream cheeks in the palm of his hand. "You're Pollyanna, Sherlock Holmes, Miss America and Circe all rolled into one delightful, intriguing package."

Though Ivy's heart rate had escalated and her breathing was anything but steady, she still managed to quip softly, "The first three I don't object to, but I'm not sure I like being compared to a woman who turned men into barnyard animals."

"You're turning me into a blathering idiot," he told her, his own breathing a little irregular. "Doesn't that count?"

"It counts," Ivy whispered, her eyes locking with his; she was unwilling to break the soft, magical web that enmeshed them. His hand was warm and rough, gentle and firm, all at the same time. He had leaned toward her, so close that his breath fanned her face; his eyes searched her features, looking for any sign that she objected to his caress. She didn't give him one. "Are you going to kiss me?"

"Yes."

"But you're not going to fall in love with me."

"No."

"Are you sure?"

"Yes."

"But you're going to kiss me anyway?" she asked quietly.

"The two are not mutually exclusive, Ivy. One doesn't necessarily lead to the other," Alex pointed out.

"Sometimes it does," she countered, stretching up just a little, until their lips were only a whisper apart. "Are you willing to risk it?"

Instead of answering, Alex lowered his hand, gently brushing Ivy's neck, shoulder, back and waist. He eased her up, straightening and pulling her with him, until both his arms were around her and her breasts were cradled lightly against his chest. "Do you realize, Sherlock, that this is the most carefully dissected, overanalyzed kiss in the history of mankind, and it hasn't even taken place yet?"

Ivy wove her arms around Alex's neck, sealing their bodies together. "So stop dissecting and start kissing, already."

And he did—slowly, leisurely, as though he had all the time in the world to explore the myriad facets of the woman who had completely captivated him. And Ivy kissed him back, which didn't do anything to assuage his desire. Or hers. In fact, it only made them want more.

The filaments of attraction that had been pulling them relentlessly toward this moment ignited, and the slow, sensual brushing of lips became demanding. Alex kissed Ivy as though he'd never experienced anything this potent before; Ivy's kiss was the same, but it was also tinged with the fear that she might never experience anything like it again. It overloaded their senses and diminished their capacity to think or reason effectively.

Fortunately, it did not obliterate reason altogether. Shaken, they pulled away from each other at approximately the same time. Their lips left the scene of the crime first, then their arms, and when there was some space between them, Ivy rose and moved quietly to a neutral corner, trying to recapture her breath.

There was a long, heavy silence before Alex finally slapped his knees and said, "Well! I think we've done enough detective work for one day, don't you?"

Ivy nodded and took a deep breath. "I think so. I found out that you are one helluva good kisser."

Alex flashed her a wicked smile that she thought could have been bottled and sold as an aphrodisiac. The entire width of the living room was between them, but they might as well have been in each other's arms for all the good it did them. "Should we hold a press conference tomorrow and tell that to the media?"

"No," Ivy answered. "Reporters have to have two sources before they can print news like that, and I can't bear the thought of sharing you with scum like Phil Danker."

"Then we'll keep it to ourselves for a while." Alex rose, retrieved his jacket from the back of the sofa and folded it over his arm. Ivy followed every move hungrily. "See you in the morning?"

"You can count on it."

"Well..." He moved toward the door and Ivy followed him. "Thanks for a wonderful supper."

"Anytime."

Alex opened the door, and Ivy held on to it, waiting while he stood in the doorway as though he had one last thing to say before he left but couldn't quite get it out. He turned toward the hall, stopped, then turned back to her. His look was thoughtful and serious. "Ivy... if we expect too much from each other, one of us is going to get hurt."

Ivy shook her head in mock bewilderment. "There you go, trying to warn me off again. What makes you so all-fired sure that I'm going to fall in love?"

Alex looked at her for a long moment. "What makes you so all-fired sure I was referring to you?" he asked, then turned without another word and walked down the corridor.

CHAPTER NINE

THE NEXT MORNING, Alex gathered his detective squad together to announce the results of his investigation of the crime scenes. He explained the significance of the readers' poll and discussed the possibility that there was some connection between the pages of various issues of *Perplexities* and the murder dates. He assigned Mort Adamson and Jordan Brubaker to find out everything they could about Erin Selway's missing dog.

By the next day the two detectives had discovered that one of Erin's photographer friends had given her a puppy for her birthday late in March, but Erin had given the dog away just six days before her death. Apparently, her busy schedule had made caring for the puppy difficult, and she hadn't been particularly pleased by the way the little animal left a fine coating of fur on her furniture. The day after the dog had gone back to the photographer who had given it to her, Erin had hired Dwyers Carpet and Furniture Cleaners to sanitize her house from top to bottom.

Armed with this information, Alex held a brief press conference in the corridor outside the squad room. He made no mention of the readers' poll, but for the safety of the public, he explained what little the police had learned of the Strangler's method of gaining entrance to his victims' homes. It wasn't much, but the press jumped on it greedily, and the mayor was praised for having hired someone who was, at last, getting a few results.

Through all of this, Ivy rarely left her desk. When she wasn't on the phone trying to wring information from an uncooperative *Perplexities* editor in New York, she was keying an endless sequence of potential *Perplexities* clues into her computer. She culled list after list of games and game contributors from the previous year's issues in the hope that some pattern would eventually emerge, but none did.

To the task force and the media, Alex had been quick to give Ivy the credit she deserved for the new clues they had found. He had even insisted she be present at the press conference. But on a personal level, he seemed to have erected an impenetrable wall that kept Ivy at a safe distance. He was polite, even pleasant on occasion, but he was all business, as though nothing of a personal nature had happened between them.

Ivy popped into his office occasionally to report her progress—or lack thereof—on obtaining a list of *Perplexities'* subscribers and contributors, and while she was there she would study Alex's latest move in their ongoing chess match. Alex usually turned to his computer and ignored her during those moments. He seemed to think that pretending she wasn't in the room would snap the invisible thread of attraction that bound them together. Ivy would make a countermove on the chessboard and depart, trying not to worry about the gulf Alex had placed between them.

It was incredibly disappointing, though. Ivy had no objection to keeping things strictly professional at the office, and she knew she could live without the pressure a budding romance would add to her life, but she missed the delightful camaraderie and tingling awareness that they had shared from the very first. She also missed the promise of passion that she had discovered in Alex's arms, but she could live without sex, too.

Apparently, the other members of the task force weren't aware of the moratorium. Rumors about her relationship with Alex continued to buzz annoyingly, and it infuriated Ivy that no one believed a woman could earn a superior's trust and respect by using her brain rather than her body.

By the time the weekend rolled around, Ivy was ready for a break. She kept her shopping date with her mother and managed to deflect all questions about Alex by telling Mavis that she couldn't discuss the case.

Mavis suspected that there was even more to Ivy's strained, subdued mood than the difficult Strangler case, but since she couldn't wheedle information out of her daughter, she let it drop. If Ivy had a problem, she would come to her mother sooner or later.

They spent Saturday morning hitting sales at department stores until Mavis found just the right outfit for a casual Sunday afternoon drive. They followed the shopping spree with lunch, and then Ivy went home alone to take care of her weekend chores. She puttered around her apartment and made a concerted effort to keep her mind off the case.

It was part of a pattern that she had developed during the past few months. Mondays through Fridays, she gave herself to her job unreservedly. She worked long hours and focused totally on the Strangler. But unless the Strangler struck on the weekend and she was forced to go to the station, Saturdays and Sundays were her own. She cleaned house, did laundry, gossiped with friends, worked a few puzzles and occasionally took in a movie—ordinary things that ordinary people did on ordinary weekends. It was Ivy's way of remaining sane.

This weekend, though, it was harder to leave the Strangler behind because the case was now intrinsically tied to Alex Devane, and she just couldn't stop thinking about the remarkable new lieutenant. The hours they had spent together played in her mind like a moviola—an endless loop of images that began with the moment she'd walked into his office and played straight through to the moment he'd left her apartment. Then it started all over again.

At night, she tended to linger over the time she'd spent in his arms. Her fertile mind rewrote the film script so vividly that she thought she would go crazy imagining what might have happened if she and Alex hadn't pulled away from each other.

Logically, she knew that she would never have made love with a man she'd known for only twenty-four hours, but logic didn't keep her body from wanting a fuller taste of Alex, nor did it keep her mind from wanting another encounter with his intriguing intellect, or her heart from wanting to reach out and heal him.

He didn't believe in love. Or so he claimed. Knowing that made Ivy want to prove him wrong, but she was smart enough to realize how foolish such an attempt would be. She was more attracted to him than any other man she had ever met, yet she hardly knew him. But that didn't stop erotic, sensual images from plaguing her.

Her mind created graphic scenes of Alex in her bed, kissing her, caressing her, softly urging her on as she kissed and caressed him ... She created a lover who was strong, generous and skillful, one who was secure enough of his manhood that he could allow her to be his equal—in bed and out. It was an erotic, romantic fantasy, and Ivy recognized it as such. She was taking the man of her dreams—the one she wanted to share her life with—and giving him Alex Devane's handsome face, his piercing gray eyes, his gravelly voice, his whipcord-lean body. In short, she was playing a dangerous game, and she continually reminded herself that it was important to keep the real Alex separate from the fantasy she spent the weekend building around him.

That would have been a lot easier to do if the chemistry between them had been mundane. Unfortunately, she felt a connection with Alex that was everything she'd ever hoped to feel for the man she fell in love with for the first, last and only time. As a romantic, she knew that no matter what the circumstances or the obstacles, she would find that man and share her life with him.

That attitude gave Ivy the patience to wait and see what might develop with Alex, but it didn't do anything to assuage the cravings of her body through long, sleepless, image-filled nights. It had been a long, long time since she'd been intimate with a man, and that only made the cravings worse.

In college, Ivy had used casual sexual encounters as a form of youthful rebellion against her mother, who hadn't realized that her daughter was growing up. It was also a way of punishing her absent father for deserting her. She hadn't been promiscuous, but she hadn't seen love as a necessity, either. Eventually, she had outgrown the need to rebel, and with that maturity came the knowledge that sex for the sake of anything but an expression of caring, warmth and communication was a waste of time.

Since then, her encounters with men had been few and far between because she made no attempt to hide her intellect. Most men of her acquaintance fell into two categories: those who were so intimidated by her that they ran the other way, and those who only wanted to jump into bed with her to prove their superiority. As near as she could tell, the theory seemed to be that if they couldn't dominate her intellectually, they'd dominate her sexually.

Alex certainly didn't fall into the latter category, and somehow she didn't believe that he was intimidated by her, either. Rather, he was attracted to her, but he'd obviously been burned once and he wasn't ready to risk getting burned again.

Eventually, he would take that risk, though. By Sunday night, after a weekend of thinking of little else, Ivy was certain of that. Their attraction was too strong for it to be otherwise. She was resolved to wait and see what happened. She would go with the flow, play by the rules Alex set down and let nature take its course.

THE NEXT BREAK in the Strangler case came Monday morning when the mail was dropped onto Ivy's desk. After considerable coercion, the acting senior editor at *Perplexities* had finally relented and sent Ivy the two lists she'd requested. The first, and by far the largest, was a list of all *Perplexities* subscribers who lived within a one-hundred-mile radius of Brauxton. The other was the name and address of every person who had contributed a puzzle or feature article to the magazine in the past two years.

Without bothering to study either list, Ivy scooped them up and headed straight for Alex's office. "They're here," she announced enthusiastically, then stopped dead still. The office was an absolute shambles. Coffee cups littered the desk, computer printouts were scattered like gigantic snowflakes, issues of *Perplexities* were spread out on every surface and, clothes were strewn over both chairs.

Ivy took in the disaster area, amazed. "What happened in here?" She stepped toward the desk, removed a rumpled jacket from one chair and tossed it onto a pair of jeans in the other chair. "Did you have an orgy and forget to invite me?"

Alex swiveled away from the computer and regarded Ivy with barely concealed irritation. His clothes were rumpled, he had two days' growth of beard, and there were dark circles under his eyes. Compared to Alex, the room looked great. "Where the hell were you this weekend?" he demanded.

Stunned, Ivy fought an impulse to take a step back, away from his anger. This was an Alex she hadn't seen before. "I was at home. Where should I have been?"

"Here," Alex said succinctly.

"This is the first I've heard of it. I'm not normally scheduled for duty on the weekends," she explained, keeping her tone equitable. No one had told her she was supposed to work, so she refused to get defensive. "If you wanted me to come in, why didn't you call?"

That was a good question, Alex thought, more irritated with himself than with Ivy. Friday afternoon when she had left for the day, he'd fought the impulse to go after her and invite her out to dinner. He'd rationalized the impulse by telling himself that he only wanted someone he trusted, someone he connected with intellectually, to discuss the case with.

He'd gotten as far as the door when he realized that he would only be using the case as an excuse to be with her. All week long, thoughts of her had been taking his mind away from the case, which should have been his only focus, and he had resolved not to give in to his desire to be with her, to get to know her better, to bask in the warmth of her dazzling personality. Ivy Kincaid was as dangerous as an addictive drug, and Alex was not going to become hooked.

Holding on to that resolve, he had spent most of the night in his office going over case notes from the six months that preceded his arrival on the task force. In the wee hours of the morning, he'd gone home, slept for all of three hours, then showered, shaved and returned to the office with a change of clothing he knew from experience he'd need sooner or later.

He'd spent Saturday going over more case notes and looking out his door whenever he heard a voice in the squad room. Every time he discovered that the person he heard talking wasn't Ivy, he became more and more disappointed. The only sleep he'd gotten Saturday night had come while he'd camped out on the cramped sofa by the door. By Sunday night, when Ivy failed to put in an appearance, Alex was exhausted, frustrated with the case and irritated by his obsession with Ivy.

This morning, after a second night on the sofa, his disposition hadn't improved. But that wasn't Ivy's fault, he reminded himself.

"Sorry," he muttered. "I shouldn't take my bad temper out on you."

Ivy glanced at the sofa behind her, noting the blanket and pillow that had undoubtedly come from the prisoner holding tank downstairs. "Did you spend the whole weekend here?"

"Most of it."

"And you're mad at me because misery loves company, and I didn't come down on my own to be miserable with you."

"Something along those lines," Alex admitted. "You look disgustingly rested, refreshed and ready to face the world."

"Really?" she asked dryly.

Alex couldn't keep from laughing, but was so tired it came out as little more than a weak huffing sound. "That's why I missed you this weekend. I needed someone to make me laugh."

"What you needed was to get out of here and get your mind off the case, Kemo Sabe. You can't work twenty-four hours a day and expect to remain sharp enough to catch this killer."

Alex shrugged. "I tend to be rather single-minded when I'm in the middle of something."

Ivy gave him a wise look. "There's a difference between being single-minded and being obsessive."

"That's a distinction I have a little trouble making sometimes," he confessed.

Ivy smiled and rested one hip on the arm of the chair. "Should I take it upon myself to let you know whenever you start obsessing?"

"Go right ahead, but it won't do you any good. I'm stubborn, too." He pointed to the computer printouts she was holding against her chest. "What have you got?"

"Oh." Ivy had completely forgotten about the lists she'd worked so hard to procure. "That idiot editor finally came across with the *Perplexities* subscriber and contributor lists, thanks to Mort Adamson. He called a friend on the force in New York, who in turn called the editor and put on a little pressure."

"Did you find anything interesting on the lists?"

Ivy stepped around his desk and placed them in front of him. "I haven't even looked. I figured you'd want first crack at them."

Alex grinned and felt his knotted insides loosen. Fighting his attraction for Ivy had made him miserable and unable to concentrate. Maybe he'd be better off if he didn't fight it quite so hard. "That's what I like, a flunky who understands chain of command."

Ivy clicked her heels together and saluted. "All hail to the chief."

Chuckling, Alex glanced at the printouts and decided to start with the contributor list. He split the list in half, handed *M* through *Z* to Ivy and said, "Sit and look. It shouldn't take us long to find out if any of *Perplexities'* puzzle creators live in Brauxton."

Ivy accepted the computer sheets and returned to the chair in front of his desk. She went through the list entry by entry. Most of the names were familiar to her—she'd been solving their puzzles for years—but knowing that Danica Nikel lived in Palo Alto, California, and Lewis Raney lived in Whynot, Mississippi, did not bring her any closer to finding someone who might be the Strangler.

Fortunately, Alex had better luck in the *A* through *L* section. In the *C*'s, to be exact. "Got one!" he shouted, almost coming out of his chair with excitement. "Norme Canyon, 998 Bridgetree Road, Pendleton Heights." The suburb of Pendleton Heights was just across the river. If the expressway was clear, it was a ten-minute drive into the city. That didn't make Norme Canyon guilty of six murders, but it did make him a suspect worth investigating.

Ivy recognized the name. Canyon constructed logic puzzles for a couple of the game periodicals she subscribed to. He was one of her favorites, but she hadn't realized he lived in the area.

"No comment?" Alex asked when Ivy didn't respond to his discovery.

"I'm sorry. I guess I'm just in shock. I've been working on Norme Canyon's puzzles for so long that he seems like part of my family. Thinking that he could be the Strangler is a little like trying to imagine Uncle Ambrose as Jack the Ripper."

Alex grinned. "Do you have an Uncle Ambrose?"

"No, but if I did, I wouldn't want him to be a serial killer."

"Does that mean that you have no desire to question your old friend Norme in connection with the Strangler case?"

Ivy sat up straight in her chair. "Are you kidding? I'd question God if I could get a private interview!"

Alex's grin turned into a full-fledged smile that made Ivy's heart do a somersault. "In that case, why don't you grab your purse and we'll head out to Pendleton Heights."

Ivy was a little shocked by the invitation. "You mean that?"

"Of course. Why wouldn't I?" Alex asked, his smile fading.

Ivy's lips pursed into a thoughtful bow. "Well…you have sort of been avoiding making eye contact with me since our expedition to the murder sites…"

He glanced away from her, looking distinctly uncomfortable. They both knew that his withdrawal had nothing to do with their day at the murder sites and everything to do with what had happened that night. "I've been busy catching up on the case files. I'm sorry if I've seemed preoccupied."

Ivy accepted his answer for the lame excuse it was and let it drop. "No problem. I'm glad that's all it was. I'd hate to think that I'd done something to damage our working relationship."

Alex met her eyes, wondering if he could do so without becoming lost in their depths. "Nothing that I know of." He stood. "Now, shall we go talk to Norme?"

"I'll get my purse." She stood and glanced at the chessboard on the wall. The game was still in its early stages, and it took only a second to evaluate Alex's last move. She countered it with her queen's bishop and calculated that she'd checkmate her opponent in four moves unless he did some creative manipulation. She turned to him and found that he was watching her and the board closely.

"Do you really think I'm stupid enough to fall for a cheap trick like that?" he asked, reaching out to capture one of her knights.

"It was worth a try," she answered, grinning. "I never use an expensive trick if a cheap one will work just as well. It helps me evaluate the skill of my opponent."

"Did you underestimate me?" he asked, coming around from behind his desk.

"No, but I'm still evaluating."

Their eyes caught and held. The room was suddenly overflowing with the awareness of each other that they were both coming to expect. They weren't talking about chess anymore. "And when you finish evaluating?"

"Then I'll close in for the kill and take what I want."

"What do you want?"

"When I'm sure, you'll be the first to know."

"And if I don't want the same thing?" Alex asked, his voice hushed. Sensual tension flowed between them like the currents of a swift river.

"Then you're a fool, and we'd both lose."

Alex shook his head ruefully. "You're awfully sure of yourself, Detective Kincaid."

"No, I'm not, Alex," she replied, her voice soft and a little sad. "It just appears that way because you're so unsure of yourself. Maybe one of these days you'll tell me why."

An image of Brenda floated through Alex's consciousness. And with that image came the painful memories of the way he'd failed her, the way she'd betrayed him with another man, the way she'd taken her life because neither her husband nor her lover had been able to see how desperately she'd needed their help.

"Don't count on it, Ivy. I played this game once and lost. I don't intend to play it again."

Ivy leaned her hip against his desk, watching him closely. "Is that why you tried so hard to pretend I didn't exist last week?"

Alex's gaze didn't wave. "Yes."

"And because of that, you had an absolutely miserable weekend," she pointed out. "Doesn't that tell you something?"

"What?"

"That you're already well into the middle of the game, whether you want to play or not."

Her words had the ring of absolute truth. "That game being love, in your opinion?"

Ivy shrugged. "'Love' is probably too strong a word at this point in the game."

"Then what *is* the game?" he asked, his voice hard and serious.

"*Life*, Alex. Whether we like it or not, we play it from the moment we're born until the moment we die. Sometimes we win a few rounds, sometimes we lose a few. But win or lose, it's not a game we can refuse to play just because the going gets tough." She straightened and stepped toward him. "And the really good thing about the game, Alex, is that nobody knows the rules, so we all take the same chances."

"When the game is over, how do you know if you've won or lost?"

Ivy shrugged expansively. "You don't. You only know if it was a good life or a bad life. If you were happy or sad. But one thing that usually comes near the end is time to reflect on the mistakes you made and the chances for happiness you let slip by. The really big winners are the ones who took the most chances—the ones who took the biggest risks with their hearts."

Alex studied her lovely, animated face and realized she believed every word she'd said. And strangely enough, so did he. But knowing that winning the game of life meant taking risks didn't mean that he would ever be able to put his heart in jeopardy again. On the other hand, according to Ivy's philosophy, he didn't have much choice in the matter.

"We have a Strangler to catch, Sherlock," he said finally, putting some distance between himself and that disturbing thought. "That's the only game I'm interested in at the moment."

Ivy smiled and gestured toward the door. "Then by all means, let's start playing. That's another game I have no intention of losing."

"Now there's something we completely agree on," Alex said as he started out the door.

"That's a start," Ivy mumbled under her breath, following him.

Alex glanced at her over his shoulder. "What did you say?"

"Nothing! Nothing at all," she exclaimed brightly, trying to hide a smile. Alex Devane liked her a lot more than he wanted to admit. Whether that was good or bad remained to be seen.

CHAPTER TEN

FINDING NORME CANYON took most of the morning. Because Alex looked as though he'd slept in his clothes—which he had—and hadn't shaved for two days—which he hadn't—he and Ivy made a quick detour to his house so that he could shower, shave and change before rushing off in pursuit of the Strangler investigation's first genuine suspect.

Ivy waited patiently while Alex transformed himself into something approximating a presentable police lieutenant. Patience was no problem, since she had his home to explore for keys to his personality while she waited. What she learned was baffling. Alex's home was spacious, attractive and relatively expensive looking, yet there was nothing much about it that suggested anyone lived there. What should have been a formal living room was set up as an office, and in the connecting room, which should have been a dining area, was a second office. Both rooms were overflowing with books, file cabinets and computer hardware.

When Alex had left her alone in the "living room" with the admonition to make herself at home, Ivy had been tempted to ask, "Where?"

She wandered through the offices, looking with casual interest at his eclectic collection of books. The shelves were filled with everything from anatomy texts to tracts on Oriental philosophy to cordon bleu cookbooks. Apparently, he also liked mythology, history, astronomy and psychology. As far as Ivy could tell, there was no general subject on the face of the earth that was neglected in Alex's vast library. Amazing.

But where did he *live*? There was no television, no stereo, no plush sofa and no easy chair in which he could curl up to enjoy one of his good books. There were just two desks, two computers, six file cabinets, a love seat, a couple of chairs and thousands of books.

Leaving the library behind, Ivy went through a door in the second office and found an antiseptically modern kitchen. It was characterless, but it seemed to contain all the normal things one would expect to find in a kitchen.

She went through another door to the right of a breakfast nook and finally found a sofa and a TV, though what she should call the room she hadn't a clue. It wasn't a family room, because there was no sign of a family having ever set foot in the place; not a single photograph occupied any surface. It wasn't a den, because a den created an image of a cozy room with comfortable old leather chairs and a fireplace, whereas this room was as sterile as the kitchen. It couldn't be a living room, because it didn't look lived-in.

It was just a big room with a TV and some furniture that had a solid, expensive look to it.

There was an arch in one wall, and Ivy went through it and found herself in a corridor. She heard the faint sound of water running and guessed that the bedroom or bedrooms were to the left. She went right and found herself in the entry hall adjacent to office number one, which was now occupied by an attractive, middle-aged woman wearing a summery skirt and blouse. She was humming a lively but unrecognizable tune as she raided one of the file cabinets, and Ivy decided that the woman was either Alex's housekeeper, his secretary or the happiest burglar she'd ever encountered.

Ivy stepped into the room tentatively. "Hello?"

Her arms loaded with files, the woman turned at the sound of an unfamiliar voice and looked at Ivy questioningly. "Who are you?"

Ivy smiled her most innocent, reassuring smile. "Detective Ivy Kincaid. I work for Lieutenant Devane, who, by the way, is in the shower."

"Maureen Fitzpatrick." She dropped the files onto her desk and stepped toward Ivy with her hand extended. "It's nice to meet you, Detective Kincaid. I saw Alex's squad car in the driveway, but I didn't realize he'd brought a guest home with him."

Ivy explained that Alex had spent the night in his office and had wanted to change clothes before going out on a call. "I'm just along for the ride." She gestured toward the desk and the book-filled walls. "Do you work here?"

Maureen nodded as she returned to the desk and sat. "I'm sort of an underpaid secretary and housekeeper."

There was a chair beside the front windows, and Ivy took it. "Forgive me for being presumptuous, but what kind of work does Alex do that requires a secretary?"

"Before he returned to the police force, he was a very successful professional researcher. But if he doesn't get back to work soon, he's going to be a bankrupt one. I'm in the process of finishing up two projects that are both overdue, and last week I had to turn down three more."

Ivy was fascinated. It had never occurred to her to wonder what Alex had done with himself in the three years he'd been away from police work. "What does he research?"

Maureen rolled her eyes to the heavens. "Anything. Doctoral dissertations, historical novels, corporate environmental impact issues, genealogies... You name it, we research it. We were a small but viable business until Len Eversall convinced Alex that if he didn't come back to the force and catch the Strangler, all subsequent deaths would be on Alex's head."

"That's horrible," Ivy said, wondering if Alex really had bought into that kind of guilt trip or if Ms Fitzpatrick was exaggerating. "I take it you've known Alex for quite some time."

"About ten years," Maureen told her. "He and my late husband were partners on the force when Alex was just a rookie. He's been like family ever since."

Obviously, the woman across the desk from Ivy knew Alex quite well. She would certainly know if there were any other women in his life, and she probably knew what had happened to him to make him so determined never to fall in love again.

The urge to pump Maureen for every scrap of information she possessed was almost more than Ivy could control. She was a trained investigator, and Alex's secretary seemed like a friendly, talkative person. It wouldn't take much to find out at least some little tidbit of information about him, but Ivy refused to stoop to guerrilla warfare. If she couldn't drag information out of Alex, or if he didn't open up to her of his own free will, there was nothing to be gained by gathering intelligence covertly.

So instead of leading their conversation onto personal topics, like why his wife had committed suicide, Ivy asked questions about his current research project. Maureen was only too happy to answer.

"I thought I heard voices in here." Looking handsome, refreshed and as close to unrumpled as he ever got, Alex appeared at the door. "Hello, Maureen. I thought you were going to be at the library all day today."

"I finished that on Saturday. I'm ready to start typing today."

"Wonderful." He crossed to the desk. "I guess you two have introduced yourselves."

"Mmm-hmm. Maureen was telling me about your research," Ivy told him. "It sounds fascinating."

Alex looked at her, wondering if that was what they had really been talking about. "It is fascinating. Most people would find it dull, but I enjoy it. Look, Ivy... would you mind waiting for me in the car? I've got a couple of business things I need to discuss with Mo. I'll be out in two minutes."

"Of course." Ivy stood and looked at Alex's secretary. "It was a pleasure meeting you, Ms Fitzpatrick."

"Call me Maureen," she insisted. "And it was a pleasure meeting you, too."

Ivy left with a wave, and when Alex heard the front door close, he sat on the edge of Maureen's desk and looked at her thoughtfully. "What do you think of her, Mo?"

The question obviously surprised her. "Detective Kincaid? I think she's nice. Very outgoing and personable..." Realizing why Alex was asking, Maureen smiled. "Very pretty, too," she said knowingly. "Or are you going to tell me you hadn't noticed?"

Alex gave a short, humorless chuckle. "Oh, I noticed, all right."

"Well, it's about time. Are you noticing seriously or casually?"

He glared at her. "We just met last week."

"What does that have to do with anything?" Maureen asked sternly. "It only takes a few minutes to determine whether a woman is type A or type B."

This was a philosophy Alex hadn't heard from Maureen before, and he was curious. "What's type A?"

"They're the ones you have trouble remembering the morning after."

"And type B?"

"The ones who are impossible to forget. Would I be wrong in assuming that Detective Kincaid falls into category B?"

"No, you wouldn't be wrong."

"Does that mean you've already progressed to the 'morning after' stage?"

Alex threw her a disgusted glance. "Not yet. Right now it's pure speculation."

Maureen smiled devilishly. "Knowing you, I can't imagine that 'pure' enters into anything."

"Thank you for that uncalled-for, insensitive appraisal of my character."

"You're welcome. Now did you really have business to discuss, or did you just want to chat about that charming detective who's outside, sweltering in the heat?"

Alex looked decidedly uncomfortable. "Actually, I wanted to ask you about Ivy... Did she... say anything about me?"

Maureen sighed disgustedly. "Alex, we weren't having a slumber party. We didn't get around to discussing boys."

"I meant, did she ask any questions about me? Personal questions?"

"Oh, I get it. You want to know if she put me under hot lights and grilled me about your secrets. Do you leave the cap off the toothpaste? Do you put on clean underwear every morning? That sort of thing."

Alex ran one hand through his still damp hair. "You know what I mean, Mo."

Maureen looked at him, growing serious. "She didn't ask about Brenda, but it wouldn't hurt you to tell her about it yourself. Talking about it isn't going to make it happen all over, and *not* talking about it isn't going to make it go away. Only you can do that."

"With the help of a good woman?" he asked sarcastically.

"No, Alex. You have to exorcise Brenda's ghost all by yourself. Being free to love the right woman is nothing more than an incentive."

"Horsefeathers," Alex said as he stood and started for the door. "Heaven save us from romance-minded females."

"No need to be insulting! You're the one who started this conversation!" she called after him, chuckling as the door slammed in his wake. It was about time somebody gave Alex Devane a good shaking up. He'd been sitting on the shelf far too long.

NORME CANYON'S HOME was a modest, attractive structure in a subdivision where all the houses looked as though they'd been stamped from the same cookie cutter. Ivy and Alex found 998 in the center of a cul-de-sac. They also found Norme Canyon's wife and a five-year-old son, but Norme wasn't home. Not that the detectives had expected him to be. Creating puzzles was a great hobby and a nice way to supplement an income, but it was doubtful that anyone could make a decent living at it.

Without alarming Mrs. Canyon, Ivy and Alex discovered that Norme was an accountant for a nationally known chain of tax consultants. They got the address of his office and bade a somewhat puzzled Mrs. Canyon good day.

"She seemed like a nice, normal lady," Ivy commented as they headed for downtown Pendleton Heights.

"You mean she hardly seems the sort to be married to a serial killer."

"Right. When people think of a mass murderer, they conjure up an image of a brooding recluse who sleeps during the day and roams the streets at night, not a suburban accountant."

"You're stereotyping," Alex said accusingly. "Generally, the most striking thing about psychopaths is that to most of the world they seem perfectly normal. They're masters at keeping their insanity hidden behind a veil of normalcy."

"I know, but if Norme Canyon does develop into a viable suspect, I'm going to hate having to go back to his wife and question her about his habits, idiosyncrasies and whereabouts on the evenings of six murders."

"You're too softhearted for your own good, Sherlock."

"Yes, but I'm a fascinating human being," she said with an impish grin.

"True," Alex muttered wryly.

They found Norme's office without any difficulty and were ushered in to see him almost immediately. He was a pleasant, average-looking man—average height, average weight—with no distinctive features except for his receding hairline, unusual only because he was in his very early thirties. His office was so tiny that there was barely room for the three of them, but after a round of introductions and handshakes, Norme sat behind his desk, Ivy took the chair in front of it, and Alex stood to the side and slightly behind her.

"Devane?" the accountant said, as though questioning his memory. "Aren't you the new head of the Strangler task force?"

"That's right."

"I don't envy you your job, Lieutenant. From what I read, it's a really complicated case."

"Do you follow the case closely?" Ivy asked casually, noting that Canyon didn't seem the least bit nervous about having the head of the task force in his office.

"How can anyone avoid it? It's the lead story on the six o'clock news every night of the week," he told her, then looked at Alex. "But what can I do for you officers?"

"If you've been following the case, you're probably aware that there's a game angle connected with each of the murders," Alex said.

Canyon nodded. "I know the killer leaves a game piece by each victim, but the news media usually doesn't say what kind of game."

"That's because we're keeping as much information as possible under wraps in order to avoid copycat killings," Alex explained. He gestured toward Ivy. "Detective Kincaid and I have been pursuing the game angle, though. We're questioning everyone in the area who might be said to have a more than average interest in games."

Canyon's slightly puzzled look vanished and was replaced by an enthusiastic smile. "I see! Someone told you I invent logic puzzles as a hobby, and you thought I might be a suspect. This is great!"

Ivy and Alex looked at each other and both gave a little shrug. Canyon's excitement was hardly the reaction of a guilty man—or an innocent one, for that matter. Alex cleared his throat uncertainly. "We're not here to make any accusations, Mr. Canyon."

"Oh, call me Norme, please," he said.

"All right, Norme," Alex replied evenly. "We just wanted to ask you about your connection with the magazine *Perplexities* and see if your hobby ever brought you into contact with anyone who might fit the Strangler profile."

Norme's face fell. "You mean you don't want to ask me where I was on the nights of the murders?"

His disappointment was so keen that Ivy had to suppress a smile. "Mr. Canyon, I get the impression that you like the idea of being a suspect. Why on earth would you want anyone to think you were the Brauxton Strangler?"

"Because nothing exciting ever happens out here in the suburbs—not to me, at least."

"Being a suspect isn't what most people would consider exciting," Alex pointed out. Like Ivy, he was having trouble hiding a smile. If Norme Canyon was guilty of six murders, he either had a split personality or was the best actor Alex had ever met.

"You don't know how boring life can be in Pendleton Heights," the accountant replied sadly.

"Well, in that case, would you object to telling us your whereabouts on the nights of January 17, February 25..."

As Alex went through the whole list, Norme jotted the dates on a scrap of paper, then consulted his desk calendar. "Offhand, I'd say that on most of those nights I was at home with Betsy and the kids. Except for the fourteenth of April. That weekend Bets and I drove the kids up to New Hampshire to attend my in-laws' wedding anniversary. I remember hearing about the fourth murder from someone at the party." He scribbled an address on another sheet of paper and handed it to Ivy. "I'm sure you'll want to check out my alibi."

"We'll do that," Ivy promised, amazed at his attitude. Apparently in the suburbs being suspected of being a serial killer was some kind of status symbol.

Norme was still leafing through his calendar, checking the murder dates against his business and social schedule. Ivy wasn't sure if he was hoping to find alibis or not! He did come up with a weekly Wednesday night pinochle game that accounted for his whereabouts until midnight on the sixth of March.

"Of course, if the murder was committed after midnight, I could have slipped across the bridge into Brauxton after I took the baby-sitter home," he said, clearly trying to be helpful to the stymied detectives.

"We'll be sure and check out that possibility," Ivy promised.

"Would you like to search my house?" he asked hopefully. "I can't leave the office right now, but I could call Bets and tell her to let you in. You won't need a warrant or anything. We have a lot of games stored in the linen closet—you might want to see if any of the pieces are missing. You know, ones that would match the pieces that were left at the scene of the crimes.''

Ivy started to protest that such action wouldn't be necessary, but Alex surprised her by taking Canyon up on the offer.

"Great!" He reached for the phone. "I'll tell Bets to get all our games out of the closet so you can look at them."

"I'd prefer it if she didn't do that," Alex said sternly. "There may be a great deal we can learn from seeing how they're stored—whether there's any dust on them, that sort of thing."

"Oh, right." Norme punched out his phone number and with considerable relish told his wife what was going on. From the one side of the conversation they could hear, Ivy and Alex concluded that Betsy was far from enthusiastic about being married to a Strangler suspect. Apparently, Mrs. Canyon wasn't as bored with the suburbs as her husband.

"She's expecting you," Norme told them as he replaced the receiver. "She said you'd already been to the house once, but she hadn't realized who you were or what you wanted."

"We didn't want to alarm her unless it became necessary," Alex explained. Ivy cast him a sidelong glance, wondering why he suddenly sounded like a script from a bad cop show. Could he actually believe that eager-to-please Norme was the Strangler? To Ivy, it was inconceivable.

"We'll be going now, Norme," Alex said, lightly touching Ivy on the shoulder. She stood. "And we'll be sure to include your cooperative attitude in our report."

"Glad to be of help. Boy, the guys at the club are going to love this."

"Glad to be of help," Ivy said dryly, and received a subtle poke in the ribs from Alex.

They left quickly, moving past rows of other cubicle-size offices, past the receptionist, through the lobby and out the front door. They were on the street before Ivy finally gave in to the laughter she'd been holding in check for the past ten minutes. The merry sound rolled out of her in waves, making her shake so hard that Alex had to take her arm in order to keep her on a steady course toward their car.

"'We'll be sure to include your cooperative attitude in our report'?" Ivy said between cackles of laughter. "You can't seriously believe he's the Strangler?"

"No, I don't," Alex told her, starting to laugh himself.

"Then why are we going to waste our time seeing how much dust has accumulated in his linen closet?"

"Because it would be foolish not to." Alex started the car and pulled into the flow of traffic. "He gave us a couple of alibis, true. But we don't know if they're valid. Psychopaths can be fiendishly clever. Maybe he only offered to let us check his game collection because he thought we'd refuse."

"You really believe that?"

"No," he replied. "But he's the first suspect we've had, and he deserves to be investigated thoroughly."

Ivy's laughter was under control, but she was still chuckling every now and then. "I don't think I'll ever again be able to work a Norme Canyon logic puzzle with a straight face."

Alex glanced at her curiously. "Do you do *anything* with a straight face? Isn't there anything you take seriously?"

"Yes," Ivy answered, thinking about the past few nights and the serious consideration she had given to making love with the man beside her.

"What might that be?"

Ivy turned on the seat and tilted her head in a gesture that was unconsciously coquettish. "Believe me, you don't want to know."

Alex took his eyes off the traffic long enough to look at her again. Her eyes were twinkling and she wore a devastating wisp of a smile. In that moment, she was all woman—soft, alluring and utterly irresistible. He glanced back at the road quickly. "You're right. I don't want to know."

Ivy's soft laughter floated around in the car, enmeshing Alex in its magical, musical web.

"Would you like to have dinner with me tonight?" he asked before really being conscious of the intention to ask her.

The laughter died away. "I'd love to."

"Good. I'll make reservations at Maison Blanche for eight o'clock."

"Wonderful," Ivy said, delighted by his choice of restaurant. Maison Blanche was more famous for its romantic atmosphere than its fine food. It had been a long time since she'd had to dress for dinner—and what might come afterward.

CHAPTER ELEVEN

WHEN IVY STEPPED out of the shower that night at six forty-five, her phone was ringing. Wrapped in a towel, she ran into the living room, wondering if the caller could possibly be Norme Canyon wanting to know if he was still a suspect. She and Alex had spent fifteen uneventful minutes at his house, during which time Canyon had called his wife twice to ask if the detectives were still there. For the quiet, suburban Canyon family, it had been a day of high drama. For Ivy and Alex, it had been a waste of time and energy. All they'd gotten out of Norme Canyon was a good laugh.

"Hello?" Ivy half expected the caller to have given up by the time she reached the phone, but no such luck.

"Hello, dear. I see you're home at a decent hour tonight."

"Yes, Mother, I'm home—but not for long. I'm getting ready for a date."

"Really? Anyone I know?"

Ivy sighed and reminded herself that all mothers were nosy. Hers more than most, but that was beside the point. "I'm having dinner with Alex Devane."

"Your new lieutenant?" Mavis sounded a little stunned. "Is it a business meeting or something?"

"I certainly hope not. We're going to Maison Blanche, and unless the maître d' wants to confess to being the Strangler, this should be just a cozy little dinner for two."

There was a little pause, and Ivy could visualize her mother frowning as she searched for the proper words. "I was afraid of something like this Saturday when you were so subdued. Ivy, dear, do you think it's wise to become involved with a man who is, essentially, your employer? Remember what happened with that desk sergeant a few years ago."

Ivy rolled her eyes and prayed for patience. "That's an incident I find hard to forget, Mom, but you're talking about apples and oranges. Sergeant Wiskowski was a pig. Never in my wildest nightmares would I have considered dating him. Alex Devane is anything but repulsive."

"Be that as it may, you still work for him."

"That was nothing to do with our having dinner."

"But, Ivy—"

"No 'buts,' Mom. You're the one who keeps complaining because I'm an old maid. How am I ever going to rectify that situation if I don't date?" Ivy wasn't actively searching for a husband, but she knew it made her mother feel better to at least know that the possibility of grandchildren existed.

"And is Lieutenant Devane husband material?"

Ivy heaved a sigh that sounded slightly regretful to both herself and her mother. "Probably not. But he's extremely intelligent and he has a wonderfully dry wit." *And he makes my insides turn to jelly,* she added silently. "Don't worry, Mom. I know what I'm doing. If I make a mistake in handling my relationship with Alex, I'll live with the consequences," she said.

"You've known him only a week, and already you have a 'relationship'?"

"It was a figure of speech, Mother. We're not going to pick out a china pattern, we're just going to dinner," Ivy said with a laugh.

Mavis laughed, too. "All right, I give up. Just be careful, dear. I don't want to see you get hurt."

"I'll try not to, Mom, I swear. Now, I've really got to run. I just got out of the shower, and Alex is due here any time. I'll try to come by one night this week—or maybe I'll do bingo with you this weekend."

"Oh, that sounds like fun," Mavis said, overjoyed at the prospect. "It'll give you a chance to meet Gil."

"That's exactly what I had in mind," Ivy said slyly. She had spent an hour on the phone the previous night listening to her mother rave about the divine Gil Hatchet, and now she was anxious to meet him.

Mavis laughed again. "Why is it that you get to pass judgment on my love life, but I can't say anything about yours?"

Ivy grinned at the phone. "Goodbye, Mother."

"Goodbye, dear. I'll talk to you later in the week."

I'll bet you will, Ivy thought as she hung up. Mavis wouldn't give up until she'd wrung every detail of her date with Alex out of her. And as she finished getting ready, Ivy wondered if it would be the kind of date she could discuss in minute detail with her mother or one that Mavis would be better off not knowing too much about.

The latter, I hope, Ivy thought as she pulled a sinfully sexy set of undies out of her lingerie drawer.

"I wonder if Alex likes red lace?" she asked the empty apartment as she disappeared back into the bathroom.

IT WAS GETTING harder now. What had started as something ridiculously uncomplicated had evolved into a game of mind-boggling complexity. It was harder to locate victims who fit the requirements. It was harder to follow them without being noticed. It was harder to arrange the intricate details that made everything go like clockwork when the time was right.

Most of all, it was getting harder to wait. Everything had to be done in a prescribed sequence, strictly according to the plan. No deviations could be permitted. Yet waiting for the right time was becoming nearly impossible. The pressure to do it, the need to do it and to have it over and done with was intense. And every day, it got worse.

In fact, the only thing that got easier was the actual killing—the moment when the waiting was over and the need to kill was finally satisfied. The rope around her neck was easy. The brief, panicked struggle she put up was pure pleasure. The quiet afterward, and the sense of peace, were wonderful.

The clue left behind was icing on the cake. The police were baffled by the genius of the Brauxton Strangler—a silly name, but appropriate. Even the supposedly brilliant Alex Devane hadn't come close to finding his quarry. No one knew when or how or why—no one but the one person who had been clever enough and bold enough to invent the most devious, exciting, wonderful game in the world.

The figure—dressed entirely in black—surveyed the home of Colette Elizabeth Romalanski. The living room was quiet now. The peaceful, lifeless body was on the floor exactly where it should be. The Scrabble board was beside her. It was done, and it was wonderful.

Time to sit back and laugh as the police tried to figure it out.

Time to start planning the next one.

IT WAS NEARLY MIDNIGHT when Alex returned Ivy to her apartment. The silence in the elevator as he accompanied her to the fourth floor had been palpable, and what had been a delightful, relaxed evening of dinner and a concert in the park suddenly became tense as they both tried to anticipate how the night would end.

With Alex right behind her, Ivy opened the door, flipped on the lights, tossed her purse onto the chair in the tiny foyer and turned to him, smiling uncertainly. "I had a wonderful time. Thank you."

"My pleasure." Alex leaned against the door frame, studying Ivy as though he meant to memorize every detail of the way she looked backlighted by the bright light of the apartment. She was still as stunning as she'd seemed when he'd arrived to pick her up several hours ago. The clingy dress she wore was fire engine red, with a draping bodice that dipped low in front and even lower in back. Alex had spent much of the night wondering how much pressure it would take to disengage the precarious, silky fabric from her shoulders leaving all of her torso exposed.

A wide belt emphasized her narrow waist, and the short, fitted skirt displayed her incredible legs to devastating advantage. She looked sleek and sexy, and Alex wanted her. But that was nothing new. He'd spent the better part of the previous week wanting her and thinking up reasons why he couldn't have her.

At this moment, only one of those reasons seemed valid: if they went too far, too fast, someone was going to get hurt.

"Would you like to come in for a drink?" Ivy asked. "I think I still have some wine in the fridge."

"I don't think so. It's getting late and we have to work tomorrow," Alex said, wondering where his sudden burst of self-control had come from.

"All right." Ivy accepted his decision gracefully, unsure whether she was relieved or disappointed. "Then I'll see you tomorrow morning. Thanks for a terrific evening."

"Thank *you*."

They stood there, rooted like statues, both remembering what had happened the last time Alex was in this apartment, both feeling like insecure, inexperienced adolescents on their first date.

"Well..." Ivy shifted from one foot to the other, wondering if, after Alex finally left, she would find this amusing. "Good night."

"Oh, what the hell," Alex muttered, stepping forward abruptly and sweeping Ivy into his arms. Ivy released the door she'd been holding open so that she could eagerly wrap her arms around Alex's neck; neither of them heard the spring-action door close of its own accord.

This time, there was nothing gentle or exploratory about their kiss. Their lips parted eagerly so their tongues could mate. The strength of Alex's arms sealed their bodies together, and Ivy's blood began singing through her veins so sweetly that every nerve ending in her body came to vivid life.

It felt right in his arms. And it felt good—better than anything she could ever remember. It made her breathless; it made her ache. It was a kiss that unleashed the kind of fire and passion that only two people who were right for each other could generate.

Hot and impatient, Alex's lips left Ivy's and blazed a trail of fire down her throat. One of his hands moved up, caressing the expanse of her back and shoulders left bare by her dress, while the other hand moved lower, urgently pulling her tighter against his hardening loins. He nudged the shoulder of her dress, and when the silky fabric fell onto her arm, he brought one hand between their bodies to cup and fondle the breast that had been exposed.

"Oh, Alex..." Ivy moaned as she whispered his name. She wove her fingers through his hair and tugged hard, bringing his head up and her lips back to his. He kissed her deeply as his hand continued to gently knead her breast through the almost nonexistent fabric of her lacy bra. The friction he created made Ivy gasp with pleasure, but the sound was lost in Alex's mouth.

She strained against him, arching into his hand and grinding her hips against his. There was heat and hardness there, and Ivy wanted to touch him. She wanted to strip away his jacket and shirt and trousers...remove all the barriers between them and savor that heat. But she knew there were more significant barriers than their clothing. The greatest barrier was Alex's fear of being hurt. Ivy knew that it was absolutely right for them to be together; Alex wasn't sure of that yet. He wanted her, and his desire was over-powering his need to keep his distance, yes. But that didn't mean once they had made love he would suddenly realize how good they could be for each other.

So Ivy struggled with control. It could have been so simple, so natural for her to touch him as intimately as he was touching her, and in so doing, inflame him to the point of no return. But she didn't. She couldn't. She had to let Alex take the lead, so that if they did end up in a tangled mass of naked limbs on her bed, he would never be able to accuse her of having enticed him into that intimacy.

But God, that was hard to do. The ache for completion that burned between her thighs was sharp and painful, but oh, so delicious.

Alex thought he must be going insane. He prided logic and reason above all else, yet what he was feeling had nothing to do with either. Sex had never been an overpowering need before. He'd never known a desire to possess a woman that was as all-encompassing as what he felt for Ivy. He'd always been in control of every moment, but he had no control now, no restraint, not a single shred of moderation. He felt like a primitive caveman who had no ability to think past this one moment of intense, sensual awareness—a moment he felt as though he'd spent his whole life waiting for.

He touched Ivy, moved against her, inflamed her, felt her desire grow, and yet he also felt her restraint. He wanted her to touch him, but she didn't. She was waiting for him to make the final move. She was waiting for him to ask her to make love with him or to pull her wordlessly to the bed to complete the act he had started with a single kiss. She was waiting. She was kissing him fervently, clenching and unclenching her hands in his hair, occasionally running one of those hands across his back, but no more. She was waiting for his decision.

"Damn it!" Alex's curse was a guttural cry as he tore his mouth away from Ivy's. He grabbed her hand and pulled her toward the bed while he jerked at his tie and tried to struggle out of his jacket all at the same time.

Ivy's heart was pounding so loudly that she could barely hear herself think. The decision had been made, but she knew that it wasn't a decision Alex was happy with. He wanted to have sex with her. He wanted a hot, hard, fast release from the incredible passion that had built between them. There was no tenderness in him as he pulled her toward the bed. He wanted her, but he hated himself for that uncontrollable wanting.

In the moment she realized that, Ivy thought she might actually die from the pain of her disappointment.

"No," she said firmly, pulling her hand out of his grasp.

Alex turned toward her, frowning fiercely, but there were unshed tears brimming in Ivy's eyes, and he took a deep breath, wondering when his passion had turned to anger. There was no denying that was what had happened. There was no denying that Ivy had realized it.

He tried to ignore the painful pressure in his loins.

"I'm sorry, Alex," Ivy said, taking a step back and trying to straighten her dress. "I didn't mean to give you mixed signals, but there's a particularly ugly four-letter word for what we were about to do, and I don't think we'd like ourselves or each other very much if we did it."

"No... I'm the one who should apologize," Alex replied haltingly between more deep breaths. "I came at you like a caveman."

"You didn't 'come at me,' Alex. You kissed me, and I kissed you back, because that's what I wanted. I also wanted to make love with you."

"I wanted that, too, Ivy."

"No, you didn't," she said sadly, finally succeeding in fighting back the threat of tears. "You most specifically did not—and *do* not—want to make love with me. You want me physically, sexually, but you're so damned determined not to feel any emotion that making *love* is the last thing you want. That implies a degree of tenderness and caring. I have that for you, Alex. I care. You excite me intellectually, emotionally and sexually, and I care a lot. In fact, I could probably care a *whole* lot if you'd let me. But what I won't do," she hastened to add when he seemed about to interrupt, "what I won't do is satisfy an ache tonight and wake up tomorrow morning with you hating me for what we've done."

Alex's face was as hard as granite. "I told you, Ivy, I'm not going to fall in love with you. I don't believe in love."

"But you never told me why—specifically, not philosophically," she added hastily.

Alex straightened his jacket and tie. It was a long time before he answered. "I'm not capable of giving a woman what she needs—the devotion, the depth of commitment, the kind of caring that is so all-encompassing, so exclusive that it obliterates the need for work, family, friends, dreams, everything."

"My God, Alex," Ivy said, aghast. "Is that really what you think every woman wants?"

"Yes! But I can't *give* that much. I tried once, and a very lonely woman is dead because I failed."

"Your wife."

"Yes."

"She killed herself because you were a bad husband. You were neglectful. You didn't love her enough."

Alex's jaw was clenched tight. "That's right."

"I hate to be the one to tell you this, Alex, but wives with rotten husbands usually opt for divorce rather than suicide." Ivy knew the statement sounded callous, but Alex was feeling enough pity for the both of them. He was taking the blame for his wife's death and wasting his life in the process.

"Brenda had problems," Alex admitted. "I should have seen how desperately ill she was, but I didn't. I was too wrapped up in myself and my work to realize that she needed help."

Ivy shook her head, trying to make sense of what he was saying. "Alex, I think you're the one who needs help. You can't spend the rest of your life being eaten up by guilt. I don't know what happened to your marriage, but even if you *did* contribute to Brenda's death in some way, you've got to learn how to accept your mistakes and get on with your life."

"That's what I am doing!" Alex said sharply. "But just because I don't see marriage or commitment as part of that life doesn't mean I need to see a psychiatrist!"

"Oh, really?" Ivy said, quirking her eyebrows skeptically. "Then why are your emotions about me so jumbled?"

"Because you want more than I can give you."

Ivy shook her head. "No, Alex. The only thing I asked of you was a chance to work on the Strangler investigation. Everything else that's happened has been a natural result of the attraction we feel for each other. You're the one who first brought up the subject of love, not me. You're the one who talked about marriage and commitment. Apparently, what you feel for me goes beyond simple lust, and you're so afraid of having an honest emotion that you're fighting with yourself every step of the way—but I'm the one who's getting the fallout."

"That's ridiculous."

"Is it? You want me, Alex, but you resent me because of it, don't you?"

Alex ignored the question because it sounded too much like the truth. "I think I'd better go. This is getting us nowhere."

He started for the door, and Ivy dug her fingernails into her hands to forestall the tears that suddenly pooled in her eyes. Clearly, a relationship with Alex was hopeless, and that realization hurt her more than she could have imagined possible. She wanted to beg him to stay and talk this out, but there was no point. His guilt was too deep. He was so enmeshed in the past that he had no future. At least, not one that could ever include her.

Heartsick, she followed him to the door. "I'm sorry the evening turned out so badly, Alex," she said quietly.

Alex opened the door and turned to her. "Me, too. You deserve better than this."

Ivy stiffened her jaw against the threatening tears. "So do you," she murmured.

"Good ni—"

The beeper in Alex's pocket began squawking, and they both froze. It was midnight, and there was only one reason why the dispatcher at Police Central would be summoning the head of the task force. The Strangler had struck again.

Ivy's throat constricted painfully, but she stepped back and pointed toward her bedside table. "The phone's over there."

Alex silenced his beeper as he rushed across the room and dialed the dispatch number. He didn't see Ivy kick off her shoes and unclasp her belt as she ran for her dressing room, but by the time he finished his call, she was back. Jeans, an oversize summer sweater and deck shoes had replaced her evening ensemble. She was hurriedly transferring the contents of her red evening bag into her regular purse.

"I'm going with you," she said firmly as he returned her cordless phone to its base.

Alex's first instinct was to tell her no. This wasn't going to be easy, and he wanted to shield her from the ugliness that was to follow. But Ivy was a cop, and a good one. He wanted her perceptions and her insights. The case needed her, and the case had to come first.

"All right. Let's go," he said, and they hurried into the night.

CHAPTER TWELVE

"THE DISPATCHER patched me through to the scene," Alex explained as they headed across town. "I told the uniform on duty to keep everyone out of the house until I get there. I don't want *anything* disturbed until I've seen whatever there is to see."

Ivy nodded, but it was doubtful that Alex caught the movement. He hadn't looked at her once since they'd left her apartment. "Who discovered the body?"

"Apparently it was a hot line tip."

"Anonymous?"

"That's what the dispatcher said."

Ivy twisted on the seat toward him, barely able to conceal her excitement. "That's wonderful! It could mean either there was a witness to the murder this time, or it was the Strangler himself. Maybe he couldn't wait for someone else to find the body."

"That's a distinct possibility," Alex conceded. "We'll know more when we get there. The rest of the senior detectives on the task force are being called in right now. I'll put someone on getting a voiceprint of the hot line call immediately."

Other than the victim's address, Alex had no further information to impart, and they completed the drive in silence. Their personal conflict paled in comparison to the death of a seventh innocent young woman, yet neither of them could completely erase the events of the past hour.

Ivy did her best to put all of her emotions on hold. She had a job to do. There was no time to think about her disappointment, no time to release that ache with tears. She forced herself into the state of calm detachment she would need in order to do what had to be done, because it was going to be a long, grueling night.

One entire block of Fremont Street, between Oak and Elm avenues, had been cordoned off by the time Ivy and Alex arrived, and the scene was a madhouse. The area was illuminated by the eerie, flashing red lights of police cruisers. Gawkers in housecoats or hastily donned jeans and T-shirts swarmed the area like ants on a marshmallow. No one had any doubts about what had happened.

Alex pulled up to one of the barricades, flashed his identification and was ushered through, but he still couldn't get close to the house because of the emergency vehicles that clogged the street. When he had come as close as he could get, he parked the car. He and Ivy jumped out and hurried through the crowd of milling policemen.

"Alex! Over here!" Jordan Brubaker waved one hand above the heads of the crowd.

"What have we got?" Alex asked when he finally succeeded in reaching the senior detective.

When Brubaker realized that Ivy was with Alex, he gave her a hard, questioning look. She was dressed casually, but she was wearing more makeup than usual, and a pair of dangling earrings sparkled in the flashing lights. He noted, too, that Alex was dressed in an expensive suit, as though he'd been out for an evening on the town when he'd received the call. Obviously, it was Ivy he'd been out with, and since she had changed clothes and Alex hadn't, it didn't take any great feat of detection to realize that they had been together at her apartment.

Brubaker was already resentful of the deferential treatment Alex had shown Ivy, and this didn't improve his disposition. Still, he had a job to do. "The neighbors say the victim's name is Colette Romalanski. Single, lives alone. Works as a legal secretary somewhere downtown. The medical examiner and forensics are waiting around back. These are Officers Wylie and Carson. They were the first on the scene."

"Report," Alex ordered as he started across the lawn toward the rear of the house, with the officers, Brubaker and Ivy hurrying to keep pace with him.

"Yes, sir," Carson replied briskly. "At 11:41 my partner and I responded to a call from the dispatcher. There were no lights on in the house, but when we checked the doors we found a point of entry in the back—a patio door had been jimmied. No one answered when we knocked, so we entered through the broken door and found the body in the living room. Female Caucasian, blond, approximately thirty years of age, strangled, no pulse."

"Did you search the house?"

"No sir," Wylie answered briskly. "We're under strict orders not to violate the scene of the crime if there's even the slightest suspicion that it might be a Strangler killing. As soon as we verified that a crime had been committed and that the victim was dead, we left the house, called for backup and covered all possible exits. No one has gone in or out of the house since we arrived, sir."

"Good. Keep it that way," Alex ordered as they reached the patio, which was almost as crowded as the front lawn. "Carson, I want you to stay by this door and see that no one goes in without my permission. Wylie, you go back around front and wait for Detective Mort Adamson. Tell him I said to get whatever men he needs to interrogate every one of those people out front and at the barricades. I want all their names and addresses. The Strangler may be among them, watching the furor he created."

"Yes, sir."

"Lieutenant Devane?" A good-looking man in his early thirties stepped forward. "I'm Dr. McCrary from the coroner's office. I understand that we're waiting for you."

Alex shook his hand. "You got gloves?"

"Right here." One of the forensics technicians handed Alex, Ivy and Brubaker pairs of surgical gloves.

"Ivy, Jordy, I want you with me," Alex said, struggling into the gloves as the others did the same. He turned and raised his voice. "The rest of you, stay here until I say otherwise." He stepped to the open patio door and looked at Ivy. "Are you ready?" he asked softly.

"I can do my job," she answered.

"Then let's do it." He pushed the door open wider and stepped inside. There was a light switch on the wall beside the door. He carefully flicked it on and found himself in a spacious kitchen. There were a few dirty dishes by the sink, and a woman's purse was sitting on the counter near a door that led through a utility room to the garage. Nothing else looked out of place. Alex moved on, conscious of Ivy and Brubaker right behind him.

Swinging doors led out of the kitchen into a dining room. The living room was to the right, toward the front of the house. As Carson had said, the body was there. Colette Romalanski was lying just inside the door from the dining room. One leg was twisted beneath her, the other was extended partially across the doorway so that Alex had to step over her to get into the room. He found the light switch and took stock of everything in the room before turning his attention back to the victim.

She was a pretty girl. A mane of golden-blond hair was splayed over the rust-colored carpeting. Her eyes were still open, and it was easy to imagine the terror that had been in them in the last moments of her life. One hand was clenched at her side, and the other was stretched out toward the back of a sofa several yards away. Beside the outstretched hand was the Strangler's calling card.

"Jeez," Brubaker said quietly as he surveyed the scene from the arched entrance to the dining room. "You were right, Alex. Scrabble was the next game."

"A lot of good knowing that did her," Alex said bitterly.

Summoning all the objectivity she was capable of, Ivy stepped across Colette Romalanski's body so that she could get a better look at the clue left by the Strangler. It was chillingly elaborate. The first six game clues had been single tokens from board games. This time, he had left an entire game. A Scrabble board complete with an integrated network of words spelled out a message. The first word that clearly jumped out at Ivy was the name Devane.

The Strangler had left a personal message for Alex.

"What does it say?" Brubaker asked. From where he stood, the puzzle was upside down, and he couldn't make sense of the jumble of words.

Alex felt sick inside. He'd been hired to put a stop to this, but all he'd succeeded in doing was capturing the attention of an arrogant maniac. He had to clear his throat before reading the crossword message. "It isn't whether you win or lose, Lieutenant Devane, it's how you play the game."

"One hundred and ninety-one," Ivy said absently, mesmerized by the game board.

Alex turned toward her. "What?"

"Points. Counting double word and double letter scores, that layout represents 191 points."

Jordan snorted loudly. "For Pete's sake, Kincaid, nobody's keeping score."

Ivy looked at him, her gaze sharp and cold. "The killer is, Jordy. Strangler, seven—cops, zero."

Brubaker didn't seem to have an answer to that, and they fell silent. Jordy knelt for a closer look at the rope that was scored into the victim's neck, while Ivy and Alex looked at the body, then at each other. Colette was wearing a simple short-sleeved shirtwaist dress of bright red. Average height, blond hair... red dress. Ivy and Alex were both remembering the red dress Ivy had worn earlier. They were both thinking that this dead woman could just as easily have been Ivy.

That knowledge passed silently between them, and just as silently they both pushed the grim, terrifying thought from their minds.

"Ivy, would you care to hypothesize?" Alex asked. Brubaker looked up at him sharply through narrowed eyes but said nothing.

"All right," Ivy said, glad to have something to focus on other than dismal thoughts about her own death. "Obviously the Strangler came in through the back door while Colette wasn't at home. He waited for her there." She pointed to a section of wall beside Brubaker that was covered in a tasteless gold-and-red flocked wallpaper. "She entered the house through the garage and utility room, turned on some lights, left her purse on the kitchen counter and was surprised by the Strangler as she came into the living room. He killed her, set up the Scrabble board, turned out the lights and left the same way he'd come in."

"That would be my guess, too," Jordy said, trying to hide his irritation that Alex had asked Ivy, not him.

"And mine," Alex said in agreement. "But where's the dog?"

"Dog?" Jordy questioned.

"My God, that's right," Ivy said. "He only breaks in if there's a dog that has to be silenced first. Unless, of course, this is a break in the pattern."

"Jordy, you and Ivy look for the dog," Alex ordered. "I'll bring in forensics and the coroner."

"Right." Brubaker stepped over Colette's inert body, skirted the Scrabble board and headed across the living room toward a hallway that led to the rest of the house. Ivy was right beside him.

"Nice earrings, Kincaid," Jordy whispered. "Did you and the lieutenant have a good time tonight?"

Startled, Ivy brought one hand to her earlobe. She had completely forgotten about the dangling crystal earrings. "That's none of your business, Jordy."

"You take over my position on the task force and then have the gall to tell me it's none of my business? That's rich."

Ivy glanced at him, aghast. "I've done no such thing! Just because Alex has asked for my opinions doesn't mean—" She stopped herself in midsentence. "Oh, forget it. You're going to believe what you want to believe, no matter what I say. I won't dignify your insinuations with a response."

They were in the hall, which had a mirrored closet at one end, two doors on the left and one door on the right. Two bedrooms and a bathroom, Ivy guessed. "You're the senior officer here. You choose which side you want. I'll take the other."

Disgusted, Brubaker opened the door to his left and entered a bedroom without a word. Ivy took the door to the right, which was slightly ajar. Putting Brubaker's attitude out of her mind, she carefully turned on the light and realized she was in Colette's bedroom. The bed was unmade, and clothing was scattered everywhere. Neatness apparently hadn't mattered much to victim number seven.

Ivy walked slowly through the room, around the bed. She checked the closet and when that yielded nothing, she turned toward a closed door, which she surmised led to a private bathroom. She stepped toward it, skirting a nightgown that was hanging over the edge of the bed.

The carpeting was a uniform beige, and just in front of the bathroom door, Ivy spotted a dark, irregular smudge about the size of a quarter. She knelt and gingerly touched it. Tiny brown flakes rubbed off onto her gloved finger, but as she probed deeper into the pile, she found that some of the substance hadn't completely dried. It was sticky and deep red.

Blood.

But from where? The blood was fresh, no more than an hour or two old. Colette hadn't made it any farther than the living room. Had she managed to gouge the Strangler's flesh with her fingernails? Had he come to the bathroom to wash away the blood?

Not logical, Ivy told herself. Her thoughts were flying faster than the speed of light as she asked and answered her own questions. If the Strangler had needed a wash basin, he would have used the sink in the kitchen. And besides, this wasn't a *drop* of blood on the carpet, it was a smudge—a smear that might have been left by blood on the sole of a shoe. Ivy quickly looked around and found a smaller, fainter stain a few feet farther away from the bathroom door. There were no other marks, which meant that the blood had probably come from the bathroom.

And there was a dog missing.

But no one had searched the house to be certain the Strangler still wasn't inside, either, Ivy remembered.

She was fairly sure that the blood had come from inside the bathroom, but she wasn't sure enough to risk her life.

Ivy didn't want to know what was on the other side of that door, but it was her job to find out. Reaching into the side pocket of her purse, she extracted a 9mm Smith & Wesson automatic.

"Brubaker! In here!" she called, proud of the control in her voice. She slipped the safety off, stepped to the wall beside the door, grasped the doorknob and threw the door open wide. When nothing happened, she left the safety of the wall and stepped into the doorway.

The blood was everywhere. And there was so much of it that her stomach turned over and threatened to disgrace her. Blood was drying in dark pools on the floor and ran in crimson streaks down the walls. In the sink the blood was a diluted pink, and crumpled towels on the floor gave testimony to the effort the Strangler had made to clean some of the blood off himself.

And in the corner by the shower stall was what was left of Colette Romalanski's brutally mutilated dog. Ivy didn't even try to figure out what breed it had been.

"Good Lord!"

Ivy jumped at the sound of Brubaker's voice at the door behind her. She hadn't realized that she had stepped into the bathroom, but Jordy's presence pulled her out of her trance and she turned. "I found the dog," she said flatly, brushing past him.

"I heard you call to Brubaker," Alex said to her as he hurried into the bedroom. "What did you find?"

"See for yourself." She was as pale as a sheet, and Alex approached her with concern.

"Are you all right? What happened?"

She jerked her head toward the bathroom, and Alex stepped to the door.

"Some mess, huh?" Jordy asked. He was just inside the doorway, surveying the carnage.

"Get forensics in here," Alex ordered. Brubaker came out of the bathroom and hurried back toward the hall. Alex gave the bathroom a quick but thorough glance, then turned back to Ivy. She was in the center of the bedroom, and Alex's eyes went automatically to her right hand hanging limply at her side. When Ivy realized that she was still holding her gun, she gave him a sheepish smile and replaced the weapon in her purse.

"Was that necessary?" he asked, not returning her smile.

"What?"

"Drawing your gun?"

She shrugged. "It seemed like a good idea at the time. I found some splotches of blood on the carpet, and no one had checked the house to be certain the Strangler wasn't still inside."

He didn't seem entirely pleased with her answer, but he made no other comment.

"Alex?" Brubaker stuck his head into the bedroom. "I've got a second forensics team on the way, and Mayor Jablonski and the commissioner are outside waiting to see you. They're anxious to give a statement to the press."

"Great. Just what I need—murder with a side order of politics." He sighed heavily. "Tell them I'll be right there." Brubaker vanished and Alex started toward the door. "Go through the rest of the house and see what you can find," he instructed Ivy as he swept past her. "And keep your gun holstered. This isn't the O.K. Corral. There's been enough bloodshed here already."

Ivy's mouth dropped open, but Alex was gone before she could respond.

"THE MUTILATION of Ms Romalanski's dog is another symptom of the incredible pressure that is building within the Strangler," Dr. Geraldine Franklyn said. She was a no-nonsense woman with graying hair and piercing blue eyes that gave the impression she missed nothing. If ever a woman looked the role of psychiatrist, it was Gerri Franklyn.

"Could you be a little more specific about this supposed...pressure, Doctor?" Alex asked, shifting uncomfortably in his chair. Ivy was beside him looking cool and composed, and Alex couldn't help remembering that only two days ago she had told him he needed to seek professional help. And now, here they were in a psychiatrist's office. They were here to discuss the Strangler case, nothing more, but Alex didn't like the way it made him recall the unpleasant scene with Ivy.

Dr. Franklyn tapped a pencil lightly on her desk blotter, wondering why the handsome lieutenant was so uncomfortable. In her experience, the only people who were ill at ease in the presence of a doctor of psychiatry were those with unresolved personal problems. Considering what she had read about his past in the newspapers recently, she figured she could make a logical guess at the source of his problems, but she knew better than to play guessing games. There was considerable tension between the lieutenant and the attractive detective with him, the Gerri would have loved to ferret out the source of that tension.

But she hadn't been asked to do that, she reminded herself. She was a consultant on the Strangler case, not part of the task force that was trying to catch him. She forced her mind back to Alex's question. "Until the killer is apprehended and I've had a chance to evaluate him, I won't really be able to define the nature of that pressure, Lieutenant. I'm sorry. Without a doubt, we will discover that it is rooted in some traumatic incident—or series of incidents—from his childhood. My guess is that it's an unresolved conflict about his mother. The only way he can deal with his inner rage is by killing women who are somehow representative of her. He is extracting retribution. And I would imagine that there is some intermediate woman involved, too."

"Intermediate woman?" Ivy asked.

Dr. Franklyn nodded. "A wife or lover—also representative of the mother—who rejected, betrayed or disappointed him, thereby feeding his inner rage. The rage feeds on itself, building until he must kill his 'mother' in order to relieve the pressure."

"But why mutilate the dog?" Alex asked, getting back to the original issue. He was consciously fighting the feeling that this was all a waste of time.

"You must understand that we are dealing with a highly intelligent, complex and rigid mind. The Strangler has invented a game that he believes is dazzlingly clever. He made the rules, and because they are his rules, he must play by them or forfeit the game.

"Which means—" she paused for emphasis "—that there are two distinct and separate forces warring within him. The need to kill and the need to play by his own set of rules. Each murder he commits brings him less and less satisfaction. Compare it to a drug addiction, if you like. At first a small quantity of the drug—in this case, murder—is enough to satisfy the rage within him. As time goes on, though, he needs more and more violence to satisfy his 'habit.' Since he has established very strict guidelines about the method in which his victims are killed, his only recourse was to take his excess rage out on the dog."

"Is there a chance he might start mutilating his victims if there is no animal to absorb his excess rage?" Alex asked.

"That's highly unlikely," Dr Franklyn said with a firm shake of her head. "It wouldn't be playing by the rules. No, it would be more logical that he would carry out the threat he made in June."

Alex remembered the arrogant note Len Eversall had shown him. "You mean he might start killing two women each month."

"Precisely. I believe that threat is his way of dealing with the increased pressure on him. And, of course, subconsciously he knows it provides the police with a greater motivation to figure out his game and catch him."

Ivy shuddered at the possibility of two murders in one month. "That means we have fifteen days or less to find him or someone else will die."

"He will strike again this month, yes," Dr. Franklyn said emphatically. She studied Ivy seriously for a moment before speaking again. "You fit the Strangler profile, don't you, Detective Kincaid?"

Ivy straightened in her chair. "Yes."

"That must be difficult for you since you work on this case exclusively."

Ivy managed a smile. "It does give me an added incentive for catching the Strangler as quickly as possible."

Dr. Franklyn returned the smile. "I'm not trying to drum up business, Detective, but if you ever feel the need to talk about your anxieties, I'd be happy to make time to see you."

Ivy was startled. Did her anxieties show that much? Did she look like someone who was tottering on the edge of a nervous breakdown or something? It was unsettling to have a psychiatrist insinuate that she needed professional help. "I'll keep that in mind, Dr. Franklyn. Thank you," she said, hoping she didn't sound as defensive as she suddenly felt.

Alex rose and shook hands with the doctor, thanking her for her time and assistance. Ivy stood, too, and they left the office via a private door that circumvented the reception room.

"What are you smiling at?" Ivy asked as they headed toward the elevator.

"I was just wondering how it felt to have the shoe on the other foot," he said, looking at her with a mixture of smugness and something else that Ivy couldn't quite define.

"What do you mean?"

Alex shrugged. "How does it feel to be told you need to see a shrink?"

They reached the elevator, and Ivy gave the Down button a vicious poke. "It's not a comfortable feeling," she admitted with a touch of petulance. "But if the shoe fits, maybe it should be worn."

A crowded elevator arrived, and they rode to the lobby in silence, but once the doors opened and everyone spilled out, Alex resumed the conversation as though it had never been interrupted. "Meaning you still think I should seek professional help?"

Ivy sighed deeply. During the course of the past two days, she'd done her best not to think about the dreadful scene in her apartment. There was so much work to be done on the Strangler case that she'd had plenty to concentrate on, instead, and she still wanted to focus on that. She didn't want or need another confrontation with Alex. "What I think is that we should drop this," she said tersely. "You've made your feelings on the subject of 'us' perfectly clear."

"Ivy, my feelings are anything but clear."

"Then that's your problem, Alex. I don't intend to make it mine," she replied as they stepped outside into the furnacelike heat of a mid-July day. "Relationships are difficult enough when both people involved are willing participants. They're impossible if one of those participants doesn't really want to be involved."

"You're right," he said as they went to their separate sides of his unmarked cruiser. As they settled inside and adjusted their seat belts, he added, "But I don't want what happened the other night to ruin our working relationship, Ivy."

"I wasn't aware that it had."

"Oh, really? Then why are you being so aloof?"

"I'm not being aloof—I'm trying to be professional!" Ivy shouted, irritated because he was absolutely right. She had been cool toward Alex these past two days, but it was only because she was trying to do her job without allowing her emotions to get in the way. "Look, what do you want from me, Alex? Do you want me to admit that I'm upset about what happened between us Monday night? All right, I admit it. I also admit that I'm so disappointed it actually hurts.

But I'm not angry—at least I'm not angry about what happened at my apartment," she amended.

"Then what are you angry about?"

"Frankly, I'm a little ticked off because of that crack you made at Colette's about the O.K. Corral. I'm a good cop. I never pull my gun unless it's necessary, Lieutenant, and I don't appreciate you second-guessing my judgment call just because you've got a hang-up about guns."

There was a long pause before Alex replied. "You're right. I shouldn't have said that. I'm sorry."

"Apology accepted," Ivy replied tersely. "Now let's just drop the whole subject and forget about Monday night."

"Fine," he said succinctly, but it wasn't fine. Not really. There were a lot of things he wanted to say about what had happened between them Monday night, but he wasn't even sure what they were.

For her own emotional protection, Ivy had placed a chasm between them, and Alex didn't like it one bit. He missed her effervescent smile, her sparkling wit. He'd known her such a short while, but in that time she had come to mean something very special to him. He didn't want to lose that, yet he was afraid to allow his feelings to progress. It would be better to do as Ivy was doing—put all emotions on the back burner and concentrate on solving the Strangler case.

But that was easier said than done.

CHAPTER THIRTEEN

THEY COMPLETED THE RIDE BACK to the station in stony silence. There, Alex briefed the other detectives on Dr. Franklyn's opinions while Ivy returned to her desk and continued cross-referencing the data that trickled in on Colette Romalanski's murder. As with the previous murders, there was very little.

The Strangler had been covered in blood after slaying the dog, and forensics found a few black clothing fibers on the towels he had used when he'd tried to wipe off the blood. The fabric was a common cotton/polyester blend that was impossible to trace. Forensics also found traces of blood in several places throughout the house, particularly on the wallpaper by the door to the dining room, where he had waited to ambush Colette.

The Scrabble board had been completely free of fingerprints, and the rope used to strangle the victim was the same common variety sold at every hardware store in the city. An autopsy on the dog indicated that he had been killed by a stilettolike instrument, the same device that had been used to jimmy the back door. It was also determined that the dog was old and probably partially deaf. A piece of uneaten, arsenic-laced meat was found in the bathroom, and considering other small pieces of evidence found, forensics speculated that the dog had been asleep on a rug in the bathroom when the Strangler surprised him. He had attacked before the killer could coax him into eating the poisoned meat, and his attack had unleashed the Strangler's pent-up violence.

None of Colette's neighbors would admit to having seen or heard anything out of the ordinary, and after a careful examination of the hot line call that had reported the murder, it was determined that message was an artificial voice produced by a recently developed, very expensive computer software program. As Ivy had suggested on the night of the murder, the Strangler apparently hadn't been able to wait for the body to be found. He had wanted someone to play his game immediately.

The computer voice was the best hard lead they'd had to date, but it wasn't much. Mort Adamson was leading the team that was tracking down every computer outlet in the city that sold the software, but it was far more likely that the Strangler had obtained it through one of the hundreds of mail-order houses that specialized in computers. They would follow the lead as far as it took them, but they would only get lucky if the Strangler had done something monumentally stupid, like buying the software program at a local store.

In a private meeting with the mayor and Len Eversall, Alex argued that the Strangler's threat to kill two women this month should be made public. With Colette Romalanski's murder, the city had breathed a collective sigh of relief because they felt they had a reprieve until August. If they weren't informed of this new threat, women would lower their guard, Alex argued.

Eversall replied that being on guard hadn't stopped the Strangler yet, but finally Alex won the argument by convincing the mayor that he would be political dead meat if the public discovered that he had been aware of the added threat and hadn't issued a warning.

Jablonski held the press conference, and as he had feared, the media did not take kindly to having been kept in the dark about the Strangler's threat. For the remainder of the week, evening news broadcasts and morning headlines denounced the mayor's special task force as a band of incompetent bunglers. One editorial even went so far as to suggest that members of the task force couldn't catch a cold in flu season.

The negative press coverage was demoralizing. The detectives were all working as hard as they could, following every minuscule lead as far as it would take them, and the added media pressure didn't make their jobs any easier.

Ivy, like everyone else, was physically and mentally exhausted. All week long she had devoted herself singlemindedly to the case in the hope that when she surfaced for air, her feelings for Alex would have changed. She wanted her attraction to him to vanish. She prayed that her desire to be with him would dissipate. She wanted to be able to look back on the time she had spent with him and smile at the folly of having imagined they shared some sort of bond. She wanted to stop thinking of him as someone she could love.

Unfortunately, none of those things happened. What she felt for Alex still seemed all too real.

"That's it, I give up," Alex said, tossing a sheaf of computer printouts onto his desk. He leaned back in his chair as far as it would go and stretched.

Ivy picked up the papers he had discarded and tried not to notice the way his shirt tightened over his broad chest. It was late Saturday night, and most of the other detectives had left the office hours ago. Only the skeletal night crew remained. Ivy had canceled her bingo date with her mother, hoping that she would be able to spend a quiet night at home catching up on lost sleep, but when Alex had suggested that they spend a few minutes trying to find the key to their *Perplexities* clue, Ivy had agreed.

Now, she was sorry she had. The office door was closed and the shades were drawn. The setting was entirely too intimate.

"I think we were wrong, Ivy."

The statement startled her out of thoughts she shouldn't have been having. "About what?"

Still leaning back in his chair, Alex reached for one of the copies of *Perplexities* on his desk. "About this, what else? We've examined these issues from every conceivable angle, and other than the readers' poll, there is simply no connection between the magazine and this case."

"What about the April Risk article?"

"Coincidence."

One part of Ivy agreed, but another part kept insisting that there was something in the magazines they had overlooked—something so simple that they would probably feel like fools if they ever figured it out. "Are you suggesting that we give up on *Perplexities* altogether?"

"No, not entirely, but it's probably not worth the sleep we've lost over it."

"In that case—" Ivy stood and stretched the kinks out of her back "—I'm going home, and I'd advise you to do the same. You spend too much time here, Alex."

"No more than you," he pointed out.

"Wrong. A lot more than me. I've worked late every night, but at least I've gone home to sleep. How many nights have you spent on that sofa this week?"

"Two or three."

"Well, don't do it tonight, okay? Go home. Fix yourself a decent meal. Get some sleep."

"All right."

Ivy gave a tired laugh. "Gee, that was the easiest argument I ever won. My powers of persuasion must be improving."

"No, I'm just too tired to argue," Alex replied, happy to see Ivy laughing again. It felt like an eternity since he had seen her smile.

"Do you want me to come in tomorrow?"

"I don't see any reason. Stay home and rest up. Next week we're going to interview more people who were gathered at the scene of the murder. And there are several friends of the other victims I want you to help me question."

"All right," Ivy said, but Alex caught the strange look that passed over her face. He was fairly sure he knew what had caused it.

"Is there a problem with that?"

"No," she said a little too quickly. "None at all. I'll be sure to wear a comfortable pair of shoes this time." She headed for the door.

"Ivy...."

She stopped and turned. He was frowning. "Yes."

"I've heard some...rumors this week. About us. You've heard them, too, haven't you?"

She glanced away from him, unable to meet his eyes. "We weren't exactly inconspicuous when we arrived together at the Romalanski house Monday night."

"They're saying that you slept with me because you wanted to be more involved in the case."

"I know." This time her smile was filled with irony. "I've done a pretty good job of not mixing business with pleasure here at the office, and it's coming back to haunt me."

"You've turned down a lot of dates from fellow officers?"

She nodded. "Jordan Brubaker, in particular."

"Is he the one spreading the rumor?"

"Probably, but he might not be the only one."

A small silence stretched into a long one as Alex contemplated what he should do. Unfortunately, there wasn't anything to do. Punching Brubaker in the mouth wouldn't stop the rumors. Even having an official "chat" with him would only make matters worse. There was nothing Alex could do but apologize. "I'm sorry."

She looked at him, surprised. "Sorry for what?"

"That I've damaged your reputation."

"*You* damaged it? How do you figure that? I'm the one who waltzed in here and asked for more responsibility on the case. I proved to you that I had knowledge that could be useful, and you capitalized on a resource. If a bunch of narrow-minded chauvinists want to make something dirty out of that, then let them. I have absolutely nothing to feel guilty about, and I have no intention of changing who I am and what I do to please anyone."

Alex respected her attitude. She was an incredibly strong, self-confident woman, but despite her brave words, being the subject of vicious gossip couldn't be pleasant. "Nevertheless, I've handled this whole thing badly, and I'm sorry."

"Oh, for crying out loud," she muttered, advancing a couple of paces toward his desk. "You know what your problem is, Alex? You accept too much responsibility for things. You allowed Len Eversall to guilt-trip you into taking responsibility for catching the Strangler. You're eaten alive with remorse over a tragic accident that took the life of a little girl, and you're carrying around a whole truckload of guilt because you weren't clairvoyant enough to realize that your wife was going to commit suicide. You probably even think that you're responsible for world hunger and the situation in the Middle East."

She placed her hands on his desk and faced him squarely. "Well, I've got news for you, fella. The sun does not rise and set on Alex Devane. The weight of the world does not rest on your shoulders, and you are not responsible for any life other than your own."

Alex's jaw was clenched again—a sure sign that Ivy had struck home. "I didn't ask for a sermon, Ivy, so get off your soapbox. I was only trying to apologize."

"For something that isn't your fault."

"Fine!" Alex slapped his hands against the top of his desk as he rose. "I retract the apology. I'm *not* sorry your reputation is being dragged through the mud." He ran a hand through his hair in frustration. "Damn it! You are the most stubborn, opinionated, self-reliant woman that it has ever been my misfortune to meet!"

"Oh, and I suppose you prefer your women pliant and submissive. Well, I'm sorry that I'm not some shy, retiring clinging vine who can't take a breath of air unless she gets your permission first!"

Alex's frustration turned to raw anger. "Leave Brenda out of this," he said hoarsely.

His comment caught Ivy by surprise, and her irritation drained away. Only sadness and frustration remained. "I wasn't even thinking of Brenda," she said softly. "Is that what she was like?"

Alex closed his eyes as his own anger evaporated. "I don't want to talk about her, Ivy," he said wearily.

"Maybe you should."

He shook his head and eased into his chair. "No. You and I are picking fights with each other because we're frustrated by our feelings. Brenda has nothing to do with that."

Alex suddenly looked so tired, so haunted and lost and lonely that Ivy wanted to cry. "Oh, Alex," she whispered, her voice filled with tender, loving emotions. "Brenda has *everything* to do with it. Can't you see that she's what's standing between us? Whatever we could have together... be to each other...would never be the same as what you and Brenda had, because I'm not Brenda."

"No, you're not," Alex said softly, sadly. "But that doesn't mean you and I could make a relationship work."

Ivy shrugged helplessly. "You're never going to know that for sure unless you try."

Alex wanted to look away from her, but he couldn't. She was so pretty, so sincere. She was everything a man could possibly want. But once upon a time, when he was much younger, Alex had thought that sweet, submissive Brenda Harkness Devane was everything he could ever want in a woman. He'd been wrong, and he wasn't sure he could survive a second dreadful mistake.

"I'm sorry, Ivy. I can't. I don't want to try again."

Ivy dug her fingernails into the palms of her hands to keep from crying. "I know." Somehow she managed a smile. "You and I are a waste of a lot of good old-fashioned lust, Alex."

He smiled, too. Sadly. "Maybe we should get the name of that computer dating service vice is investigating and blow off a little steam."

"Nah." Ivy shook her head. "With our luck, the computer would match me up with you, and we'd be right back where we started." She gave him a halfhearted wave and started for the door. "Good night, Kemo Sabe. I'm going home to bed. Alone. Just me and my gargoyles." She opened the door, stopped and looked at Alex over her shoulder. "If you change your mind, you know where to find me."

THE NEXT WEEK, the Strangler investigation slowed to a more sedate pace. Teams of detectives tracked down even more spectators who had come to gawk at Colette Romalanski's house on the night of her murder, but nearly all of them were people from Colette's neighborhood who had been roused out of bed by the sound of police sirens. On Monday and Tuesday, Ivy and Alex conducted interviews with several friends of the previous victims, but they learned no more than the original investigating officers had. No one snapped under pressure and confessed to being the Strangler.

During that week, the relationship between Ivy and Alex took on a different timbre. Their talk on Saturday night had eroded the cool wall Ivy had erected, but a chasm of sadness tinged with longing had replaced it. The tension between them occasionally erupted into arguments that were as mercurial as heat lightning—full of fury, signifying nothing except a mutual desire that wouldn't go away.

Alex threw himself into his work with an obsession that worried Ivy. With each day that passed, the fear that the Strangler would strike again before the month was out grew into a kind of paranoia that affected every member of the task force, but Alex seemed to be taking it personally, as though he alone bore the responsibility for the Strangler's actions.

Media attention kept the heat on and raised the public paranoia level to new heights, as well. A full-scale war between the media and the task force provided the public with something new to read about every day—and the worst of the attention was focused on Alex. He was blamed for suppressing the information about the Strangler's threat, even though he hadn't been with the department when the note was left on Erin Selway's body. Mayor Jablonski was only too happy to allow him to take the heat, and no one seemed to pay much attention to the statement of support Commissioner Eversall issued in Alex's behalf.

On Wednesday, a police photograph of the Scrabble board message fell into the hands of the press, and the media went wild. They sensationalized the Strangler's personal challenge to Alex, turning the case into a contest between an unorthodox detective with a haunted past and a brilliant madman who was too clever for Alex to catch. Some papers demanded Alex's resignation, but most were content to rehash his past. Details of his wife's suicide were made public, as were insinuations that he had spent time in a mental hospital after Brenda's death and the shooting of Tanya Ringwald.

The publicity sickened Ivy, but she could only imagine the effect it was having on Alex because he refused to discuss it. She wanted to wrap him up in a protective cocoon, but she knew those feelings were totally inappropriate.

And equally inappropriate was the realization that despite Alex's warnings and her repeated denials, she had fallen in love with him. The stupidity of it made her want to scream. She couldn't love a man who didn't want to be loved, yet she did.

And what was worse, it didn't feel like the kind of love that was going to lie down and die a quiet death. It felt like the kind of love that would hurt for a long, long time.

"What are you brooding about, Ivy?" Mort Adamson sank into his chair in front of Ivy's desk and swiveled toward her. He looked as exhausted as everyone else on the task force.

Ivy had been staring off into space, and the question startled her. "I'm not brooding, Mort. I'm just trying to catch up on my sleep."

"Yeah, sure," he said skeptically. "I know exactly what you're thinking about."

Ivy swallowed hard. Was she really that transparent? "What's that?"

"You're thinking that there are only six days left in this month, and the Strangler is going to strike again at any minute."

She smiled and tried to hide her relief. "You caught me, Mort. That's exactly what I was thinking. You should take your mind reading act on the road."

Mort chuckled. "It doesn't take a mind reader to know what's on the minds of everyone in this room, kiddo. We're all checking the days off our calendars. No one can think about anything else—except maybe Alex.''

"Alex?" At the mention of his name, Ivy glanced toward his office. The door was open, but the blinds were closed, blocking her view of his desk. "What makes you think that Alex isn't focusing on the case?"

"Would you be able to concentrate on the case if you'd gotten the kind of adverse publicity he's been getting? Tomorrow is the third anniversary of his wife's death, and the papers are making the most of it. A day like that is hard enough to face without having it heralded in every headline in the city." Mort shook his head sadly. "Tomorrow is also Saturday. I hope he takes the day off and gets blind-stinking drunk. Alex is the most laid-back guy I know, but lately he's been as surly as a wild boar."

Ivy swallowed the bitter knot of guilt that rose in her throat. The case and the ugly publicity weren't the only factors that had contributed to Alex's foul mood. This week it had been impossible for them to spend any time together without quarreling. *But that's not my fault,* Ivy reminded herself. The interviews they had conducted together on Monday and Tuesday had gone smoothly enough, but the time between the interviews had been grueling. The sensual tension they had both enjoyed so much in the beginning had turned into a torturous labyrinth of frustrated desires and confused emotions.

When Ivy had learned from the newspapers that the anniversary of Brenda's death was approaching, she had understood a little better why his late wife had been on his mind so much recently; but when she had urged him to talk about it for his own sake, Alex had once again accused her of pushing him. No matter what she said to the contrary, he wouldn't believe that she was just concerned about him, that she only wanted to ease some of the incredible burden he was carrying.

Mort was right about one thing. Alex did need to blow off some steam. But getting drunk wasn't the answer, and she didn't think Alex was the type to resort to artificial forget-fulness. He needed to get away from the squad room and relax. He needed to do something fun that had absolutely nothing to do with the Strangler case.

Considering the circumstances, Ivy was probably the last person he would be able to do something fun with, but she felt compelled to take action. She couldn't bear the thought of Alex being alone on a day that was certain to bring back painful memories he thought about too much, anyway.

"Ivy?"

Mort's voice startled her again. She looked at him but barely saw him. "What?"

"Where did you go to? You were off in space again."

"I'm sorry, Morty. I was thinking about something else." She started rummaging through the papers on her desk, pretending to look for something. When she found a likely looking sheaf of computer printouts, she stood. "Listen, Morty, I'll catch you later. I've got to show these to Alex."

"Sure," he said, but Ivy was already gone. Now, what on earth was that all about? he wondered as he swiveled around to his own desk. He was pretty sure the rumors about Ivy and Alex were true—parts of them, at least. They did like each other more than a little; that much was clear. But Mort didn't believe that Ivy had bartered her body, as Jordan Brubaker was contending.

No, whatever was between them was real and apparently very complex, Mort decided, but he had no idea just ex-actly what their relationship was. One thing he was certain of, though. Ivy wasn't going to Alex's office to discuss computer printouts.

CHAPTER FOURTEEN

WHEN IVY ENTERED his office, Alex was rereading the updated Strangler profiles that had been submitted by Geraldine Franklyn and the other psychiatrist who was consulting
on the case. Both professionals seemed to be in complete
agreement, and Alex couldn't find anything that was particularly enlightening.

"What have you got there?" he asked when Ivy rapped
on his open door. As usual when he saw her, his heart
slammed against his rib cage and he felt a familiar, aching
constriction of his loins.

"This?" Ivy waved the computer sheets as she approached his desk. "This is nothing. I needed an excuse to
talk to you and I didn't want to walk in here empty-handed
in case anyone is watching."

"Everyone is watching," Alex said, glancing past her into
the squad room.

"Figures. We're a hot item, and no one can figure out
what's going on."

"Least of all us," Alex muttered under his breath.

Ivy smothered a humorless smile. "Right." Just for show,
she put the computer sheets in front of him and sat on the
corner of his desk with her back to the door. Just for show,
Alex flipped through the pages and pretended to find
something interesting, but all he was really aware of was
Ivy's nearness.

"What did you need to see me about?" His voice was
suddenly as scratchy as gravel.

"I'm about to do something monumentally stupid," she told him.

"Such as?"

"Ask you out." Alex looked at her with surprise, but she forged on quickly. "I promised Mother that I'd go to the community center with her tomorrow night to play bingo. Why don't you come with us? You need to get out of this office and relax. You're working too hard."

"The newspapers say I'm not working hard enough," he pointed out.

"They don't know what they're talking about. I do. Please join us," she said entreatingly. "No strings attached. Mother is the ideal chaperon—we'll have a perfectly innocuous time. With her along, we won't be able to talk about anything relevant. We certainly won't be able to fight. It'll put us on our best behavior. What do you say?"

Alex was surprised by the invitation, and he was torn. Spending time with Ivy was the most appealing thing he could think of, and she was right—having her mother along might dissipate a lot of the tension between them. It could be a wonderfully fun, relaxing evening, and that was exactly what he needed.

But unfortunately, the very innocence of the date would make it all the more intimate. They would be two people pretending they had a comfortable relationship, when, in fact, they didn't. Still, he understood what had motivated her to invite him, and he appreciated her gesture.

"Thanks for asking, Ivy, but I can't. I...already have plans." Telling a lie was easier than hurting her feelings.

"Oh." Ivy struggled to hide her disappointment. Was he lying, or did he have a date? she wondered. Was he seeing some nice, safe, uncomplicated woman who didn't expect too much from him? Was he sleeping with her?

Ivy slipped off the desk, suddenly tortured by images of Alex in the arms of another woman. "Well...I hope you have a nice time. It'll do you good to get your mind off work for a while.''

"Yes," Alex agreed, but he didn't mean it. The twenty-seventh of July was one of the hardest days of the year for him. Thanks to this case and all the painful publicity he'd been getting, it was going to be even harder this year. "I appreciate the invitation, though. Thanks," he said as Ivy headed for the door.

She stopped and turned toward him. "You're welcome. I just couldn't stand the thought of your being alone tomorrow, that's all."

"I know. Thank you."

"No big deal," she told him with a brightness they both knew was false. "See you later."

"Right."

When she left, the room felt very empty. And so did Alex.

IT RAINED SATURDAY—not a brief summer thunderstorm, but a slow, dreary, monotonous drizzle that turned everything in the city gray and ugly. Despite the rain, the temperature stayed in the mid-nineties, and the heat and humidity made breathing unbearable.

After a nearly sleepless night, Alex rose early that morning and gave his body a thorough going-over at his health club. From there, he went to the office and accomplished nothing. His mind wouldn't focus on the case or anything else it should have focused on. He couldn't stop thinking about Brenda, and on the few occasions when he did, Ivy took her place, filling his head with images of sweet possibilities. But then the memories of Brenda would return, and the sweet possibilities he saw with Ivy turned into bitter reminders of how something right could quickly turn into something painfully wrong.

The office walls closed in on him, and at noon he gave up all pretense of working. He left the station and, without really giving it any conscious thought, headed straight out of town.

The weather south of Brauxton wasn't any better than that which blanketed the city, but at least on the old coast road there were open spaces and frequent glimpses of the vast, gray ocean. The traffic was light, and Alex drove as though he were being pursued by the hounds of hell. The memories grew more persistent. His guilt became so palpable that it left a bitter taste in his mouth, but the faster he drove to escape the memories and the guilt, the more overpowering they became.

There has to be a way to leave them behind, he thought with growing desperation. The needle on his speedometer hit ninety, then ninety-five.

He left the city far behind, but the guilt remained.

IVY TWISTED BOTH ARMS behind her back like a circus contortionist. No matter which way she wiggled, no matter how much she squirmed, she simply could not unstick the zipper of the dress she'd bought that morning. Halfway up, it had jammed, and now it refused to budge. The shopping spree had been impulsive, and so had her purchase. She'd needed something to lift her spirits, and an aggressive sales clerk had convinced her that the white eyelet square-necked sundress with its fitted bodice and full, calf-length skirt was just the thing.

"That clerk should be taken out and shot," Ivy muttered, rising on tiptoe as though that would somehow help. "Now I know why women get married. Men do have certain—" she grunted as she yanked the zipper to no avail "—limited functions around the house. Argh!" Frustrated, she let both arms go limp and glared at her reflection in the full-length mirror that took up one wall of her tiny dressing room. "I wonder what dispatch would say if I called 911?"

The doorbell rang, and her face lighted up. "Eureka! The cavalry has arrived." Not caring who was at the door as long as it was someone who could handle a zipper, she hurried into the living room and checked the security peephole.

Her heart skipped a fraction of a beat when she saw that her would-be rescuer was Alex, but she quickly unlatched the door and threw it open. He looked tired and weary and wonderfully handsome. "Hi." Her smile was tinged with uncertainty.

"Hi." Alex was a little uncertain himself. He'd spent a miserable afternoon trying to run from his memories, only to discover that there was no place to hide. All he'd really learned was that he couldn't bear being alone any longer. Thoughts of Ivy had drawn him like a magnet, and for tonight, at least, he had to be with her. "Is your invitation for an evening of fun and frivolity still open?"

Ivy leaned against the edge of the door and regarded him speculatively. "I thought you had other plans."

"I lied."

"Oh." She grinned. "In that case, you're welcome to come along—on one condition."

"What's that?"

She did a 180-degree pirouette and presented her back to him. "Fix this broken zipper, and not only will I let you be frivolous, I will become your humble, willing slave."

God, the woman was magic, he thought as he stepped forward to work on the zipper. "For how long?" Amazingly, his voice was as light as hers despite the hammering of his heart.

Ivy allowed the door to drift shut, and she shrugged to camouflage the shiver that ran up her spine when Alex's fingers grazed her back. "Depends on how good you are at fixing zippers."

Alex gently tugged the zipper up and down, trying to free the fabric that had caught in its teeth. The smooth, flawless expanse of Ivy's back was exposed from her neck almost to her waist, leaving no doubt that she was wearing this dress without a bra. The realization brought a lump to Alex's throat and a sweet, stinging pain to his groin. Her hair was casually swept up into a loose ponytail that bared the long line of her neck, and he had an overpowering urge to lower his lips to her throat to find out if she tasted as sweet and sexy as she smelled. His fingers grew clumsy, and it took a little longer than he would have liked to free the material and zip the dress.

"How's that?" he asked. The words came out as little more than a croak, and he cleared his throat.

Ivy turned to him, wondering if he could tell that she was trembling. "Great. Thank you." She smiled, and Alex felt his heart expand in his chest.

"So, how much slave time do I get for my good deed?"

"How much do you want?" she asked impishly. She was ridiculously happy that Alex had changed his mind, yet she wasn't exactly sure what he'd changed his mind about. Was he here for the innocuous evening of no-strings-attached fun she had promised, or had he finally decided to stop fighting their mutual attraction and let nature take its course? She couldn't bring herself to ask. She had promised him an uncomplicated evening, and that was what she was going to deliver. If things became complicated later on, it would have to be his decision.

"Let's see ... how much slave labor do I want?" Alex frowned as though he was considering the question seriously. "I think a few hours would be sufficient—after all, it was a pretty short zipper."

"All right. A few hours it shall be. How would you like me to start? Can I interest you in a peeled grape? Do you have a barge that needs to be toted? A bale that needs lifting?"

Feeling better than he had in a long time, Alex played his role of lord and master to the hilt, swaggering toward the sofa with a proprietorial air. "A grape first, I think. Several, in fact. Peeled, stomped, fermented and chilled."

Ivy bowed elaborately. "Your wish is my command, sahib. Red or white?"

"You choose," Alex said with an airy wave. "These executive decisions are so taxing."

"Rest your weary gray matter, sahib. I shall return anon." Still bowing comically, Ivy backed into the kitchen and quickly poured two glasses of white wine. She returned, sat at the opposite end of the sofa and handed the glass to Alex with a flourish. "Your libation, sahib."

He raised one eyebrow imperiously. "Since when is it appropriate for a slave to drink with the master?"

Ivy's eyes narrowed dangerously. "Don't press your luck, bud, or you may have a revolt on your hands."

Alex laughed, but the sound died away quickly and he grew serious. "Thank you."

"For the wine?"

"No, for accepting my presence without asking any questions," he said quietly.

Ivy's heart turned over, and she resisted the urge to reach out and stroke the lines of fatigue and pain from Alex's handsome face. "I promised you a no-strings-attached evening of fun. I assume that's why you're here."

"I'm here because I can't seem to stay away from you, and I'm tired of trying," he admitted honestly.

"And you didn't want to be alone tonight," Ivy added.

"That's right."

Smiling gently, Ivy raised her glass to his and the crystal rang delicately. "I'm glad you came."

"So am I."

They sipped their wine and let the conversation slip into polite small talk about the weather until Ivy excused herself to finish getting ready. She disappeared into the bathroom and returned a few minutes later with her hair in its usual casual style and her makeup lightly applied. Alex watched her as she transferred some of the contents of her huge purse into a smaller straw bag that matched the colorful sandals she had donned. One thing she did not transfer, he noted, was her Smith & Wesson automatic.

"What time are you supposed to pick up your mother?"

"I'm meeting her and Gil at the community center at 7:20."

"Gil? You didn't tell me this was a double date."

"You didn't ask," Ivy answered with a grin. "Do you mind?"

Alex shook his head and finished his wine. "Not at all. So long as he doesn't cheat at bingo or tell me how to run the Strangler investigation, I'm sure we'll get along fine."

"I tell you what. We'll make the Strangler investigation a taboo subject tonight. No shoptalk, just good clean fun."

"You've got a deal." He stood. "Are you ready to go?"

"Ready." Ivy started toward the door, but when Alex placed one hand lightly on her arm, she stopped and turned to him expectantly. "Is something wrong?"

"No. . . ." He studied her face for a moment before stepping closer. "I just wanted to look . . . You are so beautiful, Ivy," he said, his voice whisper soft. "So very beautiful. . . ." Gently, he brought one hand to her cheek, cupping it lightly as he lowered his lips to hers.

The kiss was so sweet and tender that it nearly brought tears to Ivy's eyes. His mouth moved over hers for just a moment—long enough to make her want to cry out for more—and then he pulled away. Their eyes met, but Ivy found no answers, only questions, in Alex's sad gaze. He wanted her, but was he ready to take the risk?

"We'd better go or we'll be late," he said softly.

"Better late than never," Ivy replied, but she wasn't referring to the engagement with her mother. She lifted her face and pressed a brief, poignant kiss to his lips, then turned and started for the door. Alex followed and reached for the light switch when Ivy stepped into the hall, but she stopped him.

"Leave the lights on, please. Lately I've developed a dislike for coming home to a dark apartment."

Alex captured her eyes, and they stood silently in the doorway for a long moment before he spoke. "Then don't come home at all tonight. Come home with me."

Ivy's breath caught in her throat, and her heart pounded like thunder. Suddenly, she was hot with longing and cold with fear. But fear was meant to be conquered, and her longing for Alex had reached the point of absurdity. She couldn't say no.

Without speaking, she leaned past him and flipped the light switch, plunging the apartment into the dreary gray dusk of evening.

GIL HATCHET WAS EVERYTHING Mavis had told Ivy he was. The retired businessman was reserved but very charming and personable. He was also remarkably attentive to Mavis, which pleased Ivy immensely. It pleased her, too, that her mother took an immediate liking to Alex. The two couples met in the lobby of the Riverside Community Center—a bank building that had been converted into a senior citizens' center—and after a round of introductions, they proceeded into the main hall, where a dozen long tables were set up.

Alex and Gil purchased bingo cards for their group while Mavis and Ivy searched for a place to sit. The room was crowded, but they managed to find four vacant chairs, two on each side of a table near the back of the room.

"Your gentleman friend is very handsome, Mother," Ivy commented as she waved to Alex and Gil, who were just leaving the registration table by the entrance. Gil was only a few inches shorter than Alex, with a lean build and a pleasant, angular face. He was laughing at something Alex had said to him, and his smile was open and welcoming. Ivy waved again to get their attention, and once she was sure they had seen her, she took a chair across the table from Mavis and sat.

"I hope you'll like him, Ivy. He's one of the most interesting men I've met in a long time," she replied. "And speaking of interesting men, I was surprised when you showed up with Lieutenant Devane."

Ivy frowned. "Is that disapproval I hear in your voice?"

"Of course not, dear."

"Good. He's under a lot of pressure, Mom," she said, leaning forward with her voice lowered confidentially. "You know how the papers have been crucifying him lately. I brought him here to get away from all that for a while. He needs to have a little fun and get his mind off work."

Mavis reached out to cover her daughter's hand. "He's very important to you, isn't he?"

Ivy found that she couldn't maintain her mother's steady, penetrating gaze. She glanced down, remembering the unspoken commitment she'd made to spend the night with Alex. "Yes, Mother, he is. Very important."

"Are you in love with him?" Mavis asked.

Ivy glanced up, but before she could decide whether she should tell Mavis the truth, Gil and Alex joined them. "Would you ladies care for something to drink before the games begin?" Gil asked, standing beside Mavis's chair. "Coffee? Iced tea? A soft drink?"

"Iced tea would be nice," Mavis answered.

"What about you, bright eyes?" Alex asked as he placed four bingo cards—two for each of them—in front of Ivy. He had one hand resting on her shoulder, and just that light touch sent her pulse racing.

"I'll have the same," she said. The men headed for the concession stand on the other side of the room, leaving a palpable silence in their wake despite the noise of the crowd.

"Well?" Mavis said, watching Ivy closely as her daughter carefully inspected the bingo cards as though she'd never seen one before.

Ivy looked up. "Well, what?"

"You know perfectly well 'what.'" Mavis sighed with exasperation. "I asked you a question."

"And I didn't answer it."

"So I noticed. Do you plan to?"

Ivy pursed her lips and looked at her mother thoughtfully. "Do I *need* to?"

Mavis shook her head. "No, I don't suppose so. It's written all over your face every time you look at him." She reached for Ivy's hand again. "Darling, be careful. I don't want to see you get hurt."

"Too late, Mom. The die is already cast."

"Is he in love with you?"

"I honestly don't know," she answered, her confusion obvious. "But even if Alex does love me, he's a long way from making a commitment to any woman. I'll just have to wait and see what happens next."

"But Ivy—"

"Shush, Mom," she said when she saw their escorts returning. "Here they come. No more questions—and don't you dare give Alex the third degree. We're here to have fun."

"All right, dear," Mavis said, putting her doubts aside for the moment. There would be time later to worry about whether or not her daughter was headed for a broken heart.

CHAPTER FIFTEEN

IVY GLANCED AT ALEX and wondered if he was as nervous as she was. The bingo game had ended nearly an hour ago, and Gil—who had won the final one-hundred-dollar jackpot of the evening—had insisted on taking his companions out for coffee at a quaint Hungarian restaurant just down the block from the community center. Alex had seemed to be enjoying himself so much that Ivy had happily agreed to the suggestion, but now that it was getting late she kept remembering the moment in her apartment when she had reached past Alex and turned out the lights. With that simple gesture, she had promised to spend the night with him. She felt no sense of regret at having done so, but there was a rising feeling of panic that she couldn't quite shake.

Panic probably wasn't the right word. Fear seemed to be more accurate, because she was taking a dangerous risk with her heart. Alex had said he was tired of fighting his attraction to her, but that didn't mean he had changed his mind about relationships. Today was the anniversary of his wife's death, and he simply hadn't wanted to spend a long night alone.

And Ivy didn't want to be alone any longer, either. She was tired of only imagining what it would be like to feel Alex's body joined to hers. She had fallen in love, and she wanted the chance to express that love—if not in words, at least in deeds. There was a chance that Alex would never be able to let go of the past and return her love, but that was a risk Ivy was willing to take.

Mavis and Alex laughed at something Gil had said, and Ivy forced her thoughts into the present. She chuckled politely, only vaguely aware that Gil had been talking about his youngest grandson's exploits on the soccer field.

"Oh, Gil, I do envy you," Mavis said sweetly. "It must be such a comfort to have grandchildren. I wish I did."

The pointed remark captured Ivy's complete attention. "Mother..." she said in a quiet, cautionary tone of voice.

Mavis glanced at her daughter ingenuously. "I wasn't implying anything, Ivy, I was just making a statement of fact. I *do* want grandchildren someday—hopefully while I'm still young enough to enjoy them."

Ivy's gaze darted to Alex to see if he was taking any of this personally, but all she discovered was amusement in his clear gray eyes. "Need I remind you, Mother, that you were older than I am when you had me?"

"Yes, dear, but I had been married for nearly six years. You're still single."

Mavis looked so adorably innocent that Alex couldn't keep from laughing outright. "She has you there, Ivy."

She fixed him with a comically menacing glare. "You'll stay out of this if you know what's good for you."

Alex laughed again and Gil joined him. "Does she talk to you like that when you're at work, too?" he asked.

"Always. The woman has no respect for authority."

"That's right," Ivy said waspishly. "And she also doesn't like to be talked about as though she weren't present."

Alex smothered his grin and tried to look properly chastised. "I'm sorry."

"I'm sorry, too," Gil said, chuckling as he reached across the table to pat her hand comfortingly. "Why don't we change the subject. I've been dying to ask about the Strangler case. It's not every day that I have access to the head of the task force and one of his chief detectives."

Ivy stiffened. She had promised Alex there would be no shoptalk tonight, and until now, everything had been going so smoothly. Alex seemed more relaxed than she'd seen him in weeks, and she didn't want to spoil his pleasant mood.

But Alex didn't seem disturbed. "Actually, Gil, there's not a lot we can tell you beyond what you read in the newspapers."

Gil made a disgruntled huffing sound. "I don't rely too much on the papers, Alex. They seem a lot more interested in stirring up trouble than in reporting the facts. You've been taking it on the chin quite a bit lately, and it just doesn't seem fair."

Alex shrugged noncommittally. "The public wants action, and the media is responding to that pressure."

"The media is trying to sell papers," Mavis said, clearly sympathetic with Alex. "They have no right to delve into the personal life of anyone on the task force. Ivy doesn't discuss the case in specific terms, but I know how hard all of you are working. Doesn't the press understand that they're only making your job more difficult?"

"Apparently not," Ivy said.

"You know, what fascinates me about the case is the game angle," Gil said, tactfully drawing the topic away from Alex's negative media coverage and earning Ivy's undying gratitude. "That Scrabble message the press got hold of was something else. Have all the other game clues been that elaborate?"

Alex shook his head. "No. As the press has reported, the others were single game pieces."

Gil looked thoughtful. "I don't suppose that Pentathlon was one of those games, was it?"

Ivy and Alex looked at each other quickly, then back at Gil. "Why would you think that?" Alex asked carefully.

"Just curiosity," Gil said with a shrug. "I know the guy who invented Pentathlon, and I've always wondered if his game was one that the Strangler had used. I mean, it would be a strange coincidence—with him living in Brauxton and all.''

A coincidence, indeed. A Pentathlon gold medal had been found beside the sixth victim, Erin Selway. Excited by a potential lead, Ivy leaned forward. ''The creator of Pentathlon lives in Brauxton?''

''Yes,'' Gil said with a nod. ''His name is Benjamin Drummond. He lives in one of those creepy old mansions on Riverside Drive.''

''How do you know him?'' Alex asked.

''I've worked on several of his projects during the past couple of years.''

''Printing?'' Ivy inquired, remembering Gil telling them that until recently he had run his own printing company. When he retired, he had turned the everyday operation of the firm over to his sons, but he still kept his hand in the business to keep from becoming bored.

''That's right,'' he affirmed. ''Whenever Drummond invents a new game, he hires us to make the prototype—you know, board layout, cards, rule sheets...that sort of thing.''

''What do you know about Drummond personally?'' Alex asked.

Gil sat back and looked from Alex to Ivy. ''Pentathlon was one of the games, wasn't it?''

Ivy glanced at Alex, leaving it up to him as to whether or not he would disclose that piece of classified information. ''Yes, it was,'' Alex said. ''But even if it wasn't, we'd be interested in anyone who invented games for a living. As you said yourself, it's a coincidence that bears investigating.''

''I don't want to get anyone in trouble....'' Gil said hesitantly. Part of him was pleased that he'd given the head of the Strangler task force a piece of information he hadn't already possessed, but another part of him was regretting having brought up the subject.

"Mr. Drummond isn't in trouble," Ivy reassured him. "Unless he happens to be the Strangler, of course. In which case you'd be doing everyone a great a favor by telling us what you know."

"Ivy Lane Kincaid!" Mavis exclaimed with exasperation. "Don't you dare give Gil the third degree. You sound just like a cop."

"Mom, I am a cop," Ivy reminded her patiently.

"It's all right, Mavis," Gil said. "I'm the one who started this. And I guess that if the truth were told, I've been thinking a lot about Drummond and the Strangler case— you know, putting two and two together. After that last murder, I even considered calling the hot line, but the very idea made me feel like a kid telling tales out of school."

"What made you connect Drummond to the Strangler case?" Alex asked.

"Well, he's just so—" he paused, searching for the right word "—strange."

"In what way?"

Gil shrugged, clearly uncomfortable. "He's a very disagreeable person. He never talks much when he comes into the shop, and I don't think I've ever seen him crack a smile—all brusque and businesslike, you know? He's a real good-looking son of a gun, but he's got a big chip on his shoulder, particularly where women are concerned."

"Oh?" Ivy said, prompting him to continue. "Have you heard him make negative remarks about women?"

"Not remarks, exactly... it's more of an impression he gives off. He's very cold, uncomfortable almost, around the women who work in the front office. He's fairly young and extremely handsome, so the girls used to sit up and take notice whenever he came in. They practically fell all over themselves trying to see who could get to him to wait on him first, but he's been so rude to them that now they dread seeing him coming."

"Anything else?" Ivy asked.

Gil nodded. "One thing.... About a year ago Drummond and I were in my office waiting for some card proofs to be cut, and just to make conversation I asked him what his wife thought of the new game we were printing up. He let me know rather abruptly that he wasn't married. Never had been, never would be, he said. Then he got this very...severe, distant look on his face, as though he was remembering something unpleasant. He didn't say anything else, but I happened to glance down at his hands, and he had them clenched so tightly into fists that his knuckles were turning white."

Alex asked a few more questions, but Gil didn't seem to have anything else to add.

"Are you going to investigate him?" Mavis asked.

"We'll check him out," Alex answered with an easy smile. "We're not so overwhelmed by suspects that we can afford to let any long shot slip by. But don't worry, Gil, if we decide to question him, we won't let him know that you were the one who brought him to our attention."

"I appreciate that. I can't believe he's the Strangler. I mean, if I'd been convinced that he was, I'd have contacted the police a long time ago. Now, I feel bad for having brought the subject up in the first place."

"Don't worry about it," Ivy said sympathetically. "If Mr. Drummond has nothing to hide, he won't mind a few questions. In fact, he may welcome them," she said wryly, remembering Norme Canyon.

Alex remembered, too, and laughed. When Mavis and Gil looked at him curiously, he encouraged Ivy to relate the story of the bored puzzle creator who'd been thrilled to be a Strangler suspect. They all had a hearty laugh, and then the conversation drifted away from the investigation. Their waiter came by to refill their coffee cups, and a little while later they decided to call it a night.

"I like your mother a lot," Alex told Ivy once they were alone in the nearly deserted community center parking lot. They had accompanied the other couple to Gil's car and waved to them as they drove away.

"She liked you, too," Ivy said, linking her arm casually through Alex's as they strolled toward his car. The rain had finally stopped, but the wet black asphalt gleamed under the street lamps.

"What do you think of her beau?"

"I like him," she answered brightly. "He seems very stable and sincere. I think they'll be good for each other."

Alex nodded thoughtfully. "What did you think of that Benjamin Drummond business?"

"Brauxton is a big city that attracts all sorts of people, so it's not an unreasonable coincidence that a wealthy game inventor might live here and not have anything to do with the Strangler killings, but it's definitely worth investigating."

"Agreed. In fact, I think I'll call the station as soon as we get home and have them run a computer check on him."

"Uh, good," Ivy said.

Something in her tone caught Alex's attention, and he realized that his comment had been based on a rather large assumption. They reached his car, and Alex unlocked the door on the passenger side, then turned to her. "Ivy..."

The parking lot was well lighted, and Ivy could read every nuance of Alex's solemn expression. "Yes?"

"You don't have to... I mean, about what I said earlier at your place... If you've changed your mind—"

Ivy reached out and silenced him with gentle fingertips pressed against his lips. "I turned out the lights in my apartment, Alex. That means I can't go home unless you're willing to help me search for intruders."

His smile made her go weak in the knees. "That seems like an awful lot of trouble. It will be a lot simpler if you just go home with me, won't it?"

"You haven't changed your mind?"

"No. Have you?"

"No," she answered quietly.

Alex opened the car door and turned to her. The movement brought them so close that Ivy could feel the heat of his body and the warmth of his breath on her face. "Then let's go home," he said softly. "I want to make love with you, Ivy."

"I want that, too, Alex," she said breathlessly. They stared at each other for a long moment, caught in a web of longing, until Ivy finally broke the contact, slid into the car and held her skirt as Alex closed the door.

THE HOUSE ON RIVERSIDE DRIVE was a huge old monstrosity, but it suited its owner well. Sheltered from the night by a shadowy grove of trees, a figure dressed in black looked at the darkened mansion and smiled. There was a sense of belonging here—the warm feeling of coming home after a long journey. Just before and immediately after every killing, the Strangler stood for a long moment in these shadows, gathering strength and a sense of purpose from the house.

But there would be no killing tonight. The need was strong, but it wasn't time yet. Soon, though. Very soon. And in the meantime, a walk on the lawn through the trees felt good. It gave a sense of purpose and quieted the nagging fears and anxiety.

It was also a reminder of things to come.

"YOUR HOUSE IS VERY . . ." Ivy paused, searching for the right word to describe his bland family room. If she hadn't been so nervous, she wouldn't have said anything at all, because there was very little about Alex's characterless home that she could compliment.

"Tidy?" Alex suggested with a smile as he returned from the kitchen with a bottle of wine and two glasses. He'd already called the station to start the investigation into Benjamin Drummond, and with that out of the way, he wasn't going to think any more about business tonight. Ivy was here, and just the thought of what was to come brought him more peace than he'd known in years.

Standing at the French doors that overlooked a darkened patio, Ivy turned to him and grinned. "It's a house that's full of possibilities," she said graciously. "A few photographs, a couple of throw pillows, a bowling trophy on the mantel and this place would almost be livable."

"What? No gargoyles or Japanese screens?" Alex teased as he popped the wine cork and filled both glasses.

Ivy looked him up and down appraisingly. What she saw made her heart race, but she kept her tone light. "No, you don't look like the Japanese screen type."

"Here." He held a glass out to her, and Ivy left the windows. Taking the wine from him, she eased gracefully onto the sofa.

"Why *does* your house have an un-lived-in look, Alex?"

Alex sat next to her, leaving a comfortable, respectful distance between them. "Probably...because I haven't done much living these past few years. When I bought the house about a year and a half ago, I also bought this furniture, placed it wherever it was most convenient, and it's sat here ever since. It's hardly been used at all. I spend most of my time buried under books in the office or in libraries."

"And before that?"

He shrugged. "Before that I was buried under books in a tiny furnished apartment."

"Where you and Brenda lived?" Ivy asked cautiously, wondering if she was making a grave mistake by mentioning his late wife. Alex seemed talkative, and there were things they needed to get out in the open—namely, his guilt over Brenda's suicide—but she wasn't sure if he had come *that* far. He'd brought her here to make love, and rehashing the past didn't exactly fall under the category of foreplay.

But Alex seemed to understand her motivation. "You need to talk about it, don't you?"

"About Brenda? Yes, I do."

"On the theory that shared confidences lead to greater intimacy?"

Ivy grinned. "Have you been watching *Donahue*?" It wasn't an irreverent question, just one that was meant to keep the mood from becoming maudlin. Alex almost, but not quite, returned her smile.

"What do you want to know?"

"Actually, I'd like to know everything there is to know about you—your family background, what you were like as a child, why you became a cop instead of a rocket scientist—everything. But I'll settle for whatever you want to tell me."

Alex noted that her list did not include "why your wife killed herself." She was offering him a way of easing into the subject, and he appreciated her tactics. "All right, the easy stuff first. I was the second of three children. My older brother, younger sister and I were born and raised out in the suburbs—in Templeton. My parents still live there, but I don't have much contact with them."

"Why not?"

He shrugged. "We were never really close. I was the classic middle child—you know, the one who gets lost in the shuffle. Dad wanted a son he could coach in Little League, and Mom wanted a daughter she could enter in beauty pageants. Under Dad's tutelage, my older brother, Nathan, eventually became a major league baseball player, and my sister, Janice, still looks great in frilly pink dresses and black patent leather shoes. But me—'' Alex laughed wryly, but Ivy sensed no bitterness ''—they just didn't know what to do with me.''

''Why not?''

''I didn't fit either of the molds.''

''Were you the brainy, bookish sort?'' she asked, thinking of his vast intellect and ridiculously high IQ.

''Only by default.''

Ivy frowned. ''What does that mean?''

Alex grinned. ''I loved sports, and I worked very hard at being good to please Dad, but I just couldn't compete with Nathan. He was a gifted athlete, whereas I was just an energetic, uncoordinated kid. As I grew up, everywhere I went people would say, 'Oh, yeah, you're Nathan Devane's little brother.' ''

''So you decided to work for scholastic excellence in order to get out of Nathan's shadow.''

''Exactly,'' Alex said. ''Nate was so bright that he made good grades without ever having to open a book, but when I discovered that by applying myself I could get even better grades than he did, I snapped up the opportunity to beat him at *something*. Dad was proud of me, but he didn't know how to handle a kid who was eventually labeled a genius. I think I intimidated him.''

''How did Nathan feel about your success?''

''It irritated the hell out of him,'' Alex said with a laugh. ''Somewhere along the line I skipped a couple of grades, so by the time we reached high school, I was only a year behind him. He felt threatened by me, though Lord knows, he had no reason to. I was this wimpy, academic nerd, and he was the all-American athlete, loved by all. I don't think he ever understood that I would have sold my soul for just a fraction of his popularity and our father's unconditional approval.''

Ivy formed an image of a child who was not so much lonely as needy. She didn't feel sorry for him, but she did empathize with him. She herself had grown up wanting the approval of a father who had practically ceased to exist for her by the time she was ten. "Were you still looking for your father's approval when you decided to become a cop?"

"No." Alex shook his head. "By then, I was searching for an identity with a little macho in it. I got tired of being the egghead at about the same time I discovered that girls don't swoon over brainy types."

Ivy grinned. "I can tell you from experience, boys don't, either."

"I refuse to believe that you ever had trouble getting a date," Alex said emphatically, losing himself in the seductive mischief that sparkled in her eyes. God, how he wanted her.

"Oh, I didn't," she replied. "There were always plenty of potential boyfriends hanging around as long as I batted my eyelashes and pretended I didn't have a brain in my head. Unfortunately, that was a game I hated playing, so I spent a lot of Saturday nights at home washing my hair."

"How strange...." Alex whispered, suddenly caught in a web of memories that were far less pleasant than his rivalry with his brother. Absently, he reached out and captured a lock of hair that curled at Ivy's throat. "You refused to play that game, and I married a woman who had perfected it into an art form."

His hand was lightly brushing her bare shoulder, and Ivy felt the heat of the casual touch course through her until it came to rest low in her abdomen. "You don't have to talk about it if you don't want to," she told him quietly.

"No, I do want to," he replied. "Maybe I even need to talk about her. And you certainly have a right to know."

More than anything he could have said, that last statement made Ivy impossibly happy. "I'm glad you feel that
way."

"Oh, don't read more into that than what's there, Ivy,"
he warned her when he saw the hope that had blossomed in
her azure eyes. "I just meant that you have a right to know
so that you can change your mind about me if you want to."

"That's not going to happen, Alex."

He smiled cryptically. "We'll see."

"Damn it, Alex, will you please tell me what it is that you
think makes you such a monster? Whatever it is, I haven't
seen any sign of it."

"Maybe you're only seeing what you want to see," he
said, releasing the silky strands of hair he'd been holding.

When he moved his hand, Ivy mourned the loss of that
simple contact with him, yet the heat he had generated in her
did not dissipate. "What I see is a very exciting, sensitive
man who is capable of great love and incredible remorse.
Men without conscience or honor don't feel guilt, Alex.
Why don't you just tell me about your relationship with
Brenda and let me make up my own mind about how justified your guilt is."

"All right." He reached for the wine bottle and refilled
their glasses. There was a long pause before he began talking again. "I started dating Brenda Harkness while I was in
college, still mired in my macho phase. I'd filled out considerably since high school—nature had added a few more
inches to my height and regular workouts had added a phy-
sique. And because, as we all know, a gun is an extension of
a man's...manhood, I had become better than proficient
in the use of several types of handguns and assault weap-
ons."

The venom and self-loathing in Alex's voice tore at Ivy's
heart, but she remained silent as he continued.

"I was Clint Eastwood, Burt Reynolds and John Wayne all rolled into one arrogant, overconfident superstud."

"And Brenda?" she said quietly.

Alex sighed deeply. "Brenda was everything a macho superstud could have wanted. She was sweet, shy and beautiful, with long dark hair and huge brown eyes that absolutely knocked me for a loop. And there was this air of helplessness about her that convinced me I could leap tall buildings in a single bound. She needed someone to protect her. I needed someone to protect so that I could feel like a man. It was a match made in heaven," he said sarcastically. He drained his wineglass, wishing it was filled with something stronger, but he knew from experience that alcohol didn't dull the pain or blur the memories.

He went on to briefly describe an idyllic courtship and the first few years of their marriage after he had graduated from college and the police academy. Though Alex bent over backward to be fair—clearly he did not want to speak ill of the dead—the picture of Brenda Devane that emerged was an unpleasant one.

Apparently, it hadn't taken Alex long to realize that his sweet, helpless bride was far from helpless and not especially sweet. She was clinging, possessive and extremely jealous of any time Alex did not spend with her. She demanded his total attention, and when she didn't get it, she resorted to a seemingly endless supply of manipulative tricks to bind him to her.

"It was strange," Alex said reflectively. "After a while, the harder she tried to hold on to me, the more I pulled away."

"That's not strange, Alex, that's only natural. I feel sorry for anyone who needs to depend solely on another human being for her own happiness, but it's not unusual for the recipient of all that responsibility to feel resentful."

"I know that, but don't you see how unfair I was being? It was Brenda's helplesssness that first attracted me to her. I led her to believe that her possessiveness was exactly what I wanted in a wife, and when I changed my mind, it left Brenda out in the cold."

"Alex, you grew up, you matured," Ivy said insistently. "It's not your fault that Brenda didn't mature with you. And besides, you said yourself that she wasn't really helpless—that it was all an act. When her playacting began affecting your marriage, she should have known it was time to give it up. Instead, she chose to become even more manipulative."

Alex ran an impatient hand through his hair. "Everything you're saying is true, but it was still my fault. I never really confronted her, told her how I felt. I just pulled away. I spent more and more time at the station, particularly after I made detective. She needed more than I was capable of giving her."

"Maybe she needed too much, Alex."

"She was insecure, and my rejection only made it worse," he countered hotly.

Ivy frowned, frustrated by his compulsive guilt. He was absolutely determined to take the entire responsibility for his failed marriage onto his own shoulders. "Alex, why in God's name are you doing this to yourself? It takes two people to make a marriage—or break one up."

"You're saying it wasn't my fault?" he asked skeptically.

"I'm saying it wasn't all your fault. Let Brenda bear her share of the blame, for crying out loud."

"Brenda is dead! Or don't you read the papers?" Alex practically shouted, then quickly reined in his temper. "Sorry," he said shortly as he stood and moved across the room to an oak credenza that served as a makeshift bar. Opening the lower doors, he removed a bottle of bourbon and poured a small shot into his empty wineglass.

Ivy watched as he drained the scouring liquid in one gulp, then poured another before recapping the bottle. She waited, allowing the silence to dissipate some of the tension that had erupted. Alex remained on the opposite side of the room, not looking at Ivy or anything else in particular. When he didn't say anything, Ivy finally decided to take the initiative. They'd come this far, she reasoned; they might as well get the rest of it out in the open—whatever the rest of it might be.

"Why did she kill herself, Alex?" Ivy asked softly. "The woman you've described to me sounds a lot stronger than you've given her credit for. She was insecure, yes. But she also had an iron core, or she would never have been able to manipulate you the way she did."

Alex did look at Ivy then, because she'd hit on the one thing about Brenda's death that had always troubled him most. "That's what I've always thought. In fact—" he paused, as though searching through his tumultuous emotions for the right words "—that's the very thing that makes me feel so responsible for her death. After eleven years of marriage, I had finally come to the conclusion that Brenda was as tough as nails and as hard as brass, despite all her feigned vulnerability. I was wrong. I didn't see it coming. I should have, but I didn't..."

He moved slowly, thoughtfully, toward the windows that overlooked the backyard. Ivy rose and joined him there. "You were in the process of getting a divorce when she died, weren't you?" she asked.

Alex didn't look at her. "Yes."

"Why?"

He chuckled humorlessly. "Haven't I given you enough reasons? We had a miserable marriage."

There was a truth that wasn't being told. Ivy sensed it. For all Alex's talk about how far he'd pulled away from Brenda, it was obvious that he'd tried to hang on to his marriage.

Whether it was out of love, a sense of duty, complacency or an unwillingness to admit failure, Ivy didn't know. But according to office rumors and recent newspaper accounts, Alex had been the one to initiate the divorce, and Brenda had killed herself because of it. Which meant that something had happened to make Alex realize there was nothing of his marriage worth saving.

Several pieces of the puzzle suddenly fell into place, and Ivy reached the only logical conclusion. "Brenda had an affair, didn't she?"

Alex looked at her sharply. It was a long moment before he finally answered. "Yes."

"With someone you knew," she said, but not as a question. "Someone close to you. She had an affair with the one person whose betrayal would hurt you the most, and then she probably made sure you discovered the infidelity in the most painful way possible."

The accuracy of her supposition stunned Alex. Fleetingly, he wondered if she'd learned that information from some outside source, but that was impossible. Only three people in the world had known about the affair. One of them was dead, one had moved afterward, and the last—Alex—was still too hurt and bitter to talk about it to even his closest friends.

"My God," he whispered incredulously. "You really are Sherlock Holmes incarnate. How in hell did you know that?"

Ivy shrugged and suppressed the urge to say, "Elementary, my dear Watson." Humor was definitely not called for at this moment. "Based on what you told me about Brenda, it's the scenario that makes the most sense. You were absorbed in your work and she felt left out, ignored. Since manipulating men was what she did best, it only seems logical that she would turn to another man in order to obtain the attention you weren't giving her. Choosing someone you trusted was just the icing on the cake."

"He was my best friend from college," Alex said, his voice hollow. "In fact, we were almost like brothers—we had the kind of relationship I'd always wanted to have with Nathan. Brenda never liked him, but I finally realized that she was just jealous of our friendship. She resented anyone who diverted one minute of my attention away from her."

"So she killed two birds with one stone—she got your attention and destroyed the friendship at the same time."

"Yes." Alex stepped away from Ivy and returned to the sofa. "Only her plan backfired. She destroyed the friendship, all right, but she hadn't counted on my moving out and asking for a divorce. I think she had assumed that she could manipulate me into forgiving her—you know, make my friend out to be the bad guy who had seduced her while she was lonely and vulnerable, which was my fault in the first place."

"And when you didn't buy the act?"

"She turned back to him. Briefly. But it didn't take long for him to realize that she was only using him. When he rejected her, Brenda came back to me one last time, begging me to forgive her. I wouldn't...couldn't. We had a bitter argument, and two days later...she was dead."

"And your friend?" Ivy asked softly.

Alex laughed humorlessly. "Needless to say, we aren't friends any longer. So, does that answer all your questions?"

"All but one," she answered. Moving slowly, thoughtfully, Ivy returned to the sofa and knelt beside him.

"What's that?"

Gently, she reached out and touched his face, silently urging him to look directly into her eyes. The agony she saw there nearly broke her heart. "Why is it all your fault?"

"Because I should have seen it coming. I should have realized..." His voice trailed off because Ivy was so close, and he didn't want to think anymore. He only wanted to touch her, be with her, lose himself inside her so that maybe he could wrench free from his sordid past.

"You couldn't have known, Alex. She betrayed you. She deliberately set out to hurt you, and she succeeded. No one can blame you for not seeing past that hurt. Let it go," she pleaded.

Alex reached for her, pulling her into his arms. "I can't let it go, Ivy," he whispered, bringing his lips close to hers. "But I can't let you go, either."

"I don't want you to let me go, Alex," she answered, sliding her arms around him, sealing their bodies together as her lips lightly brushed his.

Alex groaned, tortured by the fleeting, tantalizing taste of her. "I can't make you any promises," he said as their lips flirted and their breaths mingled.

"I haven't asked for any," she replied breathlessly. His body was hard and supple against hers, and Ivy thought she might die a glorious death from the aching need that blossomed inside her. "Make love with me, Alex." Her tongue darted out, painting his lower lip seductively, and Alex moaned again as he accepted what she was offering. His mouth slanted across hers, and the kiss was no longer flirtatious. It was deep and hot and urgent, just like the need they felt for each other. Their tongues mated, danced, caressed, aroused, and they strained toward each other until that one intimacy was no longer enough.

Breathing hard, Alex drew away from Ivy, stood and pulled her to her feet. "The bedroom is this way."

CHAPTER SIXTEEN

IVY WONDERED if it was possible to die from pure pleasure. Sunlight was peeking in through the drawn bedroom curtains, and Alex was still asleep beside her, but a few hours sleep hadn't diminished her memory of the night before. The individual events had blurred together in her mind, but the beauty of what it had felt like to have Alex touch her, move inside of her, cry out her name, his voice husky with passion—those were the moments that stood out in vivid detail.

The first time, the loving had been hard and fast. Mutual need had made going slowly impossible. The fire that had been nipping at them from the moment they had met consumed them both. They devoured each other greedily, and when Alex at last plunged into her, Ivy thought the heat of him might scorch her very soul.

And when the heat had subsided and they were lying close together, communicating with nothing more than sighs and gentle touches, a different kind of longing had emerged. It was a need to experience the ecstasy again, slowly this time, savoring each new sensation, each taste, every touch, until the fire was too hot to handle.

For Ivy, it was like coming home and finding a part of herself she hadn't known was missing.

And for Alex?

Carefully, so as not to wake him, Ivy shifted onto her side and looked at her lover's face. Such a strong face—handsome, compassionate, intelligent; the kind of face a woman dreamed of seeing when she woke up every morning. But would this be the only morning Ivy ever fulfilled that dream?

That was a question for which she had no answer. When Alex awoke, would he acknowledge how right they were for each other, or would the very perfection of what they'd shared frighten him away?

The thought of losing what she had held so briefly terrified Ivy, but she refused to dwell on it, refused to allow it to spoil the most perfect morning of her life. There was no way she was going to lose Alex, she swore. There was nowhere he could run from her that she wouldn't find him. They belonged to each other now, and whatever it took, she would make him see that. Deep in the night, while their bodies had still been joined together, Alex had cried out that he loved her. She would never forget that exquisite moment, and she wouldn't let Alex forget or deny it, either.

In the midst of all her ferociously determined musings about Alex and the future, Ivy's stomach rumbled with hunger, and she smothered a laugh to keep from waking him. Nature had a way of putting things in their proper perspective—if one took care of the basics first, everything else would eventually fall into place.

Starving, she inched to the edge of the bed and wondered if Alex had any food in his kitchen.

THE SMELL of freshly brewed coffee invaded Alex's sleep, but it took several minutes for the aroma to bring him fully awake. With that wakefulness came the memory of the night before, and a dozen conflicting emotions converged on him. He felt wonderful, alive…free. He felt as though last night he'd touched something sacred, something he should hold on to and never let go.

But he also felt fear—gut-wrenching fear that came from an instinctive need for self-preservation. Somewhere inside his head, a voice was shouting, *Be careful, Alex. Don't want too much, don't need too much. This is an illusion. Nothing can be as perfect as what you're feeling now.*

Prodded by that fear, Alex rose quickly and donned the terry-cloth bathrobe that hung on the inside of the door to the master bathroom. He splashed cold water on his face, then returned to the bedroom. On his way, he noted that the clothes he and Ivy had left strewn on the floor last night had been picked up and left neatly folded on the bureau. A half-slip and Ivy's sundress were nestled cozily beside his pants and shirt.

For some reason, the sight of his well-tended clothes irritated him, just as the strengthening aroma of coffee did. He hurried toward the kitchen and stopped at the door when he found exactly what he'd expected to find.

There was Ivy, cute as a bug's ear, rummaging through the refrigerator. She was wearing a T-shirt of his that skimmed her thighs provocatively. Just the sight of the long expanse of leg she displayed was enough to send a jolt of desire coursing through Alex. He felt his manhood begin to stiffen, and his inability to control his own body only increased his irrational annoyance with the woman who had given him so much pleasure the night before.

Frowning at the virtually barren refrigerator, Ivy extracted Alex's last three eggs from their lonely slots in the door. Balancing them in one hand, she checked the meat keeper and found a moldy wedge of cheddar cheese and a package of bacon in a plastic storage bag. She picked up both, thinking that she might be able to salvage enough of the cheese to make an omelet. Then she turned and saw Alex. He looked impossibly sexy with his tousled hair and half-open bathrobe, which exposed an expanse of chest that did wonderful things to her insides.

"Good morning, sleepyhead. The coffee's ready." She inclined her head toward the coffeepot on the counter between them. "I put out a cup for you there, next to mine."

"Thanks," he said, trying not to grit his teeth. *Her* cup, *her* coffee, *her* kitchen, *her* sexy-as-all-get-out jersey that had once been his. What was she going to lay claim to next?

Ivy moved to the counter by the stove. "I'm not sure if a meal can be salvaged out of this stuff or not. Old Mother Hubbard could take lessons from you." She placed the other items on the counter, opened the plastic bag and sniffed. "Whew! This must be the same Bacon who wrote when Shakespeare did!"

Quickly, she resealed the bag and dropped it into the trash can under the sink.

"I see you've figured out where everything is," Alex said tersely.

The harshness of his tone made Ivy's blood turn cold. She knew from having seen Alex after a night on his office sofa that he wasn't a morning person, but his bad mood today went deeper than waking up on the wrong side of the bed. As she'd feared, Alex had allowed her to get close to him last night and that intimacy was forcing him to push her away this morning. The only problem was, she wasn't going to let herself be pushed.

"Yes," she said brightly as she began trimming the mold off the cheese. "Your pantry is bare, but everything else is well organized. I think I can manage to scrape up an omelet, if you're game."

Alex leaned against the counter, sipped his coffee and tried to conquer his irritation and his desire. He failed on both counts. "Look, Ivy, this little domestic scene is nice, but..."

When his voice trailed off, Ivy stopped what she was doing and looked at him. "But what?"

She was absolutely gorgeous standing there with defiance etched on her freshly scrubbed face. He wanted her just as much as he'd wanted her yesterday... and the day before and the day before that. In all likelihood, he would want her tomorrow and all the days after that for the rest of his life. So why couldn't he stop fighting what he felt and accept the love he knew Ivy would be only too happy to give him?

Because there was so little he could give her in return, he realized. "I just think it's a little too soon to be setting up housekeeping, that's all," he answered finally.

Ivy arched one eyebrow and reined in her temper. "I'm fixing breakfast, Alex, not catering our wedding reception."

"Are you sure?"

Despite her determination not to be daunted by his remoteness, Ivy felt tears welling in her eyes. Didn't he realize that they could be laughing and kissing and snuggling this morning, if only he'd get past his fear of intimacy? Unwilling to embarrass herself, she bit back the tears and let anger take the place of the hurt.

"Damn it, Alex," she said, advancing on him menacingly. "If you tell me that last night was a mistake, I swear to God I'll hang you up by your thumbs, drive a stake through your heart and spread honey all over your body to draw fire ants!"

She swept past him into the living room so quickly that she didn't see his scowl evolve into silent laughter. In that moment, Alex realized that he didn't have a chance of keeping his heart shielded. He could fight Ivy's irrepressible wit, insight and intelligence, he could even fight her beauty and breezy, unaffected sexuality, but he could never win.

"Ivy, wait! Come back here." He took off after her, and despite her head start, he managed to catch her in the family room before she reached the hall. He captured her arm and swung her gently toward him, but she refused to look at him. "I'm sorry. Please don't be upset."

"Upset?" That brought her head up. "I'm not upset, I'm mad. Damned mad. Alex, sexwise last night was the best thing that ever happened to me. On a scale of one to ten, I give you a nine and a half—you lost a half a point because you had a little trouble with the zipper of my dress. Other than that, it was perfect. And on an emotional scale, it was pretty high up there, too. But that's the whole problem, isn't it?" she asked heatedly. "You just don't want to admit how good it was to feel like you're a part of someone, like you belong...like you could *always* belong if only you'd let yourself. Well, *I* felt it, Alex, and I can admit it. And I'm not going to stand here and let you tell me it was a mistake."

She jerked her arm, but Alex refused to let go. "I never said it was a mistake, Ivy," he murmured, gentling her with his voice. "You're right. Nothing that good could ever be a mistake." His hand on her arm became a caress as he pulled her close.

"Then why are we fighting?"

"Because I'm an idiot. And because...I don't really know where what happened last night leaves us."

Ivy saw the doubt that still shadowed Alex's eyes, but she had penetrated his fear, and that was good. Little by little, she would chip away at it until it was gone completely. "Do you have to go into the station today?" she asked, snuggling against him seductively.

Alex swallowed hard as his body responded predictably to the feel of her. "No."

"Then I'd say that leaves us the whole day to make love." She brought her lips close to his, and Alex accepted the invitation greedily. His mouth closed over hers, and their tongues mated in a dance that had become familiar but far from boring. Ivy made a little sound of pleasure as she

strained to get closer to him, and Alex slid his hands down
her until he reached the bare flesh below the tail of the T-
shirt. He splayed his fingers against her thighs, then slowly,
with sensuous precision, his hands moved up and he brought
the shirt with him as he lovingly caressed her hips, waist and
breasts. With her help, he removed the shirt altogether,
baring all of her to his sight and touch.

Breathing hard, Ivy captured Alex's heated gaze and
loosened the belt of his robe. A single shrug sent it to the
floor, and then there was nothing between them but heat
and hunger. Still bound to him by the force of his gaze, Ivy
ran her hands lightly up his torso, weaving her fingers sensuously through the dark hair that curled on his chest.
Alex's hands were roving, too, lightly skimming her waist,
gently brushing her breasts, teasing her with feathery
touches that made her weak with need.

Her eyes fluttered closed as she concentrated on the sen-
sations, and she grasped Alex's shoulders when he filled his
hands with her breasts and trailed moist, nuzzling kisses
down her throat. She moved her hips sensuously, savoring
the heat and hardness of him, and this time it was Alex who
moaned with pleasure. He wrapped one arm tightly around
her, supporting her weight as they dropped slowly to the
floor.

He covered her body with his, one leg resting between her
thighs. Ivy gave a low, sensuous laugh. "Here?" she asked.

Alex looked at her and discovered that her azure eyes had
turned to deep pools of sapphire. "Right here," he answered, grinning wickedly. His lips sought her throat again,
then moved lower, nuzzling her sensuously. "I thought you
were the adventurous type."

Her seductive chuckle turned into a gasp of delight when
his lips closed over the crest of one breast and his tongue
brought it to crystalline hardness. "Adventurous," she
managed to say between gasps of pleasure, "is making

love...on a beach...in the surf...in shark-infested waters. This isn't adventurous, it's just...decadent."

"We'll brave the sharks some other time," Alex replied shakily as his lips sought hers. "For now, we'll just have to settled for decadent." He kissed her deeply as his hands touched her everywhere. Ivy reciprocated, smoothing her hands over his heated flesh, kneading the tightly bunched muscles of his back and chest.

She lost all track of time as the pleasure escalated. The ache was becoming unbearable, and she arched against Alex, moving her hips in a sensuous rhythm that sent them both spiraling to a new plane of heightened desire. He touched her intimately, his fingers tangled in the silken curls between her thighs, and Ivy forgot how to breathe. He stroked her, caressed her and taunted her, bringing her to the edge of a shuddering abyss, then withdrawing until the wave of pleasure passed and there was a new, higher wave to be surmounted.

Almost frantic with the need to be joined with Alex completely, Ivy ran one hand down his flank, thinking only of giving him the same kind of joy he was giving her. But Alex had other plans. Without warning, Ivy found her wrists pinned lightly but firmly above her head, caught in Alex's unbreakable grip.

She writhed in frustration, but Alex only used that movement to heighten her pleasure. He struggled with his own waning control, held his own desires in check and caressed Ivy deeply, intimately, until she cried out his name again and again as ripples of exquisite sensation coursed through her.

And then he released her hands and pulled away slightly, watching her, reveling in her beauty as she slowly came down from the high place he had driven her to.

Barely able to breathe, Ivy opened her eyes and saw the self-satisfied look in Alex's smoky eyes. "Damn you," she whispered. Laughing wickedly, she fought the languor of her body and arched her back, raising her torso to his so that the tips of her breasts brushed his chest lightly. He slid one arm around her, and she used that moment to shift the tide of their lovemaking. Drawing one knee up, she gave a gentle push, and suddenly Alex was no longer above her.

Straddling his chest, she sat up and captured his startled, delighted gaze. "Now it's your turn," she murmured.

Smiling, Alex brought his wrists together and offered them to her. "I surrender."

Ivy wove her fingers through his and shifted her body lower. "We'll just see about that," she said menacingly, but her eyes were laughing with anticipation. She bent and kissed him, taking the initiative, and their laughter ceased. The fires that had never truly been banked flared again, and this time it was Alex who gasped with pleasure as Ivy's lips traveled over his body. She aroused him as torturously as he had aroused her, and when she finally ended the torture, sheathing him in her body, Alex was lost.

She played him like a fine violin, bringing him to the brink of release, then retreating, then coaxing him to the brink again and again, until they were both too near the edge to play the game any longer. They touched, they cried out, and they scorched each other with their heat. They found in each other the parts of their souls that had been missing. Alex poured himself into Ivy, and when the last shudder of pleasure ended, Ivy collapsed on top of him and reveled in the way his arms were wrapped around her—as though he'd never let her go.

CHAPTER SEVENTEEN

ALEX'S SMALL OFFICE was overflowing with cops and anticipation. Jordan Brubaker sat in one of the chairs in front of Alex's desk, Mort Adamson was crowded onto the sofa with two other senior detectives, two more were perched on the cluttered table to the right of the desk, the head of the forensics team was leaning against the opposite wall, and Ivy was sitting on the windowsill behind Alex's right shoulder. Only the second chair in front of his desk was vacant, and that was waiting to be occupied by Len Eversall.

The Strangler case was about to break. Alex and Ivy were the only ones in the room who knew all the particulars, but everyone else seemed to sense that something had finally fallen into place. They were here so that Alex could tell them what it was.

"What's going on? Why did you send for me, Alex?" Len Eversall asked as he rushed into the crowded room. "Has something happened?"

"Sorry to take you away from your lunch, Commissioner," Alex said without a hint of apology. "If you'll shut the door and have a seat, we'll get started. There's a very good possibility that we've discovered the identity of the Strangler."

Murmurs of excitement rippled through the room as Len sat on the edge of the vacant chair. "Who is he? What kind of evidence have you got?"

Alex shook his head. "Unfortunately, it's all circumstantial at this point, but Ivy and I have spent the past two and a half days checking him out, and what we've come up with looks pretty incriminating.''

"Who is he?" Mort asked.

"His name is Benjamin Drummond," Ivy answered, barely able to contain her excitement. She had spent a magnificent, idyllic Sunday with Alex and had returned home that night too happy to simply crawl into bed and go to sleep despite the late hour. Her mind had been filled with all the possibilities of a future with Alex, but speculation was pointless. They had agreed to take their relationship one day at a time, and Ivy meant to stick by that agreement.

Needing something to occupy her thoughts then, she had turned on her home computer, patched it into the department network and started investigating Benjamin Drummond. What she had discovered that night had resulted in the chain of events that had led to this meeting—and perhaps the solution of the case.

"He's a reclusive, thirty-four-year-old game inventor who lives on the north end of Riverside Drive," she continued. "He bought the house two years ago when he moved to Brauxton."

"Where did he live before that?" Jordy asked, trying not to be furious because Ivy had answers while he had only questions.

"New York."

"So what's the circumstantial evidence?" Len asked.

Alex tossed him a sheaf of computer printouts. "For starters, Drummond invented the game Pentathlon. That alone makes him a likely suspect. But it gets better. Not only is he a subscriber to *Perplexities*, but until several years ago he was also a frequent contributor of games and articles. He's extremely intelligent, he has a rather... controversial background, and—here's the kicker—his name went into the computer just yesterday as one of the people who had recently purchased the type of software program used for the call that reported Colette Romalanski's death."

Mort whistled softly. "You're right. We've got a suspect."

"What did you mean when you said he had a controversial background?" one of the other detectives asked.

Alex glanced over his shoulder at Ivy, and she took that as her cue. "I spent most of yesterday afternoon on the phone to New York, trying to find someone willing to talk about Drummond. I finally found an editor at *Games* magazine who was a veritable fountain of information. It seems that Mr. Drummond was the black sheep of a very wealthy family. The family business, run by his mother, Claudia Drummond, is one of the largest manufacturers of toys and games in the world."

"They manufactured Pentathlon?" Eversall asked, making the logical assumption, but Ivy shook her head adamantly.

"Definitely not. About fifteen years ago, Drummond severed all ties with the business and his family. According to my source in New York, the parting was a bitter one. Apparently, Benjamin didn't like the way his iron-fisted mother was trying to control his life. With the help of a small inheritance from his paternal grandmother, he started his own company and was actually making a success of it until his mother intervened. My source said it's common knowledge that Claudia deliberately sabotaged her son's company. By the time she got through with him, Drummond was bankrupt."

"Why did she do it?" Eversall asked.

Ivy shrugged. "My source wasn't sure, but she speculated that Claudia thought that if she proved to him that he couldn't make it on his own, he'd come back into the family fold like a good little boy."

"But he didn't."

"No, he just went free-lance, inventing games and selling them to anyone but his mother. He was only moderately successful at it until he came up with the idea for Pentathlon. That one game made him rich."

"So that's all you've got?" Jordy asked. "A game freak who hates his mother?"

Alex caught the sharp tone of voice and sent him a quelling glance. "Sounds like something straight out of the Strangler profile to me, doesn't it to you?"

"Yeah, I guess it does," he admitted reluctantly.

"But that's not all," Ivy said. "I don't have too many details yet, but about three years ago, just as Pentathlon became such a big success, Drummond was slapped with a lawsuit. A woman named Joanna Hughes, allegedly Drummond's former lover, claimed that he had stolen the idea for Pentathlon from her. Drummond filed a countersuit, charging Ms Hughes with harassment. Both cases were eventually dropped."

"He settled out of court?" Eversall asked.

"No one seems to know," Ivy answered. "The scandal dragged on for nearly a year, with some pretty ugly charges being leveled on both sides, then suddenly it died down. One day it was the talk of the industry, the next day, Drummond *and* Joanna Hughes had both disappeared."

"Don't tell me, let me guess," Mort said as he slid to the edge of the sofa. "Joanna Hughes is a blue-eyed blonde, of average height and weight, approximately thirty years old."

"Bingo," Alex said with a congratulatory nod.

"Damn," Eversall said softly. "It's him. Drummond is the Strangler. But we haven't got one single piece of evidence that would hold up in a court of law."

"No," Alex said in agreement, "but we've got enough to warrant questioning him. That's why I wanted all of you here. Commissioner, I need you to get hold of a judge who will give us a blanket search warrant—we need something that's stated in very broad terms but will hold up in court later." He looked at the forensics expert. "Daugherty, you get your team ready for the search. Jordy, I want you, Mort, Cleese and Gilliam to go with Ivy and me to Drummond's house."

"Why not have a black-and-white pick him up?" Brubaker asked.

"Because I want to question him in his own surroundings, first."

"Beard the lion in his lair?" Len asked.

"Exactly." He glanced at the remaining two detectives, who had not received orders. "I want you guys to start working on surveillance. If the search of Drummond's house doesn't give us the proof we need to nail him, the task force is going on a round-the-clock stakeout. You two start scheduling the shifts." They both nodded their assent, and Alex stood. "Do you have anything to add, Commissioner?"

Eversall cleared his throat and rose, looking around the room as he did so. "Only the obvious. Today is Wednesday, the thirty-first of July. If there's going to be another killing this month, it has to be tonight. If Drummond is the Strangler, we've got a chance to save a woman's life. Let's not blow it."

A murmur of agreement washed through the room.

"ARE YOU NERVOUS about confronting Drummond?" Alex asked as he checked the traffic, then merged onto the parkway. Behind him, in an identical unmarked car, Jordan Brubaker navigated the same maneuver. Daugherty's team was following Brubaker.

"Yes," Ivy admitted, pleased that Mort and the others were riding with Jordy instead of with Alex. Being alone with him allowed her to talk freely. "I'm also excited and a little bit scared."

Alex glanced at her quickly, then turned his attention back to the heavy flow of traffic. "Scared? About meeting him face-to-face?"

Ivy shook her head. "No, not that. If Drummond is the Strangler, there's no predicting how he'll react to our interrogation, but we've got plenty of backup. I'm not frightened for my own safety, I'm just scared that we won't be able to prove he's the Strangler."

"If he's the one, we'll prove it, all right," Alex said adamantly. "But as for the interrogation..."

His voice trailed off, and Ivy looked at him curiously. "What?"

Alex took a deep breath, knowing Ivy wasn't going to like what he had to say. "When we get to the house, I'm going to have Cleese and Gilliam cover any back exits in case Drummond tries to run, and I'm taking Jordy in with me. You and Mort will cover the front."

As predicted, Ivy did not take the news well. "Why?" she demanded. "We've been like partners on this case ever since you took over the task force, Alex. Why are you shutting me out now?"

Alex stiffened his jaw and refused to look at her. "You said it yourself. There's no predicting how Drummond will react when we show up on his doorstep. I'm not anticipating violence, but if something happens—"

"You want a big, strong, manly man there to back you up instead of a poor, defenseless, helpless female! Right?" she said hotly.

"I'm not worried about backup, Ivy, but this could be dangerous!"

"Damn it, Alex, I'm a cop! Risk is part of my job, and I don't think I care for your insinuation that I'm not capable of handling anything more dangerous than a computer console!"

"That's not what I'm saying, and you know it!"

"Then why don't you want me in that house? Because I'm a woman? Or because I'm your lover?" she demanded.

The tension level in the car was dangerously high, and Alex paused for a moment, collecting his thoughts and letting some of the tension dissipate. When he finally spoke, his voice was soft. "I don't want you confronting Drummond because when I think of something happening to you, I can't even breathe. I won't put your life at risk."

The last of Ivy's anger drained away. His attitude was infuriatingly sexist and would have to be dealt with if they were ever to have a future, but it touched her that he cared so much. "Watch it, Alex," she said, smiling gently. "If you're not careful, you're going to admit that you love me."

He fought to keep from smiling. "Ivy...I thought we agreed to take this relationship slowly—that you weren't going to push."

"I wasn't pushing, I was just commenting," she said innocently.

"In my book, 'pushing' and 'commenting' are synonymous."

"Then we've got to get you a new book."

He did smile then as he reached out and took her hand. "I don't want you to get hurt, Ivy."

"You can't protect me from life or my job, Alex. I'm a good cop, not just in the office, but in the field, too. Are you as worried about Brubaker's safety if he goes into the house?"

"No." He hated to admit it, but it was true. When he thought of Brubaker confronting the man Alex was convinced was the Strangler, his insides didn't clench up as they did when he thought of Ivy in the same situation. "But Jordy isn't a blue-eyed blonde who fits the victim profile," he reminded her.

"No, he's not," she agreed. "But if that's your reason for not letting me confront Drummond, you should have taken me off the Strangler case the night I walked into your office. Since I started working closely with you, my name and photograph have been in the paper several times. As far as I'm concerned, that's far more life threatening than entering Drummond's house with you at my side and four cops on the lawn outside."

Alex thought back to his first press conference, which he had insisted Ivy attend so that she could get the credit she deserved for having ferreted out the clue about Erin Selway's dog. At the time, he hadn't considered that he would be putting her in danger by bringing her to the Strangler's attention. Now, he realized what a mistake it had been. Ivy was right; he should have taken her off the case the moment he realized she fit the victim profile.

But if he'd done that, he never would have come to know her. He wouldn't be feeling a contentment he hadn't known in years, if ever. He wouldn't be on the brink of admitting that he was hopelessly in love. And more than likely, he wouldn't be a hairbreadth away from solving this horrendous case.

No, whatever risks Ivy had taken thus far, she had taken because she was a dedicated cop and a shrewd detective. She could handle whatever happened. It wasn't fair of him to try to exclude her now that they were closing in for the kill.

"You're right, Ivy. I'm sorry," he said, squeezing her hand. "I have no right to punish you because of my irrational fear. And besides, at this point you and I know more about the case than anyone else. I need you."

She cast him a provocative sidelong glance. "To help interrogate Drummond."

He returned the look and felt a tightening in his gut that had nothing to do with fear. "For that . . . and for other things."

Ivy's smile spread slowly, magnificently. "Hold on to that thought until later tonight, Lieutenant," she purred seductively. "But in the meantime, you'd better change lanes or you'll miss the Riverside exit."

DRUMMOND'S THREE-STORY HOUSE on Riverside Drive was something right out of a Charles Addams cartoon. Built at the turn of the century, it represented both the best and the worst of Victorian architecture. Lacy, wrought-iron spires adorned the mansard roof, dormers and the two square turrets that rose dramatically from each end of the house. The lawn was shaded by a grove of trees that was older than the house, and an enormous, well-tended hedge designed to assure the owner's privacy ran around the perimeter of the property.

"If Lurch or Uncle Fester answers the door, I'm going to change my mind about going in there," Ivy whispered as she and Alex mounted the steps to the porch.

"How could anyone who sleeps with gargoyles be intimidated by this house?"

Ivy chuckled and looked over her shoulder at Adamson and Brubaker, who were waiting just inside the ornate wrought-iron gate at the end of the sidewalk. The forensics team was piling equipment out of their van, waiting for the go-ahead from Alex, and Gilliam and Cleese had just disappeared around the side of the house. If the reclusive Benjamin Drummond was home, the stage was set for an interesting confrontation.

Alex knocked. They waited a respectable amount of time, and when there was no response, he knocked again. Almost immediately, a very solemn-faced, prim, proper and starched middle-aged woman answered the door. "May I help you?"

Alex and Ivy presented their badges to the woman, whose accent sounded British. "I'm Lieutenant Devane with the Brauxton Police Department, and this is Detective Kincaid. We're here to speak with Benjamin Drummond."

"Have you an appointment?" the woman asked placidly.

"No, ma'am, but we do have a search warrant," Alex informed her, producing the document from his jacket. "Would you please let Mr. Drummond know we're here?"

For the first time, her calm demeanor slipped. "Well...I don't know... Mr. Drummond doesn't like to be disturbed. He takes his privacy quite seriously. Perhaps if you'd call for an appointment..."

Alex fixed her with a stern gaze. "Ms...?"

"*Mrs.* Weaverly," she supplied stiffly.

"Mrs. Weaverly, I have a court order that gives me the right to enter and search this property with or without Mr. Drummond's permission. It also gives me the right to take him into custody for questioning regarding a number of bizarre murders. One way or another, I *am* going to see him. I'd appreciate it deeply if you'd make this easy on all of us and just go tell him we're here."

"Certainly." Looking quite uncomfortable, Mrs. Weaverly stepped back and allowed them to move into the darkly paneled foyer. "If you'll wait here, I'll inform Mr. Drummond of your arrival."

"Thank you," Alex said, but the housekeeper—if that was what she was—was already moving briskly down a long corridor. She turned a corner and disappeared from view.

"Did you get the impression that she was more worried about incurring her boss's wrath than she was with the fact that we're police officers?" Ivy asked.

"Yes," Alex answered, but his attention had shifted to his surroundings. The foyer featured a magnificent curving staircase in the center and sliding double doors that led to rooms on both sides of the entryway. The doors to the left were firmly closed, but on the right Alex could see into a parlor that was furnished with costly Victorian antiques. He and Ivy moved to the doorway and studied the interior. "It's almost like stepping back in time a hundred years."

"I have a peculiar fondness for anything with an intriguing history."

The words were spoken softly, but the deep, resonant voice made them sound like thunder in the open room. Alex and Ivy turned quickly and found the speaker across the foyer by the door that had been closed only a moment before. How he had managed to slide the panels back without either of them hearing him was a mystery.

They looked at him for a moment, startled by his sudden appearance—his housekeeper had walked down the long corridor to look for him. And he looked at them, surveying the interlopers as a feudal lord might have regarded his vassals. Tall and lean, with coal-black hair and startling large, dark eyes, he was without a doubt the most classically handsome man Ivy had ever seen. Every feature was perfect, but his magnificent eyes were also incredibly cold and lifeless. When he looked at her, Ivy felt the sting of that coldness and a chill ran down her spine.

"I'm Benjamin Drummond," their host announced regally. "I understand you wanted to see me."

CHAPTER EIGHTEEN

"WE APOLOGIZE for the intrusion, Mr. Drummond," Alex said, crossing the wide entry hall. Ivy accompanied him, forcing back an instinctive surge of fear. Under normal circumstances, she would have been able to detach herself from her own emotions, but the effect Drummond had on her was anything but normal. She hadn't anticipated the panic she would feel knowing she was in the presence of the man who had in all likelihood killed seven women—the man who had haunted her nightmares for months...the man she was convinced would eventually try to kill her unless he was brought to justice.

Summoning all her professionalism, she pushed those thoughts aside, reminding herself that Drummond was innocent until proven guilty. Norme Canyon had been a suspect and she hadn't reacted this way to him. But then, good old Norme hadn't had eyes that were as cold as death.

"This is Detective Kincaid and I'm Lieutenant Devane," Alex said, presenting his badge. Ivy did the same and prayed that neither Alex nor Drummond would notice that her hands were trembling. "We're with—"

"I recognize you both from the newspapers, Lieutenant. You're with the Brauxton Strangler task force." He said it as though the words left a bad taste in his mouth. "That is such an unimaginative appellation. But of course, that's not your fault, is it? The name was already in use before you took over the investigation."

"Have you been following the case closely?" Alex asked, but he was remembering the letter the Strangler had written, protesting the use of the "unimaginative" moniker.

"It's unavoidable," Drummond answered with a dismissive wave of his hand. *Very strong-looking hands,* Ivy noted. "My housekeeper mentioned something about a search warrant, Lieutenant. Perhaps we should get on with whatever business you think you have with me."

"Certainly. Detective Kincaid and I have some questions we'd like you to answer."

"Other than what I read in the papers, I know nothing about your case."

Alex smiled pleasantly, but it was all for show. "All the same, we'd like to ask the questions."

"As you wish." Drummond turned and closed the doors to the room behind him, then gestured toward the parlor across the foyer. "I think we'll be more comfortable in here." He led the way toward the Victorian parlor, with Alex at his side. Ivy followed, but she was far more interested in the room Drummond hadn't wanted them to see. From the small bit of it that had been visible to her, she guessed that it was the workroom where he invented his games.

In the parlor, Drummond motioned his guests toward the sofa, then took one of the matching chairs opposite it. "Since this isn't a social call, I'm sure you'll forgive me for not offering you something to drink. Now, how may I be of help to the task force?"

"You could begin by telling us your whereabouts on the nights of the seven murders," Alex said.

Drummond's expression betrayed nothing. It was impossible to tell what he was thinking. That, more than anything, worried Alex. "Why would my whereabouts be of interest to you, Lieutenant?"

"Because it's come to our attention that—among other things—you invented the game Pentathlon. If you've been following the case, you know that the Strangler's calling card is a game piece that he leaves beside each of his victims. Pentathlon was one of those games."

Again, Drummond gave no indication of what he was thinking. "And you find that significant? Lieutenant, Pentathlon is a popular game. Polls of game players have placed it in the top ten for the past two years."

"You're referring to the *Perplexities* readers' poll, aren't you?" Ivy asked "This year it was in fifth place and last year it was in sixth."

This time, he did react with mild surprise. "Apparently you have a head full of trivia, Detective Kincaid."

"I have a head full of facts that concern this case."

"And you think the relative popularity of Pentathlon is important to the case? I find that hard to believe."

"Believe it," Alex said. "Now perhaps we could get back to the original question. Where were you on the nights of January 17, February 25—"

"Lieutenant, you can't be serious," Drummond said, interrupting him. "Do you honestly expect me to remember what I was doing on a specific night almost seven months ago—or last month, for that matter? That's ludicrous."

"I agree," Alex replied. "But if you can provide an airtight alibi for even one of the nights, Detective Kincaid and I can leave you in peace and get on to other things."

Drummond shook his head. "I find this whole conversation insulting. You are accusing me of being the Brauxton Strangler."

"No accusations have been made," Alex said.

"You're in my home asking me to provide an alibi," Drummond said, his irritation becoming obvious. "That in itself is indicative of your suspicions. And since you brought a search warrant with you, it's obvious that you feel your suspicions are well-founded. I am being accused of murder solely because a game I invented is connected with one of the crimes.''

"That may not be the only reason for our suspicions, Mr. Drummond,'' Alex told him quietly. "Did you recently purchase a computer software program called Intelli-Voice?''

"Yes.''

"May I ask why?''

Drummond sighed. "I invent games—not just board games, but computer games, as well. I purchased Intelli-Voice in the hope that it might work in conjunction with a mystery program I've been designing. What could that have to do with the Strangler case?''

Alex ignored the question. "You also subscribe to the magazine *Perplexities*, don't you?''

"Yes.''

"And you have also been a contributor to that periodical, haven't you?''

"Yes, but—''

"Do you know a woman by the name of Joanna Hughes?''

Drummond froze. All motion ceased, even his breathing, and the look that came over his face was positively lethal. He struggled for control of an obviously violent emotion, and when he finally did move, standing abruptly, Ivy had to make a conscious effort not to shrink from his controlled fury.

"I don't know how Joanna Hughes fits into your case, Lieutenant, but this conversation is over. I will not discuss that woman with you or anyone else. If you have anything further to say to me, you can say it to my lawyer.''

Alex rose placidly. "You do have the right to have an attorney present, but this conversation is far from over, Drummond. One way or another, you're going to answer my questions.''

They stared at each other for a long moment, and the energy that radiated between them became as tangible as a fourth person in the room. When it became clear that the problem was not going to go away, Drummond somehow regained control of his anger. "I believe I would be wise to call my lawyer," he said coolly.

"Tell him to meet you at the station downtown," Alex advised. "We'll finish our questioning there."

Clearly, Drummond wasn't happy with that, but he answered with a terse nod of agreement. "Very well. If you'll excuse me, the phone is in my study." He started toward the door and Alex fell into step beside him.

"If you don't mind, I'll just tag along."

Drummond stopped, looking at him in apparent disbelief. "Surely you don't think that I'm going to try to…'make a run for it,'" he said sarcastically.

Alex grinned at him. "Of course not. And you wouldn't get very far if you did, since I have men stationed at the front and back of the house."

"Then obviously I couldn't possibly escape."

"No, but I'd like to stay with you, just the same. I've never seen the inside of an inventor's office, and I'm always looking for new experiences."

Drummond struggled to keep his temper on a leash. "My office is private, Lieutenant. No one goes in there. It may sound foolish to you, but I have been the victim of industrial espionage before. I have no intention of allowing any of my current projects to be pirated."

Alex raised his right hand. "I swear, I won't tell a soul." He lowered his hand, smoothly inserting it into his jacket pocket and removing the warrant he'd waved at Mrs. Weaverly. "And when my men search your office, I'll see to it that they don't tell anyone, either," he said with a smile as he handed the warrant to Drummond.

"All right, Lieutenant," he said grudgingly. "Come right this way. You can listen while I discuss this—" he fanned the air with the paper "—with my lawyer."

Drummond stalked out, and Alex turned to Ivy. "Wait here," he instructed her, then followed his suspect into the study.

Far from being displeased by Alex's directive, Ivy was only too happy to remain behind. While Drummond had been present, her attention had been focused totally on him; now she had a chance to inspect his intriguing parlor without distraction.

The antiques were superb—not a reproduction in the bunch, she decided. She wasn't an expert on the subject, but she knew enough to place every piece in the late 1800s. Even the wall decorations were authentic to the period. Dozens of tiny, gilt-framed pictures cluttered every space. Larger paintings and photographs were contained within ornate frames that were hung on long velvet ropes.

Though the frames were a century old, some of the pictures were not, Ivy noted with interest. Circling the room slowly, she studied the black-and-white photos. Most were landscapes depicting places she didn't recognize. The photography, however, was stunning, and she wondered if Drummond was an amateur photographer. There were a few pictures of people she didn't recognize, and pictures of Drummond receiving awards. One remarkable shot showed Drummond in full riding regalia holding a trophy. Next to him was a magnificent black horse. Apparently he was an equestrian, too.

Obviously Benjamin Drummond was a man with many interests—games, photography, horses, murder. The thought sent another chill down Ivy's spine. Shrugging it off, she continued her inspection and finally came across a picture that made the whole effort worthwhile. Again, it was a photograph of Drummond, but this time he was with another man—a man Ivy recognized. Leonin Brasiliovich, the Russian chess master, was grinning mischievously as he clapped a smiling Drummond on the shoulder.

Drummond's devilishly sexy smile was enough to make the picture remarkable, but what set Ivy's heart racing was the object in the foreground. The men were seated behind a table, and in front of them was a magnificent, Oriental-style chess set. Ivy leaned forward for a closer look and would have staked her life that the queen was the same one that had been left beside Darlena West's body.

The muted sound of Alex's voice told her that he and Drummond were returning, and she straightened.

"Ivy, would you invite the forensics team in, please?" Alex asked as he entered. Obviously, Drummond's lawyer had told his client there was no way to circumvent a search warrant.

"Of course," she answered, but she made no attempt to follow through on his request. "I was just admiring these wonderful pictures. Are you a photographer, Mr. Drummond?"

"Amateur at best," he answered stiffly.

"And I take it you're a chess player, as well. Quite a good one, I imagine."

"I've done fairly well in competition," he said reluctantly, clearly uncomfortable with Ivy's line of questioning. Alex, on the other hand, was fascinated. He couldn't imagine where Ivy was leading, but he knew she wasn't just making small talk.

"Did you take lessons from Leonin Brasiliovich?"

Drummond frowned. "Leo and I play chess by correspondence, Detective Kincaid. If it's absolutely necessary, I have the letters to prove it. Though frankly, I don't see what business it is of yours. Surely the fact that I play chess doesn't incriminate me in these murders."

Ivy shrugged. "It all depends on what kind of board you play on." She gestured toward the photograph. "This one, for example. It's quite beautiful. Is it yours?"

Drummond's expression was unreadable as he glanced at the photo. Even from across the room, he knew which picture she was referring to. "That set was a family heirloom, passed down to me from my grandfather."

"Would it be possible for me to see it?" Ivy asked. She glanced at Alex, who was crossing the room toward her, and saw that he had figured out the importance of her questions.

"I'm afraid not," Drummond answered coldly. "As it so happens, that set was stolen last year around Christmas. I reported the theft to the police, but it was never found."

Alex looked at the picture, then at Ivy, then at Drummond. "That may not be true. As a matter of fact, we have found one piece of your set. The queen in this photo bears a remarkable resemblance to the one left beside the body of the Strangler's third victim."

For the first time, Drummond seemed visibly shaken. Not angry, as he'd been at the mention of Joanna Hughes, but completely unnerved, as though he suddenly realized how desperate his situation really was. Ivy watched his reaction and decided that Drummond was either innocent or a first-rate actor. Her money was on his acting ability.

"If that's true," he said softly, "it would appear that someone is trying to frame me for murder."

"You've been inventing too many mystery games, Drummond," Alex said as he approached him. "Innocent people only get framed in bad detective novels."

"Does that mean you're arresting me?"

"I'm taking you in for more questioning. Once that's completed and we've searched the house, the district attorney will decide whether or not you should be placed under arrest."

"You have nothing but circumstantial evidence," Drummond reminded him.

"For the moment, that may be true, but if you killed those women, I'm going to prove it."

Drummond's gaze turned cold again, and he stepped toward a bellpull on the wall. A chime sounded at the back of the house, and the housekeeper appeared a moment later. "Mrs. Weaverly, I will be leaving shortly, but the police will remain behind to search. I would appreciate it if you would stay with them and make certain that their methods are not...excessive." He returned to Alex. "Shall we go, Lieutenant? My attorney is waiting for us at the station."

Alex nodded and looked at Ivy. "I'm taking Brubaker with me. You stay here. I want you to coordinate the search and interrogate Mrs. Weaverly."

Ivy nodded her assent. It was doubtful that Drummond would confess, and his attorney wasn't going to allow him to say anything even remotely incriminating. The best hope they had of proving he was guilty was to find the proof here in this house, and Ivy was flattered that Alex trusted her with that monumentally important job. "I'll meet you back at the station when we're finished."

She followed Alex and Drummond to the door, called for the forensics team and started the laborious search.

IT WAS TOO DARK.

Not a single ray of moonlight streamed in. Not a single street lamp shone its beacon through the windows. She reached for the light switch by the door, but nothing happened. She fumbled her way through the darkness to the lamp by the sofa. The switch clicked, but the darkness remained. The room was still as black as pitch.

And she wasn't alone.

The knowledge was visceral, not logical. She saw no shadows in the unshadowed darkness; she heard no sounds.

She merely knew. He was here. It was her turn. Tomorrow they would find her as they'd found all the others.

The realization that she was about to die was as stifling as the darkness. Panic coursed through her like wildfire, uncontrolled and unstoppable. She turned toward the door and willed herself to run, but her legs were suddenly lead weights that rooted her to the spot.

Then she heard him, and running was no longer an option. There was no escape. She was immobilized by fear and by the inevitability of her death. When the rope slipped around her throat and began to tighten, she screamed, but it was a hoarse, voiceless cry. No one would ever hear it. Pain seared her, and she screamed again, but this time no sound at all came out. Death encroached, and she fought it as she had never fought before, but finally death won. The darkness became absolute....

Sweating, gasping for breath, Ivy came awake abruptly. The room was dark, but not the horrible black of the dream. Light from the street lamp was diffused by the sheer curtains at her windows, but it was sufficient to cast recognizable, reassuring shadows throughout the room. Fighting back the effects of the dream, Ivy clung to the images and allowed them to bring her back to a state of reality.

The nightmares, terrifying in their stark simplicity, were getting worse.

Ivy tried to even out her breathing and realized that she was trembling. She eased to the edge of the bed and stood, moving quietly so as not to disturb Alex. His afternoon interrogating Benjamin Drummond had been every bit as frustrating as the one she'd spent searching the suspect's house. They had learned nothing that brought them closer to proving Drummond was guilty. A blowup of the chessboard photo had proved inconclusive—the queen the police found *could* have been the same one, or it could have simply been a *similar* piece.

The D.A. had insisted there wasn't enough evidence to hold Drummond, and the entire task force had watched morosely as their only suspect walked smugly away.

Maybe that was why the nightmare had seemed so real tonight, Ivy reasoned as she slipped into a diaphanous peignoir. Hugging herself tightly, she moved to the windows and looked out onto the nearly deserted street below.

Drummond is under surveillance tonight and Alex is here. No one's going to hurt you, Ivy, so get a grip, she told herself sternly. Unfortunately, that admonition didn't assuage her fears or stop the trembling. The feeling that she was still on the Strangler's hit list was as strong as ever, maybe even stronger. She was scheduled to die. No matter how often she told herself she was being irrational, the certainty wouldn't go away.

"Ivy? Is something wrong?"

The voice startled her, and her hand went to her chest as she gasped and whirled toward the bed. "Alex! I'm sorry, I didn't mean to wake you."

"It's all right. Couldn't you sleep?" he asked, sliding to the edge of the bed. He rose and padded to her, splendidly naked. Even so faintly illuminated, the sight of him did wonderful things to Ivy's insides. *It's not fair that I should be marked for death just when I have so much to live for,* she thought bleakly. The exquisite memory of the lovemaking she and Alex had shared only hours before wasn't enough to dispel the effects of the dream.

"Ivy?" Alex reached for her, and she went into his arms, holding him fiercely. "Sweetheart, what's wrong? You're trembling."

"Something woke me up, that's all," she murmured, her face nestled in the curve of his throat. The downy hair against her cheek was as comforting as his steely arms.

"What was it? Did you hear a noise in the apartment?"

"No.... It was just...a dream," she admitted reluctantly.

"You mean a nightmare, don't you?"

"Yes."

"About Drummond?"

"About the Strangler. Which is the same thing, I guess." She raised her head as a thought occurred to her. "It's odd.... I didn't see his face this time, even though I know what he looks like now."

Alex looked down at her and frowned. "'This time'? Ivy, how many nightmares about the Strangler have you had?"

She shrugged and returned her head to his chest. "I don't know. I lost count months ago."

"Ivy!" Alex took hold of her arms and held her away from him so that he could get a good look at her face. "Why didn't you tell me the case was having this effect on you? I knew you'd given quite a bit of thought to your resemblance to the victims, but I had no idea—"

"Alex, don't," she pleaded, pulling away from him entirely. "It's no big deal. I'm sorry I mentioned it."

"It is a big deal if it's doing this to you. Look at you! You're still trembling."

"Maybe that's because you're standing here with no clothes on, big guy. Did you ever think of that?" she asked with an insolent grin. She appreciated Alex's concern, but she had no intention of allowing him to coddle her. Until the case was over, she would handle her irrational fears herself.

But Alex refused to be cajoled. "Be serious," he told her sternly. "If you're having nightmares about the Strangler, you must truly believe he's going to come after you."

Ivy sighed heavily, unwilling to admit the truth. "Alex, you don't understand. Every woman in Brauxton who fits the victim profile is having nightmares. Please don't make more out of it than there is." She closed the scant distance between them. "If you really want to help, just hold me. That's all I need."

Alex enfolded her in his arms, stroking her hair gently. The trembling had stopped, but he knew she was still hiding something from him. "You know, Ivy, this isn't fair," he said quietly. "You asked me to open up to you, and I did. But you won't open up to me. That's a rotten double standard."

"You're right," she said reflectively as she realized she'd been holding back a part of herself as protection against the possibility that he might never be able to let go of the past and love her. But she had already given him so much of her heart, she realized that she might as well trust him with the rest—the secret, irrational fears that she had shared with no one.

"He's going to come after me eventually, Alex. I know it," she said, not bothering to conceal the fear she always worked so hard at hiding. "I don't know how I know it, but it's not just a feeling or an emotional reaction to my resemblance to the victims. It's like—" she looked up at him, finding his clear gray eyes in the shadows of his handsome face "—an inescapable fact. I know the sun will rise tomorrow, I know gravity will make objects fall down, not up, and I *know* that my name is on the Strangler's list. You can tell me I'm crazy or irrational or just plain paranoid, but you can't tell me it won't happen, because I know otherwise."

"You're scared to death, aren't you?" he asked, brushing his lips across her forehead.

"Yes," she admitted reluctantly. "But sometimes the only way you can live with yourself is to confront your fears and go on in spite of them. That's what I've been doing. The Strangler has invaded my dreams for months, but it hasn't kept me from doing my job."

"No, it hasn't," he said, wondering if he had ever had the kind of courage Ivy possessed. "You're a remarkable woman, Ivy Kincaid, and I'm very glad you're in my life. If Drummond wants you, he'll have to go through me to get you."

Ivy closed her eyes and let Alex's words and his strength chase away the last traces of her nightmare. "Careful, Alex. You're doing it again. Better keep quiet before you say too much."

She heard a chuckle rumble deep in his chest. "You are one pushy broad, you know that, Kincaid?"

"Yeah, but you like me anyway, don't you?"

"Yeah, I do," he admitted, wondering why he couldn't just come out and admit that he more than liked her; he had fallen hopelessly in love with her. But there was something holding him back. It had to do with Brenda's suicide and little Tanya Ringwald's death, with his disastrous marriage and his inability to solve the Strangler case. He'd failed at too many things in his life, and when Alex Devane failed, people had a tendency to die. Until he had chased that specter of death from his life, until he knew that his love would never bring Ivy anything but happiness, he would have to be content with holding her in his arms and chasing away her nightmares.

"Would you care to show me just how much you like me?" she asked seductively, fitting her body to his in all the right places.

"Like I said, you're a pushy broad, Kincaid," he muttered with a playful growl as his body responded predictably to the feel of hers. He sought her lips, kissing her hard and fast, and while their mouths were becoming reacquainted, Alex picked her up and carried her to the monstrosity she called a bed. He lowered her halfway, then abruptly dropped her.

"Oh, God, I'm getting too old for this romantic hero stuff," he groaned comically, clutching his back. "Do you think you could arrange to lose a few pounds before I do that again?"

"Aw, poor baby. Did um hurt umself?" Ivy cooed, trying not to laugh. "I'll just go get a heating pad and some horse liniment."

She scooted to the opposite side of the bed, but Alex made a miraculous recovery, diving for her and catching her around the waist. He dragged her back to the center of the bed and pinned her down by throwing one leg over hers. "Don't move, Sherlock. I'm placing you under house arrest."

His face was tantalizingly close, and Ivy wasn't sure whose heart was beating faster—hers or his. Still, she glared up at him with a defiant smile. "On what charge?"

Alex slid one hand down her body sensuously, sending shivers through both of them. "Sexual harassment and contributing to the delinquency of a gargoyle," he told her, his voice gravelly. He brought his lips temptingly close, and his breath fanned her face.

"Would you care to discuss a plea bargain?" she asked, her voice a sexy, breathless whisper.

"I think we might be able to reach some kind of agreement. Why don't you just show me what you had in mind," Alex mumbled lazily.

And she did. Deliciously.

CHAPTER NINETEEN

MARSHA DELL'S BODY was found at eight-fifteen the next morning when a friend dropped by to give her a ride to the photography lab where they both worked. Marsha wasn't waiting outside her apartment building as usual, so the friend went in and knocked on the door of her ground-floor apartment. Receiving no response, she circled the building to reach the courtyard Marsha shared with several other tenants and saw her friend's body through the sliding glass door.

Alex received the call and mobilized his team. As before, Ivy and Jordy accompanied him inside. They were with him when he found the Pictionary card beside the body and the typed note pinned to the victim that read, "Close, but no cigar, Devane. Keep up the good work."

With stone-faced efficiency that camouflaged an inner rage, Alex investigated the scene thoroughly. He gave orders in a cold, hard voice that was as chilling as the death room, and an hour later, while the forensics team was still combing the carpet and dusting for fingerprints, he followed Marsha's body to the coroner's wagon that was waiting at the curb in front of the building.

"Where are the guys who were supposed to be watching Drummond last night?" he asked Jordy harshly as the flashing red lights of the wagon cleared a path through the crowded street.

"The shift that worked four to midnight last night is taking the eight to four today, and I haven't seen the guys who got off at eight this morning. They should have reported back to the station an hour ago."

"Well, find them! I want to know how Drummond slipped away from them!"

"He didn't slip away from them," Ivy said, joining Alex and Jordy. She'd spent the past ten minutes on the radio, talking to the detectives currently stationed outside Drummond's house and the ones who had come off duty at eight. They had stopped for breakfast after their shift and had returned to the station only a few minutes ago.

"You mean they're positive Drummond was in his house all evening and all night?" Alex asked.

"On the contrary," she answered. "They know for a fact that he didn't come home until 1:49."

"They tailed him?"

"No. They were waiting for him when he arrived home in a cab," Ivy explained, hating to have to give Alex this bad news. "You see, no one was assigned to follow Drummond after he left the station with his lawyer last night. I guess we all just assumed that he would go straight home, where there was a surveillance team, but he didn't. He was either with his lawyer or was dropped off somewhere. I've got someone trying to reconstruct his movements, but the only thing we know for sure is that we have no idea where Drummond was or what he was doing between seven last night and two this morning."

Alex let loose with a string of expletives that burned Ivy's ears. "Pick him up! Now!" he ordered, charging toward his car. "I want that bastard at the station by the time I get back there. Jordy, you handle things here. Ivy, come with me!"

Ivy raced along beside him, and as soon as they reached the car she called in the order for the surveillance team to take Drummond into custody for questioning. With his siren wailing, Alex drove like a madman and beat the surveillance team to the station by a full thirty minutes. Ivy made herself scarce, using the time to track down Drummond's lawyer, while Alex paced the squad room furiously, trying to rein in his temper. It would be counterproductive to confront Drummond in this frame of mind; he had to be as calm, cold and calculating as the man who had taken Marsha Dell's life.

"Is this going to become a daily ritual, Detective Kincaid?" Drummond asked angrily when Ivy met him at the door of the squad room.

She was sorely tempted to throw a barbed retort at him, but aggravating suspects wasn't part of her job description. "Please come this way, Mr. Drummond. Lieutenant Devane has a few questions he'd like to ask you."

"May I call my lawyer first?"

"Mr. Webster is already on his way."

"Very efficient. Thank you."

Ivy tried to ignore the shiver that ran down her spine when Drummond looked at her. "Don't thank me. We have a few questions for him, too." She stopped outside Alex's door and gestured for Drummond to precede her. "After you."

He stepped into the office and glared at his nemesis, who was seated at the desk. To all outward appearances, the lieutenant seemed calm and collected, but Drummond knew enough about controlled rage to realize that in Devane's case, appearances were deceiving. "What now, Lieutenant? Shall it be thumbscrews or the rack?"

Ivy, too, realized that Alex's temper was hanging by a very short thread, but after the morning they'd had, she admired the restraint he'd summoned. She stepped inside the office and stood quietly by the door, praying that Drummond would make a slip today that he hadn't made yesterday.

"Where were you last night?" Alex asked, getting straight to the point.

"With a friend."

"How convenient. And the name of this friend?"

Drummond sat without being invited to do so and regarded Alex through narrowed eyes. "I'd rather not involve anyone else in your absurd vendetta, Lieutenant."

"That's too bad, because the Strangler took his eighth victim last night, and unless you can prove your whereabouts between the time you left the station and the time you arrived home this morning, I'm going to arrest you."

If Drummond was surprised by news about another victim, he didn't show it. "If you're going to make threats like that, Devane, I feel we should wait for my lawyer."

"Rest assured, he's on his way," Alex replied, glancing at Ivy for confirmation. She nodded once, and he returned his penetrating gaze to Drummond. "We have a few questions for Mr. Webster, too."

"That's what Detective Kincaid said. What possible questions could you have for Pat Webster?"

"We'd be interested in knowing where he took you after you left the station together last night."

Drummond sighed heavily, as though trying to control his temper. It was a long moment before he decided to answer. "He took me to the Kingsfield Mall."

Alex's eyebrows went up skeptically. "The mall? Do you always go shopping after interviews with the police?"

"I had a date, Lieutenant. Her name is Ginger Gleason and she owns a boutique in the mall called the Ginger Jar. We had arranged to meet at the Englander, near her shop, for drinks and dinner, and by the time I left the police station I was already ten minutes late. My lawyer took me there directly."

"How considerate of you not to stand her up."

"I believe in keeping my commitments," Drummond said, his jaw clenched.

"Bully for you. Did you spend the entire evening with Ms Gleason?"

"Most of it."

"How much is 'most'?"

"We had dinner and talked until about nine, when Ms Gleason had to return to work. I waited in the Englander for a while and then browsed through the mall until she closed the shop at ten-thirty. From there, we went to her house, and I returned home around two."

Alex looked at Ivy as they both recalled that the coroner had placed the time of death at roughly between ten and midnight. The Kingsfield Mall was a fifteen-minute drive from Marsha Dell's apartment. If the coroner's estimate was correct, Drummond would have had plenty of time to leave the mall, drive to his victim's home, kill her and return by ten-thirty.

"Did anyone see you while you were 'browsing' through the mall?" Ivy asked.

Drummond didn't turn to look at her but kept his eyes firmly on Alex. "I couldn't say."

"That's too bad." Alex looked at Ivy. "Detective Kincaid, would you send a squad car after Ms Gleason? I'm sure Mr. Drummond will be happy to give you her address."

Mr. Drummond wasn't happy to do it, but he did. As Ivy left to make the arrangements, she passed the district attorney on his way into Alex's office. The D.A. closed the door, and Ivy decided that her presence was no longer needed. Patrick Webster, Drummond's lawyer, arrived, and shortly thereafter the party was adjourned to a large interrogation room where a stenographer was waiting. Ginger Gleason arrived, looking polished, sophisticated and confused. Alex interviewed her in a separate room, and she was finally released.

By twos, members of the task force began drifting in from the murder site, but even though the squad room was soon filled to capacity, the noise level was remarkably low. No one was talking; each was waiting to see if there was enough evidence to arrest Benjamin Drummond for murder.

At noon, Alex came out and issued a spate of orders, sending teams off on various assignments, mostly to the Kingsfield Mall. He put Brubaker in charge of the mall contingent and made it clear to everyone that they were to report their findings to Ivy, who would remain at the station to coordinate the effort.

"How's it going in there?" Ivy asked quietly once the others had dispersed and she had Alex to herself. He was much calmer than he'd been earlier, but only because frustration had replaced his rage.

"Not good."

"For us or Drummond?"

Alex laughed humorlessly. "For us. Despite the fact that he has no solid alibi, he's coming out smelling like a rose."

"What about his girlfriend?"

"Nothing worth noting, except that when she left Drummond at the Englander, she gave him her car keys in case he didn't want to wait around the mall for an hour and a half."

"That's great!" Ivy said, not understanding Alex's disappointment. "That means he had transportation. He couldn't very well have called a cab to pick him up at the mall and asked the driver to wait for him while he killed Marsha Dell. But with Ginger's car—"

Alex was shaking his head. "She swears that her car was parked in exactly the same spot she'd left it in earlier."

"So, he got lucky and found the same parking space when he returned!" Ivy exclaimed. "Or one next to it—in a parking garage, all yellow lines look alike. She's mistaken, or she's covering for him."

"Probably, but that doesn't solve the problem of the Pictionary card we found at the scene. Unless Drummond was carrying the card in his wallet when we picked him up yesterday, he would have had to purchase a copy of the

game somewhere. Brubaker will be passing out pictures of
Drummond to every toy store in the mall, but I'd bet my last
dollar that no one will remember having sold him a game.
If we can't tie Drummond directly to this crime, the D.A. is
going to let him go. Damn it!'' Frustrated, Alex slammed his
fist onto Ivy's desk. ''That bastard is going to slip through
our fingers again!''

''No, he won't,'' Ivy insisted hotly. ''We'll get him. We
have to. We can't let him kill again!''

Alex looked at her, remembering how she'd trembled in
his arms last night after she'd dreamed of her own death. He
also remembered something else, something that made his
blood run cold, something he hadn't wanted to even think
about. ''Ivy. . . the next game clue he'll use—''

''I know,'' she snapped. She didn't want to think about
it, either.

Not caring who was watching, Alex placed his hands on
Ivy's shoulders. ''If the D.A. lets him go, we won't let
Drummond out of our sight, Ivy. I promise you that.''

She looked up at him, knowing she was doing a poor job
of hiding her fear. ''Let's not kid ourselves, Alex. You can't
promise that, because no matter how tight a net you throw
around a suspect, there's always a chance he'll escape it.''

Alex wanted to tell her she was wrong, but he couldn't.
He'd known too many criminals who had managed to evade
surveillance teams; if others had done it, Drummond could
do it, too. And when he killed again, he would choose a
victim whose profession related to the ninth game on the
Perplexities readers' poll— Clue. What profession could be
more appropriate than a detective? Instinctively, Alex knew
that Drummond would never be able to resist the irony of
choosing one of his pursuers as his next victim. Ivy had
good reason to be afraid.

''We'll talk about this later,'' he said finally, turning to
leave. He had an idea—a way of protecting Ivy from the

Strangler for at least a week, possibly two. If the D.A. released Drummond, Alex's next step would be to put his plan into action. Ivy wasn't going to like it, but that was too bad. No matter what it took, he would make sure that no harm came to the woman he loved.

ALEX WAS RIGHT. Ivy didn't like his idea one little bit.

"You want me to do *what*?"

"Damn it, keep your voice down," Alex ordered, stepping around her to close his office door. The evening shift was in the squad room, and most of the day shift was hanging around as well, making calls, finishing reports or praying for a case-solving clue to drop into their laps. They'd watched Drummond walk away an hour ago, but no one was ready to admit defeat. Particularly not Ivy.

"I am not going to New York!" she told Alex hotly.

"Yes, you are," he insisted firmly, returning to sit behind his desk. "I need someone to find out everything there is to know about Benjamin Drummond's past. You're the only one I trust to do it."

"That's a bunch of bull," Ivy said angrily. "You just want to get me out of Brauxton in case Drummond slips through your surveillance net!"

"I admit that reason did enter into my decision, but that doesn't negate the fact that I need all the information on Drummond I can get, and the only place to get it is in New York. I've already arranged it with the NYPD. They've agreed to assign a detective to work with you on the investigation."

Alex's calm was infuriating. "Damn it, I will not be shuffled off to the minor leagues like some over-the-hill pitcher who can't throw strikes anymore!" Ivy shouted. Slamming both hands onto the desk, she brought her face close to his. "How many times do I have to tell you that I can take care of myself? I am not afraid of Drummond!"

Alex captured her angry eyes with his cool gray ones. "That's a lie Ivy, and we both know it. You're so afraid of the Strangler that you can't sleep nights."

Ivy drew back as though he'd slapped her. "How dare you!" she said, her jaw clenched so that the words were little more than an angry hiss. "You can't do this, Alex. You can't be my lover at night and then use the things I say against me in the morning when you become my lieutenant again. That's not how the game is played. It's not fair."

"Fair or not, this is the way it's going to be," he said, rising, all brusque and businesslike. "You're going to New York. I want to know about the Pentathlon lawsuit, Drummond's mother, his business that failed, and—most particularly—I want to know about Joanna Hughes. Her disappearance is peculiar, and there's a distinct possibility that she was his first victim. I think he stole her game idea, then killed her when she raised a stink about it. That's what you and the NYPD are going to find out."

He moved around the desk to her. "This is an important assignment, Ivy," he said quietly, praying she would understand. "That's why I'm sending you to do it."

He tried to place his hands on her shoulders, but Ivy moved out of his reach. "I wish I could believe that, Alex, but I don't. It *is* an important assignment, but you're only giving it to me to get me out of town. If we weren't lovers, you'd never have considered this. You're allowing our personal relationship to govern your thinking, and in the process, you're demeaning me. You're insinuating that I can't do my job, that I can't handle my fears. But I've got news for you, Alex. I was handling my fear a long time before you joined the task force. I didn't need the protection of an overgrown Boy Scout then, and I don't need it now!"

"Ivy..." There was a plea for understanding in his voice, and Ivy moved toward him with an entreaty of her own.

"Please, Alex," she begged, "send Mort Adamson—he's worked in New York, he knows the city, he has friends on the force. He's the logical choice. Send him! Prove to me that you don't think I'm an incompetent idiot who's too scared of her own shadow to do her job!"

Alex reached for her again and ran his hands lightly down her arms. She didn't move away, but there was incredible disappointment and sadness in her eyes when he told her, "Competence has nothing to do with it, Ivy. I wouldn't send an idiot to New York. It's too important."

"Then prove to me that the secrets we confess to each other when I'm in your arms won't affect how we do our jobs," she pleaded softly.

For the sake of their relationship—their love—Alex wanted to change his mind. By sending Ivy to New York, he was betraying her trust, and he could see how deeply that betrayal was hurting her. They both knew that Mort really was the most logical choice for the job. The only reason he was sending her instead was because he was as frightened for her safety as she was. Probably more so, because at least Ivy was willing to stay in Brauxton and face her fear. She *needed* to face her fears, and Alex was depriving her of that.

As she had said, it was unfair. It was also unprofessional. But if he allowed Ivy to stay here, she was going to be in constant danger, and all it would take to bring about her death was one simple, stupid mistake. No one was infallible. Alex had to get her out of town because he knew he could never live with himself if he lost her. There were too many deaths on his conscience already.

"I'm sorry, Ivy, but I won't change my mind," he said, steeling himself against the hurt in her eyes. He moved behind the desk, putting distance between himself and the hurt. "What I will do, though, is arrange for Mort to go with you. You're right. His experience and contacts in New York will be invaluable."

That was the final blow. Ivy felt as though Alex had yanked her heart out, thrown it on the floor and stomped on it. With Mort along, she couldn't even pretend that her presence in New York was needed. In essence, Alex was taking her off the Strangler case and telling her to go hide out in New York, where she would be safe. He had no faith in her ability to protect herself. He no longer trusted her to be able to do her job effectively in spite of her fears. Last night she had trembled in his arms, and today he was sending her away. She had trusted him enough to tell him her fears, and he was using that trust against her.

She wasn't sure she could ever forgive him for it.

"When do I leave?" she asked, her voice cold and flat.

"First thing tomorrow morning. Pack enough clothes for a couple of weeks. I want a thorough investigation," he said. "I'll come over later and help you pack."

Ivy gave a short, humorless bark of laughter. "Don't bother, Lieutenant. Packing is woman's work."

"Damn it, Ivy, this has nothing to do with sexism!" Alex said, frustration making his voice harsh.

"Save it, boss," she snapped.

"I'm doing this for your own good!"

"Like hell you are!" She moved angrily toward the desk. "You're doing this for *your* own good!"

"Because I can't bear the thought of losing you! What's so bad about that?"

"If you don't know, I'll never be able to explain it to you," she said sadly. She moved back to the door. "See you in a couple of weeks . . . *Lieutenant*."

The door slammed behind her as she stormed out of his office and—he was afraid—out of his life.

CHAPTER TWENTY

In New York, Ivy kept abreast of the Strangler investigation by reading the Brauxton *Chronicle*, watching the evening news and listening to Mort Adamson, who spoke with Alex on the phone every day. She had no contact with Alex personally, nor did she want any. She was still too angry. Her feeling of betrayal was too great. She loved Alex Devane with all her heart, but she was finding it hard to forgive him for sending her into exile.

She remembered the phrases he'd used: *for your own good* and *can't bear the thought of losing you....* He had sent her away because, whether he could admit it yet or not, he loved her. Knowing that should have given Ivy comfort, but it didn't. As he had with the deaths of his wife and Tanya Ringwald. Alex was still taking responsibility for things that were beyond his control, and in the process, he was treating Ivy as though she were an incompetent nine-year-old. He loved her, but he didn't respect her as a law enforcement official.

Ivy hadn't entered police work lightly. It was an inherently dangerous profession, but it was something she had wanted desperately, something she had worked hard for, something she was proud of. Having the respect of her peers was important to her; having the respect of the man she loved was as vital as life and death. And equally important was having that man be someone she could talk to, confide in, share her hopes, dreams and fears with. Unfortunately, when she'd trusted him with her deepest, darkest fear and told him how important it was that she be allowed to confront it, Alex had repaid her trust by taking away her autonomy. Ivy was no longer in control of her life—Alex was.

And it wouldn't stop with this one case, she feared. Once the Strangler had been caught, she and Alex might be reassigned to different precincts, or Alex might even quit the force again and resume his research career. Either way, though, Ivy would still be a police officer. She would still face hazardous situations. If Alex couldn't accept her career and allow her to be responsible for her own life and her own actions, they had no hope of a future together.

That realization brought her more pain than she'd ever imagined she could experience. Her only salvation was keeping busy. She worked herself to exhaustion, talking to friends of Joanna Hughes, who claimed not to have seen her since Benjamin Drummond had left the city. She spent countless hours at the morgue of the *New York Times*, studying every word that had ever been written about Drummond, his family and the Joanna Hughes lawsuit. She also went over police reports and court documents, trying to piece together the bizarre chain of events that had followed the filing of that suit. Drummond had accused Joanna of harassment, claiming that she was calling him, sending him threatening letters and, in general, making his life a living hell.

If all that was true, Miss Hughes wasn't any more stable than Drummond, but Ivy could find no evidence to support Drummond's harassment charges. All of Joanna's friends claimed that she was the injured party, that Drummond had trumped up the charges to make her claim to the profits of Pentathlon look less convincing. Some of those friends even admitted fearing that Drummond had done away with his nemesis. One of them had gone so far as to report Joanna's disappearance to the police, but a subsequent investigation had shown no evidence of foul play.

Joanna Hughes had quit her job, packed her belongings, sublet her apartment and vanished from the face of the earth.

As for Drummond, Ivy and Mort talked to members of his family, former employees, friends and colleagues in the game industry. The picture they drew of him was that of an eccentric, sometimes erratic, often volatile genius—an assessment chillingly similar to the psychiatrists' profile of the Strangler. But for all the work Ivy and Mort did, they came up with nothing that would prove or disprove Benjamin Drummond's guilt.

As Ivy had known all along, the real solution to the case was in Brauxton, and she had been banished from the city, thanks to Alex Devane. She spent two lonely, frustrating, interminable weeks in New York, wondering when he was going to allow her to come home.

THE AUGUST ISSUE of *Perplexities* was lying on the table, open to the crossword puzzle on page seventeen. Danica Nikel had created it. That meant it had to be tonight, if it was going to be done according to the rules, and the rules couldn't be broken. Tonight, the seventeenth of August, another woman would die.

But not just any woman. No, there was nothing random in the choice. Only one woman fit the parameters of the game. One woman whose name, age, appearance and profession made her the only possible victim this month. It had to be tonight, and it had to be Detective Ivy Lane Kincaid, or the game would be forfeit.

But Detective Kincaid was in New York. Devane had known she was next and he'd sent her away. The need to win was as intense as the need to kill, but Devane had stolen the most critical component of the game. That wasn't very sportsmanlike. In fact that was cheating. And cheaters had to be punished.

The dark personality known to the public as the Braux-ton Strangler reached for the telephone and dialed. One way or another, someone was going to die tonight. There would be no stroll through the shadowed grove before or after, because the police were watching the house, but someone would die.

"HELLO? HELLO?" Ivy's suitcases were scattered by the front door, where she'd dropped them when she heard the phone ringing.

"Hello?" The line clicked and a dial tone replaced the silence. With a shrug, Ivy kicked off her low-heeled pumps and dialed her mother's number. "As long as I'm in the neighborhood . . ." she mumbled as the call rang through.

"Hello?"

"Hi, Mom, I'm home."

"Home? In your apartment?" Mavis asked, clearly surprised. "You left New York?"

"Yes, Mother," Ivy answered patiently. "Last night Mort finally convinced Alex that there was nothing more to be learned up there. We caught a flight out this afternoon, and now I'm back where I belong."

"I see." There was a slight pause as Mavis digested the news. When Ivy had called her two weeks ago to say that she was going to New York, Mavis had been delighted. Ivy's resemblance to the Strangler victims had been weighing heavily on her, and knowing her daughter was safely out of the city had brought her a little peace of mind. Having Ivy back meant that Mavis had to start worrying again.

Of course, saying that to Ivy would only start an argument, so Mavis held her tongue. "Well, how was the flight, dear? Did the weather give you any trouble?"

Ivy shrugged out of her suit jacket and hung it over the gargoyle on one of her bedposts. "We hit quite a bit of turbulence, but it could have been worse. The hurricane that's headed for South Carolina is wreaking havoc up and down the coast. Our flight beat the worst part of the storm, though.'' As though to punctuate her comment, a brilliant flash of lightning preceded a huge rumble of thunder, and static crackled on the phone line. It was still early afternoon, but already the sky was as black as night. There was one doozy of a storm coming.

Mavis made a comment about the severity of the weather, then abruptly changed the subject. "Have you spoken to Alex yet?"

Ivy sighed, wishing the comment was as innocent as it sounded. "No, Mother. I haven't talked to Alex since I left."

"Oh, Ivy, you're not still angry with him, are you? He was only doing what was best for you."

"He was doing what he *thought* was best for me, Mom. It's not the same thing," she replied tightly. They'd had this argument two weeks ago when Mavis had guessed the real reason Alex was sending her away, and Ivy didn't want to have it again. "I'm a grown-up. I can take care of myself. You're my mother, so I can forgive you for not understanding that, but I'm not sure I can forgive Alex."

"Darling, don't say that. Of course you can forgive him! You love Alex, and it's obvious that he loves you, too."

Ivy frowned and sat on the edge of the bed. "Have you been talking to him?"

A small pause punctuated the static on the line. "Yes, dear, I have. Actually, I called to thank him for sending you out of town."

"Mother, you didn't!"

"Of course I did. This Strangler business scares me to death, Ivy. I know you've had contact with the man the newspapers are saying is the only suspect—that makes you even more vulnerable. If this Drummond person really is the Strangler, he might come after you out of spite!"

Regardless of her irritation, Ivy had to laugh at her mother's choice of words. "Spite? Mother, the Strangler is a psychopathic killer, not a spoiled brat who kicks people in the shins when he doesn't get his way."

"You know what I mean," Mavis said impatiently. "I'm just saying that since the killer knows you personally, that could make you a much more challenging target. Obviously, Alex believes that, too. He only sent you away to protect you."

Ivy ran a hand through her hair and went back to the original argument. "Mom, that's not what I want out of a relationship with any man. I want a lover, a friend and a confidant, not a he-man protector who treats me like a child."

Ivy could practically see her mother shaking her head adamantly. "Ivy Lane Kincaid, you listen to me. In the beginning, I was a little nervous about your becoming involved with Alex, but you've found a wonderful man who loves you, and you can't throw that away just because of a silly little disagreement."

"It's not a silly disagreement," Ivy said heatedly. "It's an issue that says a great deal about how Alex views my career. When he sent me to New York, it was his way of telling me that he has no respect for me or the way I make my living."

"No, Ivy, it was his way of telling you he was concerned for your safety because he cares so much about you."

"I know that, Mother, but it's a problem that will crop up again and again unless I quit the police force, and I have no intention of doing that!"

"Well, maybe you should," Mavis said with a touch of petulance. "There's not a job in the world that's more important than having a good man in your life."

Ivy laughed wearily as she flopped back onto the bed. "Don't let Gloria Steinem hear you say that, Mother. That attitude could set the cause of women's liberation back a hundred years.''

''Horsefeathers!'' Mavis said disgustedly. ''I'm not talking about women's lib, I'm talking about your happiness, and if Alex Devane can make you happy, you'd be a fool to let him get away. You're too stubborn for your own good, Ivy.''

''I know that,'' she said with a resigned sigh. ''But you love me anyway, don't you, Mom?''

Mavis softened softened her voice, too. ''You know I do, Ivy. More than anything. And Alex loves you, too. Don't forget that.''

''How can I forget it? That's what makes all this hurt so much,'' she admitted sadly.

They talked only a minute or two longer, then Ivy signed off. She turned on the air conditioner to circulate some air in her stuffy apartment, then went to shower and shampoo her hair. By the time she had finished, the apartment was cool and she felt clean again. Wearing nothing but a towel and a turban, she padded through the main room, turned off the air conditioner and was trying to think of an excuse to avoid unpacking when someone knocked at the door.

Alex. She saw him through the peephole and for a moment considered pretending she wasn't home. Then she reminded herself that she wasn't a coward and opened the door.

''Hi.''

''Hi.'' He stood in the doorway, perusing her scantily attired body. She was beautiful. She was also still upset with him. He saw it in her wounded eyes and defensive stance. ''You just got out of the shower.''

''Brilliant deduction, Sherlock,'' she said without rancor. ''Come in.''

Alex had to step over a suitcase in order to get far enough into the room for her to close the door. Another suitcase and a garment bag were on the floor, and her shoes and the clothes she'd apparently worn on the plane were scattered hither and yon. "I thought Hurricane Jacob was supposed to come ashore farther south."

"Sorry about the mess. It's my way of marking my territory when I return from a long trip," she explained. "Please have a seat. Did Mort call to tell you we were back?"

Alex stepped over the garment bag and sat on the arm of the sofa. "Yes. If I'd known when your flight was arriving, I'd have been happy to pick you up at the airport."

Ivy shrugged and clutched her towel when it started to slip. "Mort's wife picked us up." Her turban chose that moment to start unraveling, and she grabbed at it with her other hand. "Will you excuse me a minute, Alex? I seem to be falling apart. I'll go change and be right back."

"Sure." He watched her disappear into her dressing room, and two minutes later she appeared in the doorway wearing a pair of crisp yellow pleated shorts and a matching tank top. The outfit was more respectable than the towel but just as revealing.

"So, what can I do for you?" she asked as she started combing the tangles out of her hair.

"I thought maybe we should talk."

Ivy leaned against the door frame. The physical distance between them was only about ten feet, but it might as well have been the Grand Canyon. Ivy studied him a moment, wishing the horrible tightness in her chest would go away. "I don't think we have anything to talk about, Alex. You talked to Mort every day, and I sent you written reports, so you know everything that we discovered in New York. And I know that nothing much happened here—Drummond rarely left his house, the press is eating him alive, Ginger Gleason dumped him when he became a suspect, and you've been working yourself to death. What else is there to talk about?''

"Us." He stood and moved to her. "We can talk about our relationship. I missed you."

"You could have avoided that by not sending me away," she reminded him coolly as she stepped away from the door and put some space between them. Being close to him tempted her to step into his arms and forget about their enormous problem, and she couldn't do that yet—not until she was certain that it was a problem that could be resolved.

Alex watched in frustration as she skittered away from him. "Ivy, I did what I thought was right, and if I could have justified the expense to the mayor, I'd have kept you in New York."

"Well, gee thanks," she said sarcastically. "Now we *really* don't have anything to talk about. I might have been willing to listen to an apology, but—''

"Damn it, Ivy, I am not going to apologize for trying to protect you."

"Then how about apologizing for taking away my autonomy, treating me like a child and misusing your authority to indulge a personal whim?"

"Protecting you is not a whim!''

"It is if I don't need protecting!'' she shouted, then forced herself to calm down. "You just don't understand what you've done, do you, Alex?" she asked quietly.

"No, I guess I don't."

"Well, I'll tell you what it all boils down to," she said, keeping her voice soft. "I'm not Brenda, I'm Ivy. I'm strong, capable and resilient. I don't need a macho super-stud to take care of me, because I can take care of myself. I don't want someone to control my life, I want someone to share it. And I absolutely will not be shoved into the mold of helpless female just so that you can feel good about yourself.''

She took a step toward him, then reconsidered and turned away, her shoulders slumped in defeat. "If you can't accept that, Alex, get out of my life. This hurts too much already, and it will only get worse."

There was a long pause, and when Alex finally spoke, his voice was colored with regret. "I love you," he said softly.

Ivy wasn't aware that she was so close to tears until they were already on her cheeks. "Damn you," she whispered, pulling her shoulders straight as she turned toward him. "Is that supposed to make me feel better? Is this my cue to melt into your arms? Do I say, 'Oh, Alex, I love you, too,' and forget that this problem exists?"

"No, I guess not," he said sadly as he moved to the door, then stopped. "We seem to be at an impasse. You see, I can't apologize for being afraid of losing you. I won't say I'm sorry for loving you or for wanting to protect the rarest, most precious thing I've ever had in my life." He opened the door and glanced at her one last time. "Maybe it's a question of need, Ivy. You can love someone, but you can't bring yourself to need someone in the same way you need air to breathe and food to eat. That's too much of a risk, isn't it?"

Ivy's face was wet, and her eyes were wide with misery. Through her anguish, she scrambled to find an answer to his question, but before one came, Alex was gone. The door closed softly behind him, and Ivy crumpled onto the bed, sobbing her heart out.

CHAPTER TWENTY-ONE

JAGGED STREAKS OF LIGHTNING chased each other across the sky, and thunder rumbled behind them. Hurricane Jacob was coming ashore three hundred miles south of Brauxton, but it was making its presence known, nonetheless. A hard rain pummeled the city, and power had been disrupted in many areas.

Alex turned away from his office window and glanced at his watch. Eight thirty-five, and except for the occasional brilliant flashes of lightning, it was already as dark as midnight outside. It was going to be a long night.

Tired and depressed, he returned to his desk and sat. Laid out in front of him were all of last year's issues of *Perplexities*. It had been ages since he'd looked at them, because he'd practically given up hope of finding the elusive clue they contained—if they even contained a clue. Why he'd chosen tonight to return to them, he didn't know. Or maybe he did know. Maybe it had to do with Ivy and the excitement they'd shared the night they'd found the *Perplexities* readers' poll. He had kissed Ivy for the first time that night. It was the night he had fallen in love.

It was fitting, then, that tonight he should torture himself with memories of that magical evening. He refused to believe that he had lost Ivy forever, but neither could he be certain that they would ever be able to build a future together. Sometimes, love just wasn't enough. He'd proved that with Brenda.

But Ivy isn't Brenda. She kept telling him that, and Alex kept reminding himself of it. Ivy was different—stronger, sweeter, gentler—but she was still in danger, and no matter how often Alex tried to tell himself he should let Ivy take care of herself, he couldn't escape the responsibility he felt for her. He had missed her terribly while she was in New York, but he wasn't sorry he'd sent her there. For those two weeks, she'd been safe, and if keeping her safe also meant losing her love, he would settle for keeping her safe and alive for the time being. Then, once the Strangler was behind bars, he would find some way to make Ivy forgive him.

That thought brought him back full circle to the magazines in front of him. He was no longer as sure as he'd once been that the key to the case was contained within the pages of last year's issues, but it was a possibility that was worth pursuing. Ivy had been responsible for keying all the *Perplexities* information into the computer, and since she'd been away for two weeks, no one had bothered cross-referencing the information on Marsha Dells' murder with the *Perplexities* list of July games and contributors.

Turning to his computer, Alex brought up the list that contained the victims, murder dates, corresponding *Perplexities* page and the contributor whose puzzle appeared on that particular page. He went to the bottom of the list, added Marsha Dell's name and entered the date July 31 in the second column. Next, he picked up the July issue and flipped to page thirty-one. It was filled with cryptograms, so he entered that information in the appropriate column.

Then he looked at the name of the puzzle contributor. Ed Marshall. Alex typed in the name, then froze when he realized the importance of what he'd just done. Marsha Dell and Ed Marshall. The names were eerily similar. So similar, in fact, that one was an anagram of the other. This was the key to unlocking the Strangler's puzzle! This was the clue that had eluded them! It had to be!

Feeling like a fool, Alex went to the top of the list. Beverly Coit, victim on January 17; Victor Eberly, contributor on page seventeen of the January issue. Alex grabbed a pencil and wrote both names on a sheet of paper. Quickly, he crossed off the letters the two names had in common. They, too, were identical—except for one letter. Victor Eberly's name had one too many *R*'s.

Damn! The names were too close for it to be a coincidence, but the Strangler was meticulous, and there were no loose ends in this case. That extra *R* had to be accounted for somewhere. And it was, Alex realized when he remembered that Beverly Coit's middle name was Renee. Beverly R. Coit was an anagram of Victor Eberly.

This was how the Strangler was choosing his victims! Armed with a list of *Perplexities'* puzzle contributors, he probably patched into the Department of Motor Vehicles' computer, obtained a list of all the women in Brauxton who fit his victim profile, and from there began anagramming names until he found a perfect match.

Spellbound, Alex went on to the next name and the next, unable to keep himself from admiring the complexity of the mind that had concocted such an intricate puzzle.

A BOOMING CLAP OF THUNDER rattled the windows of Ivy's apartment, and she awoke with a start to find that she was lying on the bed still fully clothed, with the radio blaring and all the lights on. Shaking her head to clear the effects of her nap, she glanced at the clock by the telephone. Nine o'clock. Too early to go to bed for real, and too late to go out for a night on the town.

Not that she wanted to go out and party tonight. She was definitely not in a festive mood. After Alex had left this afternoon, she had cried for what had seemed an eternity. The tears simply would not stop. His insinuation that she couldn't commit herself completely to a relationship rang in her ears and weighed heavily on a conscience that she finally realized was guilty as charged.

She was determined to keep her own identity, no matter what the future held with Alex, or any man. That in itself wasn't bad. It wasn't wrong to want to share a man's life rather than be swallowed whole by it. But by the same token, it was wrong to hold back too much of herself in order to keep from getting hurt. When two people loved, the commitment had to be wholehearted or love would fail.

It had taken Ivy most of the afternoon to realize that she had been holding something back all of her life. Well, not all of it. Just the past twenty years, since her father had deserted her. She'd loved him with all her young heart, and when Ed Kincaid had left without a backward glance at his adoring daughter, Ivy's world had collapsed. She'd survived by telling herself she would never love anyone that much ever again.

As she had grown up, Ivy had realized intellectually that such an attitude was absurd. Unfortunately, the heart was rarely intellectual. The human heart was made to be filled or broken, and once broken it was reluctant to place itself in jeopardy again.

Alex was right. Ivy was afraid to risk everything. Knowing that didn't take away the sting of his recent dictatorial behavior, but it did make her reexamine her reaction to it. It was unlike her to lash out or be unforgiving. It was *very* unlike her to think only of the problem instead of finding a solution. If loving Alex was worth the risk, there had to be a way to make him respect her. In time, if they loved each other enough, he would realize that she had more strength than he was giving her credit for.

That had been Ivy's last thought as she'd drifted off to sleep, and as she came fully awake, her first thought was of talking to Alex. She reached for the phone and dialed his number, but after ten rings she realized he must still be at the station. *Typical,* she thought with a smile. She should have known to try his office first.

She hung up and started dialing again, but a knock on the door stopped her. Praying it would be Alex, she threw the receiver back onto its cradle and dashed for the door. Out of habit, she glanced through the peephole as she reached for the doorknob, then she stopped her hand and looked through the peephole again.

There was a woman standing in the hall, not Alex. A woman whose blond hair had been plastered to her scalp by the rain—a woman who looked vaguely familiar. She looked up and down the hall uncertainly, almost fearfully, then knocked again. And Ivy finally recognized her from the dozens of photographs she'd seen of her in New York.

Joanna Hughes.

Amazed, Ivy opened the door. "Hello."

Smiling timidly, the rain-drenched woman wiped away some of the beads of water that were streaming from her hair onto her face. "Detective Kincaid?"

"That's right."

"I'm Joanna Hughes. I understand that the Brauxton police have been searching for me."

Ivy grinned. "That's an understatement." She stepped back, opening the door wider. "Won't you come in?"

"Thank you." The tall, willowy blonde stepped inside. "I'm sorry—I seem to be dripping all over your carpet," she said as Ivy closed the door behind her.

"That's all right," Ivy reassured her. "I'll get you a towel, then maybe you can tell me how you knew we were looking for you and why you're here."

"The first part is simple," Joanna said, raising her voice as Ivy disappeared through the dressing room into the bathroom. "I called a friend in New York yesterday, and she told me that last week a Detective Ivy Kincaid from the

Brauxton P.D. had been there to ask her about me. She also said that you were asking questions about Ben."

In the bathroom, Ivy grabbed a towel out of the linen closet and started back to her unexpected guest. Another boom of thunder seemed to shake the whole apartment, and the lights flickered, then remained steady. "But why come directly to me instead of to the police station?" she asked as she turned the corner and found that Joanna was no longer by the front door. She had moved to the dressing room door, leaving droplets of water on the carpet where she'd been pacing in the area between the living room and Ivy's bed. It was obvious that she was nervous, and Ivy even thought she detected a hint of fear in her dark blue eyes. Fear of what? Benjamin Drummond, perhaps?

"I came to you because I thought you might be the only one who could understand. What I've been thinking is crazy, insane. It makes a warped kind of sense, but I didn't think a man could understand," Joanna explained, accepting the towel with a grateful smile. She dried her hair and dabbed at the water on her shiny black raincoat as she continued. "You see, I live in Brauxton, so of course I've heard all about the Strangler. I've even seen your picture in the paper, and when my friend, Jacquie, told me you'd been to see her, I knew it had to be about the Strangler case. And I got to thinking . . . and then I got scared. Really scared."

"Scared?" Ivy prompted, watching Joanna's face crumple as her composure cracked.

She looked at Ivy with wide, horrified eyes. "The Brauxton police think Ben is the Strangler, don't they?"

"He is a suspect," she answered cautiously.

"And he's killing women who look like me," Joanna said tearfully. "I think, maybe, its his way of . . . killing me." She covered her face with her hands. "Oh, God. This isn't making any sense, is it?"

"Actually, it makes a great deal of sense," Ivy said, placing a comforting arm around her. She led her to the sofa. "Come have a seat and we'll talk. Would you like to take off your raincoat?"

Joanna shook her head as she sat. "No, actually I'm a little chilled from the rain."

Ivy shrugged fatalistically. It was only water, and her sofa would eventually dry. She sat next to her guest and tried to think of all the right questions to ask. Something Joanna had said seemed odd, out of place, but Ivy couldn't put her finger on what it was. Until she did, she'd ask questions.

"Joanna, why don't you start from the beginning? Tell me about your relationship with Benjamin Drummond. I know about the lawsuit and the harassment charges he leveled against you, but it would clarify a lot if you'd tell me your side."

"I don't even like thinking about it," she said with a shudder. "It was absolutely the most horrible period of my entire life. You see, I was in love with Ben, and I thought he was in love with me. We shared a lot of common interests. I never believed he could betray me the way he did."

"By stealing the idea for Pentathlon?"

She nodded and caught her breath with a hitching sigh. "That, and other things. Like the horrible lies he told about how I was crazy and I was harassing him. I loved him, and he did unspeakable things to me."

"What kind of things?"

Apparently, the things were so unspeakable that Joanna couldn't even bear to think of them. She covered her face again, crying, and Ivy gave her a moment to collect herself.

"Joanna, if Drummond was as horrible as you say, why did you follow him to Brauxton?"

She looked at Ivy, startled. "I didn't. He followed me. He must have. Only I didn't know it until Jacquie told me you'd been asking about him in connection with the Strangler case.

Don't you see? He's going to kill me. This whole thing, all the other victims, are just decoys! That's why he's killing women who look like me—so that when I die, I'll just be one of a group. Please, you've got to help me!" Joanna grabbed Ivy's arm with more strength than Ivy would have imagined she possessed.

"I will, Joanna, I will," she promised, gently disengaging the other woman's hand as she rose.

"Where are you going?"

"I'm going to call Alex Devane, the head of the task force," she explained as she crossed to the telephone by the bed. "I want him to hear what you have to say so that we can get you some protection."

"Please don't!" Joanna begged, rising. Thunder rumbled again, punctuating her near hysteria.

"It'll be all right, Joanna. Alex will understand. He'll want to help you." Ivy picked up the receiver and had already started dialing before she realized that the phone was dead. In the time-honored fashion of everyone confronted with a lifeless phone, Ivy jiggled buttons to no avail. "The storm must have knocked out the phone lines. I guess I won't call Alex, after all," she mumbled.

And then she saw it.

Lightning hadn't knocked out the phone. The cord had been pulled from the jack in the baseboard and was lying next to the wall. Fifteen minutes ago, Ivy had used that phone to call Alex's house. Now it was unplugged. Only one person could have done it. Only one person had a reason to do it.

Keeping her face immobile to reflect none of her fear, Ivy turned and looked at Joanna Hughes.

Now, she knew why all the other victims had let the Strangler into their homes. The psychiatrists had told the police it was a man. The police had told that to the public.

But they had all been wrong. The Strangler was a woman.

It was Ivy's turn to die.

NANCY MONROE AND NORME CANYON, Darlena West and Neal Steward, Elaine M. McNaughton and Michael N. Montaugne, S. Jean Anderson and Joanne Sanders, Erin Selway and Lewis Raney, C.E. Romalanski and Lois Ackerman—anagrams one and all.

Alex looked at the list and felt like shouting with triumph. This lovely, critical clue didn't prove or disprove Benjamin Drummond's guilt, but it did provide a way of predicting who the Strangler's next victim would be. And if the victim and the date of the crime could be predicted, a trap could be set, and the Strangler could be caught in the act.

The case was definitely in the homestretch!

Elated, Alex put the list aside and turned to the computer to call up the catalog Ivy had made of all of August's *Perplexities* contributors. Automatically, he erased every name that appeared on pages one through sixteen. Today was August 17; that was the page he would start with. And his first priority would be to make certain that none of the remaining contributors had names that could be anagrammed with Ivy Kincaid.

The computer screen winked at him, then presented the first entry. Page seventeen, Danica Nikel.

Wonderful, Alex thought, breathing a sigh of relief when he realized there wasn't a single letter *V* in Ms Nikel's name. But he scrambled the letters anyway, just to be thorough, and his relief turned to dread, and his dread to terror. Included in Danica Nikel's name were the letters *K-I-N-C-A-I-D.*

But the remaining letters were *A-N-E-L,* and none of those were in Ivy's name.

"Her middle name...what's Ivy's middle name?" he whispered, his desperation mounting as he tried to recall if he'd ever heard it. He turned to the computer, prepared to punch up her personnel file, but his eyes were suddenly drawn to the chessboard hanging just above his desk. His mind flashed back to the day Ivy had hung it there and their hard-fought battle of wits had begun.

It's my board—even has my name scratched on the back... she had said with the same impudent grin that had first attracted Alex the night before.

Heedless of the pieces that scattered, Alex grabbed the board off the wall and flipped it over. Carved into the wood in squiggly letters was the name Ivy Lane Kincaid.

A-N-E-L anagrammed into *L-A-N-E.*

Ivy was the Strangler's next victim, and tonight was the night.

His heart thundering in his chest, Alex grabbed the phone and dialed Ivy's number. As it rang, he held his breath and prayed for her to answer. But she didn't.

"Wilcox! Get in here!" Alex shouted as he bolted out of his chair. The startled detective met Alex at the office door. "Get a squad car to Ivy Kincaid's apartment. Now! She's the next victim," he said as he rushed toward the exit. "And have the surveillance team pick up Drummond immediately. Bring him to the station. I don't want him out of our sight for a moment!"

The confused Wilcox was already on the phone by the time Alex hit the swinging doors of the squad room at a dead run. Fear-induced adrenaline was pumping through every vein, but Alex suddenly stopped as the full impact of what he was doing hit him. He was a cop heading into a potentially dangerous situation; he was a man desperately trying to rescue the woman he loved.

Without giving it a second thought, he whirled and ran back to his office, threw open the bottom drawer of his desk and grabbed the .38 caliber Smith & Wesson Chiefs Special that Ivy had placed there.

CHAPTER TWENTY-TWO

IVY WAS AMAZED at her own calm. She was standing by the phone, looking at a psychopath who had already killed eight women and was here to make it nine. Her gun was nestled snugly in her purse on the coffee table, and the psychopath was now standing between Ivy and the purse.

Somewhere in the back of her mind, a voice was screaming, *If ever there was a time to panic, this is it,* but the cop in Ivy knew better. This was the time for cold rationality. This was the time for clearheaded thinking.

This was the time for stalling until she could get her hands on that damned gun!

"I'm sorry, but apparently the storm has knocked out the phone. I guess we'll have to wait to call Lieutenant Devane," she told Joanna apologetically. "Please have a seat. I promise you, you'll be perfectly safe here until we can get you some proper police protection."

Joanna seemed to sag with relief, but she remained standing at the end of the sofa. "Then you really do believe me?"

"Of course I do," Ivy replied. She moved casually toward Joanna but was careful to stay just out of her reach. Somewhere in one of the pockets of her raincoat was a length of rope and a Clue game piece. The rope worried Ivy a lot more than the game piece. "We've known for weeks that Drummond is the Strangler, we just haven't been able to prove it. Maybe you know something that will help us. Please, sit down so that we can talk."

Joanna nodded and returned to the sofa. Ivy moved to the
chair that sat at the end of the coffee table and prayed that
Joanna wouldn't think it strange that she'd changed seats.

"I don't really know what I can tell you about Ben that
will help your case," she told Ivy. "I haven't had any contact with him since I left New York."

Now that she knew the truth, Ivy had a hundred questions that would shoot holes in Joanna's story, but asking
any of them would alert Joanna that her cover was blown.
Thinking fast, she found a safer topic. "Actually, there is
one thing you may be able to do. We have a queen from a
chess set that we believe belonged to Drummond. He claims
that it was stolen last Christmas, and there's even a police
report to back up his story."

"Ben has several chess sets. Which one is it?"

"Ivory and jade."

"Oriental looking?" Joanna asked with such innocence
that Ivy had to marvel at her, considering the fact that she
was undoubtedly the one who had stolen the set.

"Yes. If we showed you the queen, do you think you
could tell if it was definitely from Drummond's set?"

"Oh, certainly. The set's been in his family for years.
They've even loaned it out to museums from time to time.
It's hand carved, you know," she added proudly.

"We suspected that it was," Ivy replied.

"It was made by a Dutch craftsman, Jarek Vorst. Each
piece bears his initials somewhere in the carving. Not only
that, he made only four sets in the Oriental style, and each
one is a little different. If the queen you have is a Vorst, it
should prove that Ben is the Strangler."

Ivy made a rueful face. "Unfortunately, the district
attorney will say that it only proves that Drummond's chess
set was stolen by the Strangler." She smiled. "But at least
it's a start." She edged forward on the chair and reached for

her purse. "Listen, do you mind if I take some notes? I really should be writing this information down."

It could have been the cautious way she leaned forward, or maybe it was her solicitous tone of voice. It might even have been the heavy clunk her Smith & Wesson automatic made when she grabbed her purse strap and the bag fell onto its side. Whatever the reason, Joanna Hughes realized that she was being led down the garden path.

"I don't think you should do that," she said harshly, leaning forward to snatch the purse out of Ivy's hand. She never would have succeeded if her abrupt movement hadn't startled Ivy, who instinctively recoiled the moment Joanna's hand snaked out. The split second it took Ivy to recover was more than enough to give Joanna the advantage.

Ivy reached for the bag again, but Joanna tossed it away, and before Ivy could make a dive for it, Joanna was standing over her with a gun in Ivy's face.

"Sit down!" she ordered, and Ivy eased back into the chair obediently. The two women looked at each other for a long moment. The only sound in the room was the rumble of nearby thunder and Ivy's frantic heartbeat. "When did you figure it out?" Joanna asked.

"The gun was a dead giveaway," Ivy answered.

The other woman shook her head and laughed. Ivy could hear the madness. "No, you knew before. You must have seen the phone jack."

"Yes."

"You're a very good actress. I'd applaud you—if I had both hands free," Joanna said as she backed away a step or two. "Actually, you're facing your death quite bravely."

"Thank you. I come from a long line of stoics," Ivy said, wondering if there was any point in trying to stall further. Staying alive even one minute longer seemed like reason enough. "Tell me, Joanna, why are you doing this? Why did you kill those women?"

She laughed again. "Really, Detective Kincaid, you've been reading too many mystery novels. Only in books and bad movies does the deranged killer feel the need to purge his conscience and confess to the hero. Or heroine, as the case may be."

"You won't even satisfy a dying woman's curiosity? That's cruel."

"And you're stalling for time," Joanna replied as she reached into her pocket and withdrew a coil of rope. It dangled from her hand eerily, and Ivy felt her heart slam into her rib cage.

Still, she managed to keep her voice strong. "Do you honestly think I'm going to just sit here and let you put that rope around my neck? I'm not some weak-kneed little church mouse that you're sneaking up on from behind. I know you're strong, Joanna, and you're about an inch taller than I and a few pounds heavier, but I'm a trained police officer. I didn't get my badge out of a box of cereal. I had to earn it." Cautiously, Ivy stood and was pleased that Joanna instinctively backed away another step. That meant the gun would be harder to reach, but it also meant that Joanna was having a few doubts.

"Sit down!" she shouted, but Ivy didn't obey this time.

"No, I don't think I will."

Joanna extended her arm, pointing the gun directly at Ivy's head. "I said, sit down, or I'll shoot!"

"You can't shoot me, Joanna. It wouldn't be playing by the rules, and this game you invented has some very definite rules. You can't break them."

The smile that spread across her face made Ivy's blood turn to ice. "Oh, but I won't. You see, I knew you might be a little harder than the others, so I came prepared." She dropped the rope onto the sofa and reached into her pocket again. This time she removed a plastic storage bag and tossed it onto the table in front of victim number nine.

Ivy glanced down at the contents and wished that Alex had been able to think of an excuse to keep her in New York for one more day. The bag contained three small items from the game Clue: a purple token, a colorful room card and a tiny silver gun.

"Professor Plum in the dining room with the revolver," Ivy muttered.

"Game, set and match, I think," Joanna said, her gruesome smile still firmly in place. "All we need to do is step into your little dining alcove, and the setting will be complete. Now, move!"

"Are you sure you don't want to tell me why?" Ivy asked, turning to step around the chair. She stopped abruptly, hoping that Joanna would have moved close enough that she could make a dive for the gun, but luck was not with her.

"Move." Thunder, almost constant now, emphasized the command.

Ivy took two more small steps, which placed her by the art nouveau floor lamp that Alex had thought was so bizarre. Not as bizarre as her gargoyles, but bizarre, nonetheless. "Listen, Joanna..." she said as she turned again and reached one hand casually toward the lamp.

"Don't touch that!" Joanna shrieked, and the last thing Ivy saw was the flash of lightning that brightened the room for a moment just as Joanna squeezed the trigger.

Two squad cars pulled up to the curb in front of Ivy's apartment at the same time Alex did. All five men hit the pavement running, with Alex shouting orders that were nearly drowned out by the din of thunder and pounding rain.

"You two, cover both exits!" he yelled. "And you two come with me!" He dashed into the lobby with two uniformed officers on his heels and ran straight to the elevator. He punched the call button repeatedly and heard the wheels grinding as it started its descent.

Then the grinding stopped as the lights flickered and failed, plunging the lobby into total darkness.

"Damn it! Give me a flashlight!" Alex ordered. Lightning silhouetted both officers as they fumbled for the lights clipped to their belts, and a second later, two narrow beams cut through the darkness. Alex grabbed the nearest light and started toward the stairwell. "Come on!"

He took the stairs two at a time, not caring if the uniforms could keep up with him. He had to get to Ivy. On the way over, he'd talked to the surveillance team, who assured him that they had Drummond safely in custody, but Alex still couldn't shake his fear. If she was home and unharmed, why hadn't she answered the phone?

He was going to feel like an idiot if he broke down the door to her apartment and discovered that she was out visiting her mother, but making a fool of himself was the least of his considerations. He had to hold her in his arms to prove to himself she was safe.

Alex was a few yards ahead of the other officers by the time he reached the fourth floor. Without slowing, he ran around the corner to Ivy's door, banged his fist against it and jiggled the doorknob.

"Ivy? *Ivy!* Open up!"

"Alex?" The voice was barely audible, but the scream that followed it pierced Alex's heart. He grabbed the gun that had been tucked into his belt in the small of his back and slammed his shoulder against the door. When it refused to budge, one of the uniforms lent his shoulder to the effort, too. Wood splintered and the door flew open.

Lightning cast eerie shadows in the room, highlighting two figures struggling on the floor. "Freeze!" Alex shouted, his gun and flashlight both trained on the astonishing sight in front of him.

There was a screaming, cursing woman on the floor, with one arm drawn up painfully behind her and Ivy's knee digging firmly into her back. A second flashlight beam fell on the tableau as the other officers crowded into the doorway.

"Anybody got a pair of handcuffs?" Ivy asked, blinking against the powerful lights. Joanna bucked against her captor and shrieked a few barely intelligible curses. Ivy responded by digging her knee in deeper and pinning Joanna's other arm behind her back, too.

"Who the hell is that?" Alex asked as he rushed forward.

"The Brauxton Strangler."

"A woman?" he asked incredulously.

"Yeah," Ivy answered ruefully. "The psychiatrists and I are going to have a nice long talk about this."

One of the uniforms knelt beside Ivy and handed her a pair of cuffs. "Thanks." She slipped them on with practiced efficiency and stood, bringing the still struggling Joanna with her. The officer took hold of Joanna, and Ivy let go, happy to let someone else grapple with the psychopath for a while. "Alex Devane, meet Joanna Hughes."

Alex cut the beam of light to Joanna. Her hair was a tangled mess and her face was a portrait of madness, but she suddenly stopped struggling and made a concerted effort to compose herself. "Lieutenant Devane," she said with a nod and a challenging, chilling smile.

"Miss Hughes, you have the right to remain silent..." Alex recited the Miranda act, then nodded at the officer. "Take her down to the car. I'll be along in a minute."

He watched the men escort their charge out of the apartment just as the electricity came back on. "Great timing," he said sarcastically.

"Don't complain. That power failure saved my life," Ivy told him. Alex turned and got his first good look at her. Her hair was a mess, her tank top was torn, there were scratches on her arms, and she had the makings of a first-class shiner on her right eye. She was also developing a case of the posttrauma shakes, but she had never looked more beautiful.

They stared at each other for a moment, both equally uncertain how to act, but when Ivy's eyes began to fill with tears, Alex swept her into his arms. "God, I have never been so scared in my entire life," he muttered fiercely, kissing her hair, her forehead, and finally, her mouth.

Ivy clung to him, letting the tears come. They washed down her face, turning their kiss salty, imbuing it with a sense of urgency. When they finally broke apart, Alex placed his hands on Ivy's shoulders and inspected her face closely. "Are you all right?"

She nodded, then realized that there was something hard and cold on her shoulder. She glanced at Alex's right hand and saw the gun he was still clutching. A fresh batch of tears began to flow. "I thought you were never going to touch one of those again."

Alex looked at the gun for a moment, then clicked the safety on and returned it to its makeshift holster behind his back. "I guess that will teach me never to say never, won't it?" His hands went to her shoulders again. "Some things are just more important than old fears."

Ivy brushed her lips against his. "Thank you." She frowned. "But how did you know what was going on here?"

"I didn't—not exactly. I just knew you could be in trouble." He explained how the final piece of the puzzle had fallen into place.

"Anagrams? I hate anagrams! No wonder I couldn't figure it out."

"You did fine, Ivy. Great, in fact," he said with a smile. He asked for an explanation of what had gone on in her apartment prior to his arrival, and she told him. He actually shuddered when she reached the part where Joanna pulled the trigger just as the lights went out. "I pushed the lamp at her as I dove to one side, and that knocked the gun out of her hand. After that, I'm not even sure what happened. I tried to subdue her and ended up with an elbow in my eye. I had just gotten her pinned when I heard you at the door."

"It was Joanna who screamed?"

"Yes. I think that's when she finally realized she had failed. Until that moment, she probably figured she could still fight me off—and she might not have been wrong. God, she's strong."

"What the devil is going on?" Len Eversall asked as he charged into the apartment and surveyed the considerable damage. "Who's that woman in the squad car downstairs?"

Alex sighed impatiently. "The Brauxton Strangler."

"Are you sure?"

Ivy smiled weakly. "Trust me, Commissioner. She's the Strangler, all right." On shaky legs, Ivy moved to her overturned coffee table and rummaged around until she found the plastic bag Joanna had brought. She picked it up by one corner so as not to smudge the fingerprints. "See. And the rope's around here somewhere, too, but she wasn't planning on using it."

Ivy once again explained what had happened, and Alex filled him in on the rest. Len was almost—but not entirely—speechless. "Amazing. The press is going to want to hear all of this, of course. They're already gathering downstairs. You'd better get Ms Hughes to the station for booking," he said, looking directly at Alex.

"Not me," Alex replied. "Ivy. This is her collar. I'm just along for the ride." He turned to her. "You'd better change clothes, Detective. You've got an interrogation to conduct."

Ivy's smile spread slowly until her entire face was alight with happiness and, most particularly, love. She'd wanted Alex's respect, and she knew she'd earned it. Nothing he could have said would have made her happier. "I won't be a minute."

Len, on the other hand, was nonplussed. "Now hold on, Devane. You can't let that girl—"

"'That girl' just captured the Brauxton Strangler single-handed, Commissioner. She deserves the right to handle the arrest from start to finish."

"You two fight between yourselves while I go change," Ivy said as she hurried into the dressing room. Both men watched her go.

"How can she be so chipper after what she just went through?" Len muttered irritably.

"Because she's tough," Alex answered quietly, still watching the spot where Ivy had disappeared. "She'll crash later, and someone who loves her will be around to pick up the pieces, but for the time being, she's a cop. A damned good one. Better than anyone—" he stopped himself and amended "—better than *I* gave her credit for. I won't make that mistake again."

Len cleared his throat, uncomfortable with the raw emotion he heard in Alex's voice. "I've heard some rumors, you know... about you and Kincaid being... involved."

Alex turned to face him. "All true, Commissioner."

"Is that why you chose her for the New York assignment? To get her out of town?"

"Yes," he admitted. "And it was the stupidest thing I've ever done in my life. If I'd left her here, she would have updated those *Perplexities* files two weeks ago, and I'm sure she would have spotted the anagram business. Even a child would have seen the similarity between the names Marsha Dell and Ed Marshall."

"And if you'd known in advance," Eversall said, following Alex's train of thought, "you could have set up a stakeout, planted an officer here in the apartment and used Ivy as bait."

"That's right. But instead, I tried to protect her and almost got her killed."

"You know what your problem is, Devane? You think you have to be John the Baptist, Saint Francis of Assisi and Robin Hood all rolled into one perfect individual. Under the word *guilt* in the dictionary, there should be an entry that says, 'See Alex Devane.'"

"Ivy keeps telling me pretty much the same thing," he replied with a grin.

"Maybe you should listen to her."

Alex shrugged. "It's better than standing around listening to you."

Len wiped one hand down his face. "Lord, I hope you're not planning on hanging around the department now that this case is over. I don't think I can stand the aggravation."

"Sorry, Commissioner, but I'm back to stay."

"Damn," he said vehemently, but there was a smile on his face when he said it.

"Okay, I'm ready," Ivy said, reappearing in jeans and a plain blue camp shirt. She located her purse in the debris around the sofa, collected the rest of her evidence and started out. "Do you think we could get somebody up here to fix my door?" she asked as she stepped over a piece of the splintered frame.

"Count on it," Alex said, smiling as he slipped one arm around her waist and accompanied her down the hall.

CHAPTER TWENTY-THREE

THE QUESTIONING of Joanna Hughes took nearly three hours. Benjamin Drummond was in the squad room when she was brought in, and the pyrotechnics that ensued when she saw him were a sight to behold. The story she had previously refused to tell Ivy spilled out in graphic detail, because Joanna wanted her former lover to know just how clever she really was.

The entire plot had been conceived as revenge, pure and simple. She had wanted to frame Benjamin Drummond for murder, and she'd almost succeeded. But the motive was what fascinated Ivy. Drummond had *not* stolen the idea for Pentathlon from Joanna. In fact, just the opposite had occurred. Joanna Hughes had been hired as an industrial spy by Drummond's mother, who was still looking for ways to ruin her son's career and bring him back into the family business.

Joanna had engaged in an affair with Drummond in order to steal the projects he was working on, but she made the mistake of falling in love with her quarry. When Drummond realized what she was up to, he broke off the affair, and Joanna snapped like a dry twig. She had begged, cajoled and professed her undying love, and when that hadn't worked, she had slapped him with a lawsuit claiming he'd stolen the idea for Pentathlon. Then she'd proceeded to make his life a living hell until he'd finally confronted his mother and threatened to have her arrested for industrial

espionage if she didn't call off the mad dog she had unleashed on him.

When Joanna had learned that Claudia was withdrawing
her support, she'd dropped the suit. Drummond had quietly left New York, and when Joanna learned where he had
gone, she followed him. In Braruxton, she changed her name
and bided her time until she could devise suitable punish-
ment for the handsome, brilliant gamesman who had
spurned her.

It was the appearance of Pentathlon on the prestigious
Perplexities readers' poll that finally set Joanna's plan in
motion. She spent an entire year planning the crime, inventing the rules of the game, choosing her victims and
learning about their habits so that when the time came there
would be no mistakes. She studied case histories of serial
killers, choosing a pattern that would convince police psychiatrists that the Strangler was a man.

Then, to personalize her crime and point the finger at
Drummond, she broke into his house and stole his chess set.
The set had, indeed, been loaned to various museums
through the years, and she had expected the police to discover that fact and trace the queen to him.

She had also assumed that a Pentathlon gold medal left
beside one of the victims would incriminate him. She hadn't
counted on Drummond's anonymity in Braruxton.

Ultimately, though, revenge had taken a back seat in Joanna's game. She had gone to Drummond's house and hid
outside in the shadows before and after every crime to re-
assure herself that her only motive was revenge, but the excuse was a weak one; she had enjoyed the killing far more
than she'd expected. Eventually, she had come to need it in
order to survive.

Throughout the evening, Ivy, Alex and the district
attorney asked one question after another, trying to get a
complete picture of the crimes and why they had been com-

mitted. Joanna refused the services of a lawyer, but the D.A. made certain that her confession would hold up in court—not that Joanna would ever come to trial. She was clearly insane, and the best that could be hoped for was that she would be committed to a state institution for life.

"God, I'm glad that's over," Alex said when Joanna was finally taken out of the interrogation room and placed in a holding cell to await arraignment.

"I know. I don't know when I've ever been this tired," Ivy replied, rubbing at the knots in her neck. The stenographer and the D.A. filed out of the room, and Ivy rose to follow. Alex was right behind her. They stepped into the squad room and spotted Ben Drummond sitting at a desk outside Alex's office. They'd already talked to him several times, clarifying parts of Joanna's story, but he was still hanging around, apparently stunned by the entire chain of events.

"I guess we have to apologize now, don't we?" Alex said to Ivy under his breath.

"You go first," she whispered.

"Drummond..." Ben stood as they approached, and Ivy's heart went out to him. He was a brilliant, intelligent man who had been betrayed by a heartless mother and victimized by a deranged lover. No wonder his magnificent, dark eyes were cold and lifeless.

"Is it over?" he asked.

"For the most part," Alex replied. "There's still the media to be dealt with and some paperwork, but the worst is over. You can go home now."

Drummond laughed bitterly. "And where might that be, Lieutenant?" Alex started to speak, but Ben saw the sympathy in his eyes and held up a hand to forestall him. "Forget I said that, please. I'm just tired." He shook his head in amazement. "I knew she was crazy, but I never realized she was capable of all this—because of me." He looked at Ivy apologetically. "I'm sorry, Detective Kincaid. I'm glad there's at least one victim I can say that to. I suppose the others will be on my conscience for the rest of my life."

"Drummond—" Alex captured Ben's eyes "—you didn't murder those women. Don't blame yourself for their deaths. Guilt's a real killer—take it from someone who knows."

Ben nodded. "Thanks."

"No—thank you," Ivy said. "You've been very patient with us, considering the kind of treatment we've been giving you these past few weeks. I'm sorry we misjudged you."

Alex added his apology, as well, and extended his hand. Drummond took it, nodded at Ivy and left. When he stepped into the hall, the reporters mobbed him, and Len Eversall came into the squad room. "Devane! Kincaid! I've got a zillion reporters out here who want to talk to you! Now!"

"Let them eat cake!" Alex quipped, grabbing Ivy's hand and propelling her into his office. He closed the door, locked it and drew the blinds while Ivy surveyed the scattered, broken pieces of her magnetic chessboard.

"What happened in here? Did you finally figure out that I'd have you in checkmate in three moves?" she asked, leaning against the front of the desk.

Alex leaned against the door, mimicking her casual pose, but there was nothing casual in the loving look he gave her. "I needed to know your middle name, and I was in kind of a hurry."

"Lane. Ivy Lane Kincaid," she said, reveling in the delicious attraction that was suddenly sizzling between them once again.

"I know. It's a nice name," Alex told her. "How would you feel about changing it to Ivy Lane Devane?"

Ivy cleared her throat to get rid of the lump of emotion that formed there. "Well . . . at least it rhymes."

"Yes, it does. What do you think?"

Ivy glanced down at her feet. "I heard what you said to Commissioner Eversall back at my apartment while I was changing clothes. Did you mean it?" She looked at him, praying for the right answer.

"Every word. I never should have sent you to New York. I underestimated you, Ivy... and the only thing I can say in my defense is that I did it because I love you more than my own life. I expect I always will." His voice was a soft caress and his eyes had misted over. He took a deep breath to dispel the threat of tears, but Ivy didn't bother. Hers were streaming down her cheeks.

"I love you, too, Alex," she said softly. "And more than that, I *need* you. I think we make a pretty good team."

"For life?"

Ivy smiled. "And whatever comes after."

She moved into his arms and felt the world open up in front of her.

Harlequin Superromance®

COMING NEXT MONTH

#418 RESCUE FROM YESTERDAY • Marisa Carroll
Book I of the Saigon Legacy
Simon McKendrick needed nurse practitioner Annie
Simpson to smuggle a valuable pearl necklace into
Vietnam—ransom for Simon's brother and sister, who
were being held captive by a corrupt government
minister. Simon promised he'd protect her, but Annie
suspected Simon could be pretty dangerous himself....

#419 TIGERS BY NIGHT • Sandra Canfield
Everyone was worried about Jake Cameron. He'd been
ordered to take a break from police work and had
volunteered to watch over preemie babies...tiny Peter
Bauer in particular. Falling in love with Peter's widowed
mother Robin, however, proved an impossible
complication. Sooner or later she would have to know
he had killed her husband....

#420 HEART OF THE WEST • Suzanne Ellison
The Living West—Book I
Teacher Mandy Larkin and steam locomotive owner Joe
Henderson both believed in the value of remembering
the past and learning from it, but in order for their love
to survive, it looked as if they were going to have to
forget about the past altogether....

#421 THE MARRIAGE PROJECT • Lynn Patrick
Gillian Flannery's marriage project worked fine with
her high school students. But when she was assigned a
partner herself, her "marriage" to John Slater quickly
ran into trouble. Between his bickering daughters
and his meddling ex-wife, John's home life resembled a
war zone. Did Gillian really want to get caught in the
cross fire?

From America's favorite author
coming in September

JANET DAILEY

For Bitter Or Worse

Out of print since 1979!

Reaching Cord seemed impossible. Bitter, still confined to a wheel-chair a year after the crash, he lashed out at everyone. Especially his wife.

"It would have been better if I hadn't been pulled from the plane wreck," he told her, and nothing Stacey did seemed to help.

Then Paula Hanson, a confident physiotherapist, arrived. She taunted Cord into helping himself, restoring his interest in living. Could she also make him and Stacey rediscover their early love?

Don't miss this collector's edition—last in a special three-book collection from Janet Dailey.

HARLEQUIN'S WISHBOOK
SWEEPSTAKES RULES & REGULATIONS
NO PURCHASE NECESSARY TO ENTER OR RECEIVE A PRIZE

1 To enter and join the Reader Service, affix the Four Free Books and Free Gifts sticker along with both of your other Sweepstakes stickers to the Sweepstakes Entry Form. If you do not wish to take advantage of our Reader Service, but wish to enter the Sweepstakes only, do not affix the Four Free Books and Free Gifts sticker to the Sweepstakes Entry Form. Incomplete and/or inaccurate entries are ineligible for that section or sections of prizes. Not responsible for mutilated or unreadable entries or inadvertent printing errors. Mechanically reproduced entries are null and void.

2. Whether you take advantage of this offer or not, your Sweepstakes numbers will be compared against a list of winning numbers generated at random by the computer. In the event that all prizes are not claimed by March 31, 1992, a random drawing will be held from all qualified entries received from March 30, 1990 to March 31, 1992, to award all unclaimed prizes. All cash prizes (Grand to Sixth) will be mailed to the winners and are payable by check in U.S. funds. Seventh prize to be shipped to winners via third-class mail. These prizes are in addition to any free, surprise or mystery gifts that might be offered. Versions of this sweepstakes with different prizes of approximate equal value may appear in other mailings or at retail outlets by Torstar Corp. and its affiliates.

3. The following prizes are awarded in this sweepstakes: ★ Grand Prize (1) $1,000,000; First Prize (1) $25,000; Second Prize (1) $10,000; Third Prize (5) $5,000; Fourth Prize (10) $1,000; Fifth Prize (100) $250; Sixth Prize (2500) $10; ★ ★ Seventh Prize (6000) $12.95 ARV.

   ★ This Sweepstakes contains a Grand Prize offering of $1,000,000 annuity. Winner will receive $33,333.33 a year for 30 years without interest totalling $1,000,000.

   ★ ★ Seventh Prize: A fully illustrated hardcover book published by Torstar Corp. Approximate value of the book is $12.95.

   Entrants may cancel the Reader Service at any time without cost or obligation to buy (see details in center insert card).

4. This promotion is being conducted under the supervision of Marden-Kane, Inc., an independent judging organization. By entering this Sweepstakes, each entrant accepts and agrees to be bound by these rules and the decisions of the judges, which shall be final and binding. Odds of winning in the random drawing are dependent upon the total number of entries received. Taxes, if any, are the sole responsibility of the winners. Prizes are nontransferable. All entries must be received by no later than 12:00 NOON, on March 31, 1992. The drawing for all unclaimed sweepstakes prizes will take place May 30, 1992, at 12:00 NOON, at the offices of Marden-Kane, Inc., Lake Success, New York.

5. This offer is open to residents of the U.S., the United Kingdom, France and Canada, 18 years or older except employees and their immediate family members of Torstar Corp., its affiliates, subsidiaries, Marden-Kane, Inc., and all other agencies and persons connected with conducting this Sweepstakes. All Federal, State and local laws apply. Void wherever prohibited or restricted by law. Any litigation respecting the conduct and awarding of a prize in this publicity contest may be submitted to the Régie des loteries et courses du Québec.

6. Winners will be notified by mail and may be required to execute an affidavit of eligibility and release which must be returned within 14 days after notification or an alternative winner will be selected. Canadian winners will be required to correctly answer an arithmetical skill-testing question administered by mail which must be returned within a limited time. Winners consent to the use of their names, photographs and/or likenesses for advertising and publicity in conjunction with this and similar promotions without additional compensation.

7. For a list of our major winners, send a stamped, self-addressed envelope to: WINNERS LIST c/o MARDEN-KANE, INC., P.O. BOX 701, SAYREVILLE, NJ 08871. Winners Lists will be fulfilled after the May 30, 1992 drawing date.

If Sweepstakes entry form is missing, please print your name and address on a 3" ×5" piece of plain paper and send to:

In the U.S.	In Canada
Harlequin's WISHBOOK Sweepstakes	Harlequin's WISHBOOK Sweepstakes
P.O. Box 1867	P.O. Box 609
Buffalo, NY 14269-1867	Fort Erie, Ontario
	L2A 5X3

Offer limited to one per household.

© 1990 Harlequin Enterprises Limited   Printed in the U.S.A.

LTY-H890

COMING SOON...

For years Harlequin and Silhouette novels have been taking readers places—but only in their imaginations.

This fall look for PASSPORT TO ROMANCE, a promotion that could take you around the corner or around the world!

Watch for it in September!

★